The Kokuran

THE KOKURAN

Jordin Mack

Vaughn Publishing

FIRST EDITION

Library of Congress Cataloging-in-Publication Data has been applied for.

ISBN: 978-0-9971544-0-5

Also available on ebook

Cover and jacket design by Elm Street Design Studio.

To all the Angels in my life, those who have loved, educated, encouraged, and inspired me.

TABLE OF CONTENTS – THE KOKURAN

AUTHOR'S NOTES

Orchids are just like women—they are beautiful, admirable and purposeful with an anatomy that's very similar to her, made to ultimately effect reproduction. It is this likeness that allows us to draw on their symbolism because in her essence she is a beautiful flower. Yet in contrast, a woman's anatomy is also used to elicit sexual satisfaction from her consensual or captive participation. The image in which she is made makes her desirable and vulnerable to his maleness; he can love her, make her, mate her or break her at any time of his choosing. Don't feel sorry for her though, because she does indeed have the ultimate control; she knows he covets the jewel in her soul. It is from that little hidden pearl where she derives her true power. But as she evolves in her relationships, she learns there are ambiguities and contradictions that surround the source of this power.

While this body of work is fiction, told through the eyes of a woman, it epitomizes many realities in our society today.

Each character is recognizable and represents someone known or familiar to you, as their experiences overlay the entire spectrum of relationships. In this story, there is pain and suffering, confusion and growth, evolution and redemption. There are sexual conquests that bring about quixotic pleasures and emotional destruction that rival tidal waves and tsunami seas, creating a painful cycle that causes hurt people to hurt people. But in living one's life, sometimes you have to go through darkness before you can see the light that shines toward the path forward.

1

THE INCEPTION OF EVERYTHING

As I sat on the winding staircase in the foyer of my home, I looked around and saw nothing but gloom and emptiness. Not even a single memory or fleeing thoughts of the love, laughter, and pain that once filled the walls of this home. The movers were gone, my furniture was gone, and now my husband, Philip and our son, Junior were gone as well. Tears filled my eyes as I realized this was the end of the final chapter of my eighteen-year marriage. Our home was the last of the marital assets to be sold and divided. In a few days, with the stroke of a pen, just like that, I would be single again and re-emerge as Astrid Josette Johnson.

However, the impending change in my marital status was bittersweet. With all the hell I had endured in my marriage, you would think that finalizing my divorce would have felt like a relief, but it didn't. I had been with Philip since I was seventeen. During that time I had lost my virginity, developed into a woman, and become a mother. Apart from my profession, I didn't know who I was in any other role besides wife and mother. Deep down inside, I was scared and afraid, filled with anxiety about what the future held for me.

As Gigi, my mother would say, "One thing for certain and two things for sure," I didn't want the next phase of my life to be a repeat of the first. This time things would be different if and when I ever got into another relationship. No more playing the role of the victim. I would be the one in control, holding the power, establishing the rules of engagement. I would play, date, make love, fuck, and define intimate relationships on my terms and my terms alone. The rules would be simple: play my way or not at all, or so I thought.

Who was I kidding? My transformation would be easier said than done. With all the shit I'd been through, I was probably a little screwed up in the head when it came to relationships with men. Perhaps, I should have sought professional help, but I didn't believe in psychotherapy. It was only really useful for crazy or weak people, and I was neither. I had survived some terrible things and was still standing tall. So, as far as I was concerned, I was good to go. Sure, life was tough sometimes, but that's why I always kept a bottle of tequila and some cannabis on hand. However, while my arsenal of spirits and herbs provided a quick fix on a bad day, they did nothing to calm the anxiety and confusion that preyed on my essence.

Although I was an accomplished lawyer, at age thirty-six, part of me felt like I was still the teenage, naïve, inexperienced girl who married Philip. It was Philip's distorted views on sex and being a husband that left me confused about my role as a woman in relationships and uncomfortable with my own sexuality. I had a lot to figure out, but I didn't quite know where to start. As Gigi would say, in order to go forward in your life, you must first understand where you've been and how you got there. I decided that's what I would do; I'd start at the beginning, a full examination of my history, the inception of everything. How I came to be and the road traveled that had me sitting in despair on the steps of what used to be my home.

The obvious place to start for my understanding was with my mother, the matriarch and true alpha female in my family.

Josette, also known as Gigi was born and raised in Louisiana. It was rumored that she was raised in a brothel and perhaps even worked there. She was a stunning beauty, and at thirteen was physically developed beyond her age. People often mistook her for a grown woman of eighteen or so. Most people said that her face and bustling DD bosom resembled Jane Russell, a reigning sex symbol of the 1940s and 1950s.

By the time she was twenty, she already had five little girls, even though she had never been married. For some reason, the girls who were old enough to speak called her "Gigi" instead of some derivative of "mother," as if to conceal the fact they belonged to her. No one knows much about Gigi's childhood or upbringing, because she refused to talk about her home life or how she came to have her first five children. She never mentioned anything about the father (or fathers) of her children. The only thing she would say about her family in Louisiana was that they disowned her at the age of twenty-one when she met and married Big John.

Gigi and Big John eloped and moved to Detroit so he could get a job in one of the auto plants. They settled into a small cold-water flat on the east side near the Black Bottom area, a low-income community. Living in this type of neighborhood was a total shock to Gigi. It was nothing like the green pristine estate on which she had grown up. Even though the neighborhood was comprised of European immigrants and other poor ethnic groups, she felt that she and her kids stood out and were treated differently from other people in the neighborhood. She despised living there from day one, and she cried and complained to Big John about it every day. Big John, with his calm, demure disposition, would say, "It's going to be all right. This house is only temporary. A fine lady like you deserves a fine house, and I promise I'll buy one for you one day soon." His kind words only served to calm her for a few hours. The next day, like a broken record, she was complaining once again.

After about six months, their relationship reached a breaking point. It happened the night Detroit had one of its worst torrential rainstorms. The storm was so bad that the roof began leaking buckets of water throughout the house. Later that night, Gigi told Big John that she'd had enough of Detroit and that as soon as she could make arrangements, she was leaving him and taking her kids back to Louisiana.

The next morning, Big John patched up the roof and took Gigi and the girls out for a drive to a place called the Boston-Edison District. It was a quiet, sedate neighborhood that contained a mixture of palatial homes ranging in size from mansions set amidst extensive grounds to two-story houses on spacious lots. All of the homes were are at least two full stories, built of brick, stone, or stucco, and set back at least thirty feet from the street. Many homes featured cut stone details, elaborate door surrounds, slate or tile roofs, and leaded glass windows. The two boulevards that formed the district were amply landscaped and shaded by overarching elm trees.

As they drove through the quaint neighborhood, Gigi smiled and nodded with approval. Without saying a word, she knew this was the neighborhood that Big John had picked out for them to live the rest of their lives. She would wait patiently for him to save enough money to move them into her dream house in the Boston-Edison District.

Shortly thereafter, Gigi became pregnant with her sixth child. That's when Big John proceeded to adopt the five girls, proclaiming them as his own. He wanted them to feel as if they were part of one big family without any references to half-brothers or half-sisters or stepchildren.

When Gigi had her sixth child, her first with Big John, all the kids began calling him "Pops." Big John was very traditional in that he saw his role as being the financial provider and left the rearing of the kids to Gigi. His only requirement was that the kids get a good education and go to college. On the few occasions when he did engage in serious conversations with the children, it was usually about education. Big John believed that having a college education was the key to success and a guarantee of economic prosperity. With so many girls in the house, he didn't want them to end up with menial labor jobs; he wanted them to go to college and become doctors or lawyers. His one and only prerequisite for Gigi was that she ensured that the children completed their studies. Apart from that, he never questioned any of Gigi's parenting decisions, even when he had cause to do so.

While Gigi was a loving wife and mother, she had some peculiarities. One of them was making botanical medicines, which stemmed from her Louisiana roots. Gigi grew all sorts of exotic plants and flowers indoors and outdoors to make her medicine. She had a number of books on growing exotic flowers outside of their natural environment. Her favorite flower was the orchid and at one time or another, she grew or attempted to grow several species of them. She used to sit around with her friends and talk about the mystical healing and sexual powers of the orchid and how she used them in many of her medicinal concoctions.

Her medicine business was quite prosperous. She made salves, tablets, smoking herbs, and even liquid medicines that people could take with a dropper or mix with food or some type of drink. Her medicines treated migraines, arthritis, asthma, diabetes, impotence, lazy libido, and everything in between. People within and outside of the community would come to Gigi to get diagnosed for some ailment before they went to see a medical doctor. Sometimes they even came after they saw a doctor.

Most of her customers called her "Dr. G," as if she was an actual doctor. Of course, a few critics and naysayers in the neighborhood called her "voodoo lady" or "witch doctor," but they were of no account to Gigi. She was in her element as a medicine woman. She embraced both the financial benefits and the adoration it provided.

While Big John was a quiet, soft-spoken man who worked eighteen hours a day to support his family, Gigi was a completely different story. She was definitely a diva and the queen bee of the house, and everybody knew it. She was beloved by everyone and somewhat eccentric at times. Although she was a stay-at-home wife, June Cleaver she was not. Her daily household attire was anything but normal. She always looked like she was going out on a date, with finely styled hair, makeup, and tight-fitting A-lined dresses and skirts with three or four-inch stilettos. She also wore beautiful lingerie long before Victoria's Secret made it popular. She slept in flowing nightgowns with matching robes with fur on the sleeves and collar. Even her house slippers had three-inch heels. Big John enjoyed every minute of her diva style. He often bragged to his friends about how beautiful she was. Everyone said the love between Gigi and Big John was so powerful that people could feel it in the air whenever they were in a room together. Unusual for the time, they were always outwardly affectionate with each other.

Big John also loved all of the kids. He didn't treat any of the kids differently except, on occasion, Dianne (nickname "Di"), Gigi's firstborn. Di was quiet and shy and did not take well to strangers. She was extremely close to Gigi, always clinging to her, holding onto her hands or her legs and only playing within sight of her. Big John felt that he had to work a little harder to gain Di's acceptance so he would sneak her a nickel sometimes or buy her bows and berets for her hair whenever he went to Woolworths.

After two years of working, Big John saved up enough money to open his own garage. He continued to work midnights at the auto plant while spending his days and weekends at the garage. The garage was nestled right in the heart of Black Bottom with the nearest auto repair shop more than twenty miles away, so Big John had no shortage of customers. Everyone from the community and surrounding areas took their cars and trucks to Big John's shop for repairs.

In no time, Big John built a reputation for being a man of integrity and doing quality work. But it was his kindness that endeared people to him. He would often extend his customers special payment terms or allow them to make some type of barter arrangement instead of paying cash.

Soon, the garage was doing so well that Big John expanded it and hired a few other mechanics to work there. By then, Big John was spending all his waking hours at the garage, but Gigi didn't mind, because she knew he was working hard to save money for her dream house.

It was about five years to the date of their arrival in Detroit when Big John finally moved the family out of Black Bottom. Big John purchased Gigi's dream house, a three-story, five-bedroom home in the Boston-Edison District.

Life was good for Gigi and Big John. By then, they had eight kids with another on the way. They had an abundance of everything—money, food, clothes, toys for the kids, and plenty of green space for Gigi's garden. She had an outdoor and indoor greenhouse as well as her exterior soil garden. All the neighbors would come by to see the rare exotic plants that Gigi had grown, especially her orchids, which were also displayed in vases throughout the home. She even let a photographer take pictures of her orchids for a garden book he was publishing. By all accounts, Gigi and Big John were living the American dream.

Over the next three years, she had two more kids, bringing the total to eleven. After giving birth to ten girls, she finally gave Big John the son he wanted, John Junior. She said her family was now complete, so she had a medical procedure to prevent her from having any more kids.

While Gigi's beauty and gardening was her priority, traditional homemaking tasks were not. She leaned on Di to help with those tasks and with the rearing of her younger siblings. At first, these responsibilities didn't bother Di, because she had taken care of her younger siblings her entire life, but that changed as she approached puberty. She started complaining about how it wasn't fair that she had to do so many household chores and also care for Gigi's kids. Eventually, she started arguing and mouthing off, which only led to more punishments and restrictions. Di was not allowed to leave the house except to attend school and church. With all the household chores she had to do—cleaning the kitchen, vacuuming, dusting, doing homework, and bathing her younger siblings—she didn't have time for anything else anyway. In Gigi's mind, consuming Di's time with household responsibilities was not meant as a punishment but to protect her from the seduction of the streets.

At thirteen, though not quite as stunning as Gigi, Di was certainly beautiful in her own right. She was also following in the footsteps of her mother, physically developed well beyond her age. It wouldn't be long before she was exploding out of her DD cups. Gigi knew that boys were looking at Di now, and she wanted to protect her innocence. She feared that a boy or possibly a grown man might seduce her into losing her virginity or worse, so she began imposing strict rules on her. Instead of the close loving relationship that they once had, Di became resentful of Gigi.

One day, Di asked Gigi if she could attend a football game at the local high school. Gigi refused, saying she needed her to stay at home and help with her younger siblings and that she had to wait until she was older to do those types of things. Di flew into a rage and started screaming at Gigi, saying she treated her like she was Cinderella and that she was tired of taking care of Gigi's kids.

"All you do is play dress up and have fucking babies for me to take care of!"

Gigi slapped her in the face. "Girl, that world out there is cruel. It will swallow your hot little ass up and spit you out like you're nothing. You need to enjoy the privileges of your life and the innocence of it. You'll get to experience being an adult soon enough. Do you want to end up like me, pregnant at thirteen 'cause some man decides he wants you, forces himself on you, and takes your innocence away?"

Gigi paused when she realized what she had said. She never intended to tell Di how she was conceived. It was at that moment that Di found out she was the product of rape and not the fairytale, romanticized love affair she had imagined.

"Liar!" she screamed. "You're just trying to scare me." Then she ran to her bedroom and slammed the door.

Later that night, when Big John came home and Di tried to talk to him about Gigi's strict rules, he responded with his typical, "You should listen to your mother; she knows best."

"I hate you," Di replied. "I wish I could find my real father."

That was the first and only time she ever spoke to Big John that way.

Big John looked at her and spoke in his usual calm voice. "I'm your real father, and don't ever forget it." He hugged her, and she didn't resist. "Just be patient, and listen to your mother. Everything will work out." He pulled back to look at her. "You should come with me to the garage on Saturday to help out."

From that point on, Di enjoyed going to the garage on Saturdays with Big John. It was her escape, time away from Gigi and her siblings. Big John would let Di go downtown with her girlfriends to see a movie or go shopping. Facilitating these occasional outings for Di was their secret, it was Big John's way of compensating for the overly strict rules Gigi imposed on her.

Over the next few years, Gigi tried to find other things to occupy Di's time, like sewing and piano lessons, but her interests in those areas wouldn't last long. Like any other teenage girl, Di wanted to hang out with her friends from school, and she enjoyed the attention of boys. In Di's case though, because of her mature build, both older teenage boys and young men were vying for her attention as well, and she liked it. About every three months, Gigi and Di had another one of what became termed as their "Cinderella arguments." Despite the many punishments Di received, it had no effect on her behavior.

By the time Di began high school, Gigi knew she was already losing the battle to control her. Contrary to Gigi's plans, instead of sending Di to an all-girls Catholic school, Big John convinced her to allow Di to attend Cass Tech, a public college preparatory high school located in the city. To seal the deal, Di also promised Gigi that she would change her behavior if she allowed her to attend Cass, but that promise was short-lived. Often, she was late getting in from school for one reason or another, and she continued to be headstrong and defiant.

By then, Gigi suspected that Di might be drinking alcohol, smoking cigarettes and probably marijuana, too. With eleven kids to raise, Gigi didn't have the time or energy to keep arguing with Di, and she was becoming increasingly frustrated with her. She knew she might have to take drastic measures to change the path of destruction that Di was on. She even contemplated sending her down South to stay with Big John's sister but decided not to, believing it was better to keep her kids close by in order to keep them safe.

After a few months of continuous arguments, Gigi finally reached her limit when Di snuck out the house to meet up with her boyfriend and then crept in just before daylight. Instead of having another pointless argument, Gigi waited to talk to Big John. She had planned to tell him later that day that they needed to send Di away to a boarding school or they would lose her to the streets for good. However, that discussion never took place—not because Gigi gave up on Di but because of what happened to Big John.

Like so many other weekend nights, Big John had gone to work at his garage and labored into the wee hours of the morning. On such nights, he usually called home to tell Gigi he was working until sunrise so she wouldn't be worried. However, this night was different; he never called Gigi.

At about six in the morning, Gigi called the garage, but no one answered, so she decided to drive there. As she approached the garage, she saw that the police were already there and had taped off the perimeter of the building. People were gathered outside, so she knew it had to be serious. She jumped out of her car and ran toward the building, but Mr. Paul, one of the mechanics, grabbed her and held her tight.

"Big John . . . he's gone."

Gigi shook her head in disbelief. "No, no, no . . . what happened?"

Mr. Paul told her that some men broke into the garage to rob it and killed Big John.

The next few weeks were filled with great sadness for Gigi and all the kids, especially Di. Of all the kids, she missed him most. He seemed to understand her, even more so than Gigi, and he definitely made her feel special, like she was Daddy's little girl.

Not only was Gigi mourning the loss of Big John, she was trying to make sense of their financial situation. Since Big John had always managed their finances and business matters, Gigi was unaware of the financial details of the garage, their mortgage, or his life insurance. After sorting through everything, Gigi learned that Big John's life insurance would not pay the full benefit and that both the garage and their home were heavily mortgaged. Gigi knew she would not be able to keep the house long, even with the small savings they had in the bank and the cash she had stashed away in her mattress and in Big John's strongbox.

She tried to start selling her medicines again to people from the old eastside neighborhood, with little success. Gigi had lost contact with most of her old friends when they moved to the Boston-Edison house. It wasn't because she cut them off; they cut her off, as if they were envious she was able to leave the old neighborhood. Even though her so-called friends knew about her financial situation, no one was in a hurry to help her. In some respects, it was as if they were glad to watch her slow downward struggle.

After a year, the money was running out, and things started getting tougher for the family. Gigi tried to stay in the big house as long as she could by selling both family cars, furnishings, artwork, the grand piano, her furs, and all the jewelry Big John had given her over the years—except the simple gold wedding band he had given her when they eloped. Her liquidation of their assets was to no avail; she was only able to stay in the house six more months before they had to move. With much dread and trepidation, she feared that she would have to move back to the old eastside neighborhood. In addition to having to deal with the memories of living there before with Big John, she was concerned about her family's safety, since many people believed that the men who killed Big John came from Black

Bottom. Since Big John's death, Gigi told her kids repeatedly that it was her job now to protect them.

One of Gigi's closest friends told her about a new housing complex for low-income families located on the far west side of town. It was called the Herman Gardens, commonly known as "the Gardens." The one stipulation for living in the Gardens was that Gigi sign up for the State Family Assistance Program (SFAP). SFAP imposed all kinds of strict conditions on her, one of which gave the State the right to take her kids if she didn't comply with the program rules. Although she found SFAP's controls on her and her children to be both humiliating and demoralizing, she knew the program was necessary for her family's survival.

Though sight unseen, the thought of moving to a completely new neighborhood lifted Gigi's spirits as she envisioned a new beginning for her family. With Gigi's love of gardening, where else would she want to live but in a place that embodied her affection for plant life and floral gardens?

However, Gigi's excitement for the Gardens was short-lived. The apartment complex was not nearly as scenic or serene as the name implied, and there were no botanical gardens anywhere to be found. It was nothing more than a low-income government housing project.

Moving to the Gardens was a major adjustment for Gigi. The only remnants she brought from the Boston-Edison house were her horticulture books and the vase that held the artificial black orchid that she had not been able to cultivate successfully in her garden. Even though they had only been away from the old eastside neighborhood for five years, it seemed like a lifetime ago. The people living in the Gardens were also dramatically different; there were fewer European immigrants and more people of color living there. And, just like her old eastside neighborhood, Gigi knew that she and her kids would stand out and potentially be treated harshly by the community. Even worse, having so many girls and no husband placed them at tremendous risk.

Gigi and her kids settled into their four-bedroom end unit apartment, but with the exception of Di, the older girls stayed close to home and did not socialize with the kids in the neighborhood. In keeping with Gigi's parenting style, she was quick to find a neighborhood church. Gigi and her kids attended church an average of three to four nights a week. It wasn't because she was devoutly religious but because she believed the church was a safe haven for both her and her kids. Like Di, the older children had to do household chores and help take care of the younger kids. The only social activities they were allowed to participate in were church events. In Gigi's mind, church would surely keep her kids off the streets and out of trouble.

Gigi had never worked or had a real job in her entire life, but SFAP required her to do so. The only job she could find was a position in a nearby hospital as a sanitation worker. She hated her job, especially because she hated doing anything that resembled house cleaning. But, true to form, Gigi always dressed and carried herself as if she was royalty. When she left and returned from work, no one knew she was doing menial labor, let alone janitorial work.

After only six months, she landed a job as a pharmacy tech aid. While her new position was more respectable, the pay was the same as her janitorial job, an insufficient amount to move out of the Gardens. It was at that time that she had thoughts about attending college, maybe even becoming a registered nurse or a pharmacist.

Each day as she walked to the bus stop, she looked around and knew the Gardens was not a safe place for her family; it was actually worse than her old eastside neighborhood. She mused often that instead of calling this place the Gardens, they should have called it the Jungle, because it had plenty of wild animals running through it. This place was full of gangs, drugs, prostitution, and unwed teenage mothers, and the worst of the worst. She realized she needed to devise a plan to get the hell out of the Gardens as quickly as possible.

Although she still had her youthful good looks, she knew she was not likely to find a suitable husband with eleven kids, so she would have to either get a better paying job or a couple of jobs. After giving it more thought, she decided that her only option was to go back to school, which she dreaded and feared, since she stopped going to school at age thirteen when she became pregnant with Di. She remembered what Big John used to say about a college education: it guaranteed economic prosperity.

After talking to a few people at work, she found a school that would accept her. In four years, she would become a registered nurse. She loved being a wife and mother and had always seen herself as a homemaker, not a career person. But due to her circumstances, that was no longer an option. Like it or not, she was about to become a career woman.

2

PRESENTING ASTRID

Di, by all accounts, was a gifted child. At four years old she could read, write and do arithmetic without the benefit of any formal education. Gigi said Di was like a sponge; she soaked up knowledge anywhere she could get it. Gigi remembered teaching Di to say and write her ABCs and how to count up to twenty, but she had no knowledge of how Di learned to read and write and do arithmetic. However, unlike her four younger sisters, she was shy and clung to Gigi. She always wanted to be held, to sit on Gigi's lap, or play near Gigi's feet. Gigi never thought there was anything strange about Di's behavior. She just assumed she was spoiled and needed a lot more affection and attention than her siblings. Gigi tried to accommodate her, spending more time alone with her, creating a close-knit relationship that lasted until Di reached puberty.

Di's behavior changed drastically after they moved to the Gardens. Shortly thereafter, she was kicked out of Cass and was supposedly attending an alternative high school. Instead of going to her classes, she spent most of her time partying, getting high, and hanging out with her friends. What concerned Gigi most was the type of men Di was dating. They were men from the streets, the type of men Gigi had sought to protect her from. Di was only sixteen, but she had boyfriends who were ten to twenty years older than her. They all looked like drug dealers—flamboyant with flashy designer clothes and jewelry and expensive luxury cars. Gigi would argue often with Di about her boyfriends and her self-destructive behavior, but Di simply ignored her, letting her words go in one ear and out the other. Eventually, she started ignoring all of Gigi's rules, especially the nightly curfew. Sometimes, she would stay away from home for days at a time. When she would come back, she and Gigi would argue. The last argument had escalated into a physical fight, and Gigi kicked Di out of the house. As Di stood at the door, she said she was leaving for good this time and never coming back.

After two weeks went by, Gigi became worried and started asking the neighbors if they had seen Di around. That's when Gigi received the most horrific news. A neighbor told her that Di was using heroin, and her pimp had her working the stroll downtown on Woodward Avenue. Gigi didn't question the validity of what she was told. She knew in heart it was true.

She began looking for Di at the cheap motels where she supposedly lived. As dangerous as it was, she even tried to find her at night working the streets. After several weeks of searching, she finally stopped when one of Di's girlfriends told her that Di had left town with her boyfriend. Gigi's heart was broken once again. That night, she cried profusely and prayed to God to please bring her baby home to her. She also felt a deep sadness. She thought she was a failure as a mother. She had failed to do what she had vowed to do: protect her children from the streets and predators.

Occasionally, Gigi asked her neighbors or Di's old friends about her whereabouts, but no one could tell her anything. For a while, Gigi kept expecting Di to knock on the door late at night, but that knock never happened—for two long years.

Then, one Sunday afternoon, Gigi responded to a knock and found Di standing in her doorway. When Gigi saw her, she hugged her as tight as she could. Without any hesitation or questions, she told her to come in, and she would fix her some dinner.

All of the other kids gathered around Di as if she was a celebrity and talked as if she had not been away the past two years. However, after a while, the obvious could not be ignored.

"Why is your stomach so big?" one of her younger sisters asked.

Di smiled and rubbed her stomach with pride. "Because I'm having a baby, and Gigi is going to be a grandma."

All of the kids were excited that Di was pregnant and swarmed around her big belly.

A few hours later, the kids went on to do their usual Sunday afternoon routines and left Gigi and Di sitting on the sofa in the living room. Di asked Gigi if she could stay there until she had her baby.

"You and the baby can stay here as long as you need to, forever if you want to," Gigi said.

Di leaned over and hugged Gigi and then laid her head on her lap and began to cry. "Ma mere, I'm so sorry for everything. I've been a bad person, and I've done some terrible things."

As Di apologized over and over again, Gigi rubbed her hands through Di's hair. She stopped when she felt a large, thick raised scar, as if her scalp had been split wide open. But she didn't say a word about it. She knew Di had been through some difficult times, beaten and probably worse things than she could imagine.

"Don't worry about it," Gigi said. "You're not alone. We've all done bad things at one time or another and made plenty of mistakes. You just have to learn from those mistakes and try to do better going forward. You're about to become a mother now. You're going to have to make sacrifices and decisions to benefit your child. It's not all about you anymore; you will have to be unselfish to be a good mother."

Di nodded and wiped away her tears. "I know, Gigi. That's why I'm here with you now."

The following day, Di told Gigi that she had been living in California and became drug-free once she found out she was pregnant. She said she was eight months along and was scared about having the baby alone, which is why she came home. She said nothing about what she had been doing the past two years or who the baby's father was.

Di seemed excited about becoming a mother and always referred to her baby as a baby girl, even though the baby's gender had not yet been determined. Di and her sisters talked and joked about different names for the baby, but Di always said she wanted to give her baby a name with a special meaning, because she knew her baby was going to do great things in this world.

"This baby is already special," she said. "It's a miracle that she made it this far."

Di told Gigi that she was thinking about going back to school, getting her diploma, and then studying to become a nurse or maybe even a doctor like Pops wanted her to do.

"You know you're gifted," Gigi replied. "You can be anything you want to be. You're still young, and you have plenty of time to turn your life around. You know I'll help you. Between your sisters and me, we can keep the baby while you work and go to school. We're your family; you don't have to do this by yourself."

"I know," Di said in a serious voice. "I have to be like you Gigi, unselfish and make my decisions to benefit my child."

A few weeks later, Di went into labor, and Gigi was right by her side through the entire birthing process. They both smiled and cried when I, Di's baby girl, entered the world. Di named me Astrid Josette Johnson. Gigi laughed and said when I was old enough to go to school, I'd be the only girl in class with that name.

Over the next few days, Gigi and the other kids visited Di and me in the hospital. At one point, all ten kids snuck into Di's room at the same time. It was like old times, back when they lived in their big house when they would gather in one room and talk and laugh together.

It had been years since Gigi felt so happy. That day, she kept saying, "Lord, thank you for bringing my family back together." Gigi was so excited about becoming a grandmother for the first time. She fixed up her room for Di and me, hanging up new pink curtains and putting on the new pink bedding for the used crib she bought for me.

The next morning, she went to the hospital to bring Di and me home, but when she entered Di's room, we were already gone. Gigi was scared, thinking Di had taken me back to California.

When Gigi asked the nurse about Di's whereabouts, the nurse told her to wait. A few moments later, a social worker came out. She told Gigi that Di had contacted her office a few weeks earlier about terminating her parental rights and transferring full legal custody to Gigi. The social worker said that the process would be straightforward unless the father contested the custody and that everything would be finalized in six months. My father was the last thing Gigi was worried about, because Di told her she was so heavy into drugs when she got pregnant that she didn't have a clue about the father's identity. She even listed the father as unknown on my birth certificate.

The social worker gave Gigi a stack of papers to sign and then gave her an envelope containing a letter from Di. It read: "You know I can't be a mother right now. I would rather give her to you so that she has a real chance at having a good life. I know you will love her and take care of her. Tell my baby girl that I loved her from the moment I knew she existed, and that's why I gave her to you to raise. Sometimes, no matter how hard you try, you just can't find your way back from darkness. Please forgive me for all the wrongs and hurts I have caused you. Love Di."

Just like that, Di was gone.

Tears flowed from Gigi's eyes as she kept re-reading the letter, trying to understand why Di left the way she did. Then she realized that Di hadn't come back home because she was scared to have her baby alone; she came home to bring her baby to Gigi to raise. Gigi fell to her knees and let out a scream as if she was in intense physical pain. She knew she would never see Di again.

While she lay bent over on the floor, still crying, in a quiet, low whisper, she begged God to watch over her baby. Then she began to say the Lord's Prayer.

A nurse gave Gigi some tissue and helped her get up. Then she gave Gigi a light hug.

"It's going to be all right; he heard you."

Gigi packed me up and took me home. Once she got me settled into my crib, she called a family meeting and told the kids about Di. She also told them that from this day forward, they could never mention Di's name again. They needed to erase her from their memories.

"Elle n'existe plus,[1]" she said. Gigi rarely spoke French but when she did, it was because she was angry or trying to convey a serious message. She also said I would be their little sister and not their niece. The kids all nodded, acknowledging Gigi's request.

Later that night, Gigi rocked back and forth in her recliner as she held me and looked at my curious little face.

"One thing for certain and two things for sure: You're going to be okay, little girl. I promised your mama I would raise you right, and I'm going to do just that."

---

[1] She no longer exists.

3

THE CATERPILLAR DAYS

My earliest memory of my childhood is from around four years of age. This time is memorable to me, because I was finally going to school like everyone else. Gigi said I used to cry every time my siblings left for school. Although I could already read and write, I longed to go to school, to this place where I could learn, have lots of friends, and play, too. All of Gigi's kids were exceptional scholars, so quite naturally, I fell in line.

Since my siblings were always studying, they kept me entertained by teaching me the three Rs. And once I learned how to read, they had no shortage of books for me. I didn't have a library card, but thanks to my siblings, I had a fresh set of books every week. Put a book in my hand, and I was quiet as a mouse. Otherwise, I was bouncing all over the house and needed lots of attention. My siblings used books to calm my precocious behavior, and it worked. I enjoyed reading books of all kinds, even those that were slightly advanced for me.

On those days when I was really restless, I attempted to read Gigi's horticulture books, which she kept in boxes packed underneath our bed. The bright, beautiful colors and unique shapes of the flowers, especially the orchid plants, fascinated me. One day, as I was looking through one of the books, I stumbled on the pages that contained black orchids. I pointed at the silk black orchid plant in our bedroom that Gigi had brought from her old house.

"I don't like that plant. It's ugly and scary to me."

"Why?"

"It's black and spooky looking. Flowers ain't supposed to be black anyway."

"This is a special plant. That's why I kept it. One day, I'm going to grow one just like it in my garden. You're too young to understand, but this plant is unique and beautiful in its own right. You will see and appreciate its beauty when you're older."

I didn't understand what Gigi was talking about. So like any four-year-old, my attention shifted quickly to something else.

Gigi saw my burgeoning intelligence and quest for knowledge and wanted to put me in pre-school, but she couldn't afford it, so she told me that I could attend the city's head start program in the fall. All summer long, I looked forward to going to school in the fall with everyone else.

When fall arrived, Gigi took me to get tested for a local head start educational program. But instead of going to head start, they put me in first grade with the older kids in the neighborhood. At first, I didn't mind because I was the same size if not taller than most of my classmates, and I already knew most of them from the neighborhood. But once I started going to school with them, they treated me differently. They began to tease and bully me. Every day, they teased me and called me names with references to "white girl." During recess, some of the kids pulled my hair, pushed and shoved me, and called me "ugly white girl."

One day I came home and asked, "Gigi, what color am I?"

"The color God made you. Why?"

"Am I ugly?"

She frowned. "No, you're not ugly. You're beautiful just the way God made you."

Even though people in church always told me I was cute or pretty, Gigi never said so. She never talked about beauty or ugliness in terms of people's physical appearance, so I had no reference point for beauty at that time. Sometimes, when I said my bedtime prayers, I asked God to change me from looking ugly and to change my skin color so that the kids at school would like me.

The teasing and bullying continued so much that I began to dislike school. I told Gigi that I was scared and that I didn't want to go back to school because the girls pulled my hair and called me names. She told me to just ignore them; people would be calling me names my entire life.

When the bullying continued, Gigi came to my school and stayed with me a few times during recess. She also made sure that one of my siblings walked me to and from school every day. That only helped for a little while, and then the bullying started again.

The only friend I had in school was Tommy, and that was only because he was being bullied just like me. Tommy and I were the same age, except that he was big, tall and extra chubby. He was also smart and could do the same math problems as high school students. Even though Tommy looked like the other kids in our school, they always hit him or pushed him around. He never fought back; he would just stand there and take it. Maybe he couldn't feel anything through his thick, chubby skin.

Tommy and I continued to be bullied over the next few years. I was still the tall, skinny, ugly white girl, and he was still "Fat Albert" or just plain "fat ass." By then I had learned to cope with it though. I stopped crying or attempting to befriend my classmates. I accepted that Tommy would be my only friend at school. Tommy and I had a lot in common. We both liked to read and play board games, but Tommy also had a love for math and science. He already knew about calculus and physics, and he was the one who helped me develop my advanced skills in math and science.

One day, Tommy and I were at the community park playing on the swings when some older girls came up and made us get off. One of the girls recognized me.

"I know who you are. You're Di's baby girl. I remember Di 'cause she was a hoe just like my sister."

"You don't know me," I said. "My mama's name is not Di; it's Gigi."

"That's your grandmother, stupid," she replied. "Your real mother died when you were a baby. Now go ask your Gigi about that."

As Tommy and I walked off, I turned around to face the girl. "Baise salope! [2]" I cried. It was one of the few French phrases I picked up from Gigi. Then we ran back to my house as fast as we could.

Later that evening, I told Gigi about the girl at the park and what she had said about Di, and then I asked her if it was true. To my surprise, she said that some of it was.

---

[2] Fucking bitch!

"I didn't give birth to you, but you're my daughter, just like all my other girls. And yes, Di was my daughter, too. She was your real mama, the one who birthed you."

I was still confused and asked where Di was.

"I'm going to talk about this one time, and then we're done with this topic forever," she replied. "Comprendez vous?[3]"

I nodded. Then she told me the whole story about Di and the man who gave her drugs and lured her into the streets and ultimately why she gave me to Gigi.

"I'm your mama now, and don't you worry about anything else. You just keep your head in those books, and everything's going to be all right."

I never questioned Gigi or any of my sisters about Di again.

By the time I was eight years old, I was taller than all the kids in my class, who were between ten and twelve years old. It seemed that the length of my hair was growing with the length of my body, and the taller I became; the more attention and bullying it brought me. It seemed none of the other girls in my class or in the entire school wanted to befriend me.

One time, some girls at school tricked me into going with them to an isolated area during recess. Once we got there, they pushed me to the ground and held me there as they tried cutting off my hair and calling me names.

"You think you're cute with all that long hair?"

"You're ugly!"

"You're skinny!"

"Stinky white girl!"

After that incident, I realized that I would probably never have any female friends—or any friends for that matter—so

---

[3] Do you understand?

I resigned myself to becoming a loner. With the exception of my cousin, Val, I had no female friends or relatives who were my age. Val's family lived in Chicago. They were Gigi's cousins, and they had also migrated from Louisiana. Val and I saw each other occasionally during the summer months and on some holidays or at family events. As kids, we were inseparable when we were together, but our closeness was limited, because we lived in different states. We only saw each other a few times a year; however, when we did connect in person, it was as if no time had elapsed between us.

Although I had my cousin Val and a house full of siblings, my spirit was slowly becoming filled with isolation and loneliness, which I saw, no end to. It was at that time that I started to become shy. I started slumping my shoulders and walking with my head down, as if to make myself smaller and less conspicuous. I even began wrapping my pigtails up so as not to draw attention to the length of my hair. I wanted to be invisible when I was in school.

By then, Tommy and I were like two peas in a pod. Gigi had also become great friends with Tommy's mother, almost like sisters, so Gigi would often let me stay over and play at Tommy's house.

Tommy had a large family, too, and he was the youngest child, just like me. His older siblings often ignored him (just like my older siblings ignored me) except for his brother Ricky, who was much older than us. Ricky was in his early twenties and worked in a mechanic shop like Big John used to have. He was especially kind to Tommy and me. He often played board games and joked around with us, always calling us his little Rugrats. Sometimes, he would take us to McDonalds and buy us Happy Meals. It seemed liked Ricky was my big brother, too.

I really liked Ricky. He was very kind to me, and he always asked me if I wanted or needed anything. I would say no, but sometimes he would surprise me and buy me stuff anyway, like when he bought Tommy a Batman backpack and me a Barbie backpack. Sometimes, he would come to the school and walk us home, walking me to my house first. I always felt safe with him, especially when we walked through the Gardens. He was big and strong like the WWF wrestlers on television. When he took Tommy and me to the park, no one bothered us. It was as if people feared and respected him. He knew that Tommy and I got bullied, so he always acted like he was our protector.

One day while I was at Tommy's house, Ricky called me into his bedroom and gave me a present. It was necklace, and he told me not to let anyone know I had it.

Before I left, he said, "You're my favorite girl, and you know I love you, don't you?"

I smiled and nodded.

Over the next few months, Ricky continued to give me gifts: bracelets, Barbie dolls, and my favorite, Nancy Drew books.

One day, Ricky called me into his room and told me he had another present for me, but this time I had to let him kiss me first.

He kissed me on my forehead and said, "You're my favorite girl, and you know I love you, don't you?"

I smiled and nodded and then went back to playing with Tommy. Ricky continued to play the forehead kiss game for a few months almost every time I was at their house.

One Saturday afternoon, Gigi and Tommy's mother went shopping, so I stayed at Tommy's house with him and his older sister.

it never did. It was as if I was hypnotized. I couldn't move or resist him. What I felt was indescribable. Even though I wasn't in pain, I still wanted him to stop, but I was too scared to say anything. The whole time he was kissing me down there I could feel my heart beating in my chest, faster and faster, as if it was going to burst. I could even hear my heart beating at times, like a loud drumbeat. The faster my heart pounded, the louder it got. I knew I wasn't supposed to be alone with boys or men, period. Gigi would kill me if she found out I was in a room with a boy or letting anyone kiss me anywhere on my body.

When he finally stopped, I fixed my panties and tried to leave the room, but he grabbed my arm.

"I'm not finished yet, and you're not going anywhere."

He pushed a chair up against the door and then threw me onto the bed. He climbed on top and straddled his legs over me. I started crying and screamed at him to get off. He put his hands over my mouth and held me down as he pulled off my panties. Then he loosened his belt and unzipped his pants.

"I'm going to let you taste me first, and then I'm going to make a woman out of you."

Just as I saw his snake come out, staring directly in my face, Tommy broke through the door and charged Ricky, knocking him off me. As he wrestled with Ricky, he turned to me.

"Astrid, go home. Run Astrid...Run!"

I ran out of their house and across the park to my house as fast as I could.

When I got home, I took a bath and put on my pajamas and got into my bed, which I shared with Gigi.

When Gigi came home, she looked at me in surprise. "Girl, what's wrong with you? I told you to stay at Annie's (Tommy's mother) house until we got back."

I told her I had a tummy ache and that I had accidently pooped in my panties, so that's why I came home.

She felt my forehead to see if I was warm and then she gave me some Pepto-Bismol. Later that night when Gigi came to bed, I turned to her and hugged her.

"Please hold me tight," I said. "I don't want to ever grow up."

She hugged me. "Child, what's wrong with you? Did you get your period?"

"What's that?"

"Never mind," she replied. Then she looked at me. "Did anyone try to bother you?"

I shook my head, "No."

The next day, I told Gigi I was not feeling well, so we stayed home from church. Throughout that day, I found myself clinging to Gigi. I followed her to every room in the house, and when she sat down, I sat in her lap or played right under her feet or beside her. Gigi was puzzled by my behavior.

"Child, what's wrong with you? I can't get my chores done with you hanging onto me." Then, without knowing that I heard her, in a quiet whisper she said, "You're acting just like Di did when we lived in Louisiana."

Gigi had always wondered why Di was so clingy when she was a small child and if someone had bothered her or molested her. That might explain why she was drawn to the lure of drugs and the street life when she got older.

"Babygirl," Gigi said, "I'm going to ask you one more time. Did anyone bother you . . . down there?" She pointed at my berrybush.

I shook my head, "No, Gigi. That's nasty; stop asking me stuff like that."

The next day at school, Tommy had two black eyes. I knew Ricky had done it.

During recess, Tommy gave me a bag. I looked inside and saw my panties, so I tossed the bag in the garbage can. Tommy said Ricky was angry with both of us and that we better not tell anyone what happened or something bad was going to happen to us. We did a pinky swear not to ever say anything about that day.

I never went over to Tommy's house again after that, but occasionally, I had the misfortune of seeing Ricky in passing. Sometimes when he saw me, he would smile or wink as if to let me know he was going to try to put his snake in me again. Whenever I saw Ricky, no matter how faint or brief, a tsunami wave of fear washed over me. I would lose my breath and gasp for air as if I were having an asthma attack.

The last time I saw Ricky was at Tommy's birthday party at the community park. I was blindfolded and trying to hit a piñata with a stick when a familiar voice came up behind me and whispered, "Little girl, I'm still waiting for you." I knew before I lifted the blindfold that it was Ricky. Seeing him that day made me feel that he could and would hurt me again, but the next time he would finish what he started. I wondered if I could ever get away from him. Would he always be lurking around corners waiting for me like the bogeyman?

I continued to have frequent nightmares over the next year. Sometimes, the nightmares were like a movie that replayed the entire scene with Ricky kissing my berrybush.

Other times, the nightmares were even worse, with him actually putting his snake inside me, causing me to have episodes of occasional bed-wetting. For the first time in my life, I felt a level of fear that had been unfamiliar to me before the incident with Ricky. But I could never tell Gigi or anyone, because I believed it was my fault. I had broken Gigi's rule and allowed a man to kiss me.

The next year, both Tommy and I received scholarships to attend Brookhaven Academy, a college preparatory school. We would go there for both middle school and high school. It was the perfect escape for us. We had to wear uniforms, and it offered the option of boarding during the academic year.

Once I found out we could live at the school like college kids, I begged Gigi to let me go. I loved my Gigi; I still slept in the bed with her even though I had a bunk bed in my sisters' room, but I wanted to leave the Gardens. I hated most of the kids there, but above all, I feared Ricky. I always felt I had to look over my shoulder and watch out for him, because I knew he would hurt me if he ever got access to me again. Gigi agreed reluctantly to let me attend Brookhaven, and thus began our daily phone calls, which carried on through my adult life.

I really liked Brookhaven. Not only was it out of our neighborhood, it had a lot more kids there who looked like me. The kids were so much nicer to us than the kids from the Gardens, too. They were gifted like us, so we weren't teased because we were smart, and most of the bullying stopped for both of us. Occasionally, some kids teased us, calling us indigents, welfare kids, or part of Brookhaven's philanthropic charity programs, but their teasing didn't bother me at all, because anything was better than the Gardens. The only drawback was Tommy's sudden departure. He developed a serious illness and had to leave Brookhaven. I never saw much of him after he left school.

My first three years at Brookhaven were swift and transformative. While there, I felt safe and normal; my nightmares about Ricky practically stopped. I even had female friends for the very first time. I began to emerge from the grips of shyness and low self-esteem that had encased my young spirit during grammar school. I was on the track team and an active member of several student organizations. However, the most noticeable change was my body's accelerated growth. I was only twelve, but my body screamed sixteen. I was five feet six inches tall wearing a D-cup. I had long, dirty blond hair, a small waistline, and thick, curvy hips, and I weighed about 120 pounds. At that time, I didn't appreciate the significance of my body measurements.

During visits home, Gigi would look at me and shake her head. "Oh my god, what am I going to do with you?"

The men and teenage boys from the neighborhood called me "jailbait." Even my siblings were concerned about me. They would make sure my body was covered with sweaters. And if a man looked at me or tried to say something to me, they would call him a pervert.

"She's a little girl; she's only twelve!"

I knew boys were looking at me, but I never had a single thought about having a boyfriend. I was slightly uncomfortable being around boys. However, that changed when I met Jeff during track practice. Since he was on the boys' track team, we sat together often on the bus en route to meets. Similar to me, Jeff's family was from Black Bottom, but his parents had become successful entrepreneurs, so he was able to attend Brookhaven without a scholarship. Jeff and I developed a close friendship, but it remained platonic and carried on through our adult lives.

Just as I finished middle school, Gigi finally finished nursing school, earning a master's degree. She purchased a new home in a northern suburb of Farmington Hills, which was close to Brookhaven. The house was a traditional four-bedroom colonial but was nestled on a spectacular one-and-a-half-acre lot. Gigi was able to have her garden again, full of nothing but beautiful orchids.

When it came to growing orchids, Gigi was as knowledgeable as any horticulturalist. Gigi had also progressed to growing even rarer and more exotic orchids; those that typically would not flourish outside of their normal environments, including several species of the genus Bulbophyllum, commonly called black orchid. These were by far her favorite flowers because of their mystique and rare beauty. Her favorite black orchid was the Liparis Nervosa, native to Japan and China. Gigi was intrigued not only by their exotic beauty but also by their mythical meanings. Perhaps it had something to do with her Creole roots, believing that having these flowers would impart their energy and powers to her and her loved ones. Whenever Gigi went into her analysis of the flowers in her garden, we just pretended to listen as if we were really interested, never hearing a word she said.

Gigi's purchase of our new home was fraught with sadness. The plan was for me to move back home with her, but I wanted to continue boarding while I attended high school. John Junior was away at college, so technically, Gigi had an empty nest. All of my siblings had graduated from high school and went away to college. At Gigi's urging, they never moved back home, and they only returned for holidays and occasional visits. Gigi had fulfilled Big John's dream of making sure all of the children attended college. Even though she had ten kids go to college, occasionally, she still felt sad because she had lost Di to the streets.

4

THE BUTTERFLY EMERGES

The next four years flew by, and by age sixteen, I had blossomed even more. I was often told that I had a "banging body." I was 5'10" and weighed about 135 pounds with a 24-inch waistline, 36-inch hips, and was exploding out of my DD cups. Banging body or not, it didn't matter, because I wasn't planning to date or have a boyfriend anytime soon. Every time I thought about possibly liking a boy, I got images of Ricky in my head. In my mind, nothing good could come from having a boyfriend. I simply could not imagine anything good about a penis going inside of me.

At the ripe old age of sixteen, I finally graduated from high school with honors. Although I received scholarships to several Ivy League schools, I decided I didn't want to attend a college out of state. Even though I had spent the last seven years in boarding school, I still didn't want to be far away from Gigi. I felt a great sense of comfort knowing she was in my backyard, only a few minutes away if I needed her.

I decided to study engineering at the University of Michigan (U of M), which was about forty-five minutes away from home, but I would enjoy the summer living at home with Gigi. By then, all of my siblings had left home. Big John would have been proud of his children. Six of them had become medical doctors while four of them were lawyers. Gigi had all of their high school and college graduation pictures posted throughout the house. As I walked through the house, I thought about Di, where she was, and what she might have become if that man hadn't gotten to her. More importantly, would she have liked me or been proud of me? Gigi was a perfect mother to me, but I still wondered about Di and my father, the sperm donor.

The trajectory of my life changed forever the summer I worked as an engineering intern at one of the auto plants in Detroit. I was excited because this was my first real job and glimpse into my future profession as an Engineer.

About a week after I started, a lady asked if I had a brother who worked in the plant. When I told her I didn't, she explained that there was a new engineer working there and that we looked like we could be brother and sister. Over the next few weeks, other people asked me the same question about this man, which aroused my curiosity. For a split second, I thought Di may have had other children besides me, and this guy really could be my brother. Then I dismissed the thought and carried on with my life as an intern.

I finally met my "long lost brother" in the cafeteria. While waiting in line to pay for my frozen yogurt, another intern pointed out this cute guy. At first glance he looked Mediterranean with his jet-black hair and olive complexion. Although he wasn't very tall, I thought he was gorgeous. He was about my height with an athletic build. I could see the muscles in his arms and chest bulging through his dress shirt. He was handsome by anyone's standards. Mr. "fine" (Philip Thornton) walked over and greeted me. To my surprise, he had a thick southern accent. At first, I thought he was kidding around, but he wasn't. He spoke with a true Mississippi southern drawl.

"You must be my little sister," he said, "the girl that everyone has been asking me about."

We laughed and did quick introductions and then went our separate ways. As I walked to my desk, I took a deep breath and whispered to myself, "That man is fine."

A few days later while I was sitting at a table in the cafeteria drinking tea and reading, Philip invited himself to join me. He said he had been working on the second shift for the last three years but had recently got a new job as a general manager on the day shift. I told him that I had just graduated from high school and would be attending U of M in the fall. He pulled out his business card, wrote his home phone number on the back of it, and gave it to me.

"You're really pretty," he said. "Almost as cute as me. Let's talk some more. Why don't you call me tonight, and maybe we can go to dinner or something this weekend."

I didn't think much about it. He seemed nice, and he was very handsome, so I called him. We talked briefly, mainly about him, his alma mater, and his home state of Mississippi. When I hung up, I smiled, feeling happy. As I lay in my bed, I realized I was experiencing my first crush and could possibly have my first boyfriend.

The next day when I got to work, I saw Philip in passing a few times, but he seemed to be ignoring me. Later that night, I called him and was shocked at his response.

"You lied to me," he said. "I thought you were going to college this fall, but you're still in high school. I could lose my job or go to jail for fooling around with you."

"Please hear me out," I said. I explained how I had graduated from high school at the age of sixteen.

"That doesn't change anything," he said. "I'm twenty-six, and you're too young for me." He continued speaking in a cocky tone. "If you're still pretty when you turn eighteen, just look me up. But don't call me anymore."

Even though we had not gone on a date or forged any type of relationship, I was deeply hurt. I felt rejected, as if something other than my age was the problem. Perhaps I wasn't pretty enough.

When I told Gigi what happened, she said he was right; he was too old for me. "Before you go thinking about dating any boy your age or older, you better give it some serious thought, 'cause one thing for certain and two things for sure, they're going to want to pop your cherry. Just be patient. In a few more years, you can have any man you want. Men are going to be lining up just to drink your bathwater." Her face wrinkled with concern. "You're going to have to be careful though. You need to learn the power of your beauty. It will make a man love you, but it'll make him try to hurt you, too."

"Please, Gigi, I can do without your sermons," I replied. "You raised me right. I'm going to finish college, marry a nice man, have a few babies, and live happily ever after just like you and Big John."

She smiled sadly. "Sweetie, I worry about you. You got a lot of book smarts, but you don't know anything about life. I don't care where you are, just remember . . ." And then she repeated her famous quote that she had told all my older sisters and probably John Junior, too: "That the world is cruel out there. It will swallow you up and spit you out like you're nothing if you're not careful. You need to enjoy the privileges of your life and the innocence of it. You'll get to experience being an adult soon enough."

I knew that quote like the back of my hand, because I had heard it a thousand times.

For the remainder of my internship, I avoided Philip, and he seemed to avoid me as well. As it turned out, he was quite a lady's man. He was dating several women who worked at the plant. Although I had probably dodged a bullet with Philip, his rejection still hurt. He was the first guy I ever liked as a boyfriend. The ten-year age difference didn't matter to me. Deep down inside, I felt there was something wrong with me. Maybe Philip had seen my defects, and that's why he lost interest in me. After all, my own mother didn't want me. She thought I was worthless, and so did Ricky. That's why he attacked me. I would forget about ever having a boyfriend and just focus on what I was good at: school. With my dual major course load and the organizations I planned to join in college, I wouldn't have time for a boyfriend. I would simply forget about Philip. I was leaving for college in a few weeks anyway.

The next few weeks passed like nanoseconds. My summer job was over and my life as a college student began. The most interesting aspect of my freshmen year at college was all the sex that was going on around me; especially with my roommate Tara, who was basking in the glory of it.

Tara had attended Catholic school her entire life and had been a cheerleader in high school, but a sweet, wholesome, innocent Catholic schoolgirl she was not. She said the only reason she came to U of M was because her boyfriend was on the football team. She and I got along well, and I liked her a lot. She was unapologetic and had an unrelenting spirit about herself. She was pretty, confident, and definitely part of the in-crowd. Thanks to her, I had the opportunity to attend a few parties that I would never have been invited to otherwise. Even more than the parties, I enjoyed hearing her talk about her sexual antics. She told me that by the time she was fifteen, she had already started having regular and oral sex. She said that when her boyfriend received his football scholarship, she celebrated with him by allowing him to have anal sex with her. That surprised me. I didn't even know straight people had anal sex. I thought only gay men did that.

Talking to Tara was better than any sex education class. She was very animated as she described her sexual exploits, which helped to chip away at my sexual ignorance. Every day she had one story or another about sex with her boyfriend, and I enjoyed hearing about every second of it. She would sneak into her boyfriend's dorm to have sex with him, and they were always experimenting with different positions, toys, and other stuff. While Tara made sex seem like it was a desirable, enjoyable experience, I couldn't imagine ever feeling that way about it. Although I was technically still a virgin, and perhaps appropriately ignorant when it came to carnal pleasures, the joys and passion of lovemaking were foreign to me, as if those feelings would always be inaccessible to me.

Deep within, I felt sexually awkward, like damaged goods. I was still uncomfortable with dating. However, I tried to pretend I was a normal, socially adjusted college freshman. I went so far as to make up a story that I had a boyfriend at Penn, which was my reason for not dating anyone on campus. I would also make up stories about visits with my fictitious boyfriend when I went home on weekends, thus began my first of many facades.

One day, Tara sat me down for a chat. "Babygirl, I know you're in love with your man at Penn, but you better try out some other dick before you settle on that one. You need to make sure you have the right dick before you get married, and you won't know that unless you try a few. I've had several and I'm still not done with my search for the 'right' one."

She said the only time a compromise should be made was when it involved money. I laughed and shook my head.

"Seriously, you better listen to me," she said. "You need to try out some other dick, at least a handful. You know when you see a grouchy, bitchy lady, like some of these professors around here, it's because they're dissatisfied; they married the wrong dick."

We laughed, and I told her that I would keep her advice in mind.

With the blink of an eye, freshman year was over. Rather than working, I decided to attend summer school and live at home with Gigi. Although I was seventeen and still not dating, Gigi and I had a blast. When she got off work, we spent the afternoons working in her garden. It was then that I gained an appreciation for Gigi's love of orchids. The color palette and arrangement in her garden and greenhouse were quiet and stunning. Sometimes when Gigi worked late, I would sit in the backyard alone and savor the beauty of her garden. Its serene view was like a bit of paradise on Earth.

Occasionally, Gigi would drink an entire pitcher of mojito as she worked in her garden. While tipsy, she would say anything, and it usually pertained to sex, including the fact she was still quite sexually active. I pretended to help in her garden so I could hear the stories about her sex life and all the drama that was going on in the hospital where she worked. It was better than any reality show.

On the weekends, we went shopping at the Eastern market and then usually stopped by an outdoor fair. She always made me a delicious dinner in the evening, and sometimes she even let me drink wine with her. While I felt that Gigi and I had gotten closer over the summer, she still refused to talk about Di. Whenever I tried to inquire about her, she shut me down. And if I persisted, she became angry and still refused to talk about her.

When I returned to school in the fall, I felt like I had matured and was looking forward to meeting someone special. I was seventeen and started transitioning into becoming a woman. No longer shy, I embraced all of my beauty, body and brains. The only thing missing was my roommate, Tara. She did not come back for sophomore year.

Over the next few months, I met a few guys and went out on a few dates and even French kissed a few times, but I had not yet met anyone special enough to become my boyfriend. This was disappointing to me. I thought I would have had a boyfriend by then. It seemed that everyone else around me thought so as well, especially my sisters.

Christmas was nearing, the one holiday that Gigi insisted we spend together. That meant all of my siblings, including those with spouses and children, would be home for about a week. We were packed like sardines in Gigi's house, and we loved every minute of it. The only snag was my sisters' obsession with my boyfriend status. I could never tell if they were being overly protective or just curious, but either way, it annoyed me. I guess it would be that way until I finished college and started my career, proof that I had survived the Di curse.

During the Christmas break, I met up with Tara again. She was still high-spirited and had moved on to dating older men, from ages forty and up. She was dating an executive who worked for one of the auto plants and invited me to a small gathering at his house.

I wore jeans and a tailored red sweater with my hair pulled back in a long ponytail. The only makeup I wore was natural peach lip-gloss. When I got to the party, to my surprise, Philip was there. Initially, he didn't recognize me. He walked up to me and started to introduce himself before he realized who I was.

"Wow, you look different," he said. He acted like he had met me for the first time. We sat down in the living room and started talking. After a few minutes, I interrupted him.

"You do know I'm only seventeen, right? I won't be eighteen for eight more months."

He smiled. "That's close enough for me."

We had our own little private party and talked for the next three hours. Before we left, we exchanged phone numbers, and then he walked me to my car.

Before I even got into my house, Philip called me. "I want to see you again. Can I see you tomorrow?"

When I told Gigi about Philip, she expressed her reservations. She still felt like he was too old for me. Since I had not yet had a real boyfriend, she thought I needed to date someone closer to my age. I reminded her that Big John had been ten years older than her, but she said she was already a mother of five when they met; she didn't have my innocence.

"Go ahead," she said finally, "but be careful. You need to learn who the man is on the inside. Don't let his outer beauty deceive you."

The next day was my first official date with Philip. I decided to pull out all the stops. I put on a short, fitted, cream-colored knit dress with matching boots. I wore my hair straight, to show off my golden blond highlights, along with subtle makeup and a pop of cherry red lip-gloss. As I looked in the mirror, I paused for a few minutes. It was the first time I saw myself as pretty and sexy. I finally felt like a grown woman.

As I was taking one final look in the mirror, my six-year old niece, Brea, who was visiting for the holidays, yelled upstairs and said that somebody was here for me. Then all I heard was chuckles and laughter. I knew my sisters, at least the three attorneys were drilling Philip.

Deana, my oldest sister (second behind Di) came upstairs and stood in the bathroom doorway. "I see you're going out with J.R. Ewing. He's handsome, but his southern accent . . ." She shook her head. "He sounds like a character right out of a country-western movie. Where the hell is he from anyway?"

I hurried downstairs and rushed him out the door before my family embarrassed me even more.

As we walked toward his black sports car, he paused and looked me over. "I knew you were pretty, but damn, I didn't know you were all that. You look like a model, or the girlfriend of a professional athlete."

I looked at him. "Am I supposed to take that as a compliment?"

He smiled. "Definitely. So, where are we going?"

While I would have preferred it if he had made reservations somewhere, I didn't hold it against him. I suggested we go to Greektown and wing it.

The weather was unusually mild, so I felt like walking a little bit. As we walked, I noticed men looking at me. I loved the attention, and I was getting plenty of it. One guy even stopped us and told Philip that he had a very beautiful lady. Philip smiled as if the guy had said he was beautiful. Finally, we made it to a restaurant.

During dinner, Philip told me that he had never dated a girl as beautiful as me. He said when he walked around with me, I made him feel important, like he was a celebrity or someone famous. No other girl had ever made him feel that way.

"Well, that's surprising. If I recall correctly, you seemed to be quite the ladies' man when we first met," I replied.

"Things are not always as they appear; I'm not a ladies man at all. But if you can't be with the one you want, you might as well just play around. That's over now. I think I'm ready to settle down and get married; at least that will get my parents off my back."

"That's not a good reason to get married."

"Oh, you misunderstood me. I'm from the South; everyone is expected to get married and start a family near age thirty. I didn't mean to digress. Let me pay the bill so we can get out of here."

We left the restaurant and went to a bar near the riverfront and listened to some live music. As the evening wound down, he asked me if I wanted to go to his apartment for a little while or go straight home. I really wanted to go to his apartment, but I was scared, so I said I needed to go home.

When he walked me to the door, he gave me a wet, juicy French kiss and then pulled back and looked me in the eye. "Next time, I want you to come home with me."

I wasn't sure if I would ever go to Philip's home. Gigi always said I shouldn't go to a man's house without the understanding that sex was likely to occur, and that I definitely shouldn't climb into bed unless I was planning to have sex with him. Gigi didn't believe in taking platonic relationships into intimate spaces. "Don't kid yourself," she'd say. "Men always have sex on the brain; they're wired that way."

Philip and I saw each other every day after our first date. He usually came over to my house after he got off work. Our intimacy was limited to French kissing, but I did let him rub me up a little bit. He kept telling me that that he wanted me to stay at his house before I went back to school. I told him I would think about it. I never told him that I was still a virgin. He probably assumed, as many people did, that I wasn't. I decided to lose my virginity when we went out the following Saturday.

That night we went out to dinner and then to a nightclub called The Sting. I was feeling nervous and anxious about the grand finale that was planned for the night, so I drank a little more than I should have. I finished off an entire pitcher of Long Island iced tea all by myself. I went on to drink a few shots of tequila as well. I knew I had gone too far when I could no longer keep my balance as I walked in my three-inch heels, which became obvious when Philip and I were slow dancing. Instead of dancing, I just stood there, my head resting on his shoulders and my arms wrapped around him.

"I think it's time to go. Do you want to go to a Coney Island restaurant and have breakfast?" Philip said.

I didn't respond. The next thing I knew, he was holding my arm and walking me to his car.

"Is it still okay for me to take you to my house while you're this way?" he asked. He was too nice to say that I was drunk as hell and totally fucked up.

"Yes, I still want to go to your place," I replied.

At some point during the drive to his apartment, I must have fallen asleep. The last thing I remembered about that night was sitting on the sofa in his living room.

When I woke up the next morning, I sat up in bed and wondered briefly where I was and how I got there. Just as I realized I was wearing a man's T-shirt with nothing else, I started to feel extremely nauseous. I jumped out of bed and ran straight for a door that I hoped was a bathroom and not a closet. Luckily, it was the bathroom, and I threw up into the sink, several times.

Philip must have heard me, because he came running to the bathroom door and asked if I was okay. He gave me a facecloth, and I told him that I should lie back down. I got back into bed, and about five minutes later, Philip brought me some Aspirin and a glass of water. Then he placed a neatly folded warm towel across my forehead. I asked him if he minded if I stayed awhile or if he was ready to take me home.

"Please stay," he said. "You can stay as long as you like. You need to drink plenty of fluids and try to eat something later."

He turned on the TV and found a show I liked and then left the room.

"Call me if you need anything," he said on his way out.

I must have fallen back to sleep, because a few hours had passed when Philip woke me up and told me that I needed to eat.

He had gone out to the store and bought soup for me. I ate a little and started to feel better. I got up and took a shower and put on some makeshift pajamas—one of Philip's T-shirts and a pair of cotton shorts—and then joined him in the living room. I apologized for my behavior and explained that I had never been intoxicated before.

"You don't need to apologize for anything," he said. "We all have had moments like that at least once in our lifetime. I'm just glad you were with me and not with someone else who might have exploited the situation."

"Why did you undress me?" I asked.

"Because you vomited all over yourself and on my sofa and carpet."

As my face reddened, he said he was worried about me. He didn't know if I was asleep or if I had passed out. After he put me into his bed, he lay beside me for a while, because he wanted to watch over me. He feared that I might be suffering from alcohol poisoning and might lose consciousness or worse. He had never seen anyone as intoxicated as I was since his frat party college days. I was so embarrassed I put my head down as he continued. He said that while I was sleeping, he had washed my panties by hand and took my dress to a quick one-hour dry cleaners. Although I felt embarrassed, at that moment, I began to see Philip in a very different light. He wasn't just good looking; he was also caring and nurturing.

That's when I told him I was still a virgin.

He looked at me in shock. "Wow. You don't look like a virgin. You seem so smart and sophisticated. Why, are you waiting to get married?"

I shook my head. "No, I just never met the right guy."

"Well, maybe we should wait so you can make sure I'm the right guy."

I smiled shyly. "I already know you're the right guy for me," I continued before he could protest. "I know it's only been two weeks, but I'm crazy about you. I wanted to be with you when I first met you. I know it seems quick, but I think I'm ready."

He paused for a few minutes and then smiled. "Now you got me feeling nervous."

I grabbed his hand and looked into his eyes. "It's ok; I'm ready now."

He walked me into the bedroom and laid a big white towel on the bed. Then we both got naked. I climbed into bed first and lay on my back.

He pulled the covers back. "I want to look at you. Turn over onto your stomach."

He kneeled down and kissed my ankles, working his way up to my back while rubbing his hands along my legs, my thighs, and my butt.

"You're so beautiful," he said. "I wish you could see how beautiful you are."

Then he turned me over onto my back. He made sure that the towel was under me, I guess to absorb the blood that would flow when he popped my cherry.

We began kissing, and then he sucked on my breast as he gently massaged my vagina with his fingers. But for some reason, I wasn't getting wet though.

"Maybe we're both nervous," he said.

That was strange, because he had made me feel wet several times before at my house when we French kissed. Then he put on a condom and began trying to penetrate me. It hurt and didn't feel anything like I thought it would.

He stopped suddenly. "I think we need a little more help here." Then he went to the bathroom and got some baby oil. He squeezed a large amount into his hands and then wiped it on my vagina and the walls of my labia. He climbed back on top, and then he was able to finally get the head of his penis inside of me. With a few painful thrusts, it was over. I had lost my virginity.

Nothing about it felt good or special. It was nothing like I had imagined. I heard it would hurt a little bit at first and then it would feel good, ethereal and indescribable, something that I would want to do over and over again. There was nothing about that experience that I wanted to repeat. Philip got up and replaced the towel that was under me with a fresh one. Then he slid over and held me until we fell asleep.

The next morning, when I walked into the house, Gigi greeted me with a stern voice. "I hope you're happy with yourself; there's no turning back now."

I didn't attempt to talk to her about the experience. I was still trying to process it, primarily how disappointing it was. I went up to my room, packed my stuff, and drove back to school.

Later that night, I talked to Philip on the phone.

"I know this sounds corny," he said, "but I think I'm in love with you. I felt something special for you when I first met you when you were only sixteen, which is why I pushed you away. If I had spent any time with you, it would have led to trouble for both of us. There's no way I could have been around you and only had a platonic relationship with you, especially with you looking like you were about twenty years old." He paused before continuing. "I know you're busy with your studies, but I would like to see you on the weekends, even if I have to drive to Ann Arbor and get a room."

"Okay," I said.

Philip and I saw each other every weekend over the next few months. It was then that I noticed he was a germaphobe. Sex with us was never spontaneous even if we were engaging in light foreplay, we would never go straight to having sex. He always made sure I showered first, and he always put a towel on the bed for me to lie on. On those rare occasions when we did not use a towel, as soon as we finished, he changed the linen. Although sex with Philip was not passionate, it didn't concern me, because I needed and liked his other qualities. He was a caretaker and a protector, and that's what I loved about him. He made me feel safe. He filled a void that I didn't know existed until he became a part of my life.

Whenever he came to Ann Arbor, he would take me shopping to buy groceries, clothing and anything else I needed or wanted. He always made sure my car had a full tank of gas and he checked to make sure it was running properly; and if it needed repairs he took care of it immediately. He even helped me with my chores around my apartment, doing laundry and vacuuming and so forth. He always wanted to take care of me in some way.

As time went on, I told Philip that I needed to spend a little less time with him and more time studying. I had fallen behind in my schoolwork. I told him that I would lose my scholarship if my grades fell below a 3.0 average. He said he understood, but his behavior contradicted his words. I didn't hear from Philip for two weeks, not even on the weekends. When we finally reconnected he said he knew I had midterm finals so he gave me time and space to prepare for my exams. He never told me what he did during his hiatus from me.

A month later, Philip moved to a new apartment in the city of Southfield, a suburb outside of Detroit. That's when he asked me to move in with him. I told him that I couldn't because of my apartment lease.

"What does that matter?" he asked. "You're not paying the lease anyway. Your scholarship is covering it."

He kept trying to persuade me to move in with him. Finally, I told him that I couldn't live with a man whom I wasn't married to.

"Well, in that case, I'm going to have to marry you now instead of later."

I smiled, but I didn't respond. Although I loved him, I wasn't sure I wanted to live with him yet.

The first weekend I spent at Philip's new apartment, he said he had something special planned for me. That night, he took me to The Whitney, an exclusive restaurant in midtown where he proposed to me. "I love you," he said, "and I want to spend the rest of my life with you."

I was speechless. I told him that I was thinking about going to law school when I finished my engineering degree and would most likely go to a school out of state.

"Not a problem," he said. "I can either take a leave of absence from work and go with you or find a new job wherever you go."

I told him that I loved him, but I wasn't sure I was ready for marriage, and that maybe I was too young. I let him put the ring on my finger, but I told him that I needed to think about it. Marriage would change my life in a way that I had not planned for at this time.

After days of continued pressure from Philip, I finally gave in and accepted his marriage proposal, but I told him that we would have a long engagement, because I wanted to finish school before we got married. He said that would be fine, it would give us plenty of time to plan an elaborate wedding.

A few days later, I woke up feeling tired and nauseous, with other flu-like symptoms, so I stayed in bed most of the day. While I was napping, Philip called, and I told him that I wasn't feeling well.

"Do you want me to come over and take care of you," he said. "You probably need to take a pregnancy test before you start taking any medicine. I noticed that your period was late. Your period is regular, and I know exactly when you get it, about every twenty-eight days.

"You're right," I said, "but I can't be pregnant, because we use condoms all the time."

"You know condoms are only ninety-eight percent effective," he replied. "Maybe we fell into that two percent."

Philip's preoccupation with the possibility that I might be pregnant annoyed me. He seemed certain I was pregnant, as if he had already given me a pregnancy test himself. But that was not possible. We had not taken any chances. I always made sure the condom was on before any sex occurred.

Since Gigi was a nurse, I called her and told her how I was feeling, hoping she could recommend something from the local drugstore. She wasn't fooled.

"Do you think you're pregnant?"

I said no and explained how Philip and I had always been responsible and extra careful. She told me what cold medicine to buy and that I should probably pick up a pregnancy test while I was there, too.

I laughed. "Relax, Gigi. You're not getting any grandkids from me any time soon."

Then I began to wonder if Philip and Gigi had been secretly talking to each other, because they both seemed obsessed with the notion that I might be pregnant.

After I returned from the store, I peed on the pregnancy test stick and waited patiently for the negative sign to appear, but that didn't happen. It brought up a big red plus sign instead.

I went back to the store and bought two more pregnancy tests made by two different manufacturers. I wanted to be certain I did it right this time. Sure enough, both tests came back positive.

As I sat in the bathroom, I put my head in my lap and began to cry, wondering how this had happened. I decided I would go to the campus clinic and take another pregnancy test before I made any decisions.

Once again, the results were the same. I was definitely pregnant and not yet eighteen. Being an unwed teenage mother was the last thing I wanted for myself. Not only had I disappointed myself, I would disappoint my entire family, especially Gigi. None of my sisters had any children out of wedlock. I guess I was really Di's daughter, following in her footsteps after all, pregnant and unmarried.

I decided I would not say anything to Philip about the pregnancy, because I was most likely going to have an abortion. I called Val to discuss my situation; she would advise and counsel me on the matter.

"Do you think the condom broke?" she asked.

"Not that I'm aware of."

When I told her about Philip's comments about me taking a pregnancy test, she said that maybe the condom slipped off or tore and he never told me about it.

I began to get upset. "This is fucked up. I can't have a baby now."

"You should think about it," she said. "It's not the end of the world if you have this baby. At least Philip has a good job, and you know he wants to marry you."

"It's not the baby; it's the timing. I don't feel like I'm ready or mature enough to be someone's mother."

More importantly, I wasn't sure if I wanted to marry Philip. And I definitely didn't want to disappoint Gigi.

Later that night, I thought about Di, how she kept me when her life was in turmoil, how she could have easily aborted me, but she sacrificed and got off drugs and the streets so she could deliver a healthy baby. Then she made the ultimate sacrifice and traveled back to Michigan to make sure she placed me safely in Gigi's arms. Things could have been a lot worst for me, but Di must have loved me when I was a tiny knot in her stomach, enough to make a decision to bring me into this world. I'm sure that Di's pregnancy with me was an accident, especially given her drug-addicted lifestyle. If she could have me, surely I could have my baby, and I wouldn't be alone. I would have my own little family.

After I finished my finals, I broke the news to Gigi, even though I had not yet told Philip.

"I'm not surprised," she said. "I was afraid something like this would happen to you. You've always had book smarts, but somehow you're missing the common sense life stuff. I tried to do everything right to educate and protect you, but I still came up short." She shook her head. "The only reason you're telling me this is because you're planning to have this baby."

"What if Di had aborted me?"

"Don't interrupt me! Just like I knew you were pregnant two weeks ago, I knew you would be thinking about Di as you were evaluating your situation. Just like I told Di, I'm here to help you, and I will also help you with your baby. You don't have to do this alone, and you don't have to marry that country-western cowboy. I really think you should experience more adult life before you get married. You're only seventeen, and he's your first everything. You haven't lived long enough to even know what you want in a husband."

She took a deep breath before continuing. "I'm going to say one last thing, and then I won't ever speak about it again. I don't think Philip is right for you. There's something about him that's unsettling to me. He's got a dark spirit. You haven't seen it yet. I think he's two-faced—one person in front of people and another person behind closed doors."

"You're wrong, Gigi," I replied. "I've spent practically every day with him the past six months. He loves me, and I know he'll take good care of our baby and me. If anything, he will be over protective of us."

Gigi shook her head. "I'm sorry, but I'm not signing any papers for you to marry him."

"It doesn't matter. I'll be eighteen in a few months, so we'll get married then, and you don't have to worry about coming to our wedding."

Later that night I went to Philip's apartment and told him I was pregnant. He was ecstatic. He jumped up and down like he had just won the lottery.

"I knew you were pregnant! My boys are strong; they can break through any condom."

He kissed and hugged me repeatedly.

"How did you know I was pregnant?"

"I just had a feeling about it." He grabbed my hands. "Baby, we're complete; we can become a real family now."

Seeing Philip's excitement about the pregnancy made me feel happy. I forgot about my worries.

"I can't wait to tell my parents that they're going to be grandparents," he said. "I'm the happiest man on the planet now that I'm going to be a daddy. I hope it's a boy, because I want the oldest child to be a boy, and then we can have a girl next time for you."

He seemed to have our family already planned out. I was still in shock; I wasn't sure how I was going to raise one child, let alone two.

We decided to surprise Philip's parents about the baby and our shotgun wedding plans when we went to visit them the following month. We agreed that I would finish my undergrad degree and then we would relocate to whatever state I chose for law school.

Shortly after I completed my final exams, I moved in with Philip and decided not to work over the summer but attend summer school instead.

My unplanned pregnancy and engagement to Philip was somewhat disheartening. I knew I had disappointed Gigi, but I think she was more upset about me getting married than being a teenage unwed mother. I knew Philip loved me and we would prove her wrong. She would see our love and eventually come around.

5

MARRYING PRINCE CHARMING

Philip had never spoken of his family in any detail. His portrayal of them was that they were a basic southern family—church on Sundays, fishing and hunting trips with his father, and lots of family dinners. He told me that both of his grandfathers had been very successful, one a lawyer and the other a farmer turned politician. He also said that both of his parents were educators, so I assumed they were schoolteachers. My vision of Philip's life was that he was raised in a middle class family that resembled The Cosby Show, except with less kids since he was an only child. Once we got to Mississippi, I realized that my perception of Philip's upbringing was wrong. From the appearance of his parents' home, it was far from basic.

As we passed through the tall iron gates that secured the perimeter of their home, I felt like I was dreaming and that we were driving into some famous movie star or hip hop musician's home. It was a beautiful grand picturesque sprawling mansion.

I turned to Philip. "Why didn't you ever tell me about your parents' home?"

He didn't respond.

"Is your family rich?"

He shook his head. "No. Don't be misled by the house. My parents work hard, but they also inherited some money from my grandfathers, which helped us out a lot. That's why it's important to build wealth, because it helps sustain the family legacy."

I didn't understand his comments, but I interpreted them to mean that Philip came from a long line of money.

While Philip had mentioned that both of his parents were educators, he failed to mention that his father was a practicing physician who also taught in medical school and his mother was a language arts professor at one of the local colleges. Philip's parents were certainly not ordinary working class people. He had grown up with wealth and privileges. While I respected Philip's modesty, it seemed that he didn't want me to know his family had money. Perhaps he wanted to make sure I wasn't a gold digger, because I came from an impoverished background.

Philip's mother greeted us graciously at the front door along with her two white Maltese pups dressed in pink tutus and bows. She hurried us in, because we were already an hour late for the brunch she had prepared for us. Philip's father arrived a few minutes later and introduced himself and gave me a hug of approval.

As we ate, Philip's father didn't say much. He simply ate and read the newspaper. He seemed to avoid engaging in any direct conversation with Philip or me. His mother was the complete opposite. She talked and questioned us about everything, especially my family background. She was obviously sizing up my pedigree.

After we finished brunch, Philip brought in our suitcases while his mother gave me a tour of the massive, seven-bedroom home, including the detached maid's quarters and the pool house. I was speechless as I took in the elegance of the home's décor. To my surprise, their driveway was not full of fancy cars. Instead, his father drove a pickup truck, and his mother drove a basic four-door sedan. With the exception of their vehicles, there was nothing simple about their lifestyle. Philip's mother was very active in local politics. She had also held several governor-appointed positions during her career. Philip's parents were the perfect picture of an American nuclear family, the kind of family I wanted to have someday. Looking at them reassured me that, while untimely, I had made the right decision about my pregnancy. I would marry my prince charming, and we would have a family and be like his parents—happy and rich. After all, I knew Philip loved me immensely, that he would always cherish me, and, of course, that he would spoil our baby rotten. Life would be good for us.

Later that afternoon, a few of Philip's friends stopped by for a visit, which turned into a small pool party. We swam and lounged around the pool all day and into the night. Everyone could see that we were happy and in love by the way we kissed and hugged whenever we were near each other. We even snuck up to his room and got in a quickie.

As the night wound down, one of the girls, Haley, walked over to me. "So, how long have you known Philip?"

"About a year," I said.

Her face took on a strange look. "Well, anyone can change."

"What do you mean by that?" I asked, a cold pit forming in my stomach.

"I just don't recall seeing Philip in love before."

"That's because he was waiting for me."

She laughed and turned to walk away. "That's certainly one explanation."

Later that night, I asked Philip about Haley's remarks, and he said not to pay her any attention. She was salty, because she'd had a crush on him since grade school, but he never had any interest in her.

"The only reason I see her occasionally now is because our parents are close friends," he said. "She's nasty to all of my girlfriends. Don't pay too much attention to what comes out of her mouth."

That satisfied me. We kissed each other goodnight and then went to our respective bedrooms.

The next morning, I woke up in my floral-covered room to the glistening sunlight piercing through the drapes. As I lay in bed, I wondered why anyone would ever want to leave this beautiful home in this wholesome Mississippi town to go live in the madness of an urban city like Detroit. I guessed it would be difficult to appreciate a place like this if one has not experienced living in an urban jungle. Perhaps that's why Philip liked Detroit so much; it was the opposite of his little hometown.

I was particularly nervous that morning because we were planning to announce our engagement at the dinner that Philip's mother was hosting later that evening. From my conversations with her, it was obvious that his family placed a high value on education and social status. Almost everyone in his family had graduate degrees from top-ranked or Ivy League colleges with equally impressive careers. Tonight, I would be in the bosom of "the Kennedys" from the South. I knew everyone would inundate me with questions, as if they were interviewing me for a job. There would be whispers and speculation as to why we were getting married so soon, since I was only seventeen.

As planned, Philip and I announced our engagement after dinner just before everyone dispersed for desert, cigars, and the various game rooms. To my surprise and relief, Philip's parents were overjoyed, and so was everyone else.

As I stood in the kitchen refilling my glass of sweet tea, Philip's cousin, Jaime, approached. Although we made idle chitchat, there was something condescending about her cordiality.

"I'm glad to see that Philip found a nice girl to settle down with instead of running around like a fool," she said. "You know we don't condone that kind of behavior in our family; that kind of nonsense. Intolerable. You know, he caused quite an uproar with that escapade he had in college. His father stopped speaking to him altogether for years."

I had no idea what she was talking about, so I shrugged off her words. Perhaps Philip's father didn't approve of his girlfriend at that time. She probably wasn't attending college, which seemed to be a perquisite to date anyone in this family. I excused myself politely so I could mingle with the other dinner guests.

Later that night, I asked Philip about his relationship with his father. I could tell there was some tension between them. They seemed to acknowledge each other but avoided having any direct conversations.

"I disappointed my father by not following in his footsteps and becoming a medical doctor like him. We were never very close, and we seemed to grow further apart once I left for college. If you don't mind, I prefer not to talk about anything pertaining to my father."

The next morning at breakfast, Philip told his parents that I was pregnant and that we were getting married in a few months after I turned eighteen. Philip's parents did not seem surprised nor did they express any concern about our situation. His mom simply asked me about my wedding plans. I told her that we were thinking about going to City Hall since we didn't have money saved for a wedding.

"If you don't mind," she said, "I would like to help you plan a small wedding, and we'll pay for everything."

"That's very kind of you," I replied, "but my school schedule is so hectic I really don't have time to plan a wedding."

"Then I'll hire a wedding planner, and you'll only have to make a few minor decisions, like choosing colors and so forth."

At her urging, I gave in, and we selected a date in September so that we could choose the wedding venue and get on with the plans. A few hours later, I had a wedding venue, caterer, colors, and bridesmaids. My wedding party would consist of Philip's family, my cousin, Val, my sister, Deana, and my brother, John Junior, who would give me away.

Before we left, Philip's parents sat us down and said they would help us in any way they could. They would pay my college tuition and help us purchase a home and do anything else to help us get established. I was astounded by their acceptance of our shotgun wedding and their eagerness to help us financially. They were actually quite enthusiastic about our marriage and becoming grandparents. His mother even made a comment that Lovey and Dovey (her pups) would be happy to have a playmate. While I appreciated their support, there was something suspicious about it. On the one hand, they were traditional and pretentious, but they were embracing behaviors that contradicted their values. Rather than fret over it, I decided to enjoy the warmth and love of my new family.

While we drove home, I told Philip that I had enjoyed spending time with his family, but I noticed his mother was a bit overbearing.

"She was acting that way because she didn't have a daughter. Now, because of you, she can help plan a wedding and do all the things that mothers do with their daughters. Giving her a grandchild is the greatest gift you can give her. She'll be eating out of your hand. Go along with her. I promise you will grow to love her, and you two will become best friends."

With my accelerated summer school courses and morning sickness, the next three months were a grind. Then our wedding date was upon us, and Philip and I were preparing to leave for Mississippi.

Unfortunately, not everyone in my family, especially Gigi, was happy about my impending nuptials. Gigi felt that I was too young to get married. She said that Philip would make me give up my dreams and try to break my spirit. I told Gigi that she was wrong, and her feelings about Philip were baseless. She said she couldn't explain it, but she had an uneasy feeling about him. I told her that I didn't believe in all that Louisiana voodoo spirit stuff, and I didn't want her badmouthing my future husband. That was the only time I had ever argued with Gigi. She said that she was not coming to my wedding; she could not give her blessings to our union. I begged her to change her mind, but she stood firm. I knew I was disappointing Gigi, but it was important to me that I raise my baby in a two-parent family. Once Gigi bailed, most of my other siblings did as well. Knowing that she was not supportive of my marriage hurt, but it did not alter my decision.

When we arrived at Philip's parents' home on Friday, his mother had everything planned out perfectly, from our welcome breakfast at the hotel to the spa day for my bridesmaids and the rehearsal dinner at the botanical gardens. With the exception of my severe morning sickness, I had a great time.

Later that night, I stopped by the hotel that Philip was staying in to take some things to the bridal suite. That's when Philip and I had our first argument, which was about his bachelor party plans. He said he was going to a strip club. I told him that if he went there, he better not do anything but look. No lap dances, no VIP treatment, no touching another woman period. To my surprise, he grabbed me by my arms and shook me.

"Listen, and listen carefully," he said. "Don't think you can place any demands on me because we're getting married. I'm the man in this relationship, and don't you ever forget it."

Then he pushed me onto the bed. I was shocked by his behavior, and I started crying.

Rather than comfort me as he left, he said, "I guess I'll see you tomorrow."

I was so confused. Who was this man? This wasn't the sweet, kind, loving Philip that I knew. All kinds of thoughts raced through my mind. Did I really do something wrong? Was I being a bad wife, or was Philip pretending to be a nice guy all this time? Did he have a split personality like Dr. Jekyll and Mr. Hyde? Was Gigi right about him? If so, what else would be waiting for me after I married him?

I drove back to Philip's parents' house and went straight upstairs to my room. I did not want to see or talk to anyone. As I lay in bed, I thought about Philip. I knew he was a kind, loving man, and he would never mistreat me. He was only acting out, because he was having pre-wedding jitters. I would go to sleep and wake up tomorrow, and the day would progress as if our conflict had never happened.

The next morning, Philip did not call me as he had done every day since our arrival in Mississippi. Part of me wondered if he had changed his mind about marrying me. I guessed I would find out at four, the time the wedding was set to begin.

At around ten, my bridesmaids and I went to the local salon for manicures, hair, and makeup. By the time we headed home to get dressed so we could be at the church by three, I still hadn't heard from Philip.

I grabbed my wedding dress and veil and climbed into the limo that was transporting Val and me to the church. When we arrived, I asked if anyone had seen Philip, but no one had. I was getting worried that Philip may have gotten cold feet. After all, I had already behaved badly by trying to place demands on him. I would never do that again.

As Val helped me get dressed, I finally told her about my argument with Philip and that I had not seen or heard from him since. "Maybe he doesn't want to marry me anymore."

"Well, his best man is already here," she replied. "If Philip was going to call things off, he would have told him. Besides, everyone knows how much Philip loves you. Every other word out of his mouth is 'Astrid'."

I smiled. "You're right; I'm worrying for nothing."

A few minutes later, the wedding planner knocked on the door. “Five minutes to show time, people. Hurry, and let’s line up.”

When Val left, I felt scared, and I had to fight back my tears. I didn’t know if they were tears of joy or sadness.

After my last bridesmaid went down the aisle, the wedding planner came and got me. John Junior was waiting for me, standing in for my invisible father, and walked me down the aisle. I was relieved to see Philip waiting for me.

Once we exchanged vows, Philip lifted my veil and gave me the most passionate kiss, as if he was ready to take me to bed.

“I’m sorry,” he whispered in my ear. “I love you, and I will spend the rest of my life making you happy.”

We took pictures, and then the limo took us to the reception venue. We ate, danced, and laughed until midnight. Philip and I finally made it back up to our bridal suite at around one. Unfortunately, my vomiting took some of the “sexy” out of the wedding night. We went to sleep instead of having sex. Philip was very understanding about it.

“We have the rest of our lives to enjoy sex with each other,” he said.

The following morning, we went back to his parents’ house for brunch and to coordinate shipping our wedding gifts back to Michigan. Then we flew home for a few days before we left for our honeymoon in Mexico.

The night we were packing for our trip, Philip and I talked about the things we needed to take care of, such as adding me to his insurance and so forth.

“You need to hurry and change your last name,” he said. “I don’t want you to hyphenate it either.”

When I told him I wasn't sure about that, he replied in a stern voice, "If you're going to be my wife, then you need to take my last name. What the fuck did we get married for if you're not going to take my name?"

Wow! Where did that come from? I didn't respond; I just went to the den to watch TV.

A few minutes later, Philip came in and sat down beside me and started talking as if nothing had happened. He showed me some house listings that a realtor had sent him.

"When we get back, we're going house hunting. Now that we're married, we need a house, especially since you're about to have a baby. And it needs to be big enough for a couple of kids, because I want at least two or three kids."

"I don't think I'm going to have any more kids until after I finish law school and get my career established," I replied.

He laughed. "That might not be in your control. Sometimes, God has a funny way of making things happen. Look at you, you didn't expect to be pregnant now, but you are." Then his tone became stern once again. "I'm your husband now. Don't I get a say in when and how many kids we have?"

I laughed. "You can have that choice when you can carry and deliver a baby."

"If that's the way you feel, maybe we shouldn't have gotten married," he replied.

"Well, maybe we shouldn't have," I whispered.

The next thing I knew, Philip was up in my face like a madman. He grabbed my face with his hand and then placed it firmly around my jaw, squeezing so hard I started sliding to the floor.

"What the fuck did you say? You need to learn when to open and shut your pie hole."

I was terrified. He must have stared at me for thirty seconds before he took his hand off my face.

"That's what I thought you said. I'm the man in this relationship, and don't you forget it. Don't ever think you can treat me like I'm a punk, because I'm the man in this relationship."

Tears streaming down my face, I got up and headed for the table to grab my purse so I could leave, but he jumped in front of the door to stop me.

"Where do you think you're going?"

"I'm leaving. I'm not going to put up with you treating me like that. I know where this is heading, and I'm not the kind of girl who believes in getting beat up by men."

His demeanor changed instantly. "I'm sorry," he said. "I was just playing with you. I love you, and I would never hurt you or the little one that you're carrying."

He got on his knees, hugged me around my waist, and started crying. "Please forgive me and promise me you'll never leave me. I have never loved anyone the way I love you. I don't think I could live without you. I was just kidding around. I won't play with you like that ever again. I swear on my grandfather's grave that I will never hurt you."

He started bawling even harder, saying he loved me over and over again. Finally, I couldn't take it anymore.

"Okay," I said. "I love you, too, and I'm not going anywhere."

Just like that, he became Mr. Nice Guy again. He told me to get some rest and that he would finish packing my clothes for me. That night when we went to sleep, we held each other as if nothing had happened.

When we made it to our hotel suite in Mexico, I opened my suitcase and saw that Philip had placed two gifts in it. I opened the jewelry box first. It was a gold ankle bracelet with charms on it. The other box was from Victoria's Secret. Inside was a purple lace teddy, my favorite color.

Philip treated me like a queen the entire time we were in Mexico. Whenever we went somewhere, he held my hand and waited on me like I was a delicate flower. This was the Philip that I knew and loved.

That night, I took a shower and slipped on my new teddy and greeted Philip as he sat on the balcony drinking a beer. We French kissed and then we walked to the bedroom. When we got in bed, we started kissing and enjoying a little foreplay. Then he stopped.

"Let me spread the towel out."

We repeated this intimate ritual of me showering and laying my body neatly on the towel before we had sex for the entire six nights of our stay.

Once we got home, we started looking for our new house. As we looked at different houses, we discussed which bedroom was going to be the nursery. We laughed and hugged each other all day while we were house hunting. I was happy and looking forward to my new life with Philip as a wife and mother.

About two months later, we moved into our new home in the affluent suburb of Bloomfield Hills, and by no means was it a starter home. Philip's parents had given us a large down payment, but Philip's mother also gave us a second gift of new furniture for the entire house. Of course, she came up from Mississippi and pretty much selected all of the furniture for us, including the furniture for the nursery. I didn't mind her overbearing personality though. I actually liked her elegant taste, and I was happy to be living in such an exquisite home. Philip and I were getting along fine and were quite happy. I guess we were still on our honeymoon, enjoying our new life together "playing house," as Gigi called it.

As I was approaching my ninth month of pregnancy, my libido shifted into overdrive. It was the first and only time I had ever craved sex from Philip. However, it was then that I noticed Philip had stopped trying to have sex with me altogether. In fact, the bigger my stomach grew, the less excited he seemed about the baby and me. As I thought about those things, it made me feel uneasy about my marriage and becoming a mother. Later that night I brought up my concerns to Philip, and it led to an argument.

"Look, I'm trying to do my best for everyone," he said. "I'm not sure I'm ready to be a father. I wanted to enjoy you and your sexy body a few years before we started having kids. Now you're pregnant, and your sexy body is gone. I'm going to be stuck with a woman who has saggy breasts and a kangaroo pouch. What the fuck do I want with that? The only reason I got you pregnant was to please my parents. When I told my dad about you, he said that you were a keeper and that I needed to marry you and get you pregnant quickly to ensure the marriage would last."

The only thing I heard was, "got you pregnant."

"You got me pregnant? What do you mean that you got me pregnant?"

"Yeah, I made sure I got you pregnant. I used a safety pin to put holes in the condoms to make sure it happened. I'm surprised it took so long, because I started doing it after the second or third time we had sex."

I stared at him in shock. I couldn't believe what I was hearing. I felt like he had stuck a dagger in my heart. Was our relationship real or a sham? This whole conversation seemed surreal to me. I couldn't get over the fact that Philip had purposely and deceptively gotten me pregnant. I started crying and told him that I was leaving him so he wouldn't be stuck with my saggy breasts or my kangaroo pouch.

I packed my duffle bag with some clothes, but when I went to leave, he grabbed my arms.

"You're not going anywhere."

I pulled away from him, so he grabbed my purse and car keys so that I couldn't leave. I cried and begged him to give me my keys, but he ignored me. I tried to grab my purse from him, and then he pushed me so hard I fell to the floor.

I struggled to get on my feet and went to our bedroom, where I got into bed with my clothes on and cried as I watched TV. He came in a few minutes later and said he wanted to talk to me. I turned the TV up and ignored him.

The next thing I knew, the power went out, and the TV, lamp, and alarm clock went dark. A moment later, Philip reappeared.

"Now you don't have any distractions, so you can talk to me."

I turned my back to him. The honeymoon was clearly over. This was the man I had married. I cried myself to sleep.

The next morning, I woke up with severe cramps. I went to the bathroom and saw that my water had broken. I went to the den, where Philip was sleeping, and woke him up. I told him that I was in labor and we needed to go to the hospital. He jumped up and was as attentive to me as ever, as if nothing had happened the previous night.

As we drove, he kept asking me if I was okay, but I didn't respond. We pulled into the emergency parking area so he could walk me into the hospital. We checked in, and then he left to move the car.

After I was examined, the doctor said the baby's heartbeat was irregular. They were going to monitor me for a few hours and then make a decision on whether or not I needed to have a cesarean birth.

When Philip came into my room, he looked nervous when he saw that I had intravenous lines and monitors hooked up to my body. I was still angry with him, so I pretended he wasn't there.

He sat next to me and then laid his head near my chest and began crying like a baby.

"I'm sorry. I shouldn't have pushed you last night," he said. "If something happens to you or my baby, I don't know what I'll do."

He continued to cry and say he was sorry, and that he didn't mean to push me. "Please forgive me. As God is my witness, I will never put my hands on you again."

I didn't say anything. I was worried about my baby, not our relationship. A few hours later, the doctors said the baby appeared to be in distress, so they would need to deliver it by cesarean.

The last thing I remembered was being prepared for surgery before I awoke hours later to a big, beautiful, bouncing baby boy.

Philip seemed so happy holding our new baby. He cried and thanked me for making him the happiest man on Earth. "Let's name him Philip Junior," he said. "We'll call him Junior."

Philip bought me fresh flowers each day I was in the hospital. He even fed and changed the baby's diapers during his visits and stayed overnight a few times as well. I could see he was sorry for his behavior, and now that the baby was here, he would be a changed man. I decided to put our rough patches behind us so that we could be a family. Now that Junior was here, we would make a fresh start. After all, I didn't know my father, and I needed to give my baby an opportunity to know his. I wanted us to be one big happy family.

When Gigi came to the hospital and saw how attentive and loving Philip was toward the baby and me, she leaned down and kissed me on the cheek.

"Maybe I was wrong about him," she said. "But time will tell."

Junior's birth seemed to eradicate the tension that had existed with Gigi and me since I had married Philip against her wishes. We resumed our daily phone calls. She also started visiting Junior and me frequently at our home, mainly when Philip wasn't there. She never spoke ill of Philip, but I could tell she still didn't fully embrace him.

6

THE HAPPY FAMILY

After Junior's birth, Philip and I started to move in different directions. I was preparing to resume my studies in school while Philip started going out to nightclubs on the weekends without me. He usually went out on Friday and Saturday nights, but I never knew where or with whom. When I asked him where he was going, he was evasive. He just said he was going out. But I didn't really care if he wasn't around. As far I was concerned, he had given me the ultimate gift, my healthy baby boy, whom I loved to pieces. My maternal needs had been fulfilled completely. Junior would be my one and only child. I could check the box as complete for fulfilling my maternal requirements.

By the time Junior was a year, I had experienced a dramatic weight loss, and my self-esteem started to decline. I had always had a thick, curvy body, but now I looked like a runway model, except I wasn't modeling. Even worse, when I was naked, I looked like a concentration camp victim. At least that's what Philip said. He said I should be glad he still wanted to have sex with me. I was skinny with saggy tits and no ass, and now I had a kangaroo pouch. He added that no other man would want me with my anorexic body. I didn't pay much attention to my appearance or the fact that I was unappealing to Philip because his constant insults had already killed my romantic and sexual desires for him.

I didn't realize my weight loss was so bad until my sister, Deana said something about it. We were shopping and trying on clothes when she looked at me in shock.

"Oh my god, what happened to you? You're so skinny!" She looked me over. "You can see the bones sticking out of your back, your ribcage is showing, and you have no breasts."

Yes, my thirty-four DDs were gone. I was surprised myself when that happened, because I had been heavy-chested since I was about thirteen years old.

"Everybody is worried about you," she said. "Maybe you're trying to do too much." She paused before continuing. "I'm going to come right out and just ask you: do you have anorexia or bulimia?"

I laughed to minimize her concern. "It's not that serious."

I told her that I knew that I had lost weight, but I hadn't really paid attention to how much weight I had lost. Since I mostly wore loose sweatpants to school and around the house, I didn't really notice. I was straight up lying to her though. I knew I had lost too much weight, which is why I started wearing loose jogging pants and dressing in layers. Although Deana and I were close, I could not tell her what was really going on. Being married to Philip was very stressful. It seemed like once I came home from hospital with Junior, my stress level increased, and my appetite decreased. The world in which I was living had consumed me, and it was out of my control. I was just trying to survive in it.

My life with Philip fell into a predictable pattern, especially when it came to sex. I always knew when Philip wanted sex because he would place a folded white bath towel next to the bed, and he would tell me to let Junior sleep in his own room instead of ours, as he did on most nights.

Junior usually slept through the night, but on one particular night, he kept waking up. Philip and I were in bed trying to have sex when Junior started crying. After he continued to cry for about five minutes, Philip told me to let him cry. He would go back to sleep on his own. Junior continued to cry, so I told Philip I wanted to get up and check on him.

"No," Philip said, "I'll do it."

As I lay there in bed, I kept hearing Junior crying off and on, so I got up and went into his room, where I saw Philip covering Junior's mouth with his hands, as if he were trying to suffocate him. I pushed Philip away and picked up Junior to check on him. Then I turned to Philip, my eyes blazing.

"Have you lost your mind? Don't you ever put your hands on my baby! You have crossed the line. I'm outta here tonight, and I'm taking my baby with me."

I took Junior into the den. Then I sat in the recliner, gave him a bottle, and rocked him in my arms. After he calmed down, I dressed him and then laid him in his bed because he had fallen asleep.

I was sitting in our room on the bed wearing nothing but a large T-shirt and wet hair when Philip came into the room. He grabbed me and dragged me down the hall.

"You want to leave? You can leave now, but you are not taking my son."

He opened the front door and pushed me outside. It was winter and very cold, and I was terrified at what he might be doing to Junior. I cried and banged on the door, begging Philip to let me in.

"I promise not to leave you! Please, just let me in!"

It was about two in the morning, and I was too embarrassed to knock on the neighbor's door to ask for help. I was really cold, and my lips started to quiver, so I snuggled down between the storm door and the wood door to stay warm.

After about fifteen minutes, Philip let me in.

"I hope you've calmed down," he said. Then he sat in his reclining chair and watched TV like nothing had happened.

The first thing I did was run to Junior's room to check on him. He was sleeping soundly in his bed. I looked him over to make sure he was not hurt in any way.

Then, without thinking, I ran to the kitchen, got a knife, and charged at Philip, trying to stab him. He jumped up and pushed me back. I kept coming at him, and I cut his hand when he held it up to protect himself.

"You're crazy!" he said. "You're really trying to kill me!"

"Hell yeah," I replied. "I will do time for mine, and don't you forget it! I will never let you hurt my baby, not ever!"

He ran out of the house. I didn't bother locking the door.

A few minutes later, he came back. "Can I come in? I need to go to the hospital. I think I need stitches."

I gave him his wallet, a towel, and his keys. "You better leave before you bleed to death."

He called one of his friends, and then he sat on the porch until his friend arrived. I locked the house and then tucked Junior in my bed. Before I went to sleep, I pushed the dresser against the bedroom door so that I would wake up if Philip tried to come in.

The next morning, I found Philip sitting in the recliner with his hand bandaged up.

"I had to get fourteen stitches," he said. "And you just missed some vital nerves that could have damaged the function of my hand. You're lucky. I told the nurse I cut myself, because otherwise you could have been arrested."

"If you ever put your hands on my son the wrong way again, I'll cut your throat. I'm leaving and taking my son with me. And this time if you try to stop me, I'm going to call the police."

He got up from his recliner. "You don't have to leave; I'll go." Then he packed a light bag and left.

As soon as Philip was gone, the house felt peaceful. I felt freer and happier; no more walking around on eggshells. Unfortunately, Philip took the checkbook and debit card, leaving me without any cash, so I rummaged through his pants and sport coats because he often kept cash there. Sure enough, I found an envelope in one of his sports coats with cash in it. I also found a business card from a bar called Ubiquitous. On the back of the card was the initials "DJ" and a phone number. At first, I thought maybe it was a DJ (disk jockey) from the business. Perhaps Philip took the information so he could hire him or refer him to someone looking for a DJ. But that was out of character for Philip. He wasn't in need of DJ services, and he wasn't thoughtful enough to keep someone's card to give as a referral. I laid the card on the dresser and went on with the rest of my day, doing chores, talking on the phone, and attending to Junior. Keeping up the facade of the happy family.

After I put Junior to bed, I looked at the business card again. I was concerned that Philip might be having an affair.

Even though our marriage was not good, I still didn't want to share Philip with another woman.

I had no knowledge of this bar except that the address was located in a suburb on the east side of town. My concern and curiosity about this person named DJ was weighing heavy on my mind, so I decided that I would call both numbers tomorrow.

The next day, around noon, I called the bar. When I asked what type of bar it was, the lady on the phone laughed and said it was a gentlemen's club. I asked her to elaborate. She said it was a regular bar that served bar food and alcohol, but their clientele was mostly men. I concluded it was most likely a topless bar. Philip always liked big breasts, and since I had lost mine, I was sure he was enjoying entertainment in that kind of place. I proceeded to ask her if they had a person who worked there by the name of DJ. She said no, so I thanked her and hung up. Then I called the number on the back of the card, but I didn't get an answer. I felt relieved that a woman didn't answer the call. I decided I would investigate further some other time. I put the business card away and forgot about it.

About a week later, Philip came back home, but he slept in the guest room. I told him that I didn't want to be with him anymore and that I wanted a divorce. I refused to speak to him over the next few weeks. During that time, he wrote me letters asking for forgiveness and bought flowers for me and toys for Junior, but I continued to ignore him until his mother paid us a surprise visit. Apparently, Philip had called her and told her what happened, so she decided to come up and help us mend our relationship.

One day while Philip was out, his mother and I had a conversation. I told her that Philip was abusive to me. She said she did not condone that kind of behavior and that she would make sure that Philip got counseling.

She asked, "If I would give Philip one more chance?"

I paused and didn't respond.

She continued, "If things don't work out, I'll buy you a condo and help take care of Junior as well until you finish school. "

Then I said, "ok."

Later that evening, I agreed to go to dinner with Philip. At the restaurant, he asked me to let him stay in the house so he could win back my love and trust. He promised he wouldn't do anything to harm Junior or me; he would spend the rest of his life making things up to me.

True to his word, Philip found a therapist, and we also started attending a church. Our life resumed to some level of normalcy, but it was very different from the way we lived before he threw me out of the house. The occasional playfulness and affection that had existed between us disappeared. I never quite felt the same way about him or looked at him the same way. I certainly didn't feel the same sense of safety or loving care that he had shown me before we were married. Most of the time I felt guarded, as if I had to be prepared for the worst, because Philip could snap at any time and possibly hurt our son or me or both of us.

As time went on, I learned Philip well enough to get along with him and not set him off, which allowed us to live a modicum of normality for the next few years.

After completing my engineering degree, I wanted to attend an Ivy League law school, but Philip would not allow me to leave the state. So, I decided to continue my graduate studies at U of M, pursuing a JD/MBA degree. Philip was not thrilled about me attending law school, and he often made condescending remarks about me becoming a lawyer. This was the first time I noticed that he was jealous of me. Just when I felt that I knew all of Philip's many faces, here was another one. I wondered if his jealousy would remain harmless or if it would manifest into something ugly and catastrophic.

Fall finally arrived, and I started my first year of graduate school. I was anxious, because it was a top-ranked program and extremely competitive. Because I was in a dual degree program, I had day classes, some evening classes, and study groups on most nights and weekends. I truly underestimated the demands of my program. It left very little time for me to be a wife and mother. Gigi often helped with Junior, so he was ok. However, my neglect of Philip began to rear its ugly head.

"You need to put those books down and pay attention to your man," Philip said one night when I was studying.

"Let me finish this last chapter, and I'll be right with you."

A few minutes later, Philip snatched my book right out of my hands. "If you can't handle your family responsibilities, maybe you need to quit school. I didn't marry you to be by myself, to have no one to talk to or go out with."

I reminded him how we agreed that my education was an investment in our family's future. He said he was tired of feeling neglected and going weeks without sex.

"I'm sorry," I replied. "I'll do better. It's just that my graduate program is much harder than my undergrad courses, which is why I have to put in so much more extra time with my studies."

"You should quit and go back later when Junior is older," he replied. "He's suffering too with you being in school all the time."

"Just let me get through this first year and then decide if I want to finish the entire program," I said. I could always finish my MBA and go back to law school later.

I knew Philip was agitated, so I took a shower, put on a teddy, and poured him a glass of wine and me a glass of sparkling water. Then I grabbed a towel and went into the bedroom to perform my wifely duties. In truth, I didn't fret over the slight disruption. I knew I could promptly resume my studies because Philip was short-winded in bed.

While Philip was quite handsome, I found him sexually unfulfilling, even though I had nothing or no one else to which to compare him. We always had sex in the same classic missionary position and usually, after about ten minutes of his thrusts, it was over. He never cared or noticed that I didn't have an orgasm. Sometimes, when he wanted to go a second round, that's when I would fake an orgasm and tell him how good he was. These antics always seemed to make him speed up his climactic process. Then I could wash up quickly and get back to whatever I had been doing earlier.

Philip and I repeated the endless cycle—have sex and become a peaceful couple for a few weeks—and then he would begin his negative comments about my school demands and the way I was neglecting my son and my wifely duties. This dysfunctional aspect of our marriage became our "normal."

After completing my first year of grad school, I felt more confident and was no longer struggling, which made my second year progress even faster. I was excited; I was literally a few weeks away from taking my final exams. Once I finished, I only had one more year of school left before I could finally start my career. However, nearing the end of my schooling did not help my relationship with Philip. It continued on a downward slope.

One evening, Philip made his normal gestures to me, letting me know it was a sex night. Earlier, I had noticed the folded white towel next to the bed, but I forgot about it. I was preoccupied with studying for my final exams the next day.

"How much longer are you going to be studying?" Philip asked. "Junior is already asleep."

"Not long," I replied.

I lost track of time; maybe thirty minutes had elapsed, and that's when Philip cut off the electricity. "Well, I guess you're done studying for the night," he said sarcastically.

I didn't respond. I just grabbed a flashlight and a few candles and then continued reviewing my notes. Philip had not counted on that, so he grabbed my books and then started toward the garage.

I followed him, reaching for my books, but he pushed me away.

"Why are you doing this?" I screamed.

"You know why," he said as he headed toward his car.

He popped the trunk open and then threw my books inside. Then he went back inside and grabbed my other books. I pulled on his arm, trying to stop him, but he pushed me so hard that I fell to the floor.

This is déjà vu, I thought.

I got up and ran toward him, and then he punched me in my face like he was in a boxing match. Startled, I tried to get up, but he hit me again, so I just laid there on the floor for what seemed like hours, but was probably only a few minutes. He didn't check to see if I was conscious or not; he just ran out of the house.

The second hit was so hard that I thought he had broken my nose or some other bones in my face. As I tried to get up, I felt blood flowing from my nose and my mouth all over my shirt.

I was in shock; I couldn't believe what was happening. I was being beaten like some pathetic housewife. I had officially become a battered woman, or at least finally acknowledged I was one. I thought I had to be dreaming. This couldn't be my life or my reality. How did I get there?

I lay on the floor crying until I heard the car pull out of the driveway. Then I got up and went into the bathroom and cleaned my face. My lips had already started to swell, and my nose and cheek were bruised. I grabbed a bag of frozen peas to use as an ice pack for my face because I knew I still needed to go to school and take my final exams the next morning.

Amazingly, Junior slept through the entire fight. I decided I would focus on completing my studies for my exams and worry about my bruised face later. Although I was in excruciating pain, I continued to study what notes I had left, and then I fell asleep.

The alarm clock went off at five thirty as usual. I showered, but it was only as I was getting dressed when I realized my face looked even worse than it did earlier. My eye was swollen and my lips had doubled in size. I couldn't let Junior see my face like that, so I tried to cover my bruises with makeup and then put on my sunglasses.

When I woke Junior for school, he didn't notice my face. He simply went on with his usual morning routine. But as I drove him to his school, he asked if a bumblebee had stung my lips.

"Yes," I said.

"Did you kill the bumblebee, Mommy? Because I don't want him to sting me."

"Yes, sweetie," I said. "You don't have to worry about any bumblebees stinging you. Mommy will always protect you."

I walked him to the door, and then I headed to class.

I had two exams that day, and in spite of the previous night, I felt prepared. I went to my first class wearing my sunglasses. As the instructor walked around the room, he asked me to take off my glasses. Perhaps he thought I was using them to cheat. I told him that I'd had an allergic reaction to some food and my eyes were swollen. Regardless, he said I had to remove the sunglasses or I could not take the exam. As I removed the sunglasses, he looked shocked, and then he asked me to step out into the hallway.

"Ms. Thornton, I'm so sorry," he said. "I can grant you an extension if you need it."

I started crying and said it wasn't necessary. I wanted to finish my exam that day.

"I'll tell you what," he said, "since you're already at a B average, I can give you that as a final grade—unless you feel that writing your exam can bring your grade up to an A."

I thanked him and told him I would accept the B grade.

"I'm really sorry for you," he said. "I hope things get better."

As I headed to the student union building, I thought that God must have intervened, because this professor had been stern the entire semester. I didn't think he had an empathetic bone in his body.

I went to the ladies room to freshen up and looked at my face. The swelling was getting worse. The right side of my face was black and blue, and my right eye was nearly swollen shut. As I looked at myself I became angry and started to cry, but I realized I needed to keep it together because I had another exam to take.

I headed to my next class, but this time my sunglasses did not garner me any special privileges. I felt the other students staring at me. However, I aced the exam and then left for home to deal with my reality.

When I got home, I saw that Philip had been there. My books were stacked neatly on the table along with a bouquet of roses. Ignoring them, I pulled up the directory on the internet to find a divorce attorney. Then I packed up a few clothes for Junior and me, set my pride aside, and went to Gigi's house.

When I got there, she looked at my face, but she didn't say a word about how I got my bruises.

"Don't sit down," she said. "You need to go to the hospital."

She drove me to urgent care where I discovered that, luckily, I hadn't suffered any serious damage; it was only swelling.

On the drive back to her house, Gigi glanced at me. "You know you can always come home." In true Gigi style, she never said the words I expected: "I told you so." She was very supportive and not judgmental, which was all that I needed from her at that moment.

Philip spent the next few weeks pleading with my family to forgive him and to convince me to come back home with him. I refused to talk to him though, because there was no apology that could fix what he did to me. I had no plans to go back to Philip. I had already retained a divorce lawyer. However, Philip must have sensed that I was planning to initiate divorce proceedings, because that's when he did the unthinkable.

I went to pick up Junior from school as usual, but he wasn't there. They told me that Philip had taken him right after I had dropped him off at eight that morning. He told them we had a mix-up and forgot that Junior had a doctor's appointment, so he was taking him to see his pediatrician.

I never suspected that Philip would kidnap Junior. I called Philip's cell phone but he didn't answer, so I called his mother and asked if she had talked to him. She said yes and that he and Junior were on their way to her house. I started crying and asked her to tell him to bring my baby back. She said Philip had told her what was going on with us, how I left him because I wanted to be single again, and that I was running the streets partying, drinking, doing drugs, and leaving Junior with all sorts of people.

"That's not true!" I cried. "I left Philip because he was a wife beater."

Her response shocked me. "Well, if he beat you, then it had to be for a good reason. You need to know your place. No man is going to let you disrespect him."

I was silent for a moment realizing that she lied to me, she condoned Philip's abusive behavior. I was not about to waste my time discussing that topic with her any further.

"I want Philip to bring my son back home immediately," I screamed.

"Junior is Philip's son, too," she replied. "He has every right to keep his son, especially when you're an unfit mother."

This bitch is crazy. I didn't have time to get angry with her or deal with her madness, so I told her to have Philip call me when he got there, and then I hung up.

Philip finally called me around midnight. I knew not to express any anger towards him, so I just said hello and asked how Junior was. He responded as if nothing was wrong between us.

"He's fine. He played with his grandparents, took a bath, and then went to sleep."

"When are you coming back?" I asked with trepidation.

"I'm not sure. That all depends on you."

"What do you mean?"

"It's been almost a month, and I want you to come home. I miss my family. I can't stop you from divorcing me, but I will never let you take my son away from me. I will fight you tooth and nail for custody of our son. And let me remind you, my family has very deep pockets. You know my family's money will outlast yours in a custody battle. Do you think I'm going to let you take my son and run around town playing family with some other man? You belong to me, and you always will. If I can't have you, no other man will. Do you really want me to show you just how serious I am?"

Then he said the words that would enslave me to him forever. "I know Junior's death would devastate you, but I can always go find another woman to give me another son."

At that moment, I knew that Philip's words were no idle threat. He would make me pay the ultimate price if I tried to divorce him.

"This isn't about Junior," I said. "You don't love him like that."

"It doesn't matter," he said, "because I don't have a problem using Junior to keep you at home with me.

His statement floored me. I was even more devastated when my attorney confirmed that there was some merit to Philip's custody threats and that, at a minimum, I might have to share joint custody with him.

The thought of sharing custody of my son with Philip scared me. I knew without a doubt that Philip was more than capable of hurting Junior or taking his life to get at me if I tried to divorce him. I had already seen some of his handiwork. I wanted desperately to get away from Philip, but I could not risk a custody-sharing arrangement. I knew that if I left him, he would hurt my child. I had to protect Junior at all costs. So, I felt I had no other choice but to reconcile with Philip.

For some strange reason though, I didn't think that Philip would ever kill me. He enjoyed taunting and torturing me too much to let it end so easily. Plus, he had the ultimate leverage over me with Junior.

The next week, against Gigi's wishes, I told her that I was going back to Philip with an agreement that we would seek marriage counseling.

"Why are you going back to him?" Gigi asked.

"It's the only way I can protect Junior."

She shook her head. "You're giving him too much power. One thing for certain and two things for sure: If a man hits you once, he'll hit you again."

I couldn't bring myself to tell her that I had married a monster and that she had been right all along. Instead, I reminded her of what she had said so often to us. "That in order to be a good mother, you have to be unselfish and make decisions to benefit your children."

"I know that quote all too well," she said, "but that's not applicable here. The problem with you is you don't know your own power. Until you figure that out, you will always be under his thumb."

I wasn't going to debate the merits of my lack of power with Gigi. She was probably right, but I had a bigger concern to deal with. I had to save my son's life even if I had to stay married to a monster to do it. I decided that I would remain incarcerated in my marriage until Junior left for college. I would do the time just like someone serving a long prison sentence.

As I left, Gigi hugged me. "I still don't understand," she said, "but this door is always open for you."

It was the perfect time for Philip and me to reconcile, because I was leaving for England in a few weeks. It would give us the necessary time apart to diffuse the tension between us and help us to get our marriage back on track again.

Months earlier, during one of our happy moments, Philip had given me permission to accept the summer fellowship at Oxford. He even purported to be happy, boasting about it to our friends and family. However, with all our recent drama, he had forgotten about it until a week before my departure. I knew he didn't really want me to go, but he pretended to be supportive of me leaving. Any behavior to the contrary would have raised flags about the sincerity of our reconciliation.

For the next few weeks, things between us were good. I returned to the normal routine of my life, taking care of Junior and waiting to see the white towel next to the bed every Friday and Saturday night. Of course, the marriage counseling was postponed until my return from England, which meant it would likely never happen.

7

AN INTERMISSION WITH CHEVALIER

The big day finally arrived: I was leaving for England. Apart from the vacations I had taken with Philip to Mexico, I had never been out of the country. I was excited about this opportunity because it was a true international course with a student body comprised of people from all over the world.

As much as I hated the thought of being away from Junior for ten weeks, I needed a break from Philip. I felt like I was sinking in quicksand, and I needed to refuel for Junior and me in order for us to survive. Going to Oxford for the summer was just what I needed. I decided that I would also use the time to try to find myself. All I knew about me was that I was Gigi's baby girl, Philip's wife, Junior's mother, and a good scholar; nothing more.

Most people arrived on campus by Saturday afternoon so they could get settled in and attend the welcome reception the following evening. My sixty-plus classmates and I were nestled in a conference room partaking in the buffet and the reds and whites. We were also wearing fashionable nametags that displayed our country and host university.

While there were about ten of us from the United States, I couldn't help but notice the tall dark man from Canada. He had a very distinguished appearance and was strikingly handsome. He was tall, just over six feet, with a slender build, a Nubian complexion, and European hair and facial features. He was simply gorgeous and looked like no one I had ever seen before. He reminded me of a dark-skinned Ken doll. As he walked around introducing himself, I noticed every non-Islamic female student gazing at him, if not out of lust then certainly out of curiosity. When he finally made his way to me, in his sexy French accent, he said his name was Chevalier, but it was okay for me to call him "Chevy," like the actor Chevy Chase. We both laughed and engaged in brief small talk before he continued his quest to meet everyone at the reception.

On the first day of class, we were split up into teams of six people, and Chevy and I were assigned to the same team. During our first break, Chevy and I had a few minutes alone when my curiosity got the best of me. I had to know his ethnicity. I asked him straight out about his racial and ethnic background. He said he was French Canadian with Caribbean ancestry. He grew up in Montreal but went to college in Toronto and had been living there since he graduated, working in their financial district. He was a fellow attending graduate school at Penn's famed Wharton Business School. He was thirty-two and never married, but he had a girlfriend at Penn. He seemed shocked when I told him that I was only twenty-three and was already married with a child. He thought I looked quite young, but he certainly didn't expect me to have a family.

The accelerated curriculum at Oxford was certainly no vacation. We had classes for six hours a day that required an additional six hours of non-class time to study and prepare for team cases. By nightfall, we were usually wiped out except on Thursday nights because we didn't have classes on Friday. Somehow, we always found the energy to go to a nearby pub and socialize. The weekends on campus were usually quiet because most people would travel. I usually spent my weekends talking to Philip and Junior or other family members on the phone. However, I managed to find time for a few extra curriculum activities during an intermission with Chevalier.

Chevy and I always seemed to find time to spend together, either walking from class to our respective dorms or grabbing a bite of dinner. On the Thursday night pub outings, we always seemed to sit together, and most often we walked or shared a taxi back to our dorms together. While unspoken, it was obvious to us and to others that we had some type of attraction for each other. What I felt for him was different from anything I had ever felt before. It wasn't merely lust; it was metaphysical. While Philip was handsome, I had never felt that kind of attraction to him. Whenever Chevy accidently touched my hand or my arm, I felt tingly all over.

One evening, a few too many of us piled into a Smart car. Chevy had one arm around me, and he kept rubbing the side of his face against mine. That's when I knew for sure I was in trouble with him, because he was feeling something for me as well.

The attraction we had for each other was solidified further the night our team was studying in a classmate's room. At one point, I left the group and went to the bathroom. And when I came out, Chevy was standing right outside the door.

As I tried to squeeze past him in the narrow hallway, our bodies facing each other, he grabbed my hand and stopped me dead in my tracks. He pulled my hands up to his face and began kissing and sucking on each of my fingers. Then he pulled me closer to his body and I felt his erection. A few minutes later, I pulled away from him and then rejoined the group. As I sat there on the floor, I felt disoriented and unable to focus. Something strange was going on with me. I felt light-headed, and my heart was beating rapidly. Then I started feeling hot, similar to the way women describe hot flashes, so I went to the fridge and poured a glass of water. After gulping it down, I still felt uneasy, so I told the group I wasn't feeling well and went back to my room. I wasn't sure what had happened to me, but I knew it had something to do with Chevy.

When I got to my room, I washed my face and then I took off my clothes, only to discover that both my vagina and panties were wet. I took an Aspirin, had a warm shower, and then went straight to bed. I had difficulty falling asleep though. I kept thinking about Chevy and how his touch made me feel. Eventually I fell asleep, but I had a dream where Chevy and I were making mad, passionate, animalistic love to each other, which culminated into an explosive orgasm.

I woke up feeling hot, sweaty and breathless. Nothing like that had ever happened to me before. I realized then that I had a sexual craving for Chevy, and I wasn't sure how to make it go away.

A few days later, on a late rainy Friday afternoon, I went to buy some food at the convenience store that was a short block away from my dorm room. As I ran through the rain, my bag tore, and my groceries hit the ground, rolling all over the place.

As I gathered up my things, Chevy appeared and helped me carry my groceries back to my room. By the time we made it there, we were both soaking wet. I gave him a towel to dry off and then made us some hot tea. Since neither of us had any plans, we decided to go out for dinner together.

After dinner, we came back to my room for coffee and dessert. We continued to talk about everything from A to Z. The hours passed like seconds. I knew it was late, but I still didn't ask Chevy to leave. To avoid the awkward quietness that was creeping into our space, I decided to wash the dishes that were piled in the sink.

As I washed, Chevy walked up and stood very close behind me. "How long are you going to keep running from me?"

I didn't answer at first.

"You can't deny what's happening with us; the chemistry is real."

I felt nervous, not because I was scared of him but because I felt an intense magnetic sexual attraction to him, a feeling that I had never experienced before, not even with Philip.

He pressed his body firmly against mine and whispered in my ear. "I don't have anything else to do, and I'm not ready to leave you, pretty lady."

He grabbed my hand and began sucking and kissing my fingers again. But then I slid out from under him.

"It's getting late," I said. "I think it's time for you to go. I'm feeling a little tired now."

"Okay," he said. "I can come back later if you change your mind." He smiled and left.

Needless to say, after Chevy left, I experienced a repeat of my last encounter with him.

The following morning, Chevy called and said he wanted to make dinner for me later and that I should arrive promptly at six. Without hesitation, I accepted his invitation. I knew I should have said no because my feelings for him were inappropriate. His sexual energy had aroused me and if I kept seeing him, I would yield to my craving. But for some reason I could not back away.

As I pondered what to wear, I started having second thoughts about the dinner. I had a family. I was a wife and a mother, and I certainly would never condone Philip cheating on me. I continued to vacillate about having dinner with Chevy. Finally, I convinced myself that there was no harm in having dinner with him. But then at the last minute, I changed my mind.

As six o'clock approached, I phoned Chevy to tell him that I couldn't make it.

"It's Saturday night," he said. "Do you really want to sit in that small room alone? I know I don't. Sometimes I feel like I'm going stir crazy in this room. There's too much rain here and not enough sunshine. It's depressing without someone to talk to and laugh with."

When I stood by my refusal, he tried another tack. "If you don't want to come here, then let's go out somewhere."

"No," I said, relenting finally. "Since you went through all the trouble to make us dinner, I'll be right over."

I threw on my white A-line sundress and made my way next door to his building.

When I walked into his room, I was surprised. The aroma of the food smelled good, and he had his desk set up like a table with white linen, candles, and flowers in a vase. He escorted me to my seat, and then he poured us each a glass of red wine. He started speaking French and pretended he was a waiter attending to me. When he brought the covered dish to the table, it smelled of garlic. When he uncovered it, it was pasta with a red meat sauce.

"This doesn't look like French cuisine to me," I said.

He laughed. "I ran out of time when I was running errands today, so I picked this up from the little family restaurant in town, but I do have French bread warming in the microwave."

We laughed, ate, talked, and continued to drink wine late into the night. By then, we were sitting on his petite sofa talking and still drinking as he massaged my feet. I knew I should have left hours earlier, but I didn't want to leave him. Just like the previous day in my room, I felt the same intense attraction for him. He must have felt it, too, because that's when he planted a wet juicy kiss on me.

As he kissed me, he pushed me down on the sofa and climbed on top of me. I felt his hard penis pressing against me. Then he stopped and pulled back.

"You're married and have a family," he said, breathing heavily. "I'm being selfish. Let's stop before we go too far and do something you might regret tomorrow."

I looked up at him, breathing heavily. "It's too late."

He stood up and dropped his pants; unveiling a beautiful work of art. He had a slim, muscular body and a nice-sized fully erect penis.

I started to unzip my dress.

"Let me help you," he said. "You look beautiful, like an angel in all that white."

As he lifted my dress over my head, he kissed my breasts. Then he kissed my thighs and caressed my butt with his hands. He took my hand and kissed it as we walked over to the bed.

As he pulled back the covers, I started to take off my panties, but he told me to wait.

"I'll get to those later."

He pulled off his undershirt, and then we climbed into bed.

"Let me look at you," he said, his eyes devouring me. "You're gorgeous."

At that moment, I forgot about how self-conscious I was about my frail body.

He kissed me, and then he slipped his hand inside my panties and massaged my vagina with his fingers. Then he pulled his hand out and put his finger in his mouth, sucking on it as if he was tasting a delectable sauce.

"Umm. The taste of perfection."

As I lay there with my eyes closed, he slid my panties down and began licking my vagina lips.

Suddenly, a frightening chill came over me. I felt like I was smothering in the fear of darkness. My heart beat rapidly. I kept seeing flashbacks of Ricky performing oral sex on me and then slamming me on his bed. I felt like I couldn't breathe, and I started gasping for air.

I nudged Chevy's head away from me. He sat up and looked at me.

"What's wrong? Are you okay? You look like you've seen a ghost."

He moved closer to me, laying his head on my pillow. He pulled me into his arms. "Let me just hold you," he said. "You're safe with me."

I didn't say a word. I couldn't speak.

As I lay in his arms, tears ran down my face. He didn't ask any questions, as if he knew exactly what was wrong. We lay in silence like that for a few minutes.

"Whatever happened to you in the past, it's over now, and you need to leave it behind," he said finally. "You're a woman, and God made your body to be admired, respected, protected, and loved, and nothing less than that, so don't let evil steal that experience from you. Lovemaking is a beautiful thing, and you can't be afraid to enjoy it."

He raised himself up on one elbow and looked at me as his fingers traced down my side. "Please, let me replace those bad images with new memories, something beautiful that you will want to have in your memory forever. Let me show you how a man is supposed to make love to you. But first my tongue and my lips must enjoy the taste of your savory juices. Making love to you would not be complete without it. I promise I won't hurt you. Let me love you tonight."

Despite the kind, loving words that passed through Chevy's sensual lips, the gray cloud remained in the room with us. I had not thought about Ricky or how he had assaulted me when I was a little girl for many years. In fact, I had worked hard to erase the incident from my mind, as if it had never happened. I wasn't sure why the memory of Ricky resurfaced at that time. Maybe it was Chevy's foreplay with my panties or the fact that this was my first real experience with a man performing oral sex on me. Perhaps I would have had the same reaction sooner if Philip had gone down on me, but that was something in which we had never engaged. Unfortunately, all the fire and desire I had been feeling moments earlier fled. All I wanted to do was get dressed and go home.

I sat up. "I need to go back to my dorm."

"It's okay," he said in his kind, gentle voice. "I understand completely. Let's get dressed, and I'll walk you back to your place."

As we walked back to my dorm, neither of us said a word. I think Chevy could feel that I was in deep thought somewhere far from him. When we got to my dorm, I planted a wet, juicy French kiss on him.

"Thank you for everything."

He smiled. "I better leave before I start begging you to let me stay so we can finish what we started."

As he walked away, he turned back. "You can call me later if you need to talk. I probably won't be able to sleep after I take my cold shower."

I didn't respond; I just smiled as I closed the door.

The next morning, I woke up with a terrible case of "buyer's remorse." Even though we didn't have sex, I felt as guilty as if we had done it. The guilt wasn't from the fact that I had betrayed Philip or my marital vows, I had betrayed the badge of honor I wore. The one thing I could always say was that I had been a faithful wife, and now that wasn't completely true. What scared me even more was how easy it had been for me to cross that line. I wondered if the abuse from Philip had pushed me into another man's arms or if I had indulged Chevy just because I had an appetite for him. At no time did I ever feel or think about being in love with Chevy. It wasn't love or lust but something else that was unrecognizable to me. Whatever the reason, I knew I had the capacity to go there, to lust after a man and commit adultery. The evening I spent with Chevy had unearthed several erotic emotions in me, but it also unleashed what I had buried many years earlier—memories of Ricky.

As I lay across my bed, I felt a physical anguish in the pit of my stomach. As much as I tried not to, I kept thinking about what had happened the previous night. In one of the most intimate moments of my life, memories of Ricky burst into my head and paralyzed me emotionally, robbing me as I tried to steal a taste of ecstasy. Of all the times Philip had me spread out on the towel, I never had the smallest, faintest inkling of memories of Ricky. I thought those memories were dead and buried. But now that monster had re-emerged in my life thanks to Chevy's beauty and his sexual magnetism. My hope was that since we didn't finish what we started things would go back to normal, and the memories of Ricky would fade back into oblivion.

Chevy called me later and asked if I was okay. I said I was, but I couldn't see him again.

"Damn," he said. "I knew you were going to say that. But it's your call. I'm not going to put it in stone. You can change your mind anytime you want."

I thanked him again for everything, but that was not going to happen. I would not be changing my mind.

"Pretty lady, I will back off and respect your decision, but you should know that you can pull me back whenever you want to, even after we leave here."

Over the remaining few weeks, Chevy and I maintained a platonic relationship. I caught him staring at me a few times, but nothing further happened. After we completed our final exams, most people left that afternoon as I did. Chevy and I didn't even say goodbye; the only contact information I had for him was the student directory.

8

BACK TO REALITY

Returning home from Oxford was bittersweet. It seemed as if the time apart had done wonders for both Philip and me. I felt refueled, and, thanks to Chevy, I felt like a desirable woman again. I think Philip actually missed me. When I came home, he had several gifts for me from Victoria's Secret, and he even took me out for a romantic dinner.

After we returned from dinner, I took a shower, put on my new sexy lingerie, and took my place in bed on top of the white bath towel. After about ten minutes of sex in our usual missionary position, we went to sleep.

The next few weeks felt like we were settling into being a happy family. I was back in school, Junior was a boy scout, and we went to church every Sunday. I had also mastered obedience and walking a tightrope at all times so as not to provoke Philip. I felt hopeful that I might do my time peacefully for the remainder of my eighteen-year sentence.

The next year went by without incident. I had graduated and landed an executive position with an original equipment manufacturer.

To celebrate my accomplishment, Gigi gave me a graduation party that was reminiscent of a wedding reception. I guess it was her way of making up for her absence from my wedding. There were over 200 people there, mostly family and close friends. I also invited a few friends I had met at Oxford. And to my surprise, all of them, including Chevy, showed up.

When I saw Chevy, it felt like my heart skipped a beat. He walked up and kissed me on the cheek.

"Hey, beautiful," he whispered, "I need to see you for five minutes alone before I leave."

"Okay," I replied without hesitation as I pretended to point out different people in the hall. "Pull your car around back in an hour."

He nodded and then went back to the group at his table.

After an hour of mingling, I snuck out the back door of the kitchen where I found Chevy waiting. We drove to Bell Isle, a nearby park, and parked in a secluded area. Then we took off our seatbelts and commenced French kissing like we were lovers.

As he kissed me, he tried to put his hands up my dress. "You have to let me taste you before we go back."

I knew what he meant, but that was not going to happen.

Finally, we stopped to catch our breath.

"I've thought about you a lot over the past year," he said. "I wanted to contact you, but I didn't know how you would feel about it."

"I was surprised to get your RSVP," I replied, "and for only one person."

He smiled. "I'm single—for the moment—and enjoying it."

He told me he had moved to Chicago recently so he could easily come to Detroit for a visit or vice versa. He said he was crazy about me and would not have missed the opportunity to see me again.

"Close your eyes and open your hands," he said. "I have a surprise for you."

When I opened my eyes, I was holding a blue Tiffany box.

"I wanted to give you a gift that would always make you think of me."

I opened the box. Inside was a Tiffany Bow Cuff bracelet.

"Wow," I exclaimed, "It's beautiful!"

He put the bracelet on my wrist and then planted another wet, juicy kiss on me. But what followed surprised me even more.

"I'm sorry. I know it's wrong, but I want to be with you, and not just for one night. I love kids, and I know I can be a good family man."

He waited for me to answer. When I didn't, he continued. "I know you want to be with me. What we have is much deeper than merely lust or a sexual attraction. I can feel it, and I know you can, too. The chemistry between us is undeniable." He took my hand. "Come and spend a weekend with me. Then you can decide for yourself what you want to do. You and your son can come live with me, and I'll help you with your divorce or you can stay with your husband, and I will disappear from your life forever."

"Where is all this coming from?" I asked.

"I felt the same way in England," he said, "but I wasn't sure how to handle it, especially with you being so young and married. I could tell you weren't happy then, and I know you're not happy now."

He kissed my hand and then looked up at me. "I can see the unhappiness in your eyes." He placed my hand on his heart. "I can feel it, too. At first, I thought what I was feeling for you was a fluke, but I haven't been able to get you off my mind, and no one else has made me feel the way you do, even though we never consummated our relationship."

I glanced at my watch.

"I know we need to get back," he said, "but I want you to think about it."

He gave me his business card and wrote his personal contact information on the back. "I want you to come and visit me in Chicago next weekend or as soon as you can." He looked into my eyes. "Promise me you'll come."

I hesitated for a moment and then took his card. "Yes, I promise."

As he pulled back into the rear parking lot, I opened my door. "I'll call you next week," I said. Then I snuck in and ran inside to the restroom.

Just like a year ago, my panties were wet. Just being around him aroused me. I took off my panties and put them in the garbage can and then cleaned myself up and rejoined my party.

Everyone was seemingly happy and excited for me except for Philip. When we got home, Philip came up behind me as I was getting undressed and hugged me.

"I'm really proud of you, earning a masters and a law degree. To top it off, you've landed a big executive job, and you're barely twenty-five. I'm so proud of what you've accomplished."

With his arms still firmly around me, he began squeezing me tighter and tighter, so tight that he began hurting my back, causing me to feel short of breath.

"Don't make me have to remind you who the man is around here, understand? You know me and Junior can be happy without you."

I knew exactly what Philip was trying to say—that my new financial independence was not going to change the dynamics of our relationship, and that he would use Junior as insurance to make sure I stayed in line. After Philip so eloquently reminded me that he still had a leash around my neck, I dismissed any thoughts of seeing Chevy again. I would just focus on my career.

My career and newfound financial success did not sit well with Philip. His disrespect and dislike towards me seemed to intensify. I knew that the peaceful times we had during the past year were over, and my walk on glass splinters for the days, weeks, and months that followed had just begun. There were more trying times ahead for me and my marriage.

One day while doing laundry, I found several pairs of thongs in the dirty clothes hamper. *What the fuck is this?* Philip must have been out screwing around and brought some bitch's thongs back with him. I knew without a doubt that they did not belong to me, because I didn't own or wear thongs. I grabbed a hanger from the closet and used it to place the thongs in a plastic bag.

When Philip came home, I was sitting in the great room folding towels. I showed him the thongs. "Care to explain?"

He glanced down at them. "Those are mine."

I put my hands on my hips. "Don't play games with me."

He stood up, unfastened his belt, and pulled down his pants. That's when I saw he was actually wearing a thong.

Without a hint of embarrassment, he said, "These are men's thin-lines, and they're quite comfortable. You should start wearing thongs. You'll like them, too."

I sat there in disbelief; unable to believe Philip was wearing thongs. I wondered what other questionable items he might be wearing. I told him that only male strippers or homosexual men wore thongs. A man wearing a thong was too feminine for me.

"You don't know what you're talking about," he said. "These are quite popular among men."

I scoffed. "Maybe gay men."

Before I could react, Philip was on top of me. With one hand covering my mouth, he hit me repeatedly in the thigh with his fist as hard as he could. When he was done hitting me, he pulled back, breathing hard.

"What did I tell you? I'm the man in this relationship, and don't you forget it. Don't you ever think you can talk to me like I'm some type of punk. You need to control that pie hole."

When he was finished, he got off me and spoke in a calm, monotone voice. "Now go wash your face before Junior comes downstairs and sees you crying."

My right thigh was throbbing as I limped to the powder room. I closed the door and pulled my pants down. A contusion was already forming on my thigh, my skin slowly turning green, blue, and purple. I sat down on the toilet seat and put my hands on my face as I cried heavily and quietly. Then I wiped my face and went upstairs to my room to finish tidying up my appearance.

As sick and crazy as it was, I never wanted Junior to know that his father was abusing me, so I did everything I could to hide it from him. In fact, I went out of my way to make sure Junior had a positive view of his father. I never spoke ill of him or said anything to suggest that Philip was anything less than a perfect husband and father. I told him often that he was lucky to have Philip as his dad. For some reason, I felt that by hiding Philip's abuse, I was helping Junior develop into a fine young man. I didn't want him to imitate Philip's bad behavior or think less of himself if he knew that Philip was really a demon. I also feared that if Junior showed dislike or any form of rejection towards Philip I would be punished for that too. I had no option except to make sure that Junior held his father in high esteem, otherwise I would have hell to pay. I felt deep in my gut that without Junior's love and adoration, Philip would have no reason to keep me around. He might snap and kill me and maybe Junior as well. I told myself often that all I had to do was hang in there until Junior left for college, and then I could make my great escape. I had survived so much pain and cruelty during my early childhood that I could surely endure Philip's wrath for ten more years. This too would pass.

By day, I lived my life as a sharp, intelligent, confident woman. By all accounts, I was a BAB (bad-ass bitch): beautiful, intelligent, and well-educated, and I had a great career that paid me a lucrative salary. However, in parallel, I was also suffering from full-blown battered woman syndrome. My mental state was so messed up that I could no longer tell when the abuse started and stopped. Even worse, I had started making excuses and telling myself that the situation with Philip wasn't that bad, that all women experienced some type of mistreatment or abuse from their men. They were like me, hiding and faking it. While my girlfriends and family admired my strength and sophistication, they would never believe that I was a battered woman, let alone understand it. I couldn't believe or comprehend my situation either.

As the years passed, my life with Philip got worse. Sometimes when I disagreed with Philip or said something he thought was flipped, he snuck up behind me and grabbed my hair so tight until I fell to the floor. His other equally degrading act was to push me up against the wall and choke me while asking, "What were you saying with that big executive mouth of yours?" His finishing remarks would always be, "See? This is what happens when you make me show you that I'm the man around here."

The other predictable trigger of his abuse was during income tax time. As Philip prepared our taxes, when he saw my income, which was four times as much as his, it would put him in a foul mood. This often led to an argument that escalated to me getting hit or choked or both. I thought that after I helped him land a higher paying position with my employer that his behavior would change, but it didn't.

Philip's abuse had expanded to include adultery. He made no secret that he was having affairs. He would often leave his cell phone lying around so that I could see that women were calling him. One name that I saw quite often was Jody. He said Jody was a great friend. She was easy to talk to, she understood him, and she was fun to hang out with. What I hated most was that Philip felt proud of his behavior. He wanted me know he was having an affair with Jody. He enjoyed rubbing my nose in it.

In spite of the decay that consumed our relationship, I still wanted Philip to respect our household and to maintain a façade of a happy marriage. Whenever I questioned Philip about his behavior or told him that I thought it was inappropriate, he ignored me.

"You're just insecure because your looks are gone," he'd say. "Your body disgusts me. You look like a skeleton, nothing but bones and saggy skin. If you had a million dollar makeover, it would be a waste of money, because you are never going to be beautiful or sexy again. You'd better hope I just cheat on you and not leave you. You should actually thank me for staying around to be your husband 'cause plenty of women out there want to take your place. Yeah, you're smart, but that's all. You can't do shit else. You sure as hell don't know how to take care of your man."

I had become numb to Philip's verbal abuse. He had completely broken my spirit. I was an emotional zombie. I only had enough emotional capacity to take care of Junior and to project a false face at work and with everyone else close to me. My friends and family would have been shocked if they knew the truth about my life.

At least once a month, I had to submit to Philip's verbal diatribe against me. I also learned to control my "pie hole" and not retaliate, because it would only make things worse. I was a weak, spineless person except when it came to protecting Junior, and there had been no need to draw on that strength since Philip had resorted to the ultimate warfare tactic, mind games. He knew what I feared most was him taking Junior away from me or a shared custody arrangement. All he had to do was suggest it, and I would roll over and sit like a well-trained puppy. But he also knew that his power was limited, because once Junior turned eighteen, he would no longer have that to hold over me.

The bell in my head should have rang years earlier, telling me that I meant nothing to Philip, but it didn't until this particular day. Philip and I were sitting around the kitchen island drinking coffee when he started questioning me about my job.

"I think you need to quit your job or find another job somewhere else with a salary equal to or less than mine."

I looked at him. "Are you crazy? Why should I quit my job? Our lifestyle requires me to have the type of salary I have. We need the money. We certainly can't manage our finances with your income."

Without saying a word, Philip acted like he was clearing his throat, and then he spit a huge wad of mucous right in my face. Then he came closer and stood over me as if he was waiting for me to say or do something to provoke him to hit me.

"That's what I think of you," he said. "You ain't shit to me. You're nothing to me."

I didn't say a word. I didn't move, and I didn't shed a tear. I sat there with my head down trying to wipe the warm, slimy mucous off my face with my pajama top.

Without another word, Philip grabbed his jacket and keys and left.

I went upstairs to my room to wash my face. I decided to take a shower instead. My whole body felt soiled and dirty. I felt like I needed to scrub with bleach to rid myself of any trace of Philip.

As I sat on the bench in the shower, the image of Philip spitting on me kept replaying in my head. *This asshole spit in my face like you spit on the ground in the street.* He was right, I meant nothing to him, and he had just showed me that. So this was what it felt like to hit rock bottom. Even at rock bottom though, I still couldn't leave him. I knew he would stop at nothing to hurt Junior to get back at me if I ever tried to leave him, so I was stuck at rock bottom a while longer.

After that incident, the abuse lessened, mainly because Junior was getting older and becoming more astute about what was going on in our household. I also think Philip was becoming preoccupied with his extracurricular activities, leaving him less time and energy to torture me. At least for the moment, his frequent absence allowed for some stillness around the house.

Over the years, I continued to go out of my way to conceal from my family, especially Gigi, the fact that I was in an abusive marriage. It wasn't very difficult since I was rarely around due to my twelve-hour workdays and busy travel schedule. However, Gigi must have sensed things were not quite right with Philip and me. Sometimes during our phone calls she would say, "Baby girl, you're weighing heavy on my heart these days. You know you can always come home even if it's just for a little while. You have to know that what's done in the dark will come to light, and good will always prevail over evil." I didn't want to engage in any discussions about my marriage, so I would find a way to cut the conversation short.

9

THE FINAL BREAKDOWN

The summer that Junior began playing basketball with the AAU traveling league was a defining time for me. My eyes were forced wide open, such that I could no longer hide behind the excuses I used to rationalize staying in my terminally ill marriage. I finally realized that Philip and I had reached a point of no return. However, my awakening would not easily provide the freedom I sought.

After being in Europe for almost two weeks on a business trip, I returned home a week early. I didn't bother to inform Philip about my change in plans, because I wanted to surprise Junior at his game in Ohio. Philip had complained often that I put my job before everything and I would regret all the time I had missed with Junior, so I hoped my surprise would win me some brownie points with Junior. Since I had taken this flight many times before, I knew I would get home about six in the morning, have enough time to take a nap, and then make the three-hour drive to Ohio.

Once I made it home, I tipped the limo driver after he brought in my luggage, and then I headed straight to the kitchen just like I always did when I came in the house. I laid my purse and keys on the island, and then I started up the stairs to the master suite.

When I got to the hallway I paused. Music and strange noises were coming from my bedroom. At first, I thought it was the television, but as I continued to listen, I could tell they were real voices and movement.

Initially, I thought it was Junior, but then I remembered that he was away with his basketball team in Ohio. I knew it couldn't be the maid. She was an older lady, and I knew she wouldn't do anything like that in my house.

As I moved closer to the door, I heard grunts and moaning. I could tell it was at least one man's voice, possibly Philip's. He kept saying, "Oh yeah, that's it, that's it."

The closer I got to the door, the faster my heart pounded, and the higher my temperature got. Beads of sweat ran down my face. My stomach started to ache, and my heart beat so fast I thought it would burst through my chest.

After a few minutes of denial, I realized it was Philip. I couldn't believe it. He had finally crossed the line. He brought another woman into our home and was fucking her in our bed. Of all the fucked up things he had done to me. I thought our home was off limits, and that he would never defile it. The thought of what lay behind those doors was so painful that I decided to turn around and leave. I didn't need to actually see Philip committing the act of adultery to know he was doing it. But something wouldn't let me go. Maybe seeing Philip like this would give me the courage to leave him. Without any uncertainty, I knew whatever was behind those doors would end our marriage for good.

I stood outside the door for a few more minutes, listening to sounds of panting and moaning. I took a deep breath, and then I opened the door. What I saw knocked me to my knees.

Unable to speak, I gasped for air. I was in complete shock. The image I saw was totally foreign to me. I had never seen hardcore porn before, let alone seen another couple or threesome up close and personal in the throes of sex. What I saw sickened me. I would not have expected to see Philip in that position in a million years. There he was in his raw nakedness—being fucked by another man.

They were lying on top of the covers, so I could see everything. Philip was lying on his stomach with his face turned away from me while a big, long-legged man rode him like a jockey on a horse in the Kentucky Derby.

I stood there for what felt like five minutes before they even noticed me. Finally, the man turned his head and saw me.

"Oh shit," he said, "your wife is here."

Philip turned around and looked at me, and then I ran out of the room.

I couldn't breathe. I felt lightheaded, as if I was going to pass out. I sat down on the steps, crying and trying to catch my breath at the same time.

Moments later, Philip came running out of the room wearing his robe. He sat next to me and grabbed my arm.

"It's not what you think," he said. "I'm not gay. I've never done anything like this before."

I looked at him through my tears. "You mean this is your first time getting fucked by another man? I doubt that. It didn't look like you were losing your virginity to me." I stood up. "You're disgusting. Just leave me alone."

I walked down the stairs, but with each step it felt like cinder blocks were attached to my feet. It seemed like it took me forever to make it downstairs and into the kitchen.

As I sat on a barstool at the island, I looked around for my keys. That's when I noticed a black leather portfolio with the initials "DJ" inscribed on it. I grabbed my purse and the portfolio, and then I got in my car and drove off. I didn't know where I was going. I just needed to get out of that house.

After driving around for about an hour, I decided to check into a hotel. I couldn't deal with Philip or anyone else right then. I needed to be alone in a calm, quiet environment.

Once I made it to my room, I took a hot shower and then slipped into the hotel's guest robe. I decided to order a bottle of wine and dinner from room service, even though I wasn't very hungry. I finished up my first glass of wine without touching my food and then fell asleep.

I woke up a few hours later and began watching the local news. Then I decided to look at the portfolio. When I opened it, I saw that it belonged to a Mr. Donald "Jody" Jodison, and it contained other documents with "DJ" in parentheses preceding his full name. From what I could tell, he was the owner of a bar called Ubiquitous. The bar name sounded familiar to me. Then I remembered years earlier when I found a business card in Philip's coat pocket with the name Ubiquitous on it. It all started coming back to me. The so-called gentlemen's club was actually a gay bar. And all these years that Philip was talking to his friend, Jody, he was actually talking to a man and not a woman, as I had suspected.

As I pondered this, I wondered how I had missed the signs that Philip was gay. At that moment, amber warning lights were blinking in my head. I saw things that Philip had done over the years that suggested he might be gay, such as his parents' eagerness for us to get married, the suggestive comments his cousin Jaime made, and the similar comments made by Haley, his high school classmate. It also helped explain Philip's strained relationship with his father. Above all, it explained Philip's conviction in all of our arguments that, "He was the man in our relationship." I knew that Philip had a lot of secrets, but I never suspected that being gay was one of them. *I completely missed that memo.* In fact, he had been homophobic and shown prejudice towards gay men. He went out of his way to avoid being around gay men, and he would say things like, "I don't want that punk around me." He would also make jokes about gay men being "fudge packers" and how disgusting two men being together was to him. Now I knew why he projected an anti-gay sentiment. He was masking his own homosexuality. He wanted to throw people off just in case he was giving off gay vibes. It was obvious that he was still struggling with his sexuality, but I was not going to be the one to help him figure that out. I was done with him.

The more I thought about Philip, the more it became obvious to me that my entire marriage had been a lie. Philip had used me to create a family to hide his homosexual tendencies. I think his parents knew he was gay and thought getting married would cure him somehow. I don't think Philip was bisexual at all; I think he was just simply gay.

Throughout our marriage, something about Philip's behavior had always nagged at me, especially him wearing thongs and face cream, but I couldn't quite put my finger on it. Or maybe I just didn't want to address it, so I just shrugged it off as him being metrosexual. Whatever issues were behind it, I was not going to take it on. Philip needed to figure out his sexual preferences on his own.

As my mind shifted toward Junior, I felt sick to my stomach. How would he handle the fact that his father was gay or bisexual? I wondered if he already knew or suspected it, since they had such a close relationship. This whole thing with Philip was surreal. I finished off another glass of wine and then went back to sleep.

Later that morning when I turned on my phone, I saw that Philip had called repeatedly and left at least ten voicemails pouring out his love for me and pleading for me to come home.

When I finally did arrive home, Philip tried to hug me, but I pushed him away. I could tell he had been crying. We sat down at the island in the kitchen.

"Please, let me explain," he begged.

"There's no explanation needed," I replied. "You're clearly bisexual or simply gay. I don't care either way. I only wish you hadn't made me a blind participant. But as Gigi would say, one thing for certain and two things for sure: this marriage is over. It's been over for a while. It's been a long, big, fat lie. I understand now why you were so abusive to me, always concerned about your manhood, letting me know that you were the man in our relationship. You were punishing me, because you were conflicted about your sexuality."

"That's not true," he said in a sad, pitiful voice. "I was frustrated, and I was wrong to take my frustrations out on you. I loved you and needed your help, but I was afraid to tell you. You can be cold sometimes, and that's why I would get so frustrated with you. I know I was wrong, but I didn't know how to handle the situation."

I was thoroughly confused. I didn't know what he was talking about and how it was connected to me. He was clearly trying to deflect his homosexuality and rationalize his abusive behavior.

I looked up at him. "So, what does all that have to do with me?"

"I needed you," he said. "I wanted to tell you everything then, how I was struggling with this thing, but you wouldn't let me."

"Well, you should have gotten some psychological help and not used me as the scapegoat for your issues," I replied. "Let me sum this up: you were frustrated so you abused me, and then you turned gay, is that it?

"No," he shouted. "Just shut your pie hole. I'm not gay."

"Stop lying and cut the bullshit," I replied. "I know about Ubiquitous and Jody. This goes back years, probably back to your high school days. Need I say more? What did you do in college that was so bad that your father stopped speaking to you? Did you have boyfriend back then too?"

He didn't say a word. His face cracked and turned three shades of red, and his mouth fell open in shock.

"At this point, I don't care if you're gay or not. I'm not dealing with your sexuality. You need to figure that out for yourself. But be assured, I do want a divorce. Our entire marriage has been a lie. You stole seventeen years of my life, and for what? Because you're selfish, you put your needs and happiness above everyone else."

"I know you've been wanting to divorce me for a while now," he said, "and now you have an excuse to do it instead of waiting until Junior leaves for college."

He stared at the counter for a moment before looking me in the eye. "Have you told anyone about what happened yesterday?"

I shook my head. "No."

"Don't say anything to Junior or tell him you're planning to divorce me. And definitely don't tell him you think I'm gay. I'm not gay, and you didn't see anything yesterday. You were hallucinating."

Wow. He really is crazy. How could he possibly deny he was gay? I had seen him in our bed having sex with another man, he frequented gay bars, and he had likely been having an affair with Jody, a man for years. In my book, that made him gay.

"I'm begging you," he said, tears flowing down his face, "please give me time to figure this out. I'll give you a divorce and everything else you want. I just don't want Junior to be hurt by this situation."

That was a lie. He didn't want his son, who idolized him, to know he was gay.

This was the first time I had ever seen Philip appear sad, broken, and defeated. I knew that look all too well though, because I had worn it on my face on many occasions during my marriage. For the first time since we were married, I had power over Philip. He was at my mercy now, because he did not want anyone on this planet to know his secret. I could get away with anything now without fear of reprisal.

In a surprise twist, Philip's escapade with Jody had somehow freed me from his psychological bondage. The pain and shock of it didn't break me; it caused me to emerge stronger. Philip was an ordinary person with flaws like everyone else. While I had acquired leverage over him, I also realized that I wasn't as powerless as I had felt all those years.

I wondered what had happened to me and how I got to that place with Philip. What had I done with all my strength? Why had I buried it? Why did I believe I had no strength or power in my relationship with him? Why did I suffer in silence, taking years of abuse and emotional beat downs from him? Thanks to Jody, I could flip the script. I could make Philip dance to the beat of my music, but I didn't want to. My newfound power over Philip was irrelevant, because I didn't want him anymore. The next item on my agenda was to find a good divorce attorney.

As usual, I conducted my morning business sitting in my kitchen at the island drinking coffee. On that particular morning, I was searching for a divorce attorney on my tablet. I had several colleagues who specialized in divorce, but I needed to maintain my family's privacy. Despite Philip's pleading, I did not want anyone to know he was gay either, at least not right away. What would that say about me, and how would Junior handle this on top of dealing with his parents' divorce? I had spent years pretending that Philip and I were this perfect couple and we had the perfect family. I wasn't quite ready to reveal the lie I had been living, nor the depth of it. Living this lie was the one thing that Philip and I shared completely. For different reasons, we both wanted to create a facade that we had a perfect family. Whenever we were in the present of others, the act was on. We would be very complimentary and affectionate. Having Junior and my fantasy perfect family were the only benefits I had from my marriage. I needed to get divorced quietly without anything tainting our image, so Philip's secret would be safe with me.

I had moved to the great room and was sitting on the sofa drinking my coffee when Philip snuck up behind me, grabbed me by my neck, and put a gun to my head.

"If you ever mention what happened with Jody yesterday or anything about me being gay to anyone, I'll kill you."

He pulled me down to the floor and tried to strangle me. "I'm not gay! Do you hear me?"

His face was red, his nose was running, and heavy tears were flowing down his face. I squirmed beneath him, trying to get away.

"I promise!" I cried while struggling to catch my breath. "I won't say anything!"

Finally, he let me go and sat back against the wall. Then he pointed the gun at his head.

"I can't live with myself. I don't want to lose my family. I know I destroyed our family, but I don't want to live without you and Junior."

"Give me the gun," I said, crying now. "We'll figure something out. We've had a lifetime together. We'll get through this."

He shook his head. "No, you're just going to leave me and take Junior away from me. He'll blame me for breaking up our family, and if he finds out about Jody, he'll hate me."

Finally, he gave me the gun and then hugged me. He continued to cry like a baby, dripping snot and tears all over my shoulder.

"Please forgive me for everything I've done to you. I don't deserve you, but I promise I'll spend the rest of my life making this up to you. You and Junior are my world; you mean everything to me."

"I forgive you," I said as he continued to cling to me. "We'll get through this. I won't leave you."

He held me tighter and tighter. "Thank you. I promise you won't regret it."

Truthfully, I had no intention of reconciling with Philip, but I needed to diffuse him. He was acting psychotic and erratic. In his state of mind, I didn't know what he was capable of, especially with a gun in such close proximity. My main concern was staying alive, keeping my sanity, and making sure that Junior was okay as I tried to navigate through this situation. I didn't know what lay ahead for Junior and me, but I knew it did not include Philip.

That night, I slept on the sofa in the great room, I wasn't sure if I could ever sleep in our bed again. The next day, I called a cleaning service and requested a deep clean. I told them that it needed to be scrubbed and sanitized like a hospital operating room. The following day, a small army of women arrived, and four hours later, they were done. Although my house had been purified, I still could not get the image of Philip and Jody out of my head. Just being in our house felt different. It was still a big, beautiful, elegant house, but it reeked with emptiness and sadness. It felt like someone had died there. I guess something had died there: my marriage to Philip. It certainly did not feel like a home anymore. I knew that even if Philip left, I didn't want to live there anymore. Unfortunately my exit strategy would not come to fruition as planned.

A year after the incident with Jody, despite our best efforts, my relationship with Philip had not improved. We had gone to marriage counseling and even enlisted the help of a spiritual counselor to save our marriage. These acts only served to restore calmness temporarily and to delay the inevitable. Our sex life was pretty much dead. Philip and I both took a HIV test (thankfully, we both tested negative), but I still couldn't bear the thought of him touching me. We had attempted to have sex a few times, but it was unfulfilling for us both. My body simply would not respond to him on an intimate level. His touch sickened me on the inside. Philip was irritated further by the fact I would not let him touch me without a condom or let him French kiss me. I could not get the thought out of my head that Philip could lay with a man the same way as he could lay with me.

With all of Philip's efforts, our marriage should have been on the road to recovery. He appeared to be faithful and dedicated to rebuilding our marriage, the abuse had stopped completely, and he went out of his way to show kindness towards me. In spite of these changes, the love I had for Philip was gone. I felt nothing but emptiness for him; his transformation came too late. The truth was that our entire marriage had been a lie. Philip only married me hoping it would eliminate his homosexual tendencies. What made it even sadder was that his parents knew about his sexuality, and yet they threw him at me anyway.

By then, Philip and I were barely speaking to each other and sleeping in separate bedrooms. I went out of my way to avoid Philip, even if it meant I did not spend much time with Junior. I would take unnecessary business trips, make out-of-town weekend visits, and I attended every wedding and funeral to which I was invited. Our communication with each other had disintegrated to using sticky notes. Most of the notes pertained to Junior or if I was going out of town.

Living with Philip was like I was holding my breath underwater. If I exhaled, I would drown in pain and sorrow.

10

THE WAR BEGINS

One cold fall morning, I woke up to find a yellow sticky note on the dresser mirror in our bedroom. It said, "I'm not happy, and I want a divorce." I tossed it aside and continued getting dressed for work. As I was leaving, I noticed that Philip's car was not in the garage. That was strange because I usually left for work about an hour earlier than him. As I thought about it, I realized I had hardly seen him at all over the past week.

I went on to work and then ran my usual errands in the evening before I went home. When I arrived, Philip was waiting in the kitchen. He was chewing gum in an exaggerated way, popping it and blowing bubbles like a young, urban ghetto girl. I knew his gum chewing meant he was either planning or had already done something mischievous or hurtful.

"Did you see my note?"

"Yes, why?"

"You haven't responded."

I shrugged. "I thought you were just angry. Plus, we agreed to stay together until Junior finished high school. It's his senior year. We've been together all this time. Surely we can make it one more year."

He shook his head. "No, I'm not happy, and I want a divorce right now. I haven't been here for the last three days, and you haven't said a word. You probably didn't even notice I was gone."

"What's the hurry?" I asked. "Did you get her pregnant too?"

"I've met someone," he replied. "She's my real soul mate, and we want to be together. I know you don't want me anyway."

"Okay, but let's not disrupt our son's life. Let's wait until he leaves for college or at least finishes out his senior year. You can even keep your girlfriend; just be discrete. If she was willing to date you while you were married, she'll wait a year to have you all to herself."

I stood up. "In fact, I've been feeling unfulfilled myself for the past few years, so maybe I'll have an affair, too. I could really use a good Mandingo fucking."

As soon as the words were out of my mouth, I became frightened. *Why did I say that*?

I must have hit a nerve, because he spit out his gum, moved closer to me and then pointed his finger at me. "I'm not going to wait around and watch you date other men. I'm going to make this divorce long and arduous for you. I'm going to make you suffer."

"You've already done that for so many years, and that's why I'm deeply repulsed by you today. I begged you for a divorce many times before, and you always said how you would take Junior away from me and then torture me in the process. You left me no choice but to sit here and count the days until Junior turned eighteen. That's how I got through it, doing time and looking forward to my release date. You were my jailer, my warden, and our home was my prison. I could lose my son or do the time, so I chose the latter."

I wasn't quite finished yet. "On top of everything else, I had to live with your secret and choke on the pain of it as I suffered in silence."

"I'm not talking about that anymore, ever. He interrupted me and said, "All you wanted was a picture that looked like a happy family—your son, your nice big house in the suburbs. You just wanted your friends and family to see that you made it out of the ghetto and you were living this affluent, fairytale life. You were content, but you didn't give a shit about me. All these years, I've tried to love you, but you pushed me away. You never let me get close to you. Besides, I've never been able to forgive you for cheating on me with that Chevy guy. That's right; I found the letters and emails he sent you over the years."

I must have looked shocked when he mentioned Chevy's name, because I thought I had hid his letters well. This time I was speechless.

"You had the nerve to invite that foreign speaking motherfucker to your graduation party and introduce him to me as your classmate, and all the time we've been married, you secretly wanted to fuck him. I'm pretty sure you've probably fucked him already, because there's no way a man's going to talk about performing oral sex on you if you haven't been intimate with him. I guess you sucked his dick, too. Now I'm going to destroy your life the way you destroyed mine. I'm going to show the world that your perfect picture was fake, and when I'm finished, I'm going to send you back to the ghetto where you came from."

"Are you really going to put that kind of energy into destroying the mother of your child?"

"You treated me like I was nothing, like your personal escort and your son's father, but nothing special to you."

"You created this situation," I replied. "I tried for years to make our marriage work, but it was a never-ending cycle with you, one crisis after another. I'm sorry I couldn't get past your sexual conflict, which finally tipped the scale and broke us for good."

"That doesn't matter," he said, "because I'm divorcing you, and you're going to regret it."

I shook my head in confusion. "I don't get it. You want a divorce, but you're going to torment me first?"

"I'm not happy, and it's your fault!" he shouted, tears streaming from his eyes. "You've left me no choice but to divorce you."

All I could think was, *this bird had finally flown over the cuckoo's nest.* "If you really want a divorce, then let's try to end on a good note. If for no other reason, let's do it for Junior. We need to make sure this has a minimal effect on him."

"I'm going to do what makes me happy," he replied. "I'm tired of living my life for other people. It's time for me to be happy. I have a woman who loves me now and believes in me, and she knows how to treat her man."

"She can't be too smart then," I responded, "because if she was, then she would know she wasn't dealing with a real man at all. I guess you'll do anything to stop feeling conflicted about your manhood.

Philip was right about one thing. His absence around the house went unnoticed by me for days at a time. Things had gotten so bad between us that I had actually started to block him out. When he was in one part of the house, I was usually in another part. He could have been having an affair for months and I wouldn't have noticed.

As time went on, Philip stopped sleeping in our home, but he refused to move out. He was too busy basking in the glory of parading his girlfriend around our mutual friends and his family. We were still legally married, sharing a home and supposedly raising our son together, but none of that gave him cause to adjust his behavior. Even though I no longer desired or wanted to be married to him, his flagrant disrespect hurt me.

As part of his torture, Philip came home every few days and packed his suitcase in front of me, as if he was going on a short business trip. He would make comments like, "Have you seen my shirt? Oh, it must be at my other place," or "I'm taking a couple of bottles of wine from the cellar with me," as if he was going to a mutual friend's house and I was agreeable to it. "The only reason I'm mentioning the wine is because I don't want you to think that Junior is taking it." He knew that bothering my wine collection disturbed me.

Philip was shrewd in his strategy to destroy me. He made it clear at the outset that our divorce wasn't about the dissolution of our marriage but about his destruction of me. He didn't care about the collateral damage to himself or Junior or anyone near me. He seemed energized by his actions. The more cruelty he slapped onto me, the happier he became. It was as if it he had won something, a victory of some sort that fueled him to plan his next attack. He was playing an intense game of dispensing hurt. He would use the entire arsenal he had accumulated over the years, knowledge of my deepest secrets and fears, and while going through the divorce process, he would keep score of the hurt touchdowns he inflicted upon me.

While I had the ultimate weapon to shut him down, I could never use it. My knowledge of Philip's homosexuality was like having an atomic bomb that I couldn't detonate. If I used it, told the world about his secret, it would destroy not only him; it would also have a catastrophic effect on the lives of other people, including Junior. I could not be responsible for disseminating that kind of pain to anyone, especially Junior, even if it meant I had to endure more pain and suffering. The most disturbing thing about this whole situation was that Philip knew no matter how bad he treated me; I would never tell his secret.

By then I was also becoming increasingly fearful of him. I came to realize that I wasn't just dealing with an angry person but a deeply mentally disturbed person. I began sleeping in my bedroom with the French doors locked. While the doors offered little real security, I felt safer with them locked. At least I would wake up if someone knocked or broke through the doors, as Philip often did. Sometimes, Philip made random visits to the house in the wee hours of the morning, and if I ignored him when he knocked, he would just kick the door in. These unwanted visits usually consisted of discussions about our impending divorce. Philip would start the conversation in a calm demeanor, and then it would escalate into some type of threat against me if I went through with the divorce.

The very first time he did it, he scared me so bad that I wet the bed. He wasn't just making an idle threat; he had a gun pointed at my head while he talked to me. His words were always the same. "You have the power to stop the divorce, and if you don't, I'm going to make your life a living hell."

He always concluded the conversation by saying things like, "This divorce is not going to free you from me. You are never getting away from me. I will be in your head forever. I will always be in your life. You will never stop being my wife." He also told me that if he caught me with another man, he would kill us both.

I believed his threats 100 percent because I knew he was crazy enough to go through with it. I would just lie there speechless and non-responsive, because if I reacted in any way, it might cause him to explode and actually pull the trigger. I had already resigned myself to the fact that Philip would probably kill me one day.

To add insult to injury, Philip managed to turn Junior against me, too. He convinced Junior that I was responsible for the breakdown of our marriage and our impending divorce. Even though Junior was seventeen, I could see that he was struggling with the divorce. He quit his basketball team, started drinking, partying, and breaking his curfew. Whenever I tried to talk to him or discipline him, he lashed out at me.

"I hate you! You ran my daddy off! It's your fault he left us to go live with another woman."

These types of rants became the extent of Junior's communications with me. I knew he was transferring his anger with his father to me, so I tried not to overreact to his outbursts. Sometimes, Junior would stay in his room all day, which was out of character for him. I knew he was depressed and grieving, but I didn't know how to help him. I found a therapist who counseled families going through a divorce, but when Philip refused to go, Junior refused, too.

Whenever I tried to call Philip to discuss Junior's problems and emotional state, he refused to talk. He always had a snide response, spoken in a nasty, cruel voice. "That's on you. You brought all this on our family. You're the one causing our son's pain, not me." It became obvious that Philip didn't give a damn about Junior's well-being either.

One of the saddest days I remember from this whole messy divorce was an incident that involved Junior. One night, Junior knocked on my door and asked if he could talk to me. He kneeled down beside my bed with tears streaming down his face.

"Mommy, please take my daddy back. Everybody makes mistakes. If God can forgive, why can't you? I just want our family back. Dad said he'll come back home if you want him to. It's up to you. Please, Mommy. Please, I'm begging you. Please do it for me. I just want our lives to get back to normal. Don't you want our family back, too?"

Seeing him crying and in so much pain, I almost said yes, but I didn't. I couldn't. Philip had pushed me to a point of no return.

I reached over and hugged Junior as tight as I could. With tears rolling down my face, I told him that his father had made too many mistakes, and the damage was irreparable.

"I know you don't understand, but your father and I are better off apart. There are so many things that happened over the years that have torn us—"

"Dad said you would try to blame him and tell lies about him, saying that he abused you and that he's gay." He pulled away from me. "You're a selfish bitch, and I hate you! This is all your fault!"

He got up, and as he was leaving, he slammed my bedroom door so hard I thought it would fall off its hinges.

A few minutes later, I got up and walked down the hall to his room and opened the door. He was lying in bed listening to his iPod.

"I wasn't through talking to you," I said.

"Well, I'm through talking to you. Can you please leave my room?"

At that moment, I wanted to tell him that his father was a liar and an evil person, but I knew he wasn't ready to hear that yet. So I told him that this was not anything he could fix, but I loved him, and that we would get through it.

Over the past year, I had become increasingly sick. My face was pale and fatigued. I lost a considerable amount of weight again and was suffering from a host of debilitating symptoms. On those occasions when Philip was home, he made sure that he saw me, and even though he could see I was sick, he showed no concern. Though not surprising, Philip's lack of concern for me still hurt. As ugly as he had treated me over the years, I would have put my feelings aside to help him if he had been ill. But that was my way of doing things, not his.

As my symptoms got worse, I finally decided to see a doctor. After several tests and a bit of surgical prodding, I was diagnosed with ovarian cancer. The doctor said that since it was caught early, my prognosis was favorable. I would be as good as new with surgery and eight weeks of chemotherapy.

I had serious reservations about having a hysterectomy; it would destroy the essence of my womanhood. It didn't help that my self-esteem was already in the lowest of low places. I couldn't handle anything else that made me feel less than a woman. I contacted a few other doctors to discuss alternate treatment options when I found Dr. Weinberg. While her diagnosis was the same, her treatment plan was more palatable. I would still need minor surgery, but not a hysterectomy. I signed the necessary papers and began treatment.

I also decided to keep my cancer a secret from everyone except Deana. I asked her to stay with me for a few months while I went through the treatments. She was the obvious choice. She still resided in Detroit, she was the most religious person in my family, and she didn't have a husband or children. I also wanted her there for moral support. Living in the house with Philip and Junior was like living in the enemy's camp. There was no love for me at all in my home.

My one-week hospital stay turned into a two-week stay. Deana begrudgingly lied to people and helped me conceal my secret. My chemo started the day after my surgery. Following my first chemo treatment, I was sick as a dog, nauseated, throwing up constantly, and dreading going through it again. The doctors finally gave me some medicine to reduce the side effects, which included Mother Nature's finest cannabis, medicinal marijuana. I had the option of choosing between a pill or marijuana cigarettes. Since I had never smoked marijuana before and it was now legal for me to do so, I decided to experience it in all its glory. I would smoke it like I was a 1960's hippie, just like Snoop Dogg and Bob Marley.

On my first night home, I sat in my bathroom with the window cracked as I attempted to smoke my first joint. After I learned how to inhale, I started feeling better immediately. I felt calm and mellow, like nothing or no one could evoke any negative feelings in me. If I had known marijuana (MJ) could make me feel like that, I would have been smoking it a long time ago. I knew from that point forward that me and MJ, my new best friend, would be together at least until my divorce was final. Thanks to MJ, I got my appetite back and felt like I was on the road to recovery.

Six weeks after my surgery, my doctor gave me approval to go back at work. I was looking forward to it, to getting on with my life.

11

LOSING THE BATTLE

It was Sunday night, and I was talking to Deana about issues I was having with Philip regarding the divorce, how Philip was begging me to stop the proceedings. She said Philip was crazy and couldn't be trusted. She said Satan had Philip in his grip, and he was lost, because a man with a relationship with Christ would not behave like him.

"You can't go to church, claim you love God, and live your life the way he's living it," she said. "There is no rationalization or acceptance for adultery no matter how you slice it. It's wrong, and he's wrong."

She went on to quote a few scriptures about adultery, and then said she had something very disturbing to tell me about Philip. She had prayed a few nights about whether or not she should say anything to me or just mind her own business since my relationship with Philip was already volatile, but she had finally decided it was time.

She said that when I was in the hospital, she told Philip that I was traveling for work and returning the following week, but he didn't believe her.

"That's when he did the inconceivable," Deana said. "He brought a woman, his girlfriend, into your home. They spent the night in the house. In the master bedroom."

She confronted him and told him that adultery was wrong, but he told her it wasn't wrong, because this woman was his soul mate, and he was planning to marry her as soon as the divorce was final. This was his house, and he could do whatever he wanted to do in it.

"You should be counseling your sister, not me," he said. "I know she's not away on business. She's out of town with that Frenchman."

At that moment she wanted to tell him the truth about me, that I was actually in the hospital, but she held her tongue because of the promise she had made to me.

Hearing what she said left me speechless, and emotionally paralyzed. He had already defiled our home with Jody, and now he was doing it again. As he had reminded me so often, there was no end to his cruelty and madness, but for some reason, I had failed to heed it.

Deana went on to tell me that a few nights earlier, Philip showed her several love letters that he had exchanged with his girlfriend professing their love for each other and how they couldn't wait to get married. Then she reached into her purse and pulled out the folded papers.

"He left these sitting on the counter, so I brought them to show you."

I knew Philip was not that careless, because he was a master at deception and manipulation. He had left those papers on the counter intentionally so that she could find them and show them to me.

The first thing I noticed was that the company email addresses were the same, and Philip was having an affair with someone who worked at the same company as him—the same company I worked at as well. That rubbed salt in my open wound. Of all the women living in Michigan, he chose to have an affair with someone in my workplace. The knowledge of this was gut wrenching, just as he knew it would be.

Until that point, Philip's behavior had made me feel sad, hurt, and disappointed, but now I was mad as hell. My priority should have been my health. Instead, I was preoccupied with Philip and his whore. I had finally reached my limit. I had been the bigger person, never speaking ill of him to other people, held my head up high despite his disrespectful behavior. That time was over. I was one breath away from fucking him up.

The next day as I drove to work I called Gigi as I usually did every morning. I told her about Philip's latest escapade, how I had discovered he was having an affair with someone at our workplace. As the words flowed out of my mouth, I began crying profusely. She was quiet and not her usual sultry self when it came to advising me on how to handle matters with Philip. This act was far too much for her to fathom as she struggled to find words to comfort me. All she could say was that she was sorry for me, and that this too shall pass.

"God is all-powerful and merciful, and he will help you get through this. No, he will make sure you get through this."

I could tell she was crying. I guess she could feel my hurt and pain, too.

"I'm sorry, but I need to call you back later," she said.

This was clearly too much for her to handle as well.

As I sat in the parking lot trying to compose myself, I wasn't having much success, so I decided to turn around and go back home. I was clearly not yet ready to return to work.

As the days passed, I felt my spirit crumbling under Philip's hand. I was going to church, prayer meetings, and even seeing a spiritual counselor, but it wasn't helping. Sometimes, out of nowhere, a dark gray cloud would descend and fill me with an unyielding sadness that left me with buckets of tears flowing. These emotional meltdowns were happening more frequently. With every day that passed, I felt more and more depressed. I felt defeated and broken, that there was no way out of this. I had prayed so many times for God to lift this burden from me, but it seemed like he was taking too long. But then I remembered what Gigi said. "God works on his time and it's always the right time." I continued to hope that the "right time" was coming soon.

Between my illness and the constant battle with Philip, things were starting to take their toll. My mind was all over the place. Occasionally, I reached such depths of despair that I considered suicide. The pain I felt was deep and endless. I was drained and felt like I was going to die soon anyway—if not from my cancer then certainly from a broken spirit. Philip's relentless mental torture was killing me, and I didn't know how to defend myself or fight through it. When I had these dark days, the only way I could get through it was to self-medicate. I would drop a Vicodin and smoke a joint. That would usually give me a good night's sleep and snap me out of that dark mental place so I could function again.

One day, I awoke to find myself in what had become an all-too-familiar depressed state. I kept thinking about all the terrible things Philip had done to me and was still trying to do to me. I decided that Philip was not worth taking my life, so I would take his instead. I wasn't sure how I would do it, but I knew it couldn't be too messy because I didn't want to traumatize Junior. I had a few hours to develop my plan before Philip got off work. I knew I would see him since he stopped by the house most evenings to check his mail and take wine from the cellar.

To help pass the time, I decided to write a letter to Junior explaining why I killed his father and another letter to Deana, naming her executor of our estate and explaining the tasks I wanted her to take care of. I placed each letter in an envelope and then placed the letters in the centerpiece on the kitchen table. Although it was early in the day, I decided to drop a Vicodin, throw back a few shots of tequila and smoke a joint while I pondered over how to get rid of Philip.

As I was seated at the table relaxing in deep thought, Gigi called. She said I had been weighing heavily on her mind.

"Baby girl, I know you're going through a rough time now. Don't do anything crazy. Nobody's worth going to jail for or dying over. I love you. I'm here if you need me."

I was high, so I couldn't engage in too much conversation. I just told her not to worry, that I was fine and would call her later. I guess my meds had kicked in, because I fell asleep with my head resting on my arms.

When I awoke, I realized I had been asleep for a few hours. I felt dazed and unsure as to whether or not I had spoken to Gigi earlier, but my thoughts were clearer regarding Philip. I changed my mind about killing him. I remembered the letters and thought I needed to destroy them, but when I looked around for them, I couldn't find them. I called Junior and Deana and asked if they had been by the house, but neither of them had.

In a panic, I looked around the floor and in other rooms in the house, and still no letters. Reluctantly, I called Philip and asked if he had been to the house. He said he hadn't been there yet, but he would stop by after work.

"Why, do you want something?"

"No," I said and hung up. I was terrified, because Philip could use these letters to destroy me, which is exactly what he wanted.

My thoughts may have seemed farfetched, but with Philip, anything was possible. He would try to hurt me by any means necessary, and those letters were all the ammunition he needed. They could implicate me as a suspect if Philip died suddenly. Worse, maybe I could be convicted of conspiracy to commit murder. Perhaps Philip had snuck into the house and took the letters to use against me as part of the divorce proceedings or to have me declared mentally unstable. I was scared. *Where the fuck were those letters?* Philip had most likely taken them, and then he was going to use them to bury me. However, I had no choice but to wait for him to reveal them.

Since I didn't want to be home when Philip stopped by, I went to the mall for some light shopping. Afterwards, I stopped by Jeff's home, my long-time friend from Brookhaven. He was also a lawyer with a successful practice in Detroit. Even though we were friends, I knew he had a secret crush on me, but we never crossed any lines.

We talked about my divorce and Philip's girlfriend. "I never said anything to you, but I've seen Philip in the streets many times over the years with other women and behaving inappropriately as a married man," Jeff said. "I thought Philip was cold-hearted. Most married men try to show some discretion when they cheat, but Philip seemed to go out of his way to be seen. One time, Philip went as far as to introduce some girl to me. That's when I realized he was a real loser," he smiled. "Not that I ever liked him anyway."

We continued to talk late into the night over a bottle of merlot.

"Do you want to stay over?" Jeff asked.

"Yes, I don't want to go home," I replied.

He gave me a robe and let me smoke my joint on his patio. Then we climbed into bed together. He held me close, but he didn't try to have sex with me. He must have known I just needed to be held.

When I got home the next morning, I looked around for the letters again, but they were still nowhere to be found. I showered, got dressed for work, and then looked for the letters one last time. It was as if they had walked out of the house and disappeared. As I thought about it, I concluded that Philip most likely came in the house while I was asleep and took them to use against me at some point. I would just have to play dumb and deny any knowledge of the letters if he brought them out later.

By then, my emotions were more intact and under control compared to the previous day, but the hurt and pain had not lessened.

As I drove to work, Gigi called, as usual, to check on me. I didn't tell her about the letters or that I had contemplated hurting Philip. I didn't want anyone to know that he had pushed me over the edge, and I wanted to forget that I even had those types of thoughts in my head. I told her that I was planning to confront Philip's girlfriend. She needed to know she was not welcome in my house and that I would *spank that ass* if I caught her there again. Gigi tried to make me change my mind. She said my issues were with Philip and that I should deal with him only and not have any contact with her at all. She said confronting that girl was beneath me. Philip did not deserve to see me behave that way. She also reminded me of my job and how my reputation could be affected if word got out that I had brought my personal drama into the workplace.

With tears flowing down my face, I told her that with all I was going through, the last thing I was worried about was my professional reputation. I became angry with her because it seemed like she wasn't supporting me, so I hung up without saying goodbye. Gigi tried calling back a few times, but I let her call go to my voicemail. I wiped the tears from my face, did a quick makeup retouch, and proceeded to my office.

When I got to my office, my assistant, Rose, closed the door behind me.

"I blocked your calendar this morning so we can go over this extra-long list of open issues you need to address," she said.

Rose and I had been friends for more than ten years. I met her when I was in law school. We attended the same church, and our sons attended the same school. A few years earlier when I landed my current position, I brought her in to work for me. While Rose was a colleague, she was also a friend and knew Philip as well.

As I looked through the pile of phone messages, Rose walked over to my desk and took my hand.

"Girlfriend, how are you doing?"

"What do you mean?"

"If you lose another pound, I'm going to have to organize an intervention."

I was about to protest, but she cut me off. "Everyone knows what's going on with you and Philip. Everyone knows

Philip is running around like a fool. People have tried to talk to him, including Dan (her husband) and Dr. Carson (the church pastor), but it didn't help, because Philip has lost his mind. He's parading that girl around church like she's the queen of England or something. During the open declaration part of the service, that fool stood up and announced that you and him were getting a divorce and that he had found his true soul mate."

"To top it off, he said, 'I want to ask my church family to open their arms to my future wife. We're getting married as soon as my divorce is final." Dr. Carson asked the associate pastor to take over the service while he talked to Philip and his girlfriend outside of the sanctuary.

"A few minutes later, Dr. Carson came back and sat up front for the remainder of service. I heard that Dr. Carson told Philip to find another church home and to take his girlfriend with him. But that fool had the nerve to come back to church the next Sunday with his girlfriend. His presence completely disrupted the service. People were lashing out at him, calling him a blasphemer and saying he and his girlfriend weren't welcome there. Finally, he left, and hasn't been back since. Thanks to your foolish soon-to-be ex-husband, Dr. Carson has been preaching on adultery and the sanctity of marriage the past two months."

Hearing that was more than I could bear. Just when I thought things couldn't get any worse, Rose let me know that they already had. I valued my privacy and believed that marital issues should be dealt with privately, but mine had been exposed to the world, my family, my workplace, and my church. Now everyone knew I was a fake.

As tears rained down from my eyes, I wiped my face and stood up. "Speaking of the girlfriend, I think it's time I paid her a visit.

"No," Rose said, her back to my office door. "Don't do that. That's not the way to deal with her."

Just then, one of the other assistants interrupted and asked to speak to Rose. When Rose stepped out of my office, I pull up the girl's information and photo. The first thing I noticed was that she wasn't even a company employee. She was a temp, a project coordinator; a glorified fucking clerk. That didn't really surprise me though because I knew Philip liked his women, and maybe his men, beneath him. Then I looked at her picture, and her face seemed very familiar to me, but I wasn't sure where I had seen her. She definitely was not in my social circle. Then I remembered that Philip had introduced her to me about a year earlier when I saw him having lunch at a restaurant with some of his colleagues. *His ass must have been having an affair with her back then.* I saw that she worked in Building Four, which was three buildings away from my office. The more I thought about her and Philip prancing around my house like I didn't live there, the angrier I became.

As much as I had tried to strip away all the remnants of the Gardens, this disrespectful bitch had pushed me right back there. It was time for her to meet me face-to-face. After all, if she was brave enough to fuck my husband in my bed, she was brave enough to take a real ass whipping, and I was the one to give it to her. I was from the Gardens, and we knew how to get respect. If I were a hood-rat chick, it would have been on-and-poppin' a long time ago. But since I was a refined lady, I had to use a more polished approach.

I had never really had a physical altercation with a female, but on this day, I felt like I could put my size nines so deep up her ass that my toes would be dangling out of her mouth. She had no boundaries. She had come into my home not once but several times with no regard for my presence or legal standing in it. She needed to know who I was. I wasn't some quiet, church-going suburban housewife she could disrespect at will. When I was done with her, she would think twice before fucking another woman's husband. While I didn't want Philip, I didn't want his girlfriend to feel she had the right to inject herself in the nucleus of my family structure while I was still in it. If she wanted to lie motionless on the towel with Philip, she could have him but the accouterments of my life were not included.

By no means was I disregarding Phillip's role in this situation. I had something planned for him, too; but first things first, the girlfriend and then Philip.

I headed straight toward Building Four. Meanwhile, Gigi was blowing up my cell phone with calls. I answered one of them and told her that I couldn't talk, because I was on my way to see Miss Mona, Philip's infamous girlfriend.

Rose continued beeping into my call with Gigi. When I finally answered, she asked where I was, and I told her the same thing.

"No, Astrid," she said. "Don't do it. She's not worth it, and neither is he. You could lose your job if you put your hands on her. You're a lawyer. You know she can file criminal assault charges against you."

"I don't care."

"Wait, let me come to you, where are—"

I hung up on her.

Still weak from the chemo, I couldn't walk very fast. When I made it to Mona's building, I had to sit down for a minute in the lobby to catch my breath. I realized I was in no shape to fight anyone. About five minutes passed, and then I took the elevator to the fifth floor where the little coordinator's cubicle was located.

I walked around the floor, but I didn't see her. I stepped into her manager's office and inquired about her. He said she was there, but she must have stepped away for a moment. I walked around the floor again, but there was still no sign of her. Then Rose ran up behind me, breathing hard.

She grabbed my arm. "Oh my God, I'm so glad I caught you." She paused to catch her breath. "I ran all the way over here, and that goddamn elevator isn't working, so I had to climb five flights of stairs. You know, I am fine and sexy, but I'm also fifty years old. I can't be running around like this."

She led me to an empty conference room and sat down to talk.

"If I have a heart attack, it's your fault." She held up her index finger for a moment and took a few deep breaths before continuing. "I have just one thing to say, and then you do what you want to. He's just trying to hurt you. Everyone knows he's jealous of you, that he wants to break you, so don't let him do it. He wants to be able tell everyone that you fell down. But everyone knows he's been riding your coattails. You made your family's life great, not him. He wants to get a reaction out of you. He knows he's going to come out of this divorce as the villain, and that he'll be exposed as the loser he is. Besides, he doesn't want that welfare girl. She's got three kids with three different baby daddies. Every free Willy dick in our church has already had her. Even Dan said Philip must be crazy. You don't parade around town with your whore, especially one that's wearing a sign that says, 'Always Open'."

I couldn't help but laugh at her comment, which encouraged her.

"He just wants to hurt you. Philip has been on a rampage for the past five years. I know at least three other women here that he's dated. He's made it no secret that he's not above cheating on you. Girlfriend, you need to know when to hold 'em and when to fold 'em. I think it's time to let him go and move on."

Apparently, she had more than "one thing" to say. "You're a smart, intelligent, beautiful, successful woman, and he just can't handle that. Some men can't handle being with a woman like you. That's the price you pay for your greatness. You have to find a man who appreciates your strength and doesn't feel threatened by it. A man who loves you will build you up, not tear you down."

She took my hand. "Sweetie, don't lower yourself to his level. Remember, your job here is not just about you. You're the second highest ranked female in this company. You're part of an exclusive club among a privileged few women in Fortune 500 companies. You represent all other women who work in this company, and you can't fall from grace like this."

Despite my anger, I had to admit that what she said made a lot of sense. "Okay," I said. "You're right. I have a bigger responsibility here than just worrying about myself and Philip or his stank ass girlfriend."

Rose laughed, still breathing heavily. She stood up, apparently sensing the crisis had been averted. "I need to get some water. You might have to take me to the hospital if my heart doesn't stop racing."

We both laughed and started toward the elevator, which was operational once again. My phone rang. It was Gigi. I told her that everything was okay and that I would call her back later. Then Rose and I continued to laugh at the thought or her running through hallways trying to catch me before I confronted Mona.

Just then, Philip called, but I ignored it. I was done playing his game. It was finally over for me.

12

SURRENDERING

As I sat in my office staring out the window in deep thought, I realized I was too distracted to be productive. I decided that I needed to take some additional time off. Juggling my job, my health, and my divorce issues required too much time and mental resources.

I spoke to my boss and told him that I needed to extend my medical leave.

"We're here for you," he said. "Take as much time as you need. You're an important part of this team, and we'll be here when you return."

Yes, they would be there when I returned, but what else would be waiting for me? A newly redesigned job? A parachute package? A promotion that required me to relocate somewhere in No Man's Land? Attempting to return to work after a leave of absence would not be easy for someone in my position. As an executive, particularly as a woman, I was expected to be super human, to never get sick, to put family second, and above all, to put the needs of the company first and foremost. I had prepared myself and tried to perform to those expectations, but it had not brought me the joy or happiness I was seeking. I always wanted a family and a fulfilling career that paid me a lucrative salary, so, on the surface, I had everything I wanted. But the happiness wasn't there, or maybe my definition of happiness had changed. I was pretty sure that outsiders looking in would think I was crazy if they heard me say I wasn't happy.

Later that evening, I decided to have a glass of wine with my dinner; however, once I was standing in the middle of the wine cellar, my mind shifted elsewhere. I'd had enough of watching Philip raid our wine cellar and disrespect me by flagrantly displaying his affair. I decided he was not taking any more wine from the cellar. I packed up most of the wine from the cellar and took the boxes to Jeff's house for safe-keeping. Then I decided that we would be charitable and make a large clothing donation to the Good Will. Philip had always been into fashion and had an amazing wardrobe, complete with expensive Italian designer brands. I loaded my trunk with some of Philip's clothes and took them to several Good Will dumpsters. I made about three trips, and I still had not put a dent in his wardrobe, but just enough damage to irritate him.

As I lay in bed that night, I snickered to myself. I thought about how Philip would react when he came home to pack his next overnight bag and realized his clothes were gone. Would he start cursing or crying? Seeing his reaction would be priceless.

Just as I expected, a few days later, Philip returned home to repack his overnight bag while I was at Sunday brunch with Tara. When I told her what I had done, she couldn't believe it.

"He's going to kill you, girl. You know how he feels about his clothes."

As expected, when Philip discovered his clothes were missing, he started blowing up my cell phone. When I didn't answer, Junior started calling.

"Dad said you took his clothes. He's going to call the police and have you thrown in jail if you don't return them."

I called Philip and asked him what he wanted.

"Where are my clothes?" he shouted.

I didn't lie. I told him I had made a donation on behalf of the family.

He called his attorney, because we had a court order not to remove any property or valuables from the home, but that backfired, because Philip had been siphoning money from our joint bank accounts for months. He had also stopped paying his portion of the household bills and had forged my name on a home equity loan. I figured Philip had stolen around $100,000 in cash. He was such a dumbass that he left a paper trail a mile long with all of his violations. He must have forgotten I was an attorney, too.

The next morning, I woke up and decided I would try to have breakfast with Junior before he left for school. But when I sat down at the table with him, he got up and headed for the stairs without saying a word. He barely spoke to me at the best of times, and when he did, it was with anger and hostility.

I grabbed him by the arm, but he pushed me away so hard I fell on the floor. Then he stood over me like he was going to hit me. That was the last straw.

"Get out of my house, and don't ever come back!"

As he was leaving, I shouted after him. "If you ever raise your hand to me again, you better be prepared to meet Jesus."

I knew he was hurting and that his father was manipulating him, but I couldn't help him, neither would he let me.

As I sat on the floor with my head in my lap, I thought about what Philip had said over the years, that he would take the person I loved most and destroy him if necessary to get at me. I had dismissed those words so often, thinking they were meant only to scare me. What man would seek to destroy his own flesh and blood? I knew Junior was in pain, but I had no strength to help him. I needed to get healthy and repair my body and soul before I could begin to help him.

Later that afternoon, I got a call from my attorney saying that Philip had filed a child abuse charge against me and that the police had a warrant to remove me from the premises. My lawyer got an emergency hearing and we were able to go before the judge the same day. Philip's lawyer said I was a danger to both my child and to Philip. Philip said he was afraid of me, which was why he had been living with his friend Mona for the past six months. He pulled out a two-inch stack of papers, about forty different complaints that Philip had filed with the local police. They also had audio-recorded transcripts that Philip had made with me threatening him and calling him various homosexual slurs. They made me sound like I was prejudiced against homosexuals, which was not true at all, but I was deeply disturbed by Philip's misrepresentation of his sexuality. Admittedly so, I didn't understand the psychology of bi-sexuality and was enraged by the manner in which I was introduced to it.

The judge asked Philip to explain the child abuse charges. Philip said that I didn't cook meals, I had taken Junior's car and his credit cards from him, and that I beat him and threw him out and threatened to kill him if he ever came back.

"Why didn't you take Junior with you to your friend's house if you thought she was such a serious threat to both you and your son?" the judge asked.

"My friend doesn't have enough room for him."

"So you would take refuge there, but you would leave your son in an unsafe environment? I'm confused."

The judge continued before Philip could respond. "Before I render my decision, if your accusations are true, your son will likely have go into temporary foster care while Children Protective Services conducts an investigation. Are you okay with that?"

"No, I don't think that's necessary," Philip said. "She just needs to give him back his credit cards, start cooking for him like a real mother, and stop threatening him."

The judge asked Junior to come into his chambers so he could talk to him in private about the alleged abuse. About half an hour later, the judge returned and asked Junior to leave the courtroom. Then he turned to Philip.

"If you ever attempt to use my court again to further your personal vendetta against your wife, I will give you ninety days in the county jail and a fine for wasting this court's time. You should be ashamed of yourself for coercing your son to make a false allegation against his mother."

Junior told me later that Philip had said that if the courts made me leave the house, then he would leave his girlfriend and come back home. Junior thought that if his dad came back home, he and I could reconcile.

The judge said I did not have to give Junior his credit cards or his car if I didn't want to, seeing as the school provided transportation for him. He also said that although I had to provide food for Junior, I didn't have to cook for him. He also said he found it hard to believe that this big, seventeen year-old young man could be physically abused by a woman as small as me.

"Both of you listen to me carefully now," he concluded. "My court will not be used to play games. I suggest that the two of you try to resolve your differences and get through this divorce peacefully. You know, there is life after a divorce."

As I drove home, I thought about what the judge said; "There is life after divorce." Ever since we started the divorce proceedings, my focus had been on strategizing to get through it, not what my life would be like after it was done. I had not given any thought to making a new home or a new life for myself or even what that new life would entail.

With everything that I was going through with Philip and our divorce, I had not paid attention to the seriousness of my illness either. Maybe I had deliberately focused on the divorce. After all, that was much easier to face than my own mortality. I decided to shift my focus to saving my life, because dying would be the ultimate victory for Philip. He would have everything he wanted: my money, my son, and the knowledge that he had broken me before I died. For the first time, I realized that Philip's distractions were literally killing me. It was time for me to surrender. From that day forward, I would focus on my health and let my lawyer deal with Philip.

Against my attorney's advice, I gave Philip everything he wanted except access to my future earnings. Financially, he netted out very well. Settling with him was worth it to gain my freedom. My doctors had already raised concerns about the slow progress of my recovery. I needed to remove all toxins from my life in order to get well, and number one on the list was Philip.

Just as Philip accepted my settlement offer, the house sold, and we were free to go our separate ways. Ironically, later that night while I was in bed watching TV, Philip knocked on the door and asked if he could come in and talk. I told him that we had nothing to talk about. He came in anyway and kneeled down in the same spot Junior had kneeled a few months earlier, pleading for me to reconcile with his father. Before he could say anything, his eyes swelled with tears, and he laid his head near my chest.

"I'm so sorry. I don't know how I let this happen to us. I still love you. You're my wife; we belong together."

"What about Mona?" I asked.

"I was confused at first, but then I realized that she's just another money-hungry whore with nothing to offer me but sex from a worn out pussy. I didn't really want a divorce. I only filed to make you see I was serious. But when you didn't flinch, I felt like I had no choice but to go through with it."

He paused as if he was waiting for me to respond, but I didn't say a word. I was stunned by his sudden change of heart. Then I said, "I'm done, and this is over for me."

He wiped away the rest of his tears. "Have it your way then. I'll see you in court. You will never escape me. I made you, and I will always be with you. I will always be in your head like an imprint on your brain. No matter where you are in this life, you will always belong to me. Don't ever forget it."

I dismissed Philip's words as more hateful rhetoric, but I hoped he wouldn't flip the script and undo all the progress we had made with our divorce settlement.

Thankfully, the next few weeks were quite peaceful. Somehow, Philip and I had managed to reach a truce. Our war of roses was over. All we had left to do was to wait for our court date and then sign the papers. Just like that, once D-day arrived, our eighteen-year marriage would be dissolved with a stroke of a pen. Then I could drop his last name and become Astrid Josette Johnson once again.

Now that the house had been sold, I needed to find a new place to live. Sometimes when I was alone, the thought of moving scared me. I had never lived alone before. I had gone from Gigi's house to a dorm with roommates and then to Philip's house. I was about to become a free single woman with everything that came with it. But this time I would be smarter and wiser as I navigated the rest of my life.

Knowing that I could finally cease my interactions with Philip was liberating. Having freedom was one thing, but knowing what do with it was quite another. I was okay moving forward with every aspect of my life except dating. I was uncertain as to whether I could ever have a healthy relationship with a man again. My concerns were not based solely on my experience with Philip. I was thirty-six years old, and I was so far behind other women my age when it came to sex and many other aspects of a relationship. Philip had groomed me to satisfy him sexually. And based on my experience with Chevy and the many conversations I had with my girlfriends, we were definitely not setting the sheets on fire. No one else on the planet used a towel when they had sex.

One thing was for sure: I didn't waver on feelings about marriage. I was never getting married again. I would never give any man that kind of power and control over me. I would never allow myself to fall in love again. Philip had been such a loving man, but when he got what he wanted, locking me down with marital handcuffs, he became Mr. Hyde. He gave me a child of perfection and condemned me to eighteen years of deception. Philip had taught me well. Love and marriage would not be in my future. I would set the rules by which I would interact with men. It would be my way or no way. No compromises.

The day after Philip and I signed the contract for the sale of our home, he and Junior drove to Mississippi to visit his parents. To avoid drama with Philip, I moved out of our home while they were gone. After the movers left, I decided to take one last walk through the house.

After strolling through the upstairs, I decided to make way down to the second level. As I started down the winding staircase, I just stood there looking over the grand two-story foyer and the elegance that surrounded it. How could this place hold so much beauty and ugliness at the same time? I sat down on one of the steps, and my mind wandered aimlessly from my past to my uncertain future.

After sitting on my steps for what felt like hours, reflecting on the evolution of my life and shedding endless tears, I realized my journey wasn't over; it was just beginning. I got up and went to the powder room where I dampened a hand towel and washed my face. As I looked in the mirror, it was obvious I had morphed into someone or something that was foreign to me. Whoever that person was or would become, I was about to find out. I took a deep breath. It was time to turn the page of my life and begin the next chapter.

I got in my car and smiled as I drove to my new apartment, trying to embrace the upside of the unknown, which I was about to embark upon.

A few months had passed, and I was feeling good. I was now in full recovery. My hair was growing back, and I had gained a few pounds. I got rid of my kangaroo pouch and even bought a new set of "twins," and they looked better than they did when I was thirteen. Since I was still on my medical leave, I decided I would simply relax and enjoy the summer before I resumed adult responsibilities. My life had been all about the grind since I was sixteen. It seemed that I never had time to simply relax, not even during vacations. I was always in school, working, or tending to Philip and Junior. Now that I had time for me, I was going to do just that—focus on me.

As I basked in the glory of my free summer days, I decided it was time for a change. I wanted and needed a new beginning, somewhere other than Michigan. I told Gigi about my plans, and then I retained a headhunter to find a new job in a new state with a warmer climate. As always, without judgment or commentary, Gigi gave me her blessing.

"I'm always a phone call or a plane ride away and my door is always open to you."

Even though I had not lived with Gigi for more than twenty years, I took great comfort in knowing she was just around the corner, always watching over me. She had been my rock and a source of strength for me. Whenever I needed her, she was there, even during those times when I didn't know I needed her. In some ways, moving to another state would be like I was leaving the nest for the very first time. While I'd had my wings for a long time, I had never really used them, so I was uncertain as to how well or how high I could fly.

13

RENEWAL & TRANSFORMATION

Tara and I started hanging out again. Our friendship had become distant after I got married, because Philip didn't approve of her. Philip hated Tara, because she contradicted what he believed defined a woman's role. She was single, beautiful, smart, and had a way with men. She seemingly only dated men who were millionaires, and she always did her homework to find them. She knew all the shakers and movers in the city, and when it came to local galas and events, she was always on the A-list. Although she had dropped out of college, she was still quite accomplished. She was an attractive, successful real estate broker with a charismatic personality. She owned a condo in an exclusive gated community and drove a convertible two-seater Benz and a complementary Mercedes SUV in the winter. She vacationed like she was a celebrity. The pages in her passport were completely stamped every year. Not to mention, she had a couture wardrobe—furs, jewelry, purses, and shoes. I loved her confidence and her independence, and

Philip hated her for all the same reasons. If there was anyone who could help me to assimilate into single life, it was Tara.

Tara invited me to a birthday party for one of her business associates. She said we could also celebrate my independence and re-birth into adult single life. Since I had not really been out in two years, I decided to go. I needed to have some fun. Plus, I wanted to show off my new body. I was back to my ideal weight, and it was time to unveil the twins to the rest of the world. Since the party theme was white, I bought a white cleavage-baring baby doll mini dress, a pair of sexy four-inch Giuseppe strappy sandals, a few white and nude simple satin thongs with matching bras, and all of the other required accessories. I went to the salon and had my hair cut into a short, sassy Halle Berry hairstyle and had a complete facial, including makeup and eyelashes. I was good to go.

After getting dressed, I looked at myself and said, "Damn girl, you're looking pretty good today. I forgot how well you cleaned up. You better be careful. You're going to pull both men and women tonight wearing that outfit." I felt good all over—hot and sexy, something that I had not felt in a long time.

When I arrived at the marina where the party was being held, it was packed. As I got out of my car at the valet parking, I saw men staring at me. The same thing happened when I strutted through the ballroom looking for Tara. Both men and women were looking at me and complimenting me on how beautiful my dress was. When I finally found Tara's table, she gave me the once over.

"Damn, girl, you trying to hurt somebody tonight with that dress." Then she pulled me close and whispered in my ear. "By the way, the twins are looking fabulous. You make me want to get a re-touch."

I laughed, and then we walked to the bar to get a drink.

As we waited in line, I spotted one of the band members checking me out. Then he approached the mike.

"I want to dedicate this next song to the angel standing at the bar wearing that teeny, tiny white dress," he said. "The song is called, 'You Make Me Feel Brand New.'" His smooth sexiness came through every melodic word that he belted out through his sensual lips.

After he finished, the band took a break while the DJ took over. He came over to my table and introduced himself. His name was Damien, and he had a voice like Johnny Mathis. He was a beautiful man. He looked Brazilian with his freshly tanned complexion. He was tall and slim with a model-like build, jet-black hair, and a complementary mustache.

We slow danced a few songs, and then we walked around the marina. He asked me to stay after the next set and then have breakfast with him. I hesitated, but then I agreed and returned to my table.

When I sat down, Tara put her hand on mine. "You should be careful with him. I hear he's a kept man. He only dates women who can take care of him, and he may be targeting you."

"Well, he's wasting his time, because I don't do one-night stands, and I'm not looking for any more dependents. I just got rid of one."

As the party wound down, I thought about what Tara had said about Damien, so I decided to leave with her.

When we were walking toward the door, someone tapped my shoulder. It was Damien.

"I thought you were going to let me take you to breakfast."

"I'm sorry, but it's late," I said. "Can I take a rain check?"

"How are you going to do that if you don't have my number? Please, let me take you to breakfast. I promise to be a gentlemen. Besides, we're only going to the pancake house up the street—unless you have some other place in mind. Anyway, I have this strange feeling that after tonight, I may never see you again. Come sit at the bar and give me ten minutes to pack up. Then we can leave."

The bartender gave me a vodka with a splash cranberry while I waited for Damien. I could tell he was in a rush as he packed his belongings. He threw some things into a duffle bag, but he handled his violin like a newborn baby as he placed it ever so gently in its case. Then he grabbed my arm and led me toward the parking lot.

As we walked, I commented on how careful he seemed while handling his violin.

"Well, she's a loyal bitch, so she deserves extra special handling," he said. "She performs on demand, she never lets me down, and she always generates a return on my investment. I am who I am because of her."

"Wow," I said, "what woman could measure up to all of that?"

"No one yet, but a few have come close." He looked at me and smiled. "Maybe you're that one."

When we reached the valet parking attendant, he said, "Why don't we jump in your car, and then you can drive me to mine. I'm parked in the back with the rest of the regular people. You can just follow me to the restaurant."

As I drove behind him, I started to feel nervous, like I was going on my first date. He was so fine. I knew that any man who looked that good was trouble.

We parked next to each other and then found a seat in the corner of the restaurant. We both ordered coffee, and he ordered an omelet, which he played with. He said he was hungry, but he was so excited by my company that he couldn't eat. We were having the usual get to know each other conversation when he interrupted me and asked if he could kiss me. I said yes, and he gave me a wet sensual kiss while caressing my thighs. While he was kissing me, I held onto his hands to make sure they didn't go too far. His tender kiss definitely woke up some emotions in my body. Then I pulled back.

"It's getting late, and I want to go to early church service, so it's time for me to leave."

"Okay," he said. "Let me be a gentleman and walk you to your car."

When we got to my car, he took my hand. "Would it be too forward if I asked you to let me kiss you again?

"Okay," I said. "One last kiss good night."

"Well, take off your panties."

My mouth dropped open. "What?"

"I've already kissed the lips on your face. Now I want to kiss your lips down there."

I smiled. "I don't think so. Maybe some other time."

"Why not?" he replied, glancing around. "No one's going to see us."

"You can't be sure of that. We could get arrested for lewd conduct if the police saw us."

"I only want to kiss her, not make love, at least not right now. I won't stay down there too long. I promise."

We were standing outside of my car on the passenger side. He opened the door and started kissing my neck and putting his hands up my dress, rubbing my butt and putting his hands inside my panties. I continued to resist him passively.

"No, no," I said in a soft voice. "Stop, we can't do this."

In truth, I was getting excited, but I continued to say no.

He stopped and looked at me. "Have you ever just let yourself go and done something risky? I know this sounds like bullshit, but I don't act like this with just any woman. You're so beautiful, and I'm feeling something for you. I don't have any expectations. I just want to make you feel good."

He continued kissing me, and then pushed me down in my seat, my feet still on the ground. He pulled me to the edge of the seat and slid my panties off. Then he kneeled down and put his head under my dress and started kissing, licking, and sucking on my clit.

For a few minutes I forgot where I was. I closed my eyes, completely absorbed in the moment. Then a frightening chill came over me. I opened my eyes and saw a flash of Ricky. It was his head that came up from under my dress. With labored breaths and a briskly beating heart, I pushed back in my seat away from Damien.

He looked up at me. "What's wrong?"

I pushed him off me. "I'm sorry, I can't do this. He stood up and looked confused and disappointed as he wiped his mouth and glossy face, lubricated from the cum that dripped from my vagina.

I grabbed his hand. "Do you want to go home with me?"

He smiled. "Yes!" Then he got in his car and followed me back to my apartment.

As soon as we got in the elevator, before the doors even closed, he started kissing and fondling me under my dress. I actually liked that I was wearing a dress without panties; there was something freeing and empowering about it. It was another first for me.

Once I closed my apartment door, he started taking his clothes off. As I watched him disrobe, I was shocked when he took off his boxer briefs. His dick was standing at full attention, and it was a big ass horse dick, the largest I had ever seen. It must have been at least nine inches long with a circumference of three to five inches.

"Wow, how do you walk around with that thing?" I asked.

He laughed. "It's not that big; you can handle it."

As I stared at his dick, I thought there was no way my kat could handle it. It would feel like giving birth, only in reverse. *What the hell, he was fine and sexy.* Besides, my kat was up for the challenge. She was already warm and pulsating. I could feel her wetness running down my thighs.

I led him to my bedroom, and then he pushed me down on my bed and started kissing me.

"Wait, I need to tell you someth—"

"What, you got a man? I already knew that, 'cause you're fine as hell."

"No, but I need to tell you something."

"What now?" he asked in a more serious voice.

I told him that I was in remission from cancer and that I hadn't had sex in over two years.

He laughed. "That explains why your juices were over flowing when I was tasting it."

"I don't know how I'm going to feel down there," I said. "I don't know if the chemo has affected me in some way."

He smiled. "There's only one way to find out. Don't worry, I still know how to handle a virgin."

We both laughed as he laid me on my back. He began kissing my breasts, my stomach, and then he pushed my legs open and started licking and sucking on my kat for what seemed like thirty minutes.

While I enjoyed the oral foreplay, I felt a wave of fear come over me again. I had a strange feeling that someone was watching us. I started to feel like I was having an anxiety attack. As my breaths became more labored, Damien continued to reassure me.

"It's okay, baby. I know you like it; just enjoy it. I'm going to give you this dick in a minute, just enjoy my tongue right now."

At that moment, I saw flashbacks of Ricky's face again, but I closed my eyes and tried to ignore them. I didn't want to freak out in front of Damien again.

I nudged his shoulder to let him know I was ready for him to penetrate me, but then he climbed up and put his dick near my face, as if he wanted me suck it. It startled me, and I turned my head.

"No, I can't do that."

He looked puzzled, but then he proceeded to put on a condom on and attempt to plunge right into me. Even though I was juicy and wet, it took a few thrusts before he was able to slide in. The girth and length of his penis was so large I could feel it in my stomach.

After about fifteen minutes, he flipped me over on my stomach and then began pounding me from the back. The intensity of his strokes was forceful and hard, almost brutal, and then he finally climaxed.

He lay down on his side and pulled me close to him. He took the condom off, and his dick was still hard. I felt him continue to ejaculate, rubbing his dick on my back and between the cheeks of my ass.

"Your pussy is so good," he said when he finished. "It's well lubricated and has great fit, form and function. It gripped my dick perfectly."

"You make it sound like some type of mechanical device."

He laughed. "It is a mechanical device, and you operate it flawlessly. As far as I can tell, you're not missing a beat. Your two-year hiatus has not diminished your sexual capacity at all."

We both laughed, and then his face turned serious. "You're going to drive a man crazy one day once you get your confidence back." He fell silent for a moment. "Baby, I love oral sex. I love giving it, and I love receiving it. You looked like you were terrified when I pulled up so you could give me some head."

"You caught me off guard," I said. "I wasn't expecting that from you. It's been a long time since I made love to a man. All of this feels new to me. My sex drive has been dormant for the last five years, and it's been even longer since a man has excited me the way you have. Besides, you're a stranger. I've never done anything like this before. I only know how to make love to my man. I'm not sure how to make love to you."

"Don't worry about it," he said. "I don't want you to do anything you're not comfortable with. We got time. I won't be a stranger for long, 'cause I'm gonna want to get at that," he pointed at my vagina, "a few more times. Relax so I can take care of you 'cause I know you didn't get yours the first time."

He reached for another condom. Then, as we lay on our sides, he penetrated me from behind and massaged my clit with his hand while kissing my ears and my shoulders. This time it felt much better. He had definitely widened the path and broken me in. We continued to make love with me climaxing to the heavens and back all through the night. Damien used his warm moist tongue to fuck me orally and his dick to penetrate me in sexual positions that I never knew existed.

After a few hours, we held each other due to sheer exhaustion. Before we fell asleep, he started singing verses from his song, "You Make Me Feel Brand New." I was feeling just that, renewed and brand new. I knew that after my eighteen-year relationship with Philip and the traumatic ending, I had gone through a metamorphosis. But deep inside, I was scared of the unknown. Who was the brand new me, and why was I having these flashbacks of Ricky again, especially when it had never happened when I was with Philip?

The next morning, I awoke to find Damien performing oral sex on me again, but this time it was okay. There were no signs of Ricky or any anxiety. Damien said he needed to beat it up one more time before he left. We made love again and then showered. Before he left, we exchanged phone numbers and said that we wanted to see each other again. We both agreed that we would keep our encounter private and not tell anyone about it. As he walked to the elevator, he made a gesture with his hand indicating that he would call me. I smiled and blew him a kiss and then closed my door, thinking this might have been my first one-night stand.

After Damien left, I made some tea and then lay in bed thinking about him with a smile on my face. I felt complete and utterly satisfied. I had a sense of fulfillment and peace, like nothing could make me sad or angry. I also wondered how I'd had sex with a stranger and enjoyed it so immensely. Being with Damien reminded me of my encounter with Chevy. So this was the ecstasy I had missed out on. It was a good thing I didn't go all the way with Chevy. Otherwise I might have had an affair with him or simply left Philip, because once the bar had been raised to this level of passion, I would have wanted it again.

I never knew I could enjoy sex without being in love or having some type of emotional connection with my partner. I didn't know Damien; he was a complete stranger. I didn't even know his last name, but for one night, he took me to orgasmic heaven and back. This was a first for me, having sex with a complete stranger, but I had no regrets or concerns. I was going to enjoy the rest of my day. I couldn't help but wonder if I was motivated by something else besides lust to sleep with Damien.

A few hours later, Tara called to ask me how things went. I told her we had breakfast and then we went to our respective homes. She asked if he tried to get me to have sex with him. I said yes, but I wasn't ready for that.

"I knew your square ass wasn't about to go home with him," she said. "He ain't shit anyway. I heard he's got a girlfriend who is about to give birth to his baby any day now."

"Girl, you know I'm not trying to start anything with anyone now," I replied. "I'm just trying to have a little fun. The last thing I need or want is drama or something serious."

We laughed and chatted a little longer and then hung up. I still couldn't stop pretending. I always made my friends think I was more confident than I actually was.

A few days passed, and I had not heard from Damien, so I left a message on his phone, but he never called me back. I decided not to bother calling him back again. Surprisingly, I wasn't angry. I was more concerned about the level of intimacy we shared and how it made me feel. I didn't know I could feel the type of sexual euphoria that I had experienced with Damien. To him, I might have been nothing more than a conquest or simply another booty call, but to me, he was like a sexual defibrillator that had resuscitated my libido. The thought of him viewing me as a one-night stand didn't upset me. In fact, I wanted to call him and thank him for the great fuck, because he had unearthed a part of me that had been buried deep inside for a very long time. What kind of person was I? I felt as if I could have sex with Damien again and again and have no feelings for him at all, or maybe with some other stranger with no expectations of love or any kind of relationship. I realized then that I wasn't the sweet, innocent woman I had been while I was married. I had changed, but I didn't know how much I had changed and what I had changed into.

A few weeks passed and my executive headhunter finally completed the negotiations for my new job. I accepted a position with a law firm with an office in Atlanta, heading up their entertainment division. This was a complete departure from what I had been doing since finishing law school. One of the perks of my new job required my attendance at major client events within the entertainment industry. My compensation package even included a wardrobe allowance for that purpose. While I was excited about my new job, I was more excited to be leaving Michigan. It would be the start of my new life. I could finally leave my past and Philip behind.

The Saturday before my move, Tara and a few of my other girlfriends took me out for drinks to celebrate my new job. We went to Floods, an upscale nightclub for the thirty-and-over crowd located downtown. It was one of my favorite clubs because it had an urban vibe with a clientele of both young and mature professionals.

As the hostess led us to our table, I noticed a man sitting at the bar smiling at us. As we got closer to the bar, I realized it was Chevy. We had kept in touch off and on over the years, and I had run into him at the airport and at a few conferences, but we had never hooked up. He was a little heavier, but he was still very handsome, like he hadn't aged at all.

"Hello, beautiful," he said as I walked over to him. "Are you ever a sight for sore eyes?" He hugged me. "Where have you been? What have you been up to?"

I told him that I had recently finalized my divorce and that I was relocating to Atlanta. He told me he had recently married for the second time and was expecting his first child.

"Wow!" I said. "Congratulations."

He smiled. "That's what happens when you marry a young hottie like yourself. I tried to wait for you to become single, but you took too long."

As we laughed, he grabbed my hands and held them tight. At that moment, I think we both knew that this chapter in our lives was finally closed. We talked a few more minutes, and then I rejoined my girls at our table.

An hour later, Chevy walked over and gave me his business card with his personal cell phone number on it. "Just because I'm married doesn't mean we can't still be friends," he said. "Don't be a stranger."

We hugged one last time, and then he left. I put his card in my purse and then continued partying with my girls. As I thought about him, part of me wanted to cry. Although Chevy and I would go years without seeing each other, in the back of my mind, I always thought that, in the end, we might find our way back to each other, have a great love affair, and finally live happily ever after. But that would never be. The fantasy would remain just that, a fantasy. Chevy would live his life happily ever after with his new family, and I would have to create one for myself. It was also rather ironic that I had been thinking about him over the past few weeks, especially after my encounter with Damien. In the past, I would have analyzed our coincidental meeting and interpreted it as some kind of sign, but on that day, I accepted it for what it was, an unplanned meeting with a friend. My girls and I continued to drink, laugh, and do all the latest hustles and line dances all night long. That was the first time I had actually stayed at a bar until closing. It's a good thing I wasn't driving, because I don't remember how I got home.

The next day, I woke up with a hangover, only to hear loud knocking on my door. The movers had arrived to pack and load my belongings.

The following day, I boarded a plane for my new home, the city of Atlanta. As I sat in my first class seat, I felt liberated, like a huge boulder had been lifted from my shoulders. I had signed my divorce papers before I left Michigan, and I did not have to go back to court or see Philip's face ever again. Now all I had to do was let God work his magic and guide me through the rest of my life. I knew that would be easier said than done, because I was a different person now. I really didn't know what to expect from this new person and what my transformation would bring.

14

TURNING IT UP IN THE ATL

Once I arrived at my corporate apartment, I was in awe. I had heard about The Carlton Hotel & Corporate Suites long ago, but I never thought I would have the opportunity to stay there. I earned a pretty nice salary, but $2,500 per night far exceeded my budget. The opulence and resort-like features of the hotel were amazing, and I intended to take full advantage of my ninety-day stay. It had a rooftop pool, a fully staffed fitness center, a dry and a wet sauna, indoor tennis and racquet courts, a full-service spa and salon, restaurants, shopping, a pharmacy, a concierge medical service, and a host of other amenities. I could actually live in the hotel and never leave except to go to my job. Above all, there were plenty of men living there. The hotel looked like the United Nations for men, since there were so few women there. The men were all nationalities from all over the world. In this case, it was nice to be in the minority, one of only a few women.

At least once a week, one of the residents sent me flowers or asked me out on a date, but I stood firm and decided to keep the dates platonic and not give up the goodies. I maintained my rules of engagement. I never played where I worked or where I stayed. Besides, I was still early in my career, and I knew I could end up working for or with one of these men one day. Some lines, no matter how tempting, should not be crossed. Once I crossed the whore line, I could never go back regardless of what VP or C-suite title I held.

While staying at my corporate apartment, I met Mr. Thomas Burke, a lawyer-turned executive image consultant. He was the CEO and founder of a public relations firm, but he had a few confidential clients that he managed personally, which was why he was in Atlanta. Burke had a brilliant mind with broad reach, and he was enormously successful. His five-foot-tall, physically-fit frame was also full of bravado. He was short in stature but tall in confidence. Nonetheless, he was still a man, intrigued by my pearl and bulging rack like the rest of his peers. While his preference appeared to be petite Asian women with a silicone D-rack, I still managed to catch his attention.

One night, after a long exhausting day at work, I decided to sit at the bar and have a glass of wine before turning in. That's when Mr. Burke walked over and introduced himself. We had acknowledged each other a few times in passing on the elevator, as he was always in the company of an Asian beauty, but nothing had ever transpired between us.

As we talked, he said I was stunning, and he seemed to know quite a bit about me already, as if he had compiled a dossier on me. After we finished our drinks, he walked me to the elevator.

"What would I have to do in order to sleep with you?"

His boldness caught me off guard, and I did not respond immediately.

"Don't look so shocked," he said. "You know that ninety percent of the men who look at you want to fuck you. That can be a curse or an asset. It depends on how you spin it."

"Wow," I said, still unsure of how to respond. "Should I be flattered or insulted?"

"Neither," he said. "It's an immutable fact. I don't have to tell you about using all your assets to be successful. It looks like you've already mastered that. You still haven't answered my question though."

I smiled. "I'll let you know when I have an answer." I stepped in the elevator, ignoring Burke. He stood there until the door closed as if he was waiting for me to say something else.

Burke and I continued to see each other in passing. While we never had any intimate encounters, we did develop a friendship. We had a unique connection, as if we were old, trusted friends. We felt very comfortable with each other, like we knew each other's secrets without ever verbalizing them. He knew I was a fake under my bold, intelligent, sexy exterior, and I knew that he was masking something, too, perhaps a Napoleon complex.

Over the next few weeks, whenever possible, I would listen to Burke talk for hours about all the nameless politicians and executives he had worked with over the years. When it came to the press, he was a true "spin doctor," a natural media manipulator, and he was paid handsomely for his skills. Not that I expected to ever need Burke's services, but if I did, he was the person that I would want to use.

Burke left the hotel a few weeks before me. On the last night of his stay, I tried to give him my contact information, but he said he already had it. I took that as a good sign, because it meant I was important to him and part of his network now, which was not easy to access. Burke made it his business to know everything about the people in his inner circle, given his work and the clientele he serviced.

"You might need my services one day," he joked as he left.

Those were not mere words. In the months to come, we usually connected for dinner or cocktails whenever he was in Atlanta.

I spent the first couple of weeks of my transition period onboarding at work and in my new hometown. At Gigi's urging, I reconnected with some distant relatives and began searching for a church. I also connected with a few old friends and made a few new friends as well. Gigi and I resumed our morning talks. I usually called her during my drive to work. But unlike before, she had become increasingly nosey. She was particularly interested in my dating life. She would often say things like, "Have you met anyone yet? You know you don't have to marry the first man you have sex with." I would just laugh and say "Okay." I think Gigi thought that I had not had sex with anyone since Philip. Little did she know I was done with one-on-one relationships; I planned to turn it up in the ATL.

As my time in my corporate apartment drew to a close, I found the perfect new place for my permanent residence. A luxury penthouse in a high-rise condominium located in the Buckhead community. My condo unit was opulent; emanating elegance, success, and sexiness, everything that defined me. It was home.

The week I moved into my new condo, my cousin Val came down from Chicago to help me get settled in. Val had grown into a beautiful, smart, successful physician. Since she was a psychiatrist, she had diagnosed half of our family as having some form of mental illness. We often laughed at her and said that her profession had made her paranoid. I had never shared my issues with Philip with her, but somehow she knew something wasn't right with him. I can recall a few occasions during the early years of my marriage when she would jokingly say that Philip was mentally disturbed. But I dismissed her words due to my denial and confusion.

"Cuz, you better watch him," she said. "He's the kind who will flip the script on you in a minute, and you're not going to know what hit you. I've seen his kind before, more often when I do my monthly visits to the state prison. These are the kind who will kill their wives and girlfriends and sometimes their kids, too. They are chronically narcissistic, they rationalize and feel justified in their actions, even if they hurt someone." As it turned out, her diagnosis and suspicion about Philip were right, but I never told her.

Val was a lot a fun. She also was a walking contradiction. She was ultra-conservative and straight-laced during the day but wild and undercover at night. Since I married so young, we didn't hang out too much, but I always enjoyed watching her live her life—free, full of confidence, and uninhibited. She was a world traveler, too, and she had a network of friends across the country, including Atlanta.

After a few days of shopping, helping me revamp my wardrobe and purchase a few sexy pieces of furniture for my new place, Val said we needed to work on my social life.

"You need a man, if not one to stay with, at least one to play with. You know, the fastest way to get over a man is to get under a new one, preferably one who knows how to use his tools. I'm an expert when it comes to moving on from ex-husbands. I've burned through two of them already, and I'm not afraid to go through two more."

We laughed and then continued talking about the social life I needed to create. She gave me a list of professional organizations I needed to join nationally and in Atlanta. She also gave me a lecture on how to date men of a certain economic means, where to find them, and how to avoid getting hurt by all the falsities and negativities that came with them. She was determined to help me find a new man. She told me not to go too long without sex either. It wasn't good for my mental well-being.

"A dilly will tide you over, but you need the real thing to keep you from going insane."

We drank more champagne, watched a few movies, laughed and cried a little, and then we went to sleep.

The next day, which was also Val's last night in Atlanta, she took me to see a play. Of course, I wasn't surprised when we pulled up and the marquis said "The Vagina Monologues." By the time the play was over, I had expanded my sexual IQ to include words like "cunnilingus," "anilingus," "rimming," "surfing," various uses of fruits, and tons of other updated terms to describe sexual positions that were not even found in the Kama Sutra.

After the play, Val took me to a private party hosted in a mansion by the Phallaceo Entertainment Group, the play's local promotion company. The party's theme was dicks, vaginas, and fellatio. All the plates and glasses and even the flatware had a design or was shaped to resemble a penis, vagina, scrotum, or some other part of the human sexual anatomy. As I looked around, I noticed that the party guests were mainly women and a few trans-gendered women. I was certainly out of my comfort zone, but I was in Atlanta, trying a few new adventures to help me find my social niche. So, for the moment, I would go with the flow.

After about an hour of listening to music, drinking, and eating, the host, who proudly called herself "Phallaceo," summoned us to the living room. She introduced herself and provided some history on her background. She'd had multiple professions—a licensed psychologist turned sexologist—and had worked in various lines of the entertainment business. For our pleasure, she brought in a special guest to demonstrate how to perform fellatio correctly, a sexual act that was unfamiliar to me. I was intrigued, because I had never watched porn or observed a couple performing any sexual acts.

The special guest, a woman who called herself Sasha, talked about the art of fellatio. It was all about preparation, muscle relaxation, the sensitivity of the head of a man's penis, and how to stroke his elongated shaft. She went on to talk about ancient myths about how women had used fellatio to cause sensory nerve damage, leaving men in a temporary inoperative state. Sasha also said she was going to demonstrate how to perform a deep throat fellatio act, the ultimate sexual high for a man. At that moment, I thought she was going to bring out a real man, but she didn't.

She said that deep-throating was better and easier if the penis was well lubricated, so we needed to take time for preparation, stimulating it such that it releases pre-cum. Alternatively, a woman could use her saliva to lubricate the entire shaft of his penis.

"Everything works better when it's well lubricated, ain't that right ladies?"

We all laughed, and then she pulled out a six-inch long vibrator. While relaxing her muscles, and sucking on it, she ingested all of it without gagging. I was amazed, but I don't think anyone else was until she pulled out the big boy. This vibrator was about twelve-inches long and three inches in diameter. It looked like a real plumbing pipe. I guess that's where the term "laying pipe" came from. We all watched in awe as Sasha ingested the massive thing down her throat without gagging or choking. Then she added the finale. As we watched her neck, it looked like she was making repeated swallowing motions. I was truly amazed, because she had a skinny body and what appeared to be a very small mouth. Like they say, you can't judge a book by its cover.

When she finally pulled it out, she received a very long applause. She explained that the movement in her neck was called "throbbing." It was similar to the muscle movement a woman uses with her vagina. It was also this throbbing technique that allows a man to journey toward his climax. Of course, she said deep-throating was not for the faint of heart. No spitting out at this time; you had to take in all the watermelon juices. This throbbing technique was also the mythical act that could supposedly cause a man to temporarily experience euphoria similar to that of a heroin addict. She also said this was something we could practice, and she had an exercise and sexual apparatus for that as well.

She closed out her performance by indulging us with a few Q&As and then providing business cards with her website information. She pointed us to table that was full of sexual how-to DVDs, books, and other sexual toys her company sold. She definitely aroused my curiosity.

Val and I went over to the table, and she started picking up different sized vibrators, massagers, gels, and a few other toys and books. Then she picked up the deep throat fellatio DVD and threw it in my bag.

"Cuz, you need to get this DVD, because you're going to have to step your game up. No more of that stay on the towel stuff."

We laughed and proceeded to pay for our items.

As we were leaving, I saw my real estate agent and her sister, Zoe, whom she had told me about. She said often that I reminded her of Zoe. We had a lot in common, and she would be the right person to help me get acclimated to living in Atlanta. We talked a few minutes, exchanged numbers, and then Val and I left for home.

The next morning after I dropped Val off at the airport, I noticed that she left a card on my seat. It read, "Time is too precious and fleeing, so don't let life pass you by. Live your best life and enjoy it and worry about regrets later." She signed it and then added a PS: "I hope you enjoy your goody bag. I knew you were too shy to buy those things for yourself, so I bought them for you. Consider it my house-warming gift to you. Enjoy!"

Once I got home, I went through the goody bag. I had never used a vibrator, massager, or any stuff like that before. I didn't recognize some of it, let alone knew how and where to use it. I decided to look at the fellatio DVD, because that activity interests me the most.

After watching it a few times, I decided it was time to try it out. I opened up the small vibrator called the Slim Jim. It was about six inches long, but it was skinny like a Slim Jim salami stick. Surely, I could handle that. To my surprise, it wasn't that easy. I started gagging right away and had to take it out.

The next time I got it in a little deeper, but then I started choking and coughing so hard that I threw up. I took a break for two days, but then, just as the DVD instructed, I continued to practice it daily over the next few weeks until I finally got it. I hoped that the act itself would be better than my practice sessions, because there was nothing exciting or arousing about it. I forgot this wasn't about me. I was supposed to derive my pleasure from pleasuring my man. I always thought that was bullshit. I never really thought about doing anything exclusively pleasurable to a man before. I thought men who engaged in cunnilingus did it because they liked it, not just for the female's pleasure. My motto had always been, sexual pleasure should provide mutual satisfaction to both parties and was never one-sided. I obviously had a lot to learn about sex and intimate relationships.

The whole time I was practicing my fellatio skills, I thought about Damien. He had left me curious. The sex had been wonderful, but how much better would it have been if I had given him the head that he wanted? Any woman could lick or suck a dick like a lollipop, but not all women could deep-throat it. I wondered if I had deep-throated Damien if it would have given me power over him. Could I have made him fall in love with me or would it simply have been a complement to a good fuck? I wondered if I saw him again if I would be able to do him. Who was I kidding? I was not about to perform fellatio or any deep throat tricks on any man. Plus, the thought of someone ejaculating down my throat disgusted me. In my mind, it was no different than letting a man pee in my mouth.

As repulsed as I was about this deep throat fellatio stuff, I was also intrigued by it. I thought about it frequently, not only the pleasure it gave men but also how I could use it to derive power, to gain control over men, since it was something they all desired from women. Throughout my life, so many men had pursued me for sex. Ricky had attempted to take it from me, and Philip had coerced me into doing it. Now I wanted to know if I could use sex to gain the dominant power in the relationship, to let him know how it felt to be powerless. I needed and wanted to experience that kind of power at least once in my lifetime.

My new private hobby became researching the psychology and physiology of sex, particularly as it related to men. It had to be more than testosterone and ego that caused men to be obsessed with sex, driving them to rape for it, lie for it, cheat for it, pay for it, and sometimes actually fall in love for it. Surely, if it could empower them, it could weaken them, too. I was curious to learn about the psyche behind a man's obsession with sex. Perhaps through this knowledge, I could become comfortable and secure in my own sexual relationships. As far-fetched as it seemed, I wanted to know how to use sex to gain power in my relationships with men. I wanted to be more than a pretty face and a great lay. I wanted to be a force to be reckoned with, someone who would stun him the first time and cause him to become addicted to it. He would do anything to have me again and again and again. I wanted him to know that my pussy had real power and it wasn't to be trifled with. I wanted to know how to fuck his brains out whenever I desired. I wanted that kind of power. It was the only thing missing to make me whole.

Online, I found a renowned, board-certified psychologist named Abigale (Abby) who specialized in sexual therapy. She was another self-proclaimed sexologist. I paid the fee to subscribe to her website and purchased her short essays on making love, taming your man's dragon, and so forth. What interests me most was her emphasis on the power women had over men in sexual conquests. Through the physical, we could conquer the mental. After dialoguing with her a few times on her blog, she gave me her private phone number.

When I finally mustered up the courage to call, we had an instant connection, and we went on to have several conversations. She made me feel very comfortable discussing my sex life, past and present, and my sexual inhibitions and curiosities. She was quite interesting. At age sixty plus, she still boasted a healthy though unconventional sex life. Later, I learned that she had worked as a high-class escort in her younger days while pursuing her college studies. To me, this so-called "field work" gave creditability to her craft.

After a few weeks, she invited me to a private weekend retreat that she hosted in her home once a year for a select group of women. At first, I was afraid to go, thinking it might be a waste of money or a scam or even something bizarre or dangerous. I checked her out, but I couldn't find anything suspicious about her, neither did I find anything that gave credence to her work. As I was about to decline the invitation, I thought about Zoe. She would be able to tell me if Abigale was legit or not.

I called Zoe and she seemed shocked that I knew about Abigale. "I know about Abby," she said. "I've even met her before at a few events here in Atlanta. She's definitely the real deal, but how do you know about her?"

When I told her about the invite I had received, she was amazed.

"Wow, it took me three years to get an invite to that retreat. So, who's the lucky man?"

"I'm still looking for him."

"Then you're about to get turned up for the turn-out."

I laughed. "Something like that."

"Well, let me know if you need help filling out that hundred-page confidentiality agreement of hers."

The truth of the matter was that having sex with same person on a towel in the same position for eighteen years had left me feeling sexually deficient. I still referred to the male and female sexual organs by their anatomically correct names. I was very uncomfortable holding a man's penis in my hands and verbalizing words like "pussy," "dick," or "head." I still referred to my vagina as a kitty kat. It was a stretch to say "coochie." When it came to my own sexuality, I was an unsophisticated girl trapped in a thirty-six-year-old's body. While some might say there was beauty in that type of innocence, I didn't see it that way. To me, it was a weakness. Even though I was obviously not a virgin, I felt like I did back in college—sexually retarded. Tara was right. I should have experienced more dicks before I married Philip.

In spite of my close encounter with Chevy and my fiery one-night-stand with Damien, I still felt scared, powerless, and insecure when it came to sex. My exterior was nothing less than a bona fide BAB. I had a successful career, and I was financially sound with plenty of brains, beauty, and booty, but on the inside, I felt quite the opposite. I knew I was sexy, because I could tell how men responded to me. It was something natural and effortless that emanated from my pores and the swerve of my curves. But where there is sexiness, there is usually true confidence, and that's where I had my conflict. While I was good at faking the front, I was tired of it. I wanted to know who I was sexually, and I wanted to engage in it freely and lovingly. The experience with Ricky in my childhood had planted a seed of fear around my sexuality and, I had been unable to grow and mature sexually with Philip, because he was secretly gay and never really wanted to lay with a woman. The sum of my sexual experience had not nurtured me but had starved and deprived me. Above all, it had taken my power from me. I needed to get past that and merge my outer-self with my inner-self so I could be whole and regain my power. I knew I would not be able to have a normal relationship with a man until I was secure with my sexuality and power within.

When I arrived at Abby's beautiful beachfront home in Martha's Vineyard, I was surprised to see how Zen, her décor, was and how beautifully plain she was. The house was tranquil, more like a spa than a clinical setting. While Abby wrote and spoke of sexual pleasures and exploits, her simple, elegant beauty was more like Liz Taylor or Jackie O, not the sexy Marilyn Monroe type that I thought she would be.

After we completed the tour, during which she spoke in her strong Swedish accent, Abby went over the itinerary and house rules. One of which included us wearing nothing but the thick white bathrobes and slippers she provided during the work sessions.

Along with a small medical staff, there were three other guests, all of whom were rich and famous due to the men to whom they were married. We each met with Abby separately and as a group to talk about the things we wanted to accomplish that weekend and to discuss our shared interests.

During group therapy or "tea time," as Abby called it, she would provide a lecture that was more like a modern day discussion around the Kama Sutra, sexual foes, myths, and how to be a sexual servant to our mate. She talked about the concept of the "non-sexual" orgasm. As she explained more about it, it reminded me of an experience I'd had with Chevy when we were studying abroad. I believe I had a non-sexual orgasm with him. She also talked about learning our mate, studying his responses to when and how we touched him in different places.

"Don't be afraid to experiment with him," she said. "Find the spots that make him go crazy. They all have them. You have to put it in your mind that it's your job and lifeline to pleasure him sexually. Through your gift of pleasuring him, you will gain power."

She fixed us all with a stern look. "Ladies, remember this: what you won't do for your man, another woman will, and he will not have any reservations about pursuing it or accepting it when presented to him. While it may sound like a cliché, a man wants a lady on his arm but a whore in his bed, and you have to be both all the times. He may not say it, but that's what he wants. It's been that way for centuries."

During my individual session with Abby, we discussed my concerns and insecurities about my own sexuality. I didn't tell her about Ricky, but I did tell her about my dysfunctional sexual relationship with Philip. I also told her about my lack of experience and my desire to have more physical control during intercourse and to feel more empowered sexually with my partner and in our relationship.

"When you were talking just now," she said, "I noticed that you always used the male and female anatomical terms or words like 'private parts,' and you often referred to your vagina as your 'pearl,' a 'kitty kat' or simply 'kat.'" She paused and smiled kindly. "First of all, you need to get comfortable with your pussy before you can make any man comfortable with it. How often do you look at and explore your own anatomy?"

I shrugged. "Never. I mean, I wash it multiple times a day and occasionally douche it."

She grabbed a large hand mirror and then told me to lie back on the sofa and look at it and then tell her what I saw.

I did as she asked and then laughed. “It looks like a big hairy mouth with layers of skin in it with a little pink tongue tucked away.”

She asked me about my libido, orgasms during sex, and masturbation. Of course, I found those topics difficult to talk about.

“Don’t worry too much,” she said. “The pussy and its helpers are very intelligent. They function like a brain, each having a role to help you climax. When the pussy seeks to have an orgasm through its many sensors, the juices, the vaginal muscles, and your body’s natural movement come together, pushing everything to the mountaintop for the explosion.”

She sat back and looked at me. “I’m puzzled by your conflict. So beautiful and yet so inexperienced at your age, but that’s okay. You will have plenty of homework when you leave here. You may need to come back a second time, but we shall see. And before I forget, no more pearls, feline names, vaginas, and penises. It’s all about your pussy and his dick or his cock, and those are the only appropriate terms to use with your man when you’re pleasuring him.”

Next, we moved on to the physical control of my own anatomy, how to use my vaginal muscles during sex. Since I did not have a vaginal birth, I could not relate to the control of pushing a baby through the birth canal, but I knew how to do Kegel exercises. In addition to doing Kegel exercises, she gave me soft exercise balls of different sizes and weights that I was to insert into my vagina to help control my muscle movements. I had to move the balls up and down my vagina and even hold them inside as I walked. This task was easier said than done. For a minute, it got really freaky as the nurse put on a pair of rubber gloves and lubricants and helped me perfect the exercise. I got it eventually though.

"I see you're a fast learner," Abby said.

The height of the retreat was on the last night when we had a cocktail party. Abby had invited additional guests, men and women, supposedly so they could share their experiences with us. In reality, they were more like human accessory devices to be used as part of the therapy. After mingling for an hour or so, Abby called for our attention.

"Ladies, this is your opportunity to try out your new skills or simply indulge in some extra curriculum activities, if you so desire."

At that moment, it started to feel more like a swingers' event than a therapeutic session. It was obvious that each "guest" had been assigned to us based on the skill or technique we were trying to master.

While I felt comfortable with my new tricks, I thought it would be a good time to get some feedback, so I took Mr. Tall, Dark, and Handsome back to my room.

As I tried to make small talk, he stripped down to his bare naked ass. I continued to make small talk nervously as he lay across the bed on his side with a full-blown erection.

"Go ahead and throw back a couple of tequila shots; it will help you relax. I'll take care of the rest," he said with a Spanish accent.

After I finished my shots, I went into the bathroom, changed into a short robe, and then climbed in bed beside him.

"Umm-hmmm, mommy, you're fine," he said, and then he went straight to work.

He put on a condom and then grabbed some lubricant. He proceeded to massage my vagina.

"Oh, we won't be needing this," he said, "because you've got white liver."

I frowned. "What? I don't have any STDs."

He laughed. "It's not an STD, but some people say it's a disease."

"Please explain."

"Your pussy stays wet. It craves sex like a nymphomaniac. A man can fuck you all day, and whether you have multiple orgasms or not, you will never get dry or tired of sex. Your pussy wants to be penetrated all the time."

"Well, that's definitely not me," I replied. "I barely have any appetite for sex. My kat—I mean, my pussy is so well-trained that when it's time to fuck, without any hesitation, she fires up, and the juices flow."

"Like I said, you have white liver, and you have either ignored or not fed it adequately. You do realize it's going to be hard for a man to keep up with your sex drive, right? You may even be too much for a very young man to handle."

"Enough about the white liver," I said. "Let's get back to the task at hand."

"Okay, we're going to start off in the missionary position to practice the movements, so try not to cum."

I nodded in agreement. The only problem was that about ten minutes into it, he must have forgotten his own rule.

"Oh, baby, this pussy feels too good," he said as his thrusts increased at a faster pace, breathing heavily. "I'm sorry, but I'm going to have to get this one off real quick. I can't help it. It's so good." Right before he exploded, he said, "I promise it will only take a few minutes for me to recover."

After he climaxed, he lay beside me for a few minutes catching his breath and wiping the sweat from his forehead. "I'm really sorry," he said. "That rarely happens to me."

"Is this an act?" I asked. "Part of the therapy to make me feel better, improve my sexual self-esteem?"

He laughed. "In my line of work, I indulge in a lot pussy, but I have never encountered a white liver before. At age eighteen, I had a girlfriend with a white liver; that's how I know what it looks like. I was too young and inexperienced to handle her, so she left me for a man in his thirties. I have not run across one that felt like yours in a long time. I can only imagine what it feels like raw. You're going to drive a man crazy one day with that right there." He pointed at my vagina. "You have a gift, and you don't even know it. You're already distracting me, making me want to do some things I'm not supposed to do."

He went into the bathroom and washed, then returned smelling fresh and ready to go again. He climbed back into bed and touched me gently with his fingers. "Do you know you have a hot lava machine down there?"

We laughed, and he penetrated me so we could start practicing the muscle movements again. After about twenty minutes, we both climaxed together.

We decided that we needed to take a break because we were simply fucking and not practicing the muscle exercises, so we got in the shower. While we were in the shower, he let me wash his body and play with his erect penis. I stared at it, rubbed it and massaged it with my hands while he enjoyed every minute of it. Something about the steamy hot shower made me want to engage in oral sex with him. I felt like dropping to the floor right there and deep-throating him, but

I didn't because I wanted to save that experience for someone special.

After we got out of the shower, we dialed down the passion and focused on the technical aspects of the business at hand.

"You're really good with and without this extra," he said. "Your challenge will be to keep your man calm when he climbs inside of you. The key for you to is to slow him down, and I guarantee that ain't happening until at least round two, with all the hot juices you're releasing."

I laughed. "I'll keep that in mind."

It was about four in the morning, and he said that he had to leave by six. House rules! "What do you want to do for the next two hours?"

"Sleep?" I suggested.

"Can I taste you first?"

As much as I wanted him to, I said no, because it would make our experience too personal, and I might be trying to call him after I left.

We laughed, and then he lay in bed and held me until I fell asleep.

When I awoke, he was gone, but he left an envelope containing a handwritten card next to my bed. The card was written in Spanish, which translated into: "Thank you for a beautiful night. You are a very special sexy woman. Hold on to your gifts. They will provide everything you're seeking in a relationship." I thought the words on the card were beautiful and that Javier had done his job well.

That morning during brunch, right before our departure, Abby shared some parting words with us. "You must be careful how you use your sexual power, especially when dealing with men. Under their brooding masculine exterior, they can be very fragile. The power that makes them love you can also make them hurt you. This type of passion is very combustible, and when the two meet, it explodes and usually leads to dire consequences."

As I flew back to Atlanta, I thought I was probably the only one who was seeking to get something out of the retreat. I think the other ladies were just there to have fun, to add a little zest to their sex lives. I was still uncomfortable with the term "pussy." I understood what Abby meant about getting rid of the feline names, but I wasn't sure I always needed to refer to my vagina as a pussy though; there was something too raw about it. It was no biggie. I would figure out what terminology worked best for me eventually.

I also thought about what Javier had said about me having a white liver. My vagina had stayed wet even before Ricky attacked me, but I thought that was normal. I recall washing my vagina as a little girl so hard it bruised. Perhaps that was my first experience with masturbation. Also, during boarding school, my panties seemed to stay wet similar to what I experienced when I was with Chevy in England. That was strange to me, because I knew for certain that boys did not start to interest me until I finished high school. I also recalled that Philip used to say he loved how aroused I was before we had sex. The sad thing was that it had nothing to do with him, because we rarely if ever engaged in foreplay. He often said my vagina always felt like new, and that's why he climaxed so fast. Perhaps his feelings were sincere and he wasn't being a selfish asshole. He really couldn't handle her. Perhaps there was some truth to me having a white liver.

I didn't know if I had acquired the skills for a "super pussy," but I certainly felt comfortable enough to conquer my fears. My sexual confidence was still a bit shaky, but Abby told me that would improve with practice. I wondered if the inner me would ever match the outer me. Time would tell, but for the moment, I felt that the retreat was money well spent.

15

PERFECTING THE PUSSY & THE HEAD

I had been in Atlanta for three months and still had not met anyone special, at least not anyone with whom I wanted to have sex. I went on a few dates, but nothing clicked. The men had impeccable resumes, but that was it. I wanted someone to make me feel the fire that Damien had ignited in me. Anything less wouldn't cut it.

The weekend was approaching, and I had nothing planned but my usual errands and spa regimen. I woke up Saturday morning and was reading the entertainment section of the Atlanta Journal Constitution when I saw that Damien's band was the opening act at the Verizon amphitheater that weekend. I took a chance and texted him, saying that I was living in Atlanta now and would love to see him if his schedule permitted. About two minutes later, he called me.

"Wow, what a pleasant surprise," he said. "I'd love to see you, too."

We agreed to meet for brunch, since he had to set up for his show later that afternoon.

I was so excited about seeing him. I had already made up my mind that I was going to have sex with him before he left town. I ran around my condo looking for the perfect "come fuck me outfit." It was about seventy-five degrees, so I decided to put on my white leather booty shorts with the matching low cut vest and my four-inch Giuseppe gladiator sandals.

When I picked him up, he got in the car and planted a big wet kiss on my lips, as if this was a regular thing with us. We drove to a nearby café. As we walked up to the door, I noticed that he was walking slightly behind me.

"Damn, girl, your ass is fine," he said. "You're nice and thick in all the right places. I know you're hurting them down here with all that booty."

I laughed. "Yes, I guess so. Something like that."

While we sat at our table drinking mimosas, Damien tried to explain why he never called me after our one-night affair. I interrupted him and said it wasn't necessary.

"No, I want to explain," he insisted. Then he told me about his on-and-off again girlfriend and that she had given birth the day after we spent the night together. He said he wasn't trying to play games with me, but things were hectic between them at that time, and he didn't want to involve me in his drama.

"Look, I'm going to be straight with you, I care a lot for her and my son, but she knows I'm not ready to settle down into a serious relationship, and she's okay with it. I'm a traveling musician, so I don't have time, nor do I want to be in a committed relationship with anyone right now. I love beautiful women, and I don't know how to be monogamous, and that's it. Anyway, how's your love life?"

"I don't really have one. I'm not looking for love or anything serious now. I just want to enjoy my life and let fate handle the rest."

He smiled and nodded. "That's what I'm talking about."

On the way out, he grabbed my hands and led me to a hallway adjacent to the restrooms. He pushed me against the wall, and then we began kissing. He placed my hands over the front of his pants and whispered in my ear.

"See what you've done to me? It's been hard since we started walking in the parking lot."

Then he turned me around with my face against the wall and pressed himself firmly against my butt so I could feel his erection. "You're driving me crazy," he said. "I could take you right now, but I know you won't let me."

"You're right," I replied. Then he turned around, and we walked to my car.

While I drove him back to his hotel, he took my hand. "I want to see you again before I leave. I need to taste those sexy lips of yours—and you know which ones I'm talking about."

I smiled. "I'd like that, too."

He dug into his pocket. "I'll give you a backstage pass, and then you can watch the show. Afterwards, you can go to one of the after-parties with me, and then we can sneak off somewhere and get reacquainted. The tour bus isn't leaving until six in the morning, so we have all night."

As I pulled up in front of his hotel to let him out, he turned to me. "You need to pull around the back and let me taste a little bit to hold me over until tonight."

"You can't wait until tonight?" I asked teasingly. "I promise it will be worth it."

He kissed me again and then got out of my car. But then he turned back. "Are you sure you don't want to come up for a minute?"

I smiled, waved goodbye, and drove off.

I ran a few errands and then went home to prepare for the evening. I decided the theme would be black and red. I put on my new black and white and python-printed Egyptian cotton sheets with a complementary black duvet cover. While running my errands, I had purchased a bouquet of red orchids, so I placed nine stems in a vase that I set on my cocktail table. Then I sprinkled the remaining petals on top of the duvet and the floor of my bathroom. I also placed black candles strategically around my bedroom and in my bathroom. For my wardrobe, I decided I would be the lady in red. I wore a red peek-a-boo tight-fitted dress with nothing underneath and a pair of Jimmy Choo stilettos. I felt sexy and on fire, something I hadn't felt since the last time I was with Damien back home in Detroit. I put a bottle of champagne in my fridge, and then left for the show.

I arrived at the amphitheater about an hour before Damien and his band were scheduled to go on. The security guard ushered me to a lounge area where other women were waiting. It wasn't a friendly group. I could feel the tension and animosity in the room. I wondered if they were groupies or if we were all there for the same purpose—to hook up with a band member for a one-night stand.

Finally, Damien came and got me. As he was about to go on stage, he told me to stand near the entrance so I could watch the show.

Damien performed for about forty-five minutes. When he was done, he came off stage and kissed me.

"How'd you enjoy the show?"

"You were great!"

He walked me to the lounge and then told me he'd be right back to get me.

Thirty minutes passed, and he had not yet returned, so I decided to find a restroom. Afterwards, I walked around backstage, hoping to find Damien's dressing room. When I found it, Damien was arguing with one of the girls I had seen earlier in the lounge.

"I invited you to the show, and that's all," he said. "I didn't make any promises to you. Now you need to leave and go watch the rest of the show because I have other plans."

"Oh, I'm not stupid," the girl said. "I saw you falling all over the bitch in the red dress. You're a piece of shit. Lose my number, and don't call me anymore."

"Look," he said, "you know how this works. You're partying with Atlanta's finest, so have fun, because that's all you want anyway."

"Fuck you, Damien," she shouted, and then she stormed out of his dressing room.

He looked at me as if nothing had happened between them. "Hey babe, come in."

He hugged and kissed me and whispered in my ear. "You know you're driving me crazy in that tight ass red dress." Then he pulled back. "We can watch the rest of the show or we can leave."

"I'm following you," I replied.

"Okay, I just need to get my violin and we're out of here, because I really don't want to see this show again."

As we walked toward the valet parking, he nudged my shoulder. "I'm sorry you had to see that. I usually invite one or two local fans backstage at each location, and you know how that goes. Like I told you, I am not the guy for a one-on-one serious relationship."

"I know that," I replied. "You're someone to play with, not to stay with."

He laughed and nodded. "Yes, at the moment anyway."

When the parking attendant brought my car, a candy apple red two-seater Benz, Damien stopped and stared at it. "Wow! Nice!"

It was a celebratory gift that I purchased for myself after finalizing my divorce and landing my new job.

He smiled. "Excellent choice. A beautiful car for a beautiful woman."

When we got in the car, I looked at him. "Where to?"

"It's too early to go to the after-party," he replied. "Maybe we can go somewhere and get a drink, or maybe you can show me your new place."

"I'd be happy to show you my new place."

After the valet parked my car and we walked into the lobby of my building, he looked around and nodded with satisfaction. "This is very nice. It's definitely you."

I pushed the elevator button that would take us to the penthouse floor.

"All right," he said, nodding with approval.

When I opened the door with my thumbprint, he said, "Wow, this is the shit. I am beyond impressed."

Using the keypad, I turned on a few dim lights, music, and the fireplace. I led him to the great room, where we sat on the sofa. He looked out through the two-story wall of windows at the spectacular view of the city skyline.

"There's no way you can ever have a restless night of sleep with this view."

I smiled. "Would you like some bubbly?"

"Yes, but only if you join me. In fact, why don't you show me the kitchen. I'll pour us a drink, and you can get comfortable."

While he poured the champagne, I lit the candles in the great room and in the master suite. Then we sat on the sofa, and he toasted me. "To a wonderful new beginning for a beautiful woman."

We smiled, sipped our champagne, and then we kissed. After a moment, he pulled back.

"Do you mind if I get a little more comfortable?

"Not at all."

He nodded toward my bedroom. "Why don't you slip into something more comfortable, too?"

I went into my bedroom and slipped on a red lace thong teddy. Then I put on my black satin robe and matching slippers and went back out to the great room. He was sitting on my sofa wearing nothing but an undershirt and his boxer briefs. He had refilled our glasses and left the bottle of champagne sitting in the bottle cooler next to the cocktail table.

When I sat down, he began rubbing and massaging my feet. "Don't get confused," he said. "It's taking every ounce of strength I have to refrain from making love to you. I want to spend some time looking at you and talking, getting to know the real Astrid." He smiled. "Trying to hold a conversation with you is very difficult, because my dick is already hard."

He asked me to stand up and take off my robe. Then he told me to turn around so he could get a look at me. As he watched, he pulled his dick out of his shorts and began rubbing it.

"Look at this," he said. "I'm hard as a mother—, and we haven't even touched each other yet."

He stood up and took off his briefs, and then he dropped to his knees and pulled me close to him. He kissed the crotch of my teddy, and then he slid it over and started sucking on my clit. While he kissed my vagina, he lifted one of my legs up and placed it over his shoulder. Then he used his tongue until I climaxed.

After I finished, he picked up the bottle of champagne and drank from it like he was finishing off a bottle of beer.

I took his hand. "Let me give you a tour of the rest of the house."

When I walked him into the master suite, he stopped and looked around in amazement. "Wow! Do you sleep like this every night? This is beautiful. It looks like something out of a magazine or a movie set. Your bed is almost too pretty to lie on."

Without a word, I pushed him down on my bed, pulled off his undershirt, and then climbed on top of him and began kissing him all over his face, his ears, and his neck. Then I worked my way down to his stomach. Finally, I began licking and sucking his penis, taking more of it in until it reached the back of my throat, but I didn't gag. I knew then that I could have deep-throated him if I wanted to, but I didn't. I still couldn't deal with a man ejaculating in my mouth, so I knew I couldn't keep doing it much longer.

I pulled my head up and started putting a condom on him, but he grabbed my hand.

"No, you have to let me taste it raw."

I shook my head and continued to put the condom on. Then I slid on top of him.

After having sex in multiple positions, both of us climaxing multiple times throughout the night, he snuggled up behind me and gave me a squeeze. "I think somebody's been practicing, because she's definitely got some new moves."

I smiled to myself, and then we fell asleep.

At around three, he woke me up. "I'm sorry babe, but you need to call me a cab so I can get back to my hotel. The tour bus is pulling out at six, and I can't miss it."

"You don't have to take a cab," I said. "I'll drive you."

We jumped up and took a quick shower together. We kissed and rubbed on each other, but we didn't have sex. I felt raw and sore anyway. I didn't think I could have taken him penetrating me one more time.

Before I knew it, we were in front of his hotel. He took my hand. "This is the awkward part," he said. "This is where we're supposed to say how much we like each other and make plans to see each other again. Then in a few weeks you get angry, because I stopped returning your calls as often or maybe completely, so you began sending me angry text messages."

"Wow," I said. "You know this script quite well."

He shrugged. "Only because I've lived it a hundred times or more."

"If I was trying to develop a serious relationship with you, then your script might be applicable to me, but since I'm not, let's just say goodbye, and I'll talk to you whenever."

"I hope you mean that," he said. "If I was in a different place in my life, I would definitely try to get into something more with you and see what's really there for us. But I've got too much on my plate right now. Besides, I need to get my shit together, because I know if I ever try to step to you, I'd better come correct."

Afterwards, I went home and took off all my clothes and climbed back into bed. I could smell Damien's cologne and body spray all over my sheets. As I lay there, I realized I had lied. I wasn't okay with him walking out of my life until whenever, because I enjoyed him and wanted to keep him around for my sexual pleasure, at least for a little while anyway. I felt that I could have a great sexual relationship with him and maintain the right amount of emotional detachment. Damien's dick fit me perfectly, and his lovemaking was equally satisfying. I wanted his dick for me and me alone whenever I wanted it, but I knew that could never be.

When I woke up, I discovered a two-page text message from Damien. "Thank you for a wonderful night. I cannot find the words to describe the way you make me feel. I wish I could say that it was your superb pussy, but it's the whole package. I felt your spirit last night. I know I could love you. You're dangerous for me. I can't afford to fall in love right now. Take care."

I didn't know what to think about Damien's text. Was he sincere or just playing games? I didn't know what to believe. It didn't matter anyway, because I was definitely not looking for a serious relationship, especially with a playboy musician. I knew a man like him could never be faithful and grateful to one woman.

"I understand, and safe travels," was all I said in response.

The postscript with Damien and me never played out, because I never called or texted him again, nor did he contact me. While I enjoyed Damien, I needed a playmate in my own backyard.

By then I had settled into living in Atlanta and established a network of friends. Most of my newfound social life was due to Zoe. She knew all the shakers and movers in Atlanta and was on the guest list at every major event and frequently invited me to accompany her. Over the next few months, Zoe took me to several "fishing" events, a term Zoe coined to describe the act of looking for a man to date or simply to fuck.

As it turned out, we were both fishing at those events. I was living a carefree single life, having fun and enjoying it. I was starting to fill up my little black book and had no shortage of dates. I even had a few one-night stands with a couple of rich and famous dicks, but they were nothing to brag about. They were merely tools to help me perfect my craft. I had four simple dating rules. One, plant the seed for the exit strategy up front. In this case, I usually told the guy that I had recently broke up with my boyfriend and was not looking to get into anything serious. Most guys were cautious when dating someone fresh out of a relationship and didn't expect anything lasting to evolve from the early phases of dating. Two, always drive my own car unless we were using a car service. Three, never invite them over to my place, keeping an appropriate distance for an emotionless, non-committed relationship. Four, sex them up no more than five times to ensure there were no emotional attachments, at least on my side. After the fifth sexual encounter, if we made it that far, I usually pulled the trigger on my exit strategy, sometimes with little notice or explanation.

While my rules worked for me, I can't say that my dates were necessarily pleased with them, nor did they always go away quietly or easily. Sometimes after ending the relationship, I received irate text messages or voicemails referring to me as a cold-hearted bitch or something equally demeaning. One guy went so far as to send a dozen black roses to my condo and my office every day for a week straight. I also had to block the phone number of a few guys

I dated. As much as I tried to establish the ground rules up front, my relationships almost never ended smoothly. There was always some bitterness on the part of the men. I realized that men had a mind of their own when it came to defining the terms of relationships. The concept of "friends with benefits" only worked when they initiated it. No matter the reason, a "cease dating action" was still a form of rejection to a man if he was not the one who initiated it. Nevertheless, their distress didn't sway me from dating or from utilizing my dating principles. I was single and dating freely, and my rules of engagement were in full effect.

As much as I attempted to hold solidly to my dating tenets, I slipped up when I met Jonathan who worked at CNN. We went out for about two months. We had lunch and dinner dates during the week and various kinds of entertainment on the weekends. I even let him spend the night at my condo. I could tell he was falling into the pussy trap. He was calling, texting, and trying to see me daily and spend weekends together like we were a couple. I even stood him up a few times while I went out on other dates, but he would still be waiting for my call like an obedient puppy. I knew it was time to split when he started using terms like "we" and "us" in our conversations and making plans for dates and trips that were months away. I wasn't ready for those types of dates with any man. Spending seven consecutive days with one man or taking exotic trips with him was a big no-no in my book. That was clearly a transition point on the relationship spectrum. Jonathan and I had finally reached the match point in our dating game.

On our last date, Jonathan told me that he really liked me and wanted to take our relationship to the next level. By all accounts, he was a very desirable man for a boyfriend or a husband. He was handsome, physically fit, great career—the complete package. But I wasn't looking for a serious relationship. I wanted only to have fun with no responsibilities or expectations. After all, I already had a corporate job, and I didn't need another one. He proceeded to give me his oral bio and list of accolades to impress upon me that he was a good catch. While he was indeed a good catch, that didn't matter to me. I was there to play and not stay. I wasn't interested in the qualities most women sought in a man. I had more than enough resources to take care of my needs and wants, so I didn't need a man for that purpose. Hence, dating him or any other rich or famous dick was not impressive to me. I only dated "successful" professional men because they were in my field of play. I could have just as easily dated a fine sexy factory worker.

As we were finishing dinner, I explained with as much decorum and compassion as possible that I was not ready for a serious relationship. He said he understood and respected my decision. In a calm, demure tone, he asked me if we could finish off the date at his place. I said sure. I had no complaints about him sexually. He was quite satisfying, which is what likely caused me to break my dating rules with him. I also liked his thoughtfulness and desire to please and accommodate me. He behaved like he was under my spell. Maybe the vaginal exercises I learned at Abby's retreat were actually working. During sex, he sought constant reassurance from me. "Am I good to you? Is this good? What else do you want me to do for you?"

When we arrived at his place, we went straight to his bedroom, but this time there was something different about him. He seemed in a rush, skipping our usual delicate foreplay. He dove in head first, with a bold ferocity in his oral stimulation, hurriedly releasing the flow of my lava. Then he put on a condom and turned me over on my knees, and we started doing it doggy style. We had done it in this position many times before, but this time he added something different. Instead of slapping my ass lightly, he began hitting it hard as if he was actually spanking me, dispensing actual pain.

I closed my eyes and thought, "I'm open to trying something new. I'll roll with it."

Then he slid what felt like a leather belt around my neck and pulled it tight, strangling me.

I fell to my stomach and put my hands between the belt and my neck to release some of the tension. I tried to throw him off, but he was too heavy. As I squirmed, he didn't say a word. He was smiling, enjoying the fear in my face as I tried to get away from him. In truth, I was scared for my life. I thought he was going to torture me sexually and then kill me.

"Calm down," he said finally. "I'm not going to hurt you." Then he loosened his grip on the belt. "Isn't this fun? I knew you'd like it."

When I was finally able to throw him off, I slapped him as hard as I could across his face.

Instead of getting angry or hitting me back, he said, "Oh yeah, that felt good, do it again, but slap me harder this time."

I shook my head. *What the hell was this?*

I grabbed my clothes and ran into his bathroom and locked the door. As I was getting dressed, he knocked on the door.

"I'm sorry," he said, "I didn't mean to scare you. You know I would never really hurt you unless you wanted me to. Please, don't go. I know you don't want a serious relationship right now. I don't have to be your man. We can just be lovers. I know you like the way I make you feel."

He's a real freak, another fucking Dr. Jekyll and Mr. Hyde. How did I miss that memo?

After I finished getting dressed, I grabbed a pair of scissors from his grooming pouch. Then I opened the bathroom door and peeked out, but Jonathan was gone.

I ran to the front door of his townhouse, but just as I was about to open the door, Jonathan jumped out and blocked it.

"Please wait, please. I'm not going to hurt you; I just want to talk to you. I wanted to share this side of me with you when we first met, but I was waiting for the right moment. I can see by your strength that you're the right woman for me. Let me show you something."

He opened the closet door, which was adjacent to where I was standing, and there was a chest on the floor. He opened the chest, with a look of excitement in his eyes.

"Look at all the great stuff I have for us to play with. I have even more goodies in my room under my bed."

The chest contained all sorts of S&M bondage toys and devices.

"You can do anything you want to me, bite me, beat me, or whip me. I don't mind an occasional golden shower or playing with your fudge either. I'm willing to go to the limit with you if you want me to. I'll even be your personal slave. Just give us a chance; you might like it. In time, you might find that you like being submissive to me, too. Let me show you how a little discomfort can bring you ecstasy beyond your imagination. Baby, it feels better than any drug. It's addictive, too. You'll experience a sexual high that creates an appetite for more. Every time you do it, not only do you want more of it, you want to intensify it, do it harder, go deeper, right to the absolute edge. On the surface, it feels bizarre and a bit painful, but it's an extraordinary connection between two people. This type of pleasure is incomparable to any orgasm."

I stood there listening to his words, stunned and afraid and still wondering how I had completely missed this part of him. I didn't respond, but with my heart racing, I opened the door and left his house, walking as fast as I could to my car.

On the way home, I thought about how I had dodged a bullet, and avoided a potential catastrophe with Jonathan. I also realized for the first time that I needed to be careful while playing my game of "love 'em and leave 'em." These men were also playing their games, perhaps with a desired outcome that was far more than I could handle. I needed to be more cautious. While I had protected my emotional well-being, I had not done the same for my physical safety. I was playing with fire and could get burned if I wasn't careful. So much for how well I had perfected the pussy and the head. That was still questionable. All this time I thought I had gained power and control over Jonathan through my sexual conquests. But that wasn't true at all, he was playing a submissive role in his S&M game and quietly grooming me to join him in his darkness. Little did he know, I had spent eighteen years receiving unsolicited beatings, and I wasn't about to sign up for anything that resembled that, not even remotely. S&M was not for me.

Jonathan attempted to call me a few times after that night, but I never answered, which infuriated him even more. He started showing up at my job and my home, and he even left notes on my car begging me to see him. One minute he was professing his love for me, the next minute I was a filthy, cold-hearted bitch. He continued these rants for days, and his behavior was becoming increasingly obsessive, causing me to become fearful of him. After I discussed the situation with Zoe, she sent him a letter on her ADA (assistant district attorney) letterhead, essentially telling him to back off or face stalking charges. He responded by leaving me one last voicemail on my cell phone, complete with expletives and demeaning obscene sexual references. I blocked his number, and I never saw or heard from him again.

After the escapade with Jonathan, I realized that I had to be more selective when choosing partners to play with. This could have had a very different ending, fatal or otherwise detrimental to me. I would have to find another approach to obtain the validation I was seeking from my sexual conquests.

The situation with Jonathan left me feeling exhausted and somewhat anxious. He had zapped all of my enthusiasm and energy for playing, so I decided to take a break from the dating game. While I no longer felt sexually awkward or insecure, something was still missing. It wasn't something I could label or define, but the void I felt was real. I still felt incomplete. My inner self did not match my outer being, and I had no idea how to bridge the two parts of me. For the moment, I would relax and let life happen on its own, follow its natural path, and see where it led.

16

OPEN LOVE WITH ANOTHER WOMAN

Zoe was an intelligent, beautiful woman who looked like a Latin Miss Universe beauty contestant. While petite, she had a huge personality and was a ball of fire. And highly accomplished as Chief ADA, with ambitions beyond Georgia's legal system. At age thirty-eight, she had never been married or had any children. She was in the third year of her engagement to Brad, a Wall Street investment banker who split his time between Atlanta and New York. While I found their relationship peculiar, it seemed to work for them. Neither of them appeared to be in a hurry to get married. They seemed quite content with their perpetual dating arrangement. Zoe spoke of Brad frequently, professing her love for him while proudly wearing her five-carat princess cut engagement ring. However, when it came to her social life, she certainly was not sitting around waiting for Brad.

Since moving to Atlanta, I had heard people say there was a shortage of single men available there, but that seemed far from correct, at least in the circle in which Zoe traveled.

One night, Zoe invited me to a 1970s-themed party. Ironically, we both dressed as Pam Grier, wearing Afro wigs and Foxy Brown outfits that were very suitable for us since we both had small waistlines, curvy hips, and DD racks. The party was held outside of the city limits tucked far off in the boonies in a mansion that was only accessible off a hidden, guarded private road. This was obviously another one of Zoe's rich and famous friends. We pulled up to have the car parked and then walked right in. At first, the party seemed quite normal, music piped through speakers in the walls, and people were mingling throughout the house.

Zoe walked around and introduced me to several people, and then she pulled me aside. "I need to tell you something," she whispered. "This is not a regular party; it's a couples' party."

I looked at her. "What do you mean?"

"You know about swingers, right?"

I nodded.

"Well, this is the same type of party. Most of the people here are married and with their spouses, mistresses, significant other, or seeking to find a third or fourth person or another couple to play with, to add something extra to their relationship. This is a very exclusive club. These are physicians, attorneys, judges, Wall Street and C-suite executives, entertainment moguls, politicians, foreign dignitaries, and anybody who's considered somebody. I actually met Brad at one of these parties."

I looked around. "Well, I hope you don't think I'm about to start swinging with these people. That's not my thing."

"I know that," she replied. "I just wanted to expose you to something different in case you ever got curious and wanted to turn it up a little."

She must have seen the anxiety and trepidation on my face. "Relax," she said, smiling, "nobody's going to hurt you or force you to do anything. In fact, we don't have to stay long. We can leave whenever you're ready." She took my hand and started walking. "Let me show you the candy store."

I stopped and pulled my hand back. "You know I don't do drugs."

She laughed. "Your ass is too square. Nobody's talking about drugs. You know what a candy store is; it's full of goodies. In this case, the goodies are sexual pleasures of any kind: sweet, varied, and satisfying—like candy. Just follow me, keep your mouth shut, and keep your eyes open.

We walked down a long narrow hallway. There seemed to be bedrooms all over the place, like a hotel. In each room, some type of sexual play or activity was going on. In some rooms, the doors were left open so that other guests could watch or join in. The rooms with closed doors meant there was a private party going on inside.

"Let me show you around some more," Zoe said. "I want to introduce you to one of my good friends."

We walked upstairs to a bedroom where several women were huddled around a table doing lines of some kind of drug.

"Where's Tammy?" Zoe asked.

"I'm right here, baby," a soft, silky voice replied.

Tammy walked over to Zoe, and they hugged and French kissed, feeling each other all over. When they came up for air, Zoe turned to me.

"Tammy, this is my girl I told you about, Astrid. I brought her out tonight to expand her mind, show her how we like party in the ATL."

I turned around to leave and said, "I'll be waiting for you downstairs."

As I walked down the hallway to the stairs, I saw the bedroom door close.

While I sat in the family room, I noticed several couples coming and going upstairs, downstairs, and down the winding halls.

I felt awkward just sitting there. I was about to get up and walk around when someone tapped me on the shoulder. It was a man wearing a white lab coat. He was quite distinguished-looking with a tall, slender build, but he was much older than me, perhaps in his mid-fifties.

"Your body is dangerous," he said. "I really thought I was looking at Pam Grier from behind. I know you're oblivious to it, but you're killing us tonight. Every man in here has been talking about you." He extended his hand to me. "I'm Doc."

I shook his hand. "I'm Astrid."

"Do you mind if I walk around with you as I try to get to know you better?"

"That's fine as long as you know that's all I'm interested in doing," I replied.

I asked him about his costume, because I didn't see the seventies connection. He said he wasn't a big fan of the men's fashion during that time period, so he decided to wear a lab coat, since the only thing he had ever wanted to be was a doctor and wearing a white coat one day.

"You really stretched far to come up with that idea," I said. We both laughed.

Our first stop was one of the rooms with the door open. Inside was a man in bed with four women. They were all rotating between each other, performing oral sex and simultaneously penetrating each other with various sexual devices. Watching them did not arouse me one bit. In fact, it made me tired. It seemed like too much work to be enjoyable, but to each his own.

"Why did you come here?" Doc asked. "More importantly, what do you think?"

"It's my first time and, well, I don't think it's really my thing."

"I know what you mean," he said. "I'm a slight germaphobe, so while I enjoy watching, I never engage. But it is a nice place to meet women with shared interests."

"What are your interests, besides voyeurism?"

"I'd rather show you than tell you," he replied. "Perhaps we can get together some other time and get to know each other better."

I didn't respond as we proceeded to another room. This one looked rather tame. It was two men and two women having regular sex. I suspected it was two heterosexual couples switching partners. We moved on to another room on the second floor, where a large group seemed to be huddled together. When I finally made my way to a part of the room where I could see what was going on, what I saw sickened me. It was three men with one woman engaging in full-on triple penetration. I made a quick U-turn.

"I think I've seen enough."

"You never answered my question," Doc said as we walked back to the family room.

"I think you have the wrong impression of me," I replied. "This is not my thing. I'm probably too square even for a guy like you."

He smiled. "I know you're not. Your innocence and anxiety about this place is what interests me about you. I don't normally do this, but I really would like to see you again."

He gave me a business card that read Dr. William Bolton, Chief Neurologist.

"So, do I call you Doc, Bill or Will?"

He laughed. "You can call me whatever you want, but my friends call me Will." Then he wrote his cell number on the card. "In case you change your mind."

I didn't want to seem rude, so I put his card in my purse, knowing that I would throw it away as soon as I got home. He seemed like a nice guy, but I was a long way from being ready to date men from that circle. Despite my recent sexual endeavors, my rating was still very low on the freak scale. I probably would have attempted to date him if I had met him in a different place, but after my ordeal with Jonathon, I needed to keep it safe and simple. I wasn't in the mood for any new adventures, especially with strangers.

As Doc and I continued to have small talk, Zoe emerged smelling of sex. She must have sensed that I wasn't enjoying the party very much. She quickly introduced herself to Doc and then looked at her watch. She turned to me and said, "It's getting late, are you ready to leave?"

"Yes, I replied."

I said my goodbyes to Doc. Then Zoe and I left the party.

As we were driving home, she glanced over at me. "I'm sorry, I thought you might like to try something different."

"I guess I'm a little square," I replied. "Orgies are not my thing."

She laughed. "Don't knock it until you try it. I'm not into orgies either, but I do like the taste of a woman occasionally, and right now I enjoy Tammy inside and out. She's married though, and the only time we can be together is at events like this."

"So you're bisexual?"

She hesitated before answering. "Yes, I guess I am, but if I had to choose, I would choose dick over pussy, and I would always choose Brad. I love Brad, and he loves me. He gets me, and he lets me be me. Brad is straight, and he loves a threesome, so you know a woman's got to like a little pussy to enjoy that."

Before I got out of the car at my condo, Zoe put her hand on my thigh and started rubbing it. "I like you, too. I would love to be your first. So if you ever want to get down with a woman or try a threesome, just let me know. Brad and I are very careful; we test regularly. I would love to turn you out for just one night."

I smiled and said goodnight without acknowledging her invitation.

Uncomfortable with Zoe's behavior, I avoided her calls over the next few weeks. She left me messages, apologizing repeatedly. Despite her sexual antics, I missed our friendship, so I finally agreed to have lunch with her.

While at lunch, she mentioned that it was Brad's birthday and that she was planning a dinner for him at the Blue Oyster, a popular sushi restaurant downtown. "I'm also planning a threesome, so if you want to join us, let me know before I invite somebody else."

She laughed at the look of disgust on my face. "It's only an invitation; you can decline or accept."

"Then I respectfully decline."

I met my date at the Oyster Bar along with four other couples who were friends with Zoe and Brad. This was my first time seeing Brad in person. He was younger and better looking than he seemed in the pictures Zoe had shown me.

When Zoe and I went to the ladies room, she told me that her "plus one" had cancelled on them at the last minute.

"I'll do it," I said jokingly.

Her eyes lit up. "Thank you so much!"

"I was kidding," I replied. "I'm not about to be sucking your man's dick or licking your twat. That's just not my thing."

"I know your ass would like to try it," she replied with a knowing look. "You're just scared. Since this is your first time, how about if we just pleasure you? All you have to do is lie back and enjoy it. Brad loves to break in a virgin."

I shook my head firmly. "No."

We had a few more drinks, and then we headed to the parking lot. I kissed my date goodnight and then I whispered to Zoe that I would do it. She smiled.

"I promise you'll enjoy it, and we can stop at any time."

As I drove to Zoe's condo, I started having second thoughts. At one point, I even thought about making a U-turn and heading home. Zoe was right though. I was curious about being with another woman. She was a beautiful woman with a sexy, curvy, petite body. If I were going to do it, she was the perfect person for me. Besides, I felt comfortable with her. She was intrigued by my innocence and inexperience. She was obviously experienced, and she would guide and teach me. I knew she would laugh with me and not at me.

When I got to Zoe's condo, I felt my heart beating rapidly. She poured us all a tequila shot, and then we sat down in her living room. A few minutes later, she called me into the bathroom.

"It's cool if you want to change your mind and go home."

"No, I'm game," I replied.

She offered me a muscle relaxer. We both took one, and then we went into the bedroom.

All three of us took off our clothes and got into bed with me in the middle. I pulled the covers over my head.

Zoe laughed. "You are so silly."

She wasted no time getting the party started. The next thing I knew, Zoe started French kissing me and then kissing my breast and massaging my vagina with her soft little fingers. Then she slid down and began performing oral sex on me. It felt really good, like a man was down there. She was also talking just like a dude, but with a soft voice, saying things like, "I knew you wanted me to taste you. I'm going to tear this pussy up. This belongs to me tonight. I knew you'd like it. I bet no man has ever eaten your pussy this way."

She was right. To my surprise, I had an orgasm. After that, I guess she needed to get hers. She spread my legs wider and positioned her vagina atop of mine, and then she thrust back and forth until she climaxed, too.

Brad stood next to the bed masturbating until semen was all over his hands.

This isn't a threesome; it's the Zoe and Astrid show. But then Zoe went over and started kissing him and licking and sucking the semen on his hands. Then she began sucking his dick until it was hard again, and that's when the party really started. Brad climbed into bed, and while I was lying on my side, he penetrated me vaginally from behind as Zoe began orally stimulating me again. At first, it felt erotic and satisfying, and then the intensity of it started to drive me crazy. The feeling was incredible, like I was in this orgasmic state but unable to climax for about two minutes. I felt my body trembling like I was having a seizure or going into a convulsion. When I finally came, the release was like an explosion. I felt like I was ready to pass out, as if I had just crossed the finish line in the Boston Marathon.

After I climaxed, we changed positions so that Brad and Zoe could have each other. I moved to the edge of the bed and tried to go to sleep, but that didn't happen. Between the constant motion of the bed moving and Zoe and Brad's moaning and abrasive pillow talk, I knew that it would be a long, sleepless night.

It seemed that Brad and Zoe fucked straight with no breaks for more than an hour. They had to be doing drugs, probably Viagra or something. Nobody had that kind of energy.

When they finally calmed down, Zoe got up and went to the bathroom so I thought they were done and we could all go to sleep. But that proved to be incorrect.

When Zoe returned, she approached me, but I pretended I was asleep. The next thing I knew, she and Brad were back at it. We had started this trois three hours earlier, and they were still going at it. The bed never stopped moving. Their adrenaline was so high they seemed to fuck and thrust all night.

I wanted to get up and leave, but I didn't think it was cool, so I lay there thinking about all sorts of things, like how I got into that position and how I was actually turned on by it. I also kept thinking about the many facets of Zoe's personality. One moment she was a picture of femininity, and the next minute she was talking shit like a cocky, arrogant man. I guessed petite women could have a Napoleon complex, too.

Despite all of the bed motion and erotic chatter, I finally went to sleep.

The next morning day, I woke up in the bed alone. I grabbed the robe that Zoe had laid out for me and walked into the kitchen where Brad and Zoe were sitting at the table drinking coffee like it was an ordinary Sunday afternoon, which it probably was for them.

Zoe poured me a cup of coffee and then kissed me on my cheek. "Good morning, pretty girl. Do you want me to make you some breakfast?"

"No, thanks," I said. "After I finish my coffee, I think I'll just take a shower and head home."

"You don't have to rush off," she replied. "You're welcome to stay as long as want. You're also welcome to have some more of what I gave you last night."

I laughed. "I think I've had enough for a while." I was afraid that if I stayed a few minutes longer, those two would have me back in the bed for another round.

As I was leaving, Brad thanked me for the birthday gift. "I'm looking forward to doing it again."

I went home and took another shower, put on some pajamas, and turned on the news. I kept thinking about the previous night. I had enjoyed the experience immensely. Quite frankly, I could have done it several more times. Even though it felt wonderfully good, to be completely honest—I wasn't sure I wanted to go down that road. Although I didn't want the marriage and love thing again, I didn't want that lifestyle either. A threesome could not be the pinnacle of my sex life. To have a need for that level of sexual satisfaction or more would take me down a path for which I wasn't sure I was ready. I decided I would put the brakes on my sexual relationship with Zoe for good.

Zoe called me later that night to check on me. I told her I was fine, that I had enjoyed the previous night, but I didn't want to do it again. I also asked if she wouldn't mind keeping that part of her life separate from our friendship. She wasn't offended. Neither did she question me about my request.

"It's cool; you're my girl," she replied. "I won't ever bring anything like that to you again. I promise."

True to her word, she never did. In fact, our friendship went right back to the way it was, as if the threesome had never occurred. We did seem to grow closer after that experience, more like sisters or cousins than friends. I even made her my local emergency contact in Atlanta.

Although I was settling into Atlanta with my new life, my heart still ached over my strained relationship with Junior. Sometimes he wouldn't take my calls, and when he did, it was usually very dry and had something to do with me sending him money. I could have easily used my money to make him see me, but I didn't. I hoped that my generosity would open his heart and he would want to resume our relationship. Instead, he acted like a Casanova taking money from a desperate woman.

The same scene with Junior and me played out several times, and every time it occurred, it sent me spiraling into a mild depression. The last time it happened, the effect of his behavior sent me into the worst depression since my divorce.

I had planned a business trip near Junior's college just so we could spend time together. When I called him to confirm, he said he had forgotten about my plans to visit him and that he had other commitments. Prior to that, he had refused all of my other invitations for him to visit me in Atlanta and refused to allow me to visit him on the east coast. When I confronted him about his constant refusal to visit with me, he said he wasn't ready. He didn't know if he could ever forgive me for what I had done to our family. When I tried to explain, he hung up on me. His words caused my heart to fall into the pit of my stomach. I realized Philip had won. He told me that he would take from me what I cherished most in the world, which was our son. No amount of money, career, or love from anyone else could fill the hole left in my spirit from the loss of my relationship with Junior. I lay in the fetal position crying and unable to get out of bed for days as I grieved over my son.

After not answering my phone or responding to text messages for a few days, I finally answered a call from Zoe. When I said hello, she could hear the pain in my voice.

"I'm on my way over right now," she said.

When she arrived she came straight into my bedroom and sat on the bed. "What's wrong, Astrid?"

I had shared with her previously that I had gone through a bad marriage and divorce and that my relationship with Junior was strained, but she didn't know the details.

"I'm here for you," she said. "What can I do to help?"

"Nothing," I replied. "How am I supposed to go on with my life without my son?"

"You know I'm not a holy roller, but I believe when everything else falls, you have to pray about it. Sometimes you have to step out on faith. The God I know will not let you linger out here in sadness without your son. Remember when we went to see Joel Osteen and he said something about how God will not bring a crisis to you without a plan to bring you through it? Well, I believe that's true."

Zoe made me some herbal tea and then ran me a hot candlelit bath. She knew I liked my aroma candles when I bathed and wanted to relax. When I got into the bathtub, Zoe sat on the side and massaged my head and my neck.

"I know you're hurting, but you can't stay like this for too long or you'll end up needing medication to function. You have to believe your son will come back to you. He needs his mother's love even if he doesn't realize it now. He's still angry and trying to process his new life. You have to own your part with your son's confusion, how you concealed your husband's abuse and perpetuated a false image of him to your son. Now you want him to undo his view of normal. It takes time to face that kind of truth and accept it."

I lowered my head. "I thought I was doing the right thing for Junior. I wanted to protect him, but all my secrets made him turn on me, ultimately causing me to lose him."

She rubbed my back. "Astrid, you're going to have to be patient and have faith, and let God handle this for you. I promise he's working on it, and he's working on your son, too. Look, don't think that I don't know or believe in God because of the way I live. I was raised in the South in a Baptist church, so I know a little something."

I smiled at her. "You're right. Things will work out eventually. I just have to be patient."

A few minutes later, Zoe asked if she could get into the tub with me, and without thinking, I agreed. She took off her clothes, flipped the switch to turn on the jets, and climbed in behind me.

As I lay back between her legs, she continued to rub my head and my neck and shoulders. In true Zoe style, she also started to massage my pussy. It felt nice, and I didn't stop her. Between Zoe's gentle touch and the pulse of the water flowing from the jets, I was totally relaxed.

After soaking for a while, we dried off and went into my bedroom. She massaged me and put lotion all over on my body, and then she paused.

"Do you want me stop?"

I didn't respond, so she leaned in close. "I'm going to stay with you tonight. I can lie here and just hold you or I can love on you or I can leave you alone and go into one of the other rooms."

"Please stay with me," I said. "I don't want to be alone."

She climbed into bed with me and continued to massage my pussy. After it was wet, she proceeded to perform oral sex on me. This time, it was much nicer than I remembered it from before. She seem to be less hurried and more relaxed. She climbed between my legs and started kissing my stomach, my breasts, and even my lips. Then I began kissing her back and became fully engaged, making love to her as if we were a regular couple. I enjoyed the softness of her touch, the silk of her skin, the taste of her wetness, and the passion of her thrusts. We continued sharing intimacies and making love throughout the night, both having multiple orgasms.

The following morning, Zoe made us coffee and had breakfast delivered. After we finished, we got dressed and went to Phipps Plaza for some much needed shopping therapy. After getting a quick mani-pedi, we dropped a few grand on our favorite designers at the mall. I felt better immediately, refreshed and energized, a feeling similar to that first cup of coffee in the morning. When Zoe dropped me off at my condo, she asked if I was going to be okay. I nodded.

"Please call me or someone else whenever you're feeling like you're sliding down that slippery slope of depression," she said. "You're not the only person to have dark moments. We all have them; we just cope with them differently."

I thanked her for everything and said I'd call her in a few days.

Zoe and I resumed our normal lives, and we never spoke of the intimacy we had shared together that weekend. In fact, we never had any form of sex again with each other after that night, but we still remained the best of friends.

17

THE PRE-SEASON GAME

Zoe invited me to a fundraiser event sponsored by the Atlanta Professional Athletic Association. According to Zoe, this was the event for single women like myself. It would put me on the radar of a certain caliber of single men; giving me access to an exclusive local millionaire's club.

As expected, the event was crowded with famous athletes and women. After we found our table, Zoe disappeared into the crowd somewhere, charming people as usual. I told her often that she was secretly preparing for a career in public office.

I decided to make my way to the ladies room, which would allow me to survey the ballroom a little more. On the way there, a man grabbed my hand. "Can I go with you, anywhere?"

Since I didn't really follow sports, I didn't immediately recognize him, but looking at his body, I figured he was likely a football player. He held out his hand and introduced himself.

"My name is Joey, but you probably already know that, don't you?"

I looked at him but didn't respond. He told me he was a quarterback for the San Francisco 49ers, but he was from Atlanta and he kept his primary residence there. He was a tall work of art. He had a beautiful smile with perfect white teeth, a handsome face, and a strong, lean, muscular body, similar to but not as extreme as a bodybuilder. He was stunning physically, but I was not impressed with him. The arrogance he displayed was a real turn off. He was the typical cocky athlete, acting as if any woman should be glad to be in his presence. I told him it was nice to meet him and then resumed my trek to the restroom. I glanced back and saw him and his friend staring at me as they whispered to each other. When I finally made my way back, I joined in the conversation with Zoe and the other ladies at our table.

When the event was almost over, Joey tapped my shoulder. "You never told me your name."

"You never asked."

"Well, I'm asking now."

After I told him my name, he sat down next to me, bold as could be. "Look, I'm just going to come out and say it. You're fine as hell, and I could sit here and have small talk and lie to you but the truth is, I really want to sleep with you. So I'm going to ask you to let me take you on a few dates, only so I can get what I really want—which is to ultimately get into those panties."

I looked at him in surprise. "I don't know if I should be offended or appreciative of your honesty. See, if you were fine and sexy (which he was), you could get away with that line, but since you're average looking and severely malnourished, I'm not going to waste my time with you." I was about to turn away, but then I turned back. "Oh, and by the way, I don't wear panties."

We both laughed, and then his face turned serious. "I would really like to get to know you. Real talk, I would like to get to know all of you."

"If you really want to get to know me like a gentleman, then you can call me. But if you're looking for a jump-off or some quick dick and honey, I'm not the one, so let's not waste each other's time."

"There's only one way to find out my true intentions: you have to go out with me."

He was an athlete, which made him just like a musician, someone to play with, not stay with. What the hell, I'd play for a minute.

I gave him my number. Before he left, he leaned in close. "Look, I'm here with someone, but she's not my girlfriend, and I'm not on a real date. If you tell me you want to leave here right now, I'll leave with you."

"What about your unreal date?"

"My friend, Marcus, will make sure she gets home all right."

"Then let's go right now," I said, calling his bluff.

"Meet me out front in five minutes," he replied.

Since I had ridden there with Zoe, I told her that I might be leaving with Joey.

When I went out front, Joey was sitting in his shiny black Ferrari waiting for me. We drove out to Johns Creek, a northern suburb, and stopped to get some ice cream. We sat at a table and began talking. He said he liked me because I didn't know who he was and I wasn't throwing myself at him.

"Well, I like you for your quirky shyness," I replied.

We both laughed, and then the conversation turned more serious. He asked me about my family, my career, my dating life, and so forth. I gave him the short, "G-rated" version of my life. I also told him about Gigi and her love of orchids, which I shared. Then I asked him to reciprocate. To my surprise, we had a lot in common.

Although we were both part of the hip-hop generation, we both liked old school classic soft rock and R&B music. Just like me, Joey was the youngest child in his family. He said his mother called him her miracle child, because she was in her late-forties when he was born, and his youngest sibling was almost twenty years older than him.

"I was, and continue to be, spoiled by my entire family. I have no sibling rivalry, and I'm everyone's favorite. However, it was my older brother, Matt, who introduced me to the game of football. He never played, but he had a great love for the sport, and it spilled over onto me. I was ten when I lost my father, so Matt stepped in and did all the father-son things with me. He taught me to play all the major sports. Of course, he put a football in my hand and started teaching me to throw and run plays as far back as I can remember. Matt actually recognized my talent early and decided to nurture it. He said I would be a great quarterback one day. He was right, and here I stand today with a career in the NFL. I know I have been truly blessed in my life. I'm living my dream as an NFL player, I have two wonderful sons, a loving family, great friends like Marcus and a few others, and now I've met a special lady, you."

"Yes, you are blessed, and so am I. So, tell me about Marcus. You've mentioned his name several times."

"Marcus used to spend the summers with his grandmother, who lived just down the street from us. He eventually moved in with his grandmother permanently, and as kids we played together and became inseparable. As Matt coached me with football, he coached Marcus as well. We played little league football together and continued to play through high school and college. The rest is history. He's family; he's like a brother to me. I can't wait for you to meet him."

"If he's anything like you, then I'm sure I'll like him, too."

"Now let's get back to you. Astrid, that's an interesting name and a lot to live up to, 'divine with Godly strength.' I like your swag."

"I'm impressed that you Googled the meaning of my name."

"Ok, now you're stereotyping me. You thought because I was an athlete, I wasn't smart. You're so wrong."

We both laughed and then he complimented me on my beauty and my intelligence. "I haven't dated many college educated professional women. You would be the first. Most of the women I usually date are models, actresses, or in some other facet of the entertainment business."

I asked him about the woman he was with that night. He said she was a good friend and their relationship was strictly platonic. She was his home girl; they grew up together.

"She's cool to hang out with or have as a plus one when I need a date at the last minute. I keep her around, because she has no expectations or a hidden agenda. I told her that I met you and that I was leaving with you, and she told me to have fun, and that was that."

"Have you ever slept together?"

"I knew that was coming. Yes, if you want to call it that," he replied. "But that was years ago. She's pretty, but sexually, well, I just didn't feel that spark or excitement with her. If I want to just get my rocks off, I prefer to use a pro. It's a lot less complicated. Sometimes it's easier just to pay to play."

He continued before I could make a comment. "Despite what you think about athletes, we're not all dogs. I'm not trying to play games or use women and throw them away when I'm done with them. I'm looking for something real, but until I find that special one, I'm going to continue my life as a bachelor." He thumped the table. "On that note, let's get out of here."

When we pulled up in front of my condo, he smiled. "I figured you to be the high-rise type and not the townhouse type."

"Care to explain?"

He grinned. "Maybe later."

By then, my impression of Joey had started to change. He was showing dribbles of decency under that arrogant exterior, or least he was pretending much better. Maybe he wasn't that bad. I gave him a soft kiss on the cheek. "Have a good night. And don't forget; you have my number."

The next day, I woke up and decided to go to the seven o'clock church service. Since it was going to rain all day, I planned to stay in and watch Lifetime and take my usual Sunday afternoon nap.

As I was leaving church, Joey called and asked me to stop by his house for brunch. At first, I hesitated, thinking I didn't know him well enough to go to his house. But then I thought, he had a lot to lose, so he wouldn't dare hurt me. He had plenty of groupies who would do anything for him, so he didn't have to resort to violence with any female. Besides, I didn't get a psychotic or predatory vibe about him.

"Okay," I replied, "but just so you know, you must be very special to me, because I have a standing Sunday date with Lifetime and never change it for anyone."

After many winding roads, I finally made it to his secluded gated mansion. His chef had an entire spread of food laid out, enough to feed ten people. When we finished eating, Joey gave me a tour of his house. It was massive and luxuriously decorated. Of course, he showed me his master suite last. He told me that, despite his many relationships, he had never let any of his girlfriends move in with him. The only woman who could live with him was his wife, and he had not met her yet. He got us mimosas, and then we went into his theatre room and watched a movie that was still playing in theatres.

I must have been tired, because I dozed off for about an hour. I woke up to Joey kissing me on my cheeks, my ears, and my neck.

"You must have been tired," he said. "You didn't even last fifteen minutes into the movie. Why don't you go upstairs, get comfortable, and watch your Lifetime channel here?"

I looked at him suspiciously. "Okay, the real you is here—the guy who really just wants to get into my panties."

He laughed and said, "What panties?" He continued smiling. "Yeah I do want that, but I also want to get to know you. I think I like you. It's nice to meet a woman who's really got her shit together and not looking at me for what I can do for her." He nodded slyly. "I did my homework on you. I know you're a big shot attorney, a senior partner, right?" He shook his head. "All that beauty, booty, and brains, why would any man want to let you go?" He paused. "I think I know why, but I want to find out for myself."

"You can't make a statement like that without explaining yourself."

"I'll explain later," he promised. "A woman like you with all those brains could really complement me; you could run the Joey empire."

We both laughed.

"I'm almost ten years older than you," I replied. "Besides, you need to experience things in life that I've already done."

"I've never been married, but I already have two sons, so I'm good on that tip," he replied. "I've got my heir and a spare. I don't need or want to have any more children. I want someone to share my life with though, someone who loves me for me and not just because I'm a pro football player." He took my hand. "What do you want?"

I thought about it for a moment and then shook my head. "I'm not sure. I just want to enjoy life and be happy. My divorce is still too new to be talking about getting into a serious relationship right now."

He smiled. "I got you; I understand."

Then he led me over to the clear glass elevator, which we took to the third floor. He walked me into the master suite and showed me a drawer where he kept his pajamas.

"You can find something to slip into. I don't sleep in PJs, but my mother buys them for me every year for my birthday and Christmas. She doesn't seem to understand that I prefer to wear shorts or sweats when I'm lounging around the house. I can't tell her that I sleep in the raw, 'cause Rollo likes his freedom. You don't know anything about Rollo though. That's old school Prince and Time music."

I laughed, and then he turned on the TV and left the room.

As I searched for the perfect pajama shirt, I felt an extraordinary connection with Joey, as if we were already a couple. It didn't feel like we were strangers at all. However, I had mixed feelings, too. I wasn't sure if he was playing a game or being genuine with me. Regardless of my ambivalence about Joey, I didn't want to run away from him. I didn't know where I was headed with Joey, but I wasn't afraid to take the ride to that destination. I would enjoy my happiness even if it was only just for the day.

I took my clothes off, slipped into a navy blue satin pajama shirt, and then climbed into his massive bed. He came back with a mimosa and made sure I was comfortable. I asked him to open a window, because I wanted to hear the sound and inhale the smell of the rain.

"I'm going downstairs," he said after he had done what I asked. "Call me if you need anything."

"Don't go," I said before he was out the door. "I don't want to lie in this big bed alone."

He smiled. "Okay, but I'm warning you, if I climb in that bed with you, we ain't watching Lifetime." He looked at me for a moment. "Are you sure?"

I nodded and smiled back at him.

He wasted no time taking off his clothes. His dick was already bone straight hard. He got in bed, took a sip of my mimosa, and then began French kissing me as I rubbed on his long, thick dick. After a few minutes, he slid under the covers and began performing oral sex on me. He was slow and gentle as he kissed and licked my labia and perineum. His movements became more intense as he sucked on my clit and fingered my anus. I knew that was a sign that he wanted anal sex. I moved his hand away from my anus as he continued to intensify his oral stimulation. He was very quiet. He never moaned or said a word.

By then my juices were overflowing and had him even more excited. He finally put on a condom and then kissed me hard. He licked and sucked my entire face just as he had done to my clit. Then he rolled me onto my back and penetrated me. That's when he started making sounds.

"Oh my god, your stuff is so good. It's gripping my dick just the way I like it."

The pace of his strokes intensified as he climaxed with sweat dripping all over his body. Between his heavy breaths, he said, "I'm sorry. I wasn't expecting it to feel so warm, so juicy, so fucking tight, and the way you moved those muscles in your pussy."

He rolled over onto his back. "Give me a minute to catch my breath, and then I'm going to take care of you, I promise. This never happens to me. I'm not selfish like that, but I couldn't help myself. Your pussy was just so fucking great. You're going to blow my mind when you let me have you raw."

He went into the bathroom and came back with a warm, soapy facecloth. He washed my vagina and the inside of my butt cheeks and gently around and inside my anus. True to his word, a few minutes later, he was right back at it. He laid on his back and then pulled me over on top of him with my butt positioned right over his face. He slid down slightly so that his face aligned with my pussy.

"I want to fuck you orally in every orifice of your body until you come, and then I want to penetrate you the same way," he said. "Just pretend my tongue is a dick, and then do your thing."

I hadn't realized it until then, but he had a long pink tongue. At first, I couldn't quite find a rhythm, because my natural inclination was to just sit on his face, but he moved me up and down and back and forth until I climaxed.

Afterwards, he climbed behind me, but instead of penetrating me, he began rimming me and licking me intensely between the base of my butt cheeks, my perineum, and my anus while penetrating my vagina with his fingers. Then he took my hand and told me to keep massaging my pussy while he put on another condom.

"Don't be shy," he said, smiling, "you know what to do."

At first, I hesitated, because I had never masturbated without a device, and I had begun to do that only recently. It seemed like seconds later that he penetrated my vagina from behind with deep, forceful strokes. It was as if he was trying to go deep inside me, inserting the fullness of his entire penis and scrotum inside me. He had me pinned down, and I was scared that he was going to penetrate me anally as well, but he didn't. He continued to pound me until he climaxed, letting out a long sigh. I fell to my stomach, and he rolled over on his back with sweat dripping from his body like he had just emerged from a sauna.

"Girl, you're going to have me back in shape before I have to report to training camp. I could make love to you every day."

After he cooled off, he slid his body next to mine. "I didn't hurt you, did I?"

"No," I replied.

"I would never ask or force you to do anything you don't want to do. A lot of women like anal sex, but I can tell you don't, and that's cool. We just need some time to grow and figure out what works for us. I have no complaints; I am more than satisfied. In fact, it was even better than I expected."

"How so?"

"I didn't expect it to be so warm and succulent and snug like a glove that fit perfectly; not too tight, just right." He paused for a moment before continuing. "I was wrong."

"Wrong about what?"

"Wrong about why your husband let you go. You're the complete package. You're sexy as hell, and you can fuck, too. I know you're the type of woman who tries to please her man, in bed and elsewhere. I guess that leaves only one thing: you're psycho, but I'm psycho, too, so I can roll with that."

We laughed, and then things got quiet. I was starting to fall into a light sleep.

"It's essential that I have sexual compatibility with my woman," Joey said, jarring me awake again. "You know I like head like any man, but I like ass, too."

"Are you bisexual?"

"Absolutely not," he replied. "I'm not gay, bisexual, down low, low down or none of that. I don't fool around with nothing but God-made pussy. I can tell you like to have your pussy eaten. Does that make you a lesbian?"

"No, I replied, but that whole anal sex thing makes me think of gay men." Of course, I thought about Philip and Jody, but I didn't dare tell Joey about Philip's closeted homosexuality. I would take that secret to my grave.

"I know that's not your thing," he replied, "but I need to let you know I won't be satisfied without it. I got to have me some ass, not all the time but sometimes, so think about it. I know you're still a virgin in that area, so I'll be patient with you."

"You seem quite confident that I'll stay around long enough to indulge in your sexual fantasy," I said.

He laughed. "Oh, it's not a fantasy, it's a requirement. I have a feeling that you're going to be around for a long time. I'm sure of it."

He turned me over onto my back, and then he went down on me again, but this time as he ate me, he slid his finger into my rectum and moved it slowly back and forth. After a while, I couldn't feel his finger, but then he added another finger, which added significantly more pressure, so I pulled back.

"That's enough for today," he said, coming up for air. "See? It wasn't so bad."

He tried to kiss me, but I turned my head. "I like you, but your breath smells like shit. I can tolerate pussy juice, but I draw the line at ass juice. I don't care if it is mine. I don't want to taste any remnants of my own shit."

He laughed. "You're funny. You need to loosen up, because you're going to be doing everything with me. There can be no limits with us."

He came up and lay down beside me. "I don't want to play games with you; I want to see you again."

"In what capacity?" I asked.

"I don't have a label for it, but I know I want to see you again. Can we deal with that for now? I know you're not looking for anything serious, so let's just see what happens, take it day by day. If nothing else, we know we like each other and we make each other feel good. We both may decide in two weeks that we feel different, and that's okay, too. Or we might decide we want to go the distance. I'm not asking you to stop dating or change anything in your life except to make room in it for me. I'll do the same for you, and then we'll see what happens."

I was on an orgasmic high, so I would have said yes to anything. Finally, I agreed.

"Okay," he said. "I'm going to run you a hot bath so you can relax some more before you leave."

While Joey was preparing my bath, I thought about his kind, loving words and the way he made me feel. It wasn't just great sex; it was something more. I was really feeling him and was nervous about it, because it was happening so quickly. My feelings also had me confused. I wasn't sure if I should jump ship or stay the course. Then I told myself to stop worrying and just enjoy my time with him. But I would need to make a decision soon before this relationship spiraled out of control.

I turned on the television that hung over the fireplace at the end of the bathtub. I was feeling good, and I closed my eyes briefly as I relaxed in my hot, steamy bubble bath, which felt more like a therapeutic Jacuzzi, with its large powerful water jets. At one point I even laid back and immersed my entire body under water.

When I came up, I was startled, because Ricky was kneeling down next to the tub. He didn't say a word; he just smiled and nodded the way he did when I was a little girl. A wave of fear came over me, and I started gasping for air and crying. "No, no, please leave me alone!"

A few minutes later, Joey brought me a glass of champagne. "Did you say something earlier?"

"No," I replied. "I just realized that I forgot to call in my script for my disposable contacts."

"It must have been the television then, because I thought I heard a woman crying.

My heart was still racing, but I tried to act normal. I didn't want Joey to know what was going on with me. We both laughed, and then he climbed into the tub with me. I was hoping he wouldn't touch me again. My body was tired, and I wanted to enjoy my lilac bath. He lay behind me, massaging my neck.

"You know you can spend the night," he whispered in my ear.

I shook my head. I wasn't prepared to stay overnight, but I told him I would take a rain check.

After we finished bathing, I was looking through one of his cabinets for a toothbrush when I noticed it was well stocked with all sorts of anal care items, such as flavored anal candies, various types of lubricants, antibacterial rinses, enemas, and other pharmaceuticals. My initial thought was that he might secretly be gay or bisexual; especially given the attention he had given to my anus and rectum. It didn't matter how well he fucked me. I was still suspicious of his sexuality. If nothing else, Philip had taught me that a man's masculinity and womanizing had nothing to do with his true sexuality. This man was serious about anal sex and clearly knew what to do with it; that is, cleanse, prep, pleasure, and maintain the wellness of it. One thing was for sure, if I stayed with him, I would have to engage in anal sex eventually.

On the way home, I thought about Joey, his age, his kids and his sexual proclivities. I enjoyed spending time with him, but I could not see a future with him or anyone else, for that matter. I wasn't trying to get serious with anyone in the near future. Besides, who was I kidding? I knew he was still the same cocky, arrogant guy I had met a few days earlier. I wasn't about to get caught up again. I would play his game as long as he wanted. I would not become a locker room story that he told to amuse his teammates, how he turned out this older woman. No way, that would not be me. But I continued to smile as I thought about him. I was feeling good, and I was actually looking forward to seeing Joey again.

Then, as I pulled into the garage to park my car and turned my head around to back in, I saw a flash of Ricky sitting in the back seat. I closed my eyes and put my head down on my steering wheel for a minute. When I opened them, he was gone. Seeing images of Ricky scared me. I didn't understand why he had resurfaced again. I would try not to give in to the craziness he was trying to stir up in me.

The next day, Joey had a bouquet of orchids delivered to me at work. The card simply read, "Thank you for everything." I was impressed that he remembered I liked orchids; most men would have sent roses.

Later that day, I called Joey to thank him for the flowers. He said he needed to see me again. He asked me to pack a bag and spend the night. I didn't respond immediately. I told him I worked long hours and usually didn't get home before eight. He must have sensed the hesitation in my voice.

"I just want to be with you. We don't have to have sex. I just want to know what it feels like go to sleep at night and wake up in the morning with you. Give me a chance. Let me show you that I'm one of the good guys. You can trust me. I'll always be truthful to you even if it hurts."

Unable to resist his offer, I went home, packed my cute little overnight bag, and headed to Joey's house.

It was late when I got there, already past my usual bedtime. Joey met me at the door, kissed and hugged me, and then marched me right up the stairs to the master suite. He put my bags down and then walked me into the candlelit bathroom, where he had a hot bath waiting for me. Lying on the chaise lounge was a beautiful cream-colored satin robe with matching slippers. He left the bathroom, closing the door behind him.

While I relaxed in the tub, I heard classic songs by Stevie Wonder playing through the bathroom speakers. A few minutes later, Joey appeared with a glass of champagne.

"You shouldn't stay in the tub too long," he said.

"I won't. Just give me a few more minutes," I replied.

When I stepped out of the bathroom, Joey told me to close my eyes, because he had a surprise for me. He took my hand and led me to his closet. When I opened my eyes, I was speechless. It was a rack of top designer clothes, everything from suits to dresses to playwear, and about ten pairs of designer shoes. Then he opened a drawer that was full of lingerie.

"I want to make it convenient for you to stay here," he said, "just in case you forget something in that little overnight bag of yours. Plus, I might want you to stay for more than one night. I know it's too soon for us to talk about living together, but I want you here with me every night—until whenever."

I smiled. "You might change your mind after you hear my snore."

"I've already heard you snore," he replied. "It's not cute, but I still want you here with me."

I laughed and shook my head. "This seems like too much too soon. Let me think about it."

"Forget all that stuff I said about you making room for me in your life while you see other guys. I want you all to myself. I want us to be exclusive, okay? That means, no slips, no dips, or weekend trips with any other man. If you're going to be my woman, then you have to be completely faithful and monogamous. I have zero tolerance for infidelity. I have a jealous side that you don't want to see, so don't ever do anything to make me jealous. Seeing you with another man would drive me crazy; I might flip out or something."

"Okay," I said. His rules didn't really matter to me, because I was there just for the day, and not for a long stay.

"I'm tired. May I go to bed now?

"Of course," he replied. "I'll join you later."

That night, to my surprise, all we did was sleep. It was nice to be held.

The next morning, I awoke to Joey devouring my pussy. He said he needed a little bit before I went to work to hold him over until that night.

The next few days fell into a pattern. I made it back to his house in time for a late dinner followed by a hot bath, a glass of champagne, and a night of passion. I must say being with Joey and making love to him every night felt nice. Every morning, I drove to work with a smile on my face and found myself looking forward to going home in the evenings. I could not recall ever feeling that way about Philip, even in the early days of our relationship.

That Friday when I got back to Joey's house, he wasn't there, so I decided to snoop around in his office. I found a large envelope from a law firm lying on his desk. I opened it and saw what appeared to be a paternity suit and a request for prenatal financial support for an unborn child. The plaintiff's name was Pilar Mendoza. As I read the complaint, I became livid. This was déja vu. He was just another lying, cheating, fucking asshole. I decided to pack my belongings and leave. I didn't need any more pain or drama in my life. I had dealt with that kind of shit when I was married to Philip. I wasn't about to go through it again.

As I was putting my suitcase in my car, Joey pulled up and looked at me in surprise. "Where are you going?"

"Home."

"Why?"

"Why don't you ask Pilar?"

His facial expression changed immediately. He looked like he had been caught in a wrongful act. "Please don't go, let me explain," he pleaded.

As Joey talked, I saw flashes of Philip's face. I felt the same pain and sadness as I felt when I was in the midst of Philip's wrath. Tears flowed down my face.

"I trusted you," I said. "I should have known you were rotten just like the rest of them." Then I got in my car and drove off.

On the drive home, I kept seeing Philip's face. Then I saw him sitting in my backseat. He was yelling at me. "I told you that you could never escape me. I made you. I will always be with you. You will always belong to me."

"Shut up! Leave me alone!"

Though not deliberate, I pressed own on the accelerator, and I almost drove off the road. I felt like I was having an anxiety attack, so I pulled over to compose myself. I sat there for about five minutes until I was calm enough to resume driving. When I got home, I drank two tequila shots, turned off my cell phone, and went to bed.

The next morning at about six, I awoke to the bellman calling my house phone. It was Joey. He had been waiting in the lobby for the past two hours. I agreed to let him come in. I opened the door and we sat on my sofa.

"I'm sorry, I didn't mean to hurt to you," he said. "I only met you a little over a week ago, and I didn't expect us to become so close so quickly. I met Pilar in California a few years ago, and we started having an on-and-off sexual relationship, but that was it. It wasn't serious to either one of us. She was never my girlfriend, and she knew it. I'm not going to lie, she was a good lay, and that's the only reason I kept her around. At first, she was easy. She wasn't trying to get into any deep emotional shit. She was a party girl, you know a THOT,* the kind I could fuck on a regular basis if I bought her stuff like designer purses and red bottom shoes and gave her tickets to celebrity events. I let her stay at my condo a few times while I was on the road, and the next thing I knew she was trying to move in with me. Then I put the brakes on us. We stopped seeing each other until about seven months ago, the night I supposedly impregnated her. Before that night, I had never slept with her in the raw, because she's been around the league with other guys.

"The next day, I asked her if everything was okay, because I knew a doctor who could give her a pill to take care of it. She said everything was okay, because she was getting those birth control shots. The next thing I knew, she called me and told me she was pregnant and keeping it. I realized then that she had set me up. I let my guard down one time, and it's probably going to cost me millions. You might not agree with me, but I'm trying to pay her off. I don't want to have anything to do with her or her unborn child even if it is mine. I made a big mistake, and now I've got pay for it.

"I'm usually very cautious with women, especially when I first meet them, but I've only known you a week and I already trust you. I've made myself extremely vulnerable to you. I have completely opened my house and my heart to you in one week. I trust you implicitly. I know this may sound corny

---

* That Hoe Over There

or like bullshit, but I feel like you're the one for me. I can have any woman I want, but I choose you. You're the one I want to wake up to, share my home with and maybe share the rest of my life with."

He knelt down in front of me. "I'm begging for your forgiveness. I don't want to lose you, not like this, not over this bullshit. I know I'm going to fall in love with you, if I'm not there already. When you left on Sunday, I felt an emptiness that I've never felt before, and that's why I wanted you to come back. I can get any woman just to fuck, but I told you I'm looking for the whole package, and I think you're it for me. But I'm not sure you feel same about me." He took my hand. "Baby, please give us more time. You owe us that; we deserve it."

My heart wanted to believe him, but my brain wouldn't let me. I kept thinking about all the years I lost with Philip, how he had deceived, manipulated, abused, and betrayed me, and how much pain he brought into my life. Joey would be just like Philip, loving and kind in the beginning and then, once he knew I loved him and needed him, he would pull out a dagger and chisel away at my heart, my spirit, and my soul. I could not fall back into that type of emotional trap again. I was through letting men walk all over me, hurt me, and destroy my essence. I decided I would play Joey's game, but he would be the one who would end up hurt this time, not me.

I put my arms around Joey and held him tight, and then I kissed him.

"I have something to show you," he said. It was a medical lab report that showed results of his blood tests, essentially showing that he did not have HIV or any STDs. "Baby, I want to give you all of me, and I want all of you, too. I need to feel and taste all of your natural juices. I need to be one with you."

"Well, what about my lab results?"

"I already have them. Please don't ask me how I got them or judge me in my approach."

"I was about to take a shower," I said. "Care to join me?"

He smiled and nodded.

I took his hand and led him to my bedroom. I turned on the shower and then proceeded to undress him. I dropped to my knees and began kissing his penis. I licked all over the head and then sucked it just enough to get his interest. Then I got up and led him to the shower.

After I doused my facecloth with liquid soap, I washed my body, and then I began washing his back, from the top of his shoulders down to his smooth, round athletic derriere. I even opened his tight cheeks and washed down inside the crack of his ass. I moved around to the front of his body and began washing his chest and stomach. Then I worked my way down to his penis and scrotum. As I was washed his dick, I dropped to my knees and began sucking it for about thirty seconds at a time. I repeated this wash and suck act a few times. After my knees started hurting from resting on the hard tile, I stood up and began kissing him, working my way down his chest and his stomach. Then I pushed him down onto the bench in the shower, threw a towel under my knees, and began giving him head again. I pulled his butt down so that I could ingest more of his penis. I felt my fingernails pressing into his butt as I pulled his penis in further, so deep that I could feel it hanging down my throat. Yes, I was actually performing my first deep throat fellatio act.

As he got close to climaxing, he pulled my hair harder and harder. I felt him throbbing back and forth, and then he ejaculated. I felt the warm, slimy, salty substance go down my throat. It seemed like he was releasing his fluids for minutes, but it was only seconds. That was the first time I heard Joey moan with such a high pitch in his voice.

"Oh, oh, oh my God . . . what the fuck!" It was like a verse in a song that he repeated over and over again.

As I felt Joey's semen make its way down my throat, it started to gross me out. At that moment, I wished I could throw back some tequila, anything to mask the taste. I pulled my head up, releasing his semi-hard dick from my mouth. Then I got up, and we stepped out of the shower, dried off, and went straight to my bed.

Joey began kissing me. "You know that you just made me love you, don't you?" he whispered. Then he slid under the covers and began performing oral sex on me. He did his usual thing of fingering my anus. I knew I would have to give up the ass one day, but not that night. I was still trying to wrap my mind around him ejaculating in my mouth and not being able to spit that shit out.

We did our usual lovemaking act, first missionary style long enough for me to climax, and then he always seemed to need to get it from the back in order to climax. This time he had me move to the edge of the bed with me sitting on my butt with my legs folded. Then he tilted me forward and pressed my back down with my chest almost touching the bed. He lifted me up slightly and then penetrated me. This position was so uncomfortable. I felt pressure on my rectum as he was stroking back and forth. There was no way my body could even go in that position if I had not taken yoga classes. Thank God he finally climaxed. I didn't think I could have stayed in that position a minute longer. We climbed into bed, and he held me tight as we fell asleep.

A few hours later, I awoke to Joey massaging my pussy with his hands.

"Damn, girl, your pussy stays wet. It wants to be fucked all the time."

"That's not true," I replied. "It simply responds to stimuli instinctively. Similar to me playing with your dick. Just because it gets hard doesn't mean you want to fuck, right?"

"Wrong. Rest assured that when my dick is hard, it wants to fuck, and that's for real."

We laughed, and then I got up and made us some coffee and poured him a glass of orange juice. We sat in bed and talked more about the Pilar situation.

"You don't have to snoop around looking for things to find out about me," Joey said. "You can ask me anything, and I'll tell you the truth, I will never lie to you."

"What about withholding information?" I asked. "You know I'm a lawyer. I could always depose you. Why don't we start with full disclosure on the things that affect your money, time, and your heart?"

He listed at least twenty famous and semi-famous women with whom he had dated over the past five years. He also told me about his first love, Karen, the mother of his two sons. He explained how he had destroyed their relationship.

"Oh yeah, I dated a model for a while. Her name was Manuela. I thought she was the real thing, but she was an imposter. Thanks to Marcus, she was exposed before it was too late. I haven't had a serious relationship, if you want to call it that, since her. So, now you see, Pilar was never my girlfriend. I could kick myself for being so stupid with her."

Joey paused as if he was thinking very carefully about what to say next.

"This time I know what to do to keep the woman I love," he said, "I'm not going to take you for granted or ever disrespect our relationship. I'll make you first, and I'll consult with you on anything that pertains to my children so as not to disrupt the equilibrium in our lives. I'm going to make you love me as much as I love you. Just wait and you'll see."

Part of me wanted to believe Joey—that he could love and cherish me, but the inner voice in my head wouldn't let me. It kept saying, "Don't trust him, he's just like Philip." Even so, something wouldn't let me leave him. I didn't want to be without him. The connection I felt with Joey was stronger than any magnetic force. I wasn't sure if it was love, but whatever it was, I had already surrendered to it. I would be with Joey until the game was over.

18

SEASON I OF THE GAME – THE FIRST HALF

Joey asked me to stay with him at his house until he left for training camp. He was home for only three more months and wanted to spend as much time with me as possible before he left so that we could get closer and put the appropriate label on our relationship.

"This feels like the real thing to me," he said, "but I want to make sure it's not just infatuation."

Flattered, I agreed. It had been years since I had a real emotional connection with a man, and I wasn't sure if I was ready or if I even wanted to be in any type of serious relationship. I felt conflicted about Joey. Part of me cared for him and wanted to explore all the possibilities, but then that faint voice in my head wouldn't stop talking. "He's trying to manipulate you so he can have power over you. You must strike first before he turns on you, because he will try to destroy you eventually; that's what men do." In spite of my feelings for Joey, I knew the voice in my head was right about him, and I needed to heed its warning.

I decided I would use the next several weeks to get close to Joey, make him love me, and then, like a boomerang, I would do to him what he was planning to do with me. I knew what Joey was up to, trying to make me fall in love with him so that he could make me his emotional slave. How long would it take before he started making old dried up pussy jokes? Nope, that was not going to be me. I would be long gone before that happened. But, like a surgical scar, he could never forget me. I would leave an imprint on his brain and heart that would be everlasting, just like Philip had done to me.

On my first night back at Joey's house, he said he had something important to talk to me about. He poured us a glass of champagne, and then we sat in the hearth room.

"I want you to stop referring to this house as my house," he said. Then he gave me a set a keys. "I want you to move in here permanently, when you're ready."

"But I have my condo downtown."`

"Then sell it, lease it, or just keep it if you want to. I know it seems like I'm moving fast, but when you find perfection, you grab it and go with it."

"What about our age difference?" I asked, eying the keys. "The eight-year age gap is insignificant now, but it could become a factor later."

"You just need to keep that sexy body and never stop fucking me," he replied. "You know women can keep sexing well into their sixties. We men slowdown in our fifties, so our ages line up perfectly. Besides, I'm going to have plenty of Viagra and Cialis on hand so we will be good in the sex department for a long time."

I laughed. "Let's slow things down a bit and let things flow naturally."

Joey grabbed my hand. "Okay. Let's start by going upstairs to let things flow naturally in bed while I taste your sweet juices."

He started tickling me as we walked up the backstairs just off the kitchen. Joey's affection and playfulness were two of the many qualities that endeared him to me.

Joey and I had been dating about three weeks when I finally met Marcus in person. Joey had left the house early to go watch his sons play soccer, so I lounged around in bed until the afternoon. Finally, I got up to take a shower. I always enjoyed showering in Joey's master bath. He had a clear glass European steam shower, large enough for six people, with water jets everywhere. I had a habit of closing my eyes whenever I showered alone, mainly because I liked the feel of the water jets spraying on my face. After I finished washing my hair, I was about to lie down on the marble bench when I noticed a man standing right outside the shower. I screamed.

The man held up his hands. "Wait. Hold up, I'm Marcus."

Then he grabbed a towel and gave it to me. Strangely, he remained in the bathroom until I asked him if I could have some privacy. He stared at me from head to toe for about thirty seconds. He smiled. "You knew I was watching you. I've been standing here for the last five minutes." Then he left.

I put on my bathrobe and then walked downstairs to the kitchen where Marcus was pouring himself a glass of orange juice.

"You must be Astrid," he said. He looked me up and down and then shook his head. "Damn, Joey didn't tell me you were fine like that. But that's okay. He always gets preoccupied when the new pussy first arrives."

He kept staring at me like a dog in heat. "You know we share everything, right?" he said in a smug tone. "I usually don't fuck with his leftovers, but I'll make an exception for you."

I looked at him with disgust. "The only way you would ever have me was if I was cold and stiff, lying in a coffin. You know how to let yourself out, right?"

He smiled and dangled a set of keys in front of me. "I come and go when I am ready."

I didn't say anything; I just turned and walked away.

I went back upstairs to the bedroom to finish getting dressed, but this time I locked the door. I stayed upstairs for another two hours until I heard Joey's voice approaching the bedroom.

"Hurry up, I want you to meet someone," he said when I opened the door.

I hugged and kissed him as if I had not seen him for days and then grabbed his hand as we made our way to the kitchen. Marcus was still there, sitting at the counter waiting patiently for us as if he lived there. In a voice like a commentator, Joey introduced me.

"This is Astrid, the first round draft choice for the wife position." He laughed and then held out his arms as if to present me. "She's beautiful, isn't she? Smart too." He smiled. "Man, real talk. I think this is the one. She's special; she meets all the qualifications."

Marcus gave me a snarly look and then spoke in a low whisper. "You're all right. Time will tell it all." He came over and shook my hand and then gave me a light, friendly hug with a fake smile. "Welcome to our family." Then he paused and whispered, "Maybe," as if to let me know I needed his approval if I wanted a long-term relationship with Joey.

Marcus reminded me that he and I had met briefly at a charity event I had attended with Zoe a few months earlier. I didn't remember him, but he clearly remembered me by the way he recalled the details of the style and color of the dress I wore that day. Although Marcus was easy on the eyes with his tall muscular build, he was not my type. There was something about him that suggested he did not hold women in high regard; they were all THOTs to him. I could tell immediately that he was nothing like Joey. He didn't have his physical attributes, charisma, integrity, or sweet, charming personality.

As it turned out, Marcus had stopped by Joey's that afternoon to pick up tickets for an upcoming event and let himself in with his keys. This was a common practice between them, since Joey was on Atlanta's A-list when it came to local red carpet events. Joey didn't really care for the limelight off the field, so he would often send Marcus in his place. Marcus reveled in the idea of representing Joey at these events and the fact that he had direct access to Joey at any time. Whenever people wanted Joey to make a special appearance at a local event, they knew Marcus was the man who could get him there. This fed Marcus' ego, that he had this special influence and connection with Joey.

Joey told me that he was anxious for me to meet his family and his two sons. The following week he took me to his sister, Melanie's home, where she was hosting a 75th birthday party for their mother. To my surprise, when we arrived, Marcus was already there with his date. When he saw us, he waved slightly to acknowledge us, but he kept mingling as if he were a part of Joey's family and not an invited guest.

Joey walked me around, holding my hands tightly and kissing me on my cheek and my hands as he introduced me as his girlfriend to all of his family, including Karen, the mother of his two sons, Joey II (age 9) and Justin (age 7). I didn't quite know what to think about Karen being there. Was she hanging around Joey's family hoping to get back with him?

As I scanned the backyard, I couldn't help but notice Marcus's behavior. I heard him call Joey's mother "Mom" frequently and refer to Joey's sisters as "Sis." I also noticed that Joey's siblings reciprocated his affection, referring to him as their brother, while Joey's nieces and nephews called him "Uncle Marcus." Marcus was definitely a part of Joey's extended family. Even though Marcus's interaction with Joey's family seemed genuine, something about him was still suspect. I knew he was not the real deal, but it didn't matter, because he had Joey's family completely fooled.

Joey was indeed the apple of the eye of his entire family. Everyone seemed to adore him, from his nieces and nephews, all the way up to his siblings and their spouses. Both of his sisters cooked his favorite foods that day so he could take the leftovers home. I could see the love his sisters had for him, behaving more like he was their son rather than their brother.

Shortly after our arrival, I knew I had to let Joey's family have him, because everyone was vying for his attention. As the little kids pulled at him, he looked at me, smiled and shrugged as if to say, "What can I do?"

"I'll be right back," he whispered.

He never came back, but that was okay with me. I made my way to the beverage table and poured myself a glass of ice tea and then I found a seat in a shaded area on the patio so that I could watch Joey horsing around, throwing the football with his nephews and his two sons.

While I sat there, I noticed that Marcus kept staring at me, but not in a flirtatious way. It was more like he was disappointed I was there. I just turned my head and looked in the opposite direction.

A few minutes later, Karen walked over and sat down. "Wow, it's nice to finally meet you in person. Joey told me about you the day after he met you. So, he must be feeling something special for you."

I didn't reply; I just eyed her curiously.

"You know, he's only brought one other girl around his family since we split. It was that tall, Brazilian model named Manuela. But it didn't last too long; she disappeared a few weeks after we met her."

Karen must have sensed that her presence and conversation were puzzling to me.

"Listen, Joey and I are strictly friends now. Whatever we had was over a long time ago, and we're both fine with it. We're just trying to raise our sons together as best as we can under the circumstances. So relax, I am not a threat to your relationship with Joey. But I will tell you this. . . " She leaned in close as if she was revealing something highly confidential. She whispered, "You'd better watch out for Marcus; he's something else. I think he had something to do with Joey's sudden breakup with Manuela."

Just as she was about to tell me more, Joey walked over and interrupted us. "What are the two of you talking about? I don't know if it's a good idea for the baby mama and the future wife to be all cozied up, talking and smiling like that."

We all laughed, and then Karen walked away.

At that moment, I realized that Joey was really falling for me, calling me his future wife even though we had only been dating a few weeks.

My plan is working, I thought. It's only a matter of time before I have the power in this relationship, and then he'll have to play on my terms.

He hugged me and kissed me and smiled. "You know you got my heart, don't you?"

I didn't reply; I just smiled back at him.

The hours passed quickly, and then Joey and I were saying our goodbyes. I was waiting in the living room while Joey packed up all the special dishes his mother and sisters made for him. Marcus walked up to me and smiled.

"I hope you enjoyed the party."

"Yes, I had a great time."

"I think it's a little too soon for Joey to be bringing you around our family and calling you his girlfriend," he said in a smug tone. "I don't know you, I don't trust you, and I'm not sure I like you. I'm going to be watching you, and if you don't act right, I'm going to send you packing like the rest of them."

Then he just walked off.

Where did that come from? I wondered. Who was he to be telling me he was going to be watching me?

As we drove home, I attempted to tell Joey what Marcus said to me, but before I could complete my first sentence, Joey interrupted me.

"I know Marcus may not come off well, but he's really a good person. He's family to me. In some ways he's closer to me than Matt. You know he's the godfather to my sons. I know Marcus is a true friend, because he took a bullet for me that could have derailed my entire career."

At first I thought he was talking about a real gunshot, but he meant it figuratively.

"I'll tell you one day," he said after I asked about it. "Then you'll understand why Marcus is my boy for life. Give him a chance. I know he's a little rough around the edges at first, but you'll grow to love him like the rest of us. I'm telling you Marcus is a good man, and he will have your back just as I do."

That's when I realized Joey had no clue about Marcus. He was right about one thing though: Marcus would love to have my back; that is, sexually if I let him.

The time I spent with Joey seemed to move at an accelerated pace. Soon, our few weeks together turned into months. Despite my lack of trust in Joey, I felt very happy. In fact, this was the first time in my life that I looked forward to leaving work and going home. My career had always been important to me to the extent that sometimes I even put it before Junior. But now, thanks to Joey I had an appreciation for living a complete life. I enjoyed work and my life outside of work as well. We had a great friendship and courtship. Joey would come into town and take me to lunch a few days during the week, and we partied and played hard on the weekends. He was also very spiritual, always saying grace before eating his meals. Often, he took me to church with him on Sundays. I was impressed by how well he knew the Bible. I even had an opportunity to play stepmom to his two sons when they spent time with us during the summer. I really enjoyed having his kids in the house. I forgot how nice the sound of kids running through the house was. It reminded me of some of the happier times I had when Philip, Junior, and I were living together. Joey and I were also having great sex. Even on those weeknights when I was feeling tired, he found a way to get me going.

"I'm sorry, but I love this pussy of yours," he'd say. "I can't sleep next to you without thinking about it, tasting it, feeling it. I know that sometimes you're tired after work and would rather I left you alone, but I can't help myself. It's your fault; your pussy shouldn't be so damn good. I'm addicted to it. It's like crack."

I smacked him playfully. "You're silly."

As good as he claimed my pussy was, he still wanted my ass. Every time we made love, he whispered that he needed my ass, too. By then, we were comfortably up to two fingers, but I still wasn't ready to lose my anal virginity. I was still afraid of the pain and losing something I would never get back. Besides, all of my thoughts of anal sex had negative connotations associated with it. The thought of a man wanting to put his dick in something as foul as a shit hole was disgusting to me. But Joey would say often that pussy could be quite foul, too, with all the blood, natural fluids, and all the other stuff that comes out when birthing a baby. It can be just as frightening. Joey did everything to try to make me feel comfortable with anal sex. He would go on the Internet and print all kinds of materials on the joys of anal sex. He even suggested that I talk to Zoe about it. He had intimated on several occasions that Zoe was a freak and that she would do anything, including anal sex. When I asked why he called Zoe a freak, he said it was because she was, and everyone knew it. Then he looked at me as if he knew something more than he was revealing.

"You know she's a freak, too. But I've never had her, and I don't want her, so that's nothing for you to worry about."

I had no concerns because the last thing I was worried about was those two fucking. Between Joey and me, I knew who Zoe preferred to be with.

Joey's sons had spent the past two weeks with us, and since they were going back to their mother's home the following day, we decided to hang out around the house.

After eating pizza, playing video games, and watching sci-fi movies all night, the boys fell asleep, and Joey and I finally managed to find some quiet time alone.

We were relaxing on the terrace while I sipped a glass of champagne and he smoked his cigar. It was around midnight and I said I was ready to turn in.

"Babe, it's a full moon tonight. We should get in the pool," Joey said.

"Okay, let me go change into my swimsuit."

He looked at me and smiled. "We don't need bathing suits tonight."

I shook my head. "Nope, let's get our swimsuits. Your boys don't sleep through the night. Remember, they almost caught us in the shower together earlier this week."

Joey smiled. "Okay, but don't expect to keep it on long, 'cause you know what I want to do."

While Joey and I enjoyed our late night swim, Marcus stopped by unexpectedly. He gave us his usual advance notice, which was calling Joey's cell phone after he came through the security gate.

"Hey man, what's up? Where are the little fellas?"

"They're knocked out, but my baby and I are in the back taking a swim."

"Okay, I'll be there in a minute."

I hated the liberties that Marcus took when it came to Joey's house or the lack of respect he showed for our relationship, but there wasn't much I could do about it, as least not then. Luckily, Joey and I still had our swimsuits on.

When Marcus arrived, I was sitting by the poolside while Joey refreshed our drinks.

"Hey Astrid, what's up?" Marcus said.

"Not much, I'm just enjoying this moonlight swim with my honey. So, what brings you by tonight?"

"I was over this way and thought I would stop by to talk to Joey about the B&H[4] party I'm having tomorrow night." He smiled pompously. "You know what that is, the kind of party where wives and girlfriends are not allowed to attend."

"On that note, I'm going to get a few more laps in before I go to bed," I said.

Joey approached Marcus and they continued talking as I swam.

"I don't think I'm going to make it tomorrow," Joey said. "I only have two months left before training camp starts, and I want to spend as much time as possible with Astrid and my sons before I leave."

"It's only one night," Marcus protested. "It won't be the same without you there. She'll understand. If you're planning to keep her around for a while, you need to teach her the rules like the rest of them. If she wants to stay, she'll get some acceptance."

"This relationship is different," Joey said. "She means a lot to me. Besides, it would be disrespectful to her for me to attend that kind of party knowing what goes on there. I wouldn't condone her going to parties of that nature, so quite naturally, I have to behave accordingly."

Marcus just stared at Joey and shook his head and whispered, "I see where this is going—another fucking Manuela."

By then, Marcus' voice was becoming louder, and I could hear everything he was saying, but he didn't care. "I know you

---

[4] Bottles & Hoes

like her, but you can't let her start controlling things. You better train her now or you'll have problems with her later."

Joey continued listening but didn't say word.

"Well, just stop by; you don't have to stay long. Everyone is expecting to see you there."

"No, just scratch me off the guest list. I told you, no more B&H parties for me."

Marcus looked startled and confused by Joey's response. I think he was more disappointed, because he knew that the real reason people hung around him or supported his events was because of Joey. He knew that his social status was questionable without him.

As I got out of the pool, Joey wrapped a towel over my shoulders. I saw Marcus looking at me. He seemed furious, not with Joey, but with me.

As we walked toward the terrace door, Marcus spoke to me in a calm, pleasant voice. "Astrid, I heard you make a lemon crème cake that's out of this world. You think I could get a slice to go?"

"Sure," I said.

As Marcus and I walked toward the kitchen, Joey ran upstairs to check on the boys. A few minutes later as I was wrapping up the cake, Marcus grabbed my arm.

"Listen, you stuck-up bitch. I know exactly what you're up to. You may have Joey fooled, but I'm onto you. I'm not going to stand around and watch you manipulate him while you elevate your status."

Before I could get a word out, I heard Joey coming toward the kitchen. Marcus, grabbed my arm again and whispered in my ear. "You better not say a word to Joey."

Marcus released my arm just as Joey entered the kitchen. "Why is it so quiet? It's not that serious."

Marcus laughed. "It's all good. I'm sorry I interrupted you two lovebirds." He grabbed his cake. "It's late; I'll let myself out."

As Joey and I were getting ready for bed, he noticed that I was upset. "What's wrong, baby?"

I knew Joey would not be receptive to hearing the truth about how Marcus really felt about me, so I soft-pedaled it. "I'm uncomfortable with your friend, Marcus. He seems a bit wild for me."

"Well, he is a bachelor, and he loves that lifestyle. I don't think he will ever be the marrying kind. But that's him, not me. I hope you're not upset about his B&H party. I told you that I would never disrespect our relationship, so I'm not going. Anyway, I have no interest in going to those types of parties anymore. I got everything I want and need with you. I hope you know that. Now get your fine, sexy naked ass in the bed so I can put a smile on that face." And he did just that.

The next morning, Joey and I got up early so that we could have breakfast together before he took his sons home. As I drank my coffee and looked at my iPad, Joey noticed me looking at pictures of Junior on Facebook. He could see the sadness in my face.

"I know you miss your son, 'cause you have pictures of him all over your condo. Why don't you invite him down here for a weekend or something so that I can meet him? You know we can always go visit him if he can't make the trip. I'll charter a plane if I have to. I'll do anything to wipe that sadness away. I know something's wrong. I see how you are with my boys, but you rarely talk about your son. Talk to me, tell me what's going on with you and your son."

That's when I told him about my strained relationship with Junior. As I talked about various aspects of my divorce and how Junior was affected by it, I was overcome with tears.

Joey grabbed me and held me tight. "Your ex-husband is crazy. I would never try to drive a wedge between my boys and Karen. In fact, I demand that they respect her, and I'm teaching them to be little men around her house and to protect their mother. Listen, you're a good person, and I know you were and still are a great mother. Your son will come around. Boys have a soft spot in their heart for their mothers; that's unbreakable. That bond is formed way before they are born. Before the year is out, you and your son's relationship will be back to normal. I promise."

I looked at him. "I hope you're right."

As the days passed, Joey intensified his mantra about anal sex. He continued trying to convince me that anal sex could be pleasurable. He would say it was quite common in heterosexual relationships. A lot of women love it, even more than getting it in their vagina. We even watched several graphic porn DVDs of couples having anal sex, but it didn't lessen my anxiety about it. Regardless of my hesitation, he was not giving up. I knew I would have to give in sooner or later, because leaving him wasn't an option. Joey had this way of making me feel like I wanted to give him everything, I guess, because he gave me everything. However, I knew that once I gave Joey my ass, he would feel that he had won, and that he had power over me. He would have my heart and soul, and then he could do with it what he wanted. That's when he would change; reveal his other side, the dark side that was hidden within every man. And he would seal my fate, first by tormenting me and then slowly and methodically killing my spirit.

Sometimes, I felt myself losing sight of reality. It felt as if we were actually building a relationship and a life together. But the truth was, the life we were living was not real. It was just a game, Joey's game to deceive and break me. The smart thing to do was to run away, but I couldn't. Deep inside, I needed what Joey was giving me, and I needed it to be real. But that could never be, because he didn't know how to be honest and sincere. Inevitably, he would change and unleash his hurt upon me just like Philip.

With each passing day, my relationship with Joey was getting more serious than I had planned and seemed to be moving beyond my control. Despite my efforts to only use Joey for intimacy and companionship, I was falling hard for him. Every day and all through the day, Joey would tell me that he loved me and how blessed he was to have me in his life. Part of me wanted to believe him, but the other part of me was too scared. I struggled constantly with this division as I kept hearing that voice inside my head saying, "The love Joey says he has for you isn't true." I was scared that Joey's romantic deceptions were working, and I was becoming vulnerable to him. I knew it was time for me to get out. I didn't want to hurt him, and I didn't want him to hurt me. I decided to break up with Joey when he left for training camp.

During our final week together, Joey took me to a resort in the Colorado Mountains for a four-day getaway. We arrived in time to start our day with a wonderful lunch and three hours of spa treatments for me. That night, a chef prepared a private dinner for us in our suite. We finished the evening by soaking in the hot tub on our private patio and then sipping bubbly and making passionate love all through the night.

The next morning, Joey took me up in a hot air a balloon. Then we spent the afternoon horseback riding. That night, we ate dinner at a local western style restaurant that was filled with famous and semi-famous celebrities and their families. To my surprise, there were no paparazzi around, which made the venue even nicer. After dinner, we did a repeat of the prior night.

While we were relaxing in the hot tub on the balcony, Joey reminisced about his days playing football in high school.

"Playing football was so natural for me, and it's still that way today. I really love the game. I don't know what I would have done with my life if I had not gone to the NFL. There was no plan B for me, at least nothing I could see back then. I probably wouldn't have the businesses I have today if it wasn't for Marcus.

"Is that why you're so loyal to him?" I asked.

"What do you mean?"

"You know, remember when you told me that he took a bullet for you one time that could have ended your career?"

"Oh that. Yes sort of. Okay, I'll tell you what happened. Marcus and I were both drafted the same year to the same NFL team. Like most rookies, we liked to party every chance we got, and this particular night the party was in my room. We had the usual, food, liquor, and plenty of beautiful women in all flavors: short, tall, dark, light and everything in between."

He smiled as he reflected on that night. "The girls came in and got butt naked, nothing but tits and ass everywhere, and just like that, the party was on."

He looked at me, slightly embarrassed, realizing he was showing too much excitement while talking about the women at the party. "I was young back then, so I didn't see any harm in partaking in those types of festivities. I thought that was part of the package, if you know what I mean.

"After a few hours, I decided I would turn in early, by myself this time. I planned to call Karen and then go to sleep. We were still together back then, and she was pregnant with baby number two, so I was trying not to be a total jerk to her.

"Marcus was seated on the sofa with two girls on his lap, kissing and doing everything you can imagine. Because we had each other's back, we always let one or the other know when we were dipping out with a chick or something. So I motioned to him that I was turning in and he nodded as if to say, 'See ya.' "Look, I'm not trying to pretend I was a saint, because I wasn't usually, but on that particular night I was, and that's for real."

I continued listening patiently, wishing he would hurry up and get to the good part of the story.

"When I went into my bedroom, I saw the light on in my bathroom. I paused and wondered, who was in my room. I told everyone that this room was off limits. When I opened the bathroom door, there was a girl lying on the floor wearing nothing but a thong. I noticed there was a small tray sitting on the bathroom sink with some kind of drugs on it. I thought she was high and had passed out, so I tried to wake her, but she didn't move. I grabbed a cup of water and threw it in her face thinking it might help, but she didn't respond. That's when I ran and got Marcus.

"As we were walking back to my bedroom, I told him what happened. He went over to the girl and kneeled down and checked her pulse. 'She's barely breathing,' he said. 'I think this bitch has overdosed.'

"I started panicking. 'What am I going to do now? Do you know how this looks? We could both get kicked out of the league for this. Marcus said, 'Man, be quiet. This is way more serious than that. You could go to jail for this, especially if she dies. This is your suite, and the police will assume that these are your drugs. Besides, this girl looks like a minor; she can't be no more than sixteen.'"

"I sat on the floor and rubbed my head in disbelief, wondering what I was going to do. That's when Marcus came up with the plan. He told me to help him get her dressed. Then he would take her to his room. 'Let's throw a coat over her, and then it will look like it always does—she's high, and she's going to my room to get fucked and to sleep it off."

"Marcus dressed her in one of my T-shirts and then put his jacket over her and walked her to his room. A few minutes later, I kicked everyone out of my suite; the party was over. I called Marcus about thirty minutes later. He said everything was okay and to just stick to the story if anyone asked. 'The last time you saw her she was leaving the party with me.'"

"Unfortunately, a few days later, all hell broke loose. Instead of taking the girl to his room, Marcus parked her in a stall in one of the restrooms along the hotel corridor. The next morning, she was found dead and traced back to my room because of the hallway security footage. However, Marcus ended up copping to it. He told the authorities that he met the girl in the lobby and invited her to the party. A few hours later they decided to go back to his room to party some more. As they were walking to his room, he noticed she didn't look well, so he helped her into the bathroom. He waited a few minutes, but she never came out, so he went on to his room. He thought she had sobered up and went home. He never thought she was seriously ill or on the verge of death."

"To make a long story short, by the time the league's legal team and spin doctors got through with the incident, Marcus walked away with a suspension and a tarnished reputation. He was also released from his contract. Since it was early in his career and he wasn't a starter, other teams were reluctant to take a chance on him. Thus began the downward spiral of his NFL career.

"In all these years, he never said a word to anyone about what really happened that night, and he has never thrown it in my face or said I owed him anything. Now do you see why I care for him, why I have his back? He sacrificed his career for mine. That night could have ruined my career, not to mention the legal ramifications.

I didn't agree with him, but I didn't dare say anything. I finally understood the hold that Marcus had on Joey. Marcus knew that Joey felt responsible for his failed NFL career, and because of Joey's kind and loyal nature, he knew that Joey would feel indebted to him the rest of his life. The guilt that Joey carried that bound him to Marcus further solidified to me that there was nothing I could ever say to convince Joey that Marcus was not his devoted, loyal friend. But knowing Marcus, it would only be a matter of time before he revealed his true self to Joey, because that was the kind of person he was—a true hater.

I wish I could say I was moved by Joey's story about Marcus's great deed, but I wasn't. My perception of Marcus had not changed one bit. Marcus was probably better off financially riding Joey's coattails than riding the bench in the NFL. The one thing the story did for me was cement just how much Joey cared for other people.

The following morning, we worked out, and then the chef prepared breakfast for us in our suite. We decided to spend our last day relaxing and doing things that tourists did. We went sightseeing and rafting in Colorado Springs and then returned to our suite to take a short nap before dinner. Later that evening, we had dinner in a restaurant that was nestled in the mountains with spectacular panoramic views. During dinner, Joey told me that the past few months had proved to be far better than he expected.

"Your genuine love, kindness, and innocence is endearing to me. You got me snowed; you're my heart, Astrid. I know you're the woman for me. I love you."

"I love you, too," I replied.

After dinner, we ordered dessert. While we were waiting, Joey pulled out a small jewelry box. I thought it was too soon for us to get engaged, so it must be a pair of diamond earrings. Then Joey grabbed my hand.

"I have thought about this since the first week you stayed at my house." He opened up the box and then slipped a ring on my finger. "Will you marry me?"

I was speechless. It was a ten-carat emerald cut yellow diamond with five carats of white diamonds nestled around it. It was beautiful; it looked exactly like the picture of the ring I cut out of the Robb Report that I had posted on my dream board.

"I saw the picture of the ring at your condo." He laughed. "Girl, you got expensive taste, but I know you're worth it. When I saw this ring initially, I thought that maybe I'd give it to you at Christmas or on your birthday, but I changed my mind, and for good reason." Sensing my hesitation, he continued. "I know it seems quick, but you can't put a time limit on love. Some people fall in love at first sight, and some people stay together for thirty years and never truly love each other. We're lucky it happened so quick for us. The time we've shared together has been spectacular, and I don't want it to end. I want to know that I can look forward to coming home to you. I know you'll love me well after my football career is over. You're it for me, so stop worrying about our ages. I love you, and I want to spend the rest of my life with you. We can go Vegas this weekend or we can have a big wedding if you want. It's your call. Just know that I want to spend the rest of my life with you."

I was too caught up in the moment to respond at first. Then I smiled and said, "I love you, too, and of course I'll marry you."

He reached over and kissed me. "Thank you for being you."

As we walked back to our room holding hands, Joey paused and kissed me. "Since it's our last night here, tonight I want everything."

I smiled. "Only if you give me everything."

He held out his arms. "Whatever you want, baby, it's yours."

"Why don't we start with a bottle of Don Julio?" I suggested. If I was going to lose my anal virginity, I needed some liquid courage. A few double shots of tequila would do the trick.

Joey called room service and ordered the tequila while I started the shower.

"Wait for me," he said. "I want to wash you tonight."

I knew what that meant. It was butt, cheeks, and ass night. Even though we had not yet had anal sex, Joey loved to rub his dick between my cheeks and the rim of my ass, especially when we were in the shower.

When the tequila came, we both took a shot before we got into the shower. Joey took the liquid body wash and poured it all over me. Instead of using a facecloth, he used his hands to wash my pubic and rectal areas. Then he turned me around, placed my hands on the wall and, standing behind me, rubbed his soapy, slippery penis up and down my butt, between my cheeks, and near the rim on my anus. For a second, I thought he was going to attempt to penetrate my anus right then and there, but he didn't.

"I promise I'll be gentle," he said while kissing my neck and shoulders. "I'll make sure you enjoy it."

He was so hard that I could tell he was anxious to get started. I hadn't seen him that excited since the first time I deep-throated him. He stepped out of the shower first and grabbed his robe. After I stepped out, he helped me to put on my robe and then held out his hand. "Let me escort you to your oasis."

When we walked into the bedroom, I saw twelve vases filled with vibrant red orchids placed throughout the room. I looked at Joey in surprise. "It's so beautiful!" Joey knew how much I loved orchids. He (or his assistant) put a lot of work into finding those red orchids, because they were not usually as plentiful as red roses.

Joey was forever Mr. Romantic. He always did something extra to make an occasion more memorable. I loved that quality about him.

We walked over to the table where the tequila was set up, and we both threw back two more shots, but this time we didn't bother with the lime. Joey could tell I was anxious.

"Don't be nervous, baby. If we start and you don't like it, we can always stop."

We climbed into the bed and bypassed our usual small talk, French kissing, and caressing. Instead, Joey went down on me immediately and began performing oral sex. He licked and kissed my perineum and sucked on my clitoris until my juices were overflowing. Then he used my juices to lubricate my anus. He continued his oral stimulation while he penetrated my rectum with one finger, two fingers, and then three fingers. Then he turned me over and had me get on all fours. I heard him squeeze what sounded like lotion or gel from a tube. Then I watched as he rubbed it all over his penis. He wiped the rest between the base of my inner cheeks near the rim of my anus. Then, little by little, he put the head of his penis in my rectum. It felt much larger than his fingers.

After a few tries he finally got the head in. I tensed up immediately.

"Relax, you made it tighter," he said.

"I'm not sure I'm ready for this," I admitted. "Maybe not tonight."

Disappointed, he laid down on his back. To help cheer him up, I massaged the length of his fully erect penal shaft with my mouth. Just as I was about to take the head in, he stopped me.

"Go get a hot soapy cloth."

That's what I loved about him. Even in moments of passion, he was always unselfish and made sure everything was clean and kosher and comfortable for me. He knew I had germaphobe tendencies, which was why I liked giving him head in the shower. Although I spit his semen in a towel most of the time, I swallowed a considerable amount of it, too. There was something I liked about the taste of soap mixed with his thick, salty semen. After washing him, I climbed between his legs and proceeded to give him head until he climaxed, which seemed to put a smile back on his face.

About an hour later as I lay next to him trying to sleep, he whispered in my ear. "The night is still early, and I'm not leaving here without my dick feeling the walls of your ass. Baby, I will do anything for you and anything to satisfy you."

"I'll do anything for you, too," I replied, "but at my own pace."

He got up and brought the tequila and the shot glasses to the bed. He poured me two shots and held them out to me. "Drink up quickly." I did, and then we both drank another shot and fell asleep.

At around four, I was lying on my stomach when I awoke to Joey performing anilingus and fingering me again. When I saw the open lubricating gel, I knew he was going to try to have anal sex again, but I had a feeling he wasn't going to stop this time.

He climbed on my back and began to penetrate my anus slowly. He put his forearm near my mouth.

"Just bite me as you start to feel the pressure."

Once the head of his penis was in, he made one strong thrust, and all of him was in. It hurt so bad that my eyes teared up, and I let out a low scream. Then I bit down as hard as could on his arm. He had me bend my knees slightly to lift my butt up, which lessened the pressure. As he continued to move back and forth gently, the pressure and pain intensified. After a few minutes of thrusting, he pulled his penis out and ejaculated onto my back. He said he could tell I was uncomfortable, so he pulled out, because the pressure of his thrusts from trying to reach his climax might be too much for me to handle my first time. When he finished ejaculating, he rubbed his semen on my back as if he was applying moisturizer.

"I told you I would be gentle and wouldn't hurt you. After the second or third time, you'll start to really enjoy it."

I didn't think there would be a second or third time. I could not imagine ever enjoying it; there was nothing pleasurable about the experience. It was just as disappointing as when I lost my other virginity. This was not an act that I would ever initiate. The only reason I would ever consider doing it was if he wanted it. He would be my first and last anal sex partner.

He got up and started the shower. Then he came back and took my hand. "Come here and let me clean you up."

When I got up to walk, I felt like I had just given birth without an epidural. I walked slowly. He asked me if I was in pain. I nodded. I felt like my rectum was swollen and open.

"With anal sex, you have to keep your rectum very clean," he said. He pulled out a pouch with a small bottle in it. "I'm going to clean you out with this anti-bacterial rinse."

The last thing I wanted was something else going up my ass, but he insisted.

When I stepped into the shower, I put my knee on the bench, and he bent me over slightly and squirted the lukewarm rinse inside my rectum. As the solution ran down my leg, I could see that it had a little blood and fecal matter in it. He also washed the rest of my body with a soapy cloth. He caressed me, kissed me, and told me repeatedly that he loved me. He would spend the rest of his life trying to make me happy. He told me to relax and stay in the shower a little longer while he changed the linen. I did just that. I wanted to be alone. I needed to process what we had done. I thought I would feel different, closer to him, happier. Instead I felt sad and melancholy and even confused.

I adjusted the shower to the hottest temperature possible. It was too hot for my body, but I didn't care. I felt unclean. I leaned my head against the marble-tiled wall and began to cry. I slid down to the floor and closed my eyes and continued crying tears of pain and confusion. I started seeing images of Philip and Ricky, both smiling at me and grabbing me. I tried to fight them off to no avail. They kept reaching for me, and then both of them overpowered me.

I opened my eyes and started gasping for air. It seemed like I was choking and suffocating from the steam. I looked around to make sure there were no signs of Philip or Ricky, and then I stepped out of the shower into a full steamy bathroom. I grabbed the thick, hooded terrycloth robe and sat down on the chaise lounge chair. My rectum felt sore. I touched it, and it felt like it had been torn. It also felt swollen. I tried to look at it, but I couldn't see it due to the steam, not even with my compact mirror. I knew it was different now that Joey's dick had penetrated it. I would see my doctor when I got home to make sure that there was no damage. The way I was feeling, I wasn't sure if I could ever make love to Joey again, let alone attempt anal intercourse.

When I finally came back into the bedroom, I noticed that Joey had ordered breakfast. He could tell I wasn't my usual self. He tried to make small talk about our wedding, but it wasn't enough to change my mood. He gave me two Tylenol and a cup of herbal tea. Then he kissed me on my forehead.

"Why don't you lie back down and get some sleep?"

I climbed into bed, but I didn't fall asleep immediately. I tried, but my mind kept racing with thoughts of Joey and my anal sex experience. Why did I allow Joey to have anal sex with me? Did I want to do it or did I do it out of pressure to please him? I remembered what Abby said about pleasing your man. "What you won't do for your man that some other woman will do and that your man will not have any reservations about pursuing it." I felt confused and powerless. I wondered if I was still playing his game.

A few hours later, Joey woke me so that we could leave for the airport. He had laid out my clothes and shoes and packed everything but my toiletries. "I told you that I would take care of you," he said.

As the limo drove us to the airport, Joey and I didn't talk much. The awkward silence continued for most of the plane ride home. At first, Joey got on his iPad to check his social media sites while I pretended to nap, but two hours into our flight, the silence still loomed between us. By then I was watching movies while Joey read the endorsement contracts his agent had sent over. When the pilot announced we were thirty minutes from Atlanta, were both breathed a sigh of relief. We could finally shift our attention away from the elephant that seemed to be lingering around us.

When we got back to Joey's house, he asked me about setting a wedding date. I told him it would be at least a year from then, because I needed time to plan the wedding.

His chef made dinner for us, and then we went to bed. It was the first time we had ever gone straight to sleep without making love. Joey and I usually had sex every night, including some nights when I was on my period.

The next morning, Joey and I were up packing. He had an afternoon flight to California, and I was moving back to my condo. Since I didn't want to stay in Joey's big empty house without him, we agreed that I would go back to my place until the season was over.

As he helped me put my things in my car, he turned to me. "Baby, I wasn't going to say anything, but I'm worried about you."

"Worried about what?" I asked.

"You often have nightmares. You cry and plead for someone to stop hurting you, and sometimes you even swing your arms. Then the next day, you seem to have no memory of it, so I don't bring it up." He took my hand. "I love you, but I think you're in some kind of pain that I can't help you with. I just want you to be happy. I think you need to see a doctor, maybe a psychiatrist."

I nodded. "Okay, I'll look into it." I didn't say much more. It wasn't a topic I wanted to discuss with Joey.

He kissed me goodbye. "I'll call you after I touch down in Cali."

Afterwards, I was shocked by what Joey said about my nightmares. I thought I was no longer having anxiety attacks, except for the one I had recently during our trip to Colorado, and I was certain that Joey didn't know about that. Prior to that, it had been months since I had experienced any visions of Ricky or Philip. I realized my anxiety attacks had shifted into nightmares. I was worried because I had no memories of these nightmares, and the last thing I wanted was for Joey to know about my molestation or my abusive relationship with Philip. I didn't want him to know how weak and broken I used to be. I didn't believe in psychotherapy, so I would rely on mind over matter to overcome my nightmares; it wasn't that serious. I was sure they would stop on their own.

As I drove home, I reflected on the time Joey and I had spent together and how it culminated into this relationship and how conflicted I felt. I cared for Joey, but I didn't feel that I loved him enough to marry him. I looked at my ring and thought about how beautiful it was, but I knew I would have to give it back. There was no way I could marry him. The eight-year age gap was problematic for me, plus the other bullshit that came with dating men, period, especially a professional athlete. On the other hand, I thought maybe he wasn't playing a game. After all, he was only thirty years old, and his behavior was actually typical of a young superstar athlete. Maybe I'd just enjoy the ride with Joey for however long it lasted. Perhaps, I didn't always need to have a firm plan for my life. Sometimes I could just go with the flow.

Later that night, Joey called and told me he loved me while we discussed me coming to San Francisco to visit him, since he could not leave while training was in session. I felt good about us and optimistic about what lay ahead.

As I lay in bed, I continued to vacillate about telling Gigi about my engagement. She knew I was dating Joey, but I had underplayed the seriousness of our relationship in my discussions with her. I called Gigi reluctantly and told her about my engagement. Initially, she didn't say anything; there was nothing but silence on the phone. I thought the call had dropped.

"Are you pregnant again?"

"No."

"Then what's the hurry this time?"

"There's no rush. We're probably going to wait until next year, since Joey wants an elaborate wedding."

"It seems too soon, but as long as you're happy, I'm happy, too. I hope I can meet him before the wedding."

"Of course you will. Don't worry, Gigi. I'm a grown woman. I was a child when I married Philip. I know how to be an adult in relationships now."

At least I hoped so. I could tell that Gigi was concerned about my sudden engagement. Her comment about meeting Joey was just so she could check him out before rendering her final opinion about him. But in true Gigi style, she tried to be supportive.

19

SEASON I OF THE GAME – THE SECOND HALF

Joey and I talked and texted daily whenever we could. Things seem to be going well until one Friday. That morning, we talked as usual, but then later that night I didn't hear from him. He didn't respond to my text messages either.

When I awoke Saturday morning, I called Joey again before I got out of bed, but he didn't answer. Finally, about an hour later, Joey called me back. He said he had gone out the previous night with a few of the guys and that he had been talking to the cleaning lady when I called earlier. He didn't sound like his usual talkative, playful, loving self. I also heard a woman's voice with a Latin accent in the background. When I inquired about the woman, he said it was the maid. I didn't believe him. I was sure it was Pilar, especially since she had recently given birth to her son and had posted pictures of him all over social media.

"Have you seen Pilar since you've been out there?"

He paused before answering. "No, I'm letting the lawyers handle the business with her. Don't be paranoid, babe. You're my fiancé, the woman I love and want to spend the rest of my life with. I told my teammates about us last night, and everyone is looking forward to meeting you."

This motherfucker is lying. He was back to playing his game. Nope, he never stopped. I had just lost sight of it. He had reeled me in. I felt angry and hurt. I had let my guard down. I started having flashbacks of Philip again. He was laughing at me. I kept seeing images of Joey, and then Philip's face would appear. I felt my breathing becoming labored, so I told Joey I had to go and that I would call him back later. I realized he had played his game so well, and now it was my turn. I wasn't sure just how or what I would do, but he would find out only when the shit hit the fan and he had lost.

Joey and I agreed that I would not come to California for a visit until training was over. He said he needed time to get focused and get in the zone for the season.

This proved to be a very trying time for us. Joey behaved differently towards me. He no longer seemed excited about our relationship. We texted each other daily, but our calls became fewer and fewer while the context of our discussions became mundane. Even though we were engaged, I felt like yesterdays' news, an ordinary girlfriend and not the future wife he had been excited about a few weeks earlier. I figured that at the rate we were going, we wouldn't last through Christmas, and the game would be over.

However, just when our relationship was on the brink of disaster, Joey pulled out all the stops to turn things around. Since he couldn't be with me on my birthday, he surprised me by arranging for Kem, a famous R&B singer from my hometown, to sing a few songs at my party, which Zoe was hosting. It didn't stop there. Joey also gave me a 38.6-carat tennis bracelet set in 18k white gold. Along with everyone else, I was speechless when Joey's personal assistant gave it to me. Knowing Joey, he had easily spent a small fortune on my bracelet.

However, the grand finale was when Joey Skyped in and sang happy birthday to me. He couldn't sing one bit, but to me, he sounded like Pavarotti. I loved the gifts that Joey gave me, but I loved his delivery even more. He never just gave me a simple wrapped gift. It was always accompanied with an over-the-top presentation. Joey said the "how" always trumped the "what." Joey's extravagance and generosity were not limited to me. He did this type of thing for his mother, his siblings, and his children.

While I was in the midst of enjoying my party, I couldn't help but notice through my peripheral vision that Marcus was grimacing at me. I knew he didn't want to be there, but Joey probably insisted that he come. When Marcus saw the bracelet, he just shook his head in disbelief. As much as he tried, he could not contain his anger. His face was contorted like he was having some type of muscular attack. A few minutes later, he left without saying goodbye.

Over the season, Joey invited me to several home games. On each trip, I usually stayed with him for about three days, and like clockwork, we would have an argument about Pilar. After the paternity results confirmed that Joey was indeed the father of Pilar's son, Aaron, he changed his mind about having a relationship with their child. When he told me about his change of heart, he said his conscience would not let him abandon his son. He would love Aaron as much as he loved his other two boys.

I could see that Pilar was already using Aaron to play games with Joey. Whenever I was in town, she conveniently disappeared or had a conflict with Joey that resulted in her refusal to let him see Aaron while I was there.

Even though Joey gave me a hellified apology gift—a new car and an oceanfront condo in Cape Cod—I was still uncomfortable with his co-parenting arrangement with Pilar. I told Joey that he should get a legal visitation agreement, but he insisted that they could work it out without going through the court. He always made excuses for her behavior, saying this was her first child and Aaron was only a baby and that's why she behaved as she did. He often made it seem like I was jealous and unreasonable for feeling as I did. The situation with Pilar was becoming a huge source of contention between us.

To make matters worse, with each of my visits to California, I noticed that there was increasingly more baby stuff in Joey's condo, as if the baby was living there. When I inquired about it, Joey always had an explanation. He wanted the baby to have everything he needed at his condo when he came for a visit. What bothered me most was when I found clothing that belonged to Pilar, such as a satin robe, blouses, and even panties, tucked in one of the drawers in Joey's bedroom. When I confronted him about it, he became upset and denied any knowledge of it. As usual, he always had some plausible explanation, such as they were probably mixed with the baby clothes she washed and left at his house. When I asked him why she couldn't drop the baby off instead of being part of the visits, he lost his temper.

"Come on, babe, you know the baby is only a few months old, and she's still nursing him. We've been over this numerous times. I thought you understood that this was only a temporary arrangement until Aaron's at least a year old."

We had similar arguments almost every time I visited him in California. The last argument we had while I was there became so heated that I cut my trip short, which led to our first of many breakups. Our breakups never lasted more than a week, because Joey never took them seriously. He called them "time outs" for me to cool off. He would usually lure me back by saying he needed me to make a public appearance with him somewhere, and then we were right back in the throes of our relationship.

Joey and I had started talking again after another one of our breakups over Pilar when he invited Zoe and me to attend his game in Seattle.

When we got to the stadium and made our way to our seats, to my surprise, Junior was sitting there.

"Hey, Mom," he said and then hugged me tight.

I began crying tears of joy.

Zoe smiled. "You two had better make up for good. I had to work very hard to coordinate this surprise for you."

After the game, I saw Joey briefly, since his team was flying right back to California.

He kissed me. "I told you I would help you fix things with your son. See? I never break my promises."

We hugged and said goodbye. Just when I thought Joey couldn't do anything to top my birthday party, he pulled off another breathtaking surprise. He kept his promise and brought my son back to me. I was slowly sinking in the sea of love into which Joey had pulled me.

Later that evening, Junior and I went to dinner. We didn't talk about the past or his behavior towards me. We made plans to visit each other and to talk or, in his case, text more often. From that day forward, Junior and I began communicating regularly. He never admitted it, but I think he missed me and had been suffering without me in his life as well.

During the flight home, I thought about Joey. I was feeling powerless in my relationship with him. With all his acts of kindness, it was difficult to keep my guard up. By now I was cooked. I was deeply in love with him, something I had not planned to let happen. As kind as Joey was to me and as much as he claimed to love me, I still questioned his sincerity. That little voice in my head would not go away. It kept saying, "Joey's feelings for you are not genuine. He's playing a game to make you love him so that he can have power over you to hurt you at his will. He's going to hurt you; he's going to try break you. You need to hurt him first before he hurts you." With these conflicting thoughts and emotions, I was so confused. I didn't know what direction to go where Joey was concerned. Whatever my decision, I could not and would not be hurt again.

Two weeks later, Gigi and I flew out to California on the final leg of her visit with me in Atlanta. She was going to meet Joey for the first time. After meeting Joey, she gave me a nod of approval. Her main concerns were all his baggage, primarily Pilar and their infant son. The only drawback of the trip was Joey's and my efforts to have some romantic time. Gigi had insomnia on Pacific Time and cleaned and cooked the whole time she was there, not to mention that she knocked on our bedroom door every hour.

As we were about to leave, Joey took my hand and whispered. "Gigi is always welcome to stay at the house in Atlanta, but if you ever bring her back to California, I'm putting her up in a hotel." He smiled and shook his head. "She's something else."

We both laughed.

I loved Joey, and he loved me. But once I returned to Atlanta, he returned to being Mr. NFL, and our relationship dialed down to his terms.

Joey and I barely survived our first football season together, but by the time it was over, he was back to the loving man I had met almost a year earlier. While it was unfortunate that his team didn't make it to the Super Bowl, it gave us more time together in Atlanta.

After spending the Christmas holidays with his two older sons, Joey surprised me with a two-week trip to Bora Bora. Then we flew straight to Saint Tropez on the French Riviera for another two weeks. Thankfully, the nature of my job provided me a great deal of latitude when it came to traveling. Socializing with celebrities was always an opportunity to bring in new clients for the firm. Of course, Joey's celebrity status on and off the field was more power for the cause. The partners in the firm reveled in the idea of me dating Joey. Perhaps, it had something to do with all the autographs and football memorabilia he signed and personal appearances he made with me at the partners' homes. It didn't matter though. I was glad to have the time for my extended weekends and extravagant vacations with Joey.

That was my Joey—kind, romantic, generous, and full of surprises. He really knew how to spoil me; not only with material gifts but also in the way that he treated me. He was very affectionate and attentive and had no problems with public displays of affection. He loved to hold hands, kiss, and hug, especially while we were on vacation, and I enjoyed the fact that the paparazzi was taking photos of us for the world, and especially Pilar, to see. Joey knew just how to get our relationship back on track, and I loved him even more for his efforts. In that month we spent together, I fell in love with him all over again. We did everything from fishing and partying on private yachts, diving, and swimming to lying around doing nothing but enjoying each other like beach bums. With the exception of having to submit to Joey's appetite for anal sex, our time together was perfect. When it was time to head home, I had forgotten about all the issues that had plagued our relationship. I even promised Joey that I would set a date and hire a wedding planner.

When we got back to Atlanta, things between Joey and I continued to proceed smoothly. I felt even closer to him and started to believe we could have a future together. Other aspects of my life were also going well, especially with Junior and me. Thanks to Joey and his NFL status, Junior and I were rebuilding our relationship. He visited me a few times and started calling me on a regular basis, sharing his life and college experience with me. It was starting to feel like a normal mother and son relationship. Life was good, but I still couldn't bring myself to set a wedding date or sell my condo, as Joey had requested. I wasn't sure why I was holding back. I loved Joey, and I couldn't imagine my life without him. But for some reason, I couldn't see the grand finale of marriage just yet.

Season two approached quickly. Just like the prior season, Joey was transitioning to Mr. NFL, a very different person from the man he was during the off-season. Football season did not strengthen our relationship; it only served to weaken it. It wasn't the bi-coastal logistics or his busy travel schedule. It was his attitude. When he was in Atlanta, he was a kind, sweet, humble, loving man, but during football season he was an arrogant bastard. To make matters worse, I knew he was secretly seeing Pilar and their baby. That's why he seldom flew me out to California.

Yes, I was Joey's public girlfriend, but there was something other than Aaron that kept him tied to Pilar. Perhaps it was because she liked anal sex more than I did. I let Joey make love to me in every orifice of my body, even though I hated it. He could tell I didn't enjoy it, but that didn't stop him from wanting it. We just didn't do it that often. I guess my sacrifice for him was not enough. He made it clear early on that his sexual needs had to be satisfied for us to have a relationship. He was not going to give me a pass on anything pertaining to sex. Although subtle, he reminded me of it constantly. I loved Joey, but I felt a lot of pressure to please him sexually. I knew Pilar was waiting in the wings, so I felt that if I made one slip-up, she would be right there to take my place. I also knew she would leverage Aaron in any way she could to get next to Joey. In my mind, she was a real threat to our relationship.

Because of social media and Joey's celebrity status, Pilar was becoming a constant fixture in our life. She had become even more bothersome to me than Marcus, particularly since Joey seemingly had developed a close co-parenting relationship with her. Over the spring and summer months, Joey frequently went to California without me to visit his son. His rationale for me not going with him was that it created too much drama, and his trips were strictly about Aaron. I didn't believe him, especially since Joey had become secretive and somewhat protective of Pilar. He would often do things for Pilar and their baby and never tell me about it, but I would find out eventually, because Pilar posted all her business on social media. While hurtful, Pilar's social media antics kept me informed of her interactions with Joey, which usually led to arguments between us. Joey's justification for not informing me about his activities with his son was always that he was trying to protect my feelings.

I knew our relationship was coming to a head when Joey refused to let me attend Aaron's christening. Joey made it seem like his christening was a small, informal event, and that's why he didn't want me there. However, I learned later that it was a very formal grandiose event attended by most of Joey's family, including his two older sons, Marcus, and a few of his other close friends. Of course, I found out all the details on social media the next day, which resulted in another breakup.

Joey and I reconciled again, but our relationship continued to be strained. It didn't help that my family, and our mutual friends, mostly other pro athlete couples, also thought Joey and Pilar were having an affair, and they assumed I was okay with it. It seemed that there were unspoken rules of engagement between athletes and their girlfriends. "Don't ask, don't tell," "Don't get caught," and "It's okay to screw a jump-off as long as you wear a condom," making it acceptable for them to cheat. But that was bullshit to me. I wasn't buying it, and I wasn't having it with Joey either. I made it very clear from the beginning that I wasn't signing up for a one-way monogamous relationship, especially when he demanded complete faithfulness from me. He said that wasn't his expectation, but his words didn't match his actions.

I continued to be plagued by Joey's co-parenting relationship with Pilar. Whenever I inquired about anything pertaining to her or Aaron, it irritated Joey. He would say I was insecure and paranoid. He would remind me that he loved me and was engaged to me. He asked me frequently why it was taking me so long to set a wedding date. "You have the prize. You will get all the benefits of a wife. You're the only one who really matters."

His efforts to reassure me only served to confirm my suspicions about him being unfaithful. I could have just walked away from him, but every time I tried to break up with him, he pulled me back in. The truth was that I had fallen in love with Joey, and I didn't know how or if I really wanted to let him go. In spite of our issues, I knew Joey loved me, too, and that's why he couldn't let me go either. But I still remained conflicted about my feelings, loving him one minute and hating him the next.

It seemed that the Pilar situation was going to become the deal breaker for us eventually. His relationship with her was starting to stress me out. He couldn't see that she was using their baby to get next to him. Her interest in him was not limited to co-parenting. That bitch was trying to get her ten carats from Joey, and she saw me as a minor obstacle in her plan. When I expressed my concerns, Joey dismissed them as imaginary. His responses only angered me further, igniting memories of Philip when he was having his affairs.

Sometimes, I felt like having an affair or creating a situation that appeared that way to make Joey jealous. I wanted him to know the anguish he caused me, but for some reason, it wasn't easy for me to fall back into my old life. Part of me wanted to give him one of Gigi's magic potions to make him love me the way I needed to be loved. The other part of me wanted to hurt him. I wanted him to know the pain he had caused me. I had only two options: wait patiently for opportunity to strike or do nothing and try to live happily with Joey.

Between Pilar and Marcus, I didn't know who was worse. Neither of them wanted to see Joey and me together. Pilar was nothing more than a modern day gold digger, so her motives were very clear. She wanted Joey's money and his celebrity lifestyle, especially since her so-called modeling and acting career was practically nonexistent. However, Marcus was quite another matter, and it was his relationship with Joey that was most disconcerting to me.

In his own twisted way, I knew Marcus cared about Joey, but I could never tell if he was protecting Joey's interests or his own interests. Marcus acted like he was the one who had nurtured Joey's talents and helped him make it to the NFL and rise to a superstar. It was as if Joey was the investment that had turned into a golden goose for him. As much as I wanted to dislike Marcus for the power and influence he held in Joey's life, I couldn't. Marcus only used the power he had over Joey because Joey gave it to him.

Recently, I had noticed Joey taking a stance for me with Marcus. However, other times it was like he was trying to please both of us. While I was certain that Joey and Marcus were not gay, their brotherhood was still convoluted to me. I knew my relationship with Joey would not stand a chance with Marcus hanging around. I needed to examine their relationship further to determine if I could learn to tolerate Marcus or if I had to figure out a way to get rid of him. As Gigi would say, one thing for certain, and two things for sure: I, and not Marcus, would be the one to determine the fate of my relationship with Joey.

20

THE TRUE HATER

From the first day that I met Joey, he talked about his friend Marcus. They had grown up together since kindergarten, attended the same high school and college, and both went on to be drafted into the NFL. However, that's where the similarities ended. Joey was a superstar quarterback in college and was a first round draft pick, while Marcus was a tight end and a seventh round pick. Marcus' football career was modest at best. He was traded around the NFL like a Saturday night whore. After a three-year stint in the league, Marcus retired, supposedly due to injury, and became a football coach at a small college in Georgia. However, leaving the NFL did not dampen Marcus' ego. He was still an arrogant show-off who thought he was God's gift to women and that his star shone brighter than it actually did.

Marcus and Joey had a true "bromance." They had a tight-knit social connection that was similar to women in the sense they talked on the phone almost daily and hung out together constantly. Marcus was also Joey's confidante. Joey sought advice from him frequently on matters regarding his personal and professional life. He trusted Marcus implicitly and valued his friendship like he was a blood related sibling. Marcus had the codes to Joey's home security gate and alarm system and free access to all of Joey's vehicles. They were even partners in a couple of small businesses.

Although Marcus was no longer in the NFL, it had no effect on their friendship. When it came to doing the guy thing, Marcus was right by Joey's side. If anyone ever spoke negatively about Joey or criticized him in any way, Marcus was there to defend him. He even got into a few physical altercations defending Joey's honor. For all intents and purposes, Marcus appeared to be a loyal devoted friend. He acted like he would risk his life for Joey if he had to, possibly die for him. Their close friendship was undeniable, and they were inseparable. They partied together, played golf together, traveled together, whored around together, and got into mischief together, the whole nine yards. They were as close as two heterosexual men could be. I knew that I would have to embrace Marcus, at least in the short term, to be a part of Joey's life.

From our initial meeting, it was obvious that Marcus was no fan of mine or of my relationship with Joey. Whenever we saw each other, he would make some type of rude comment. On numerous occasions, I thought about telling Joey about Marcus' behavior towards me, but I feared he wouldn't believe me. I had only been with Joey a short time, while Marcus had been with him a lifetime.

As time went on, my concerns about Marcus grew. I didn't trust Marcus and felt that he would betray Joey at the drop of a dime. Whenever I tried to express my concerns to Joey, he would dismiss them and say I just didn't understand Marcus. He thought I didn't like Marcus because he was living a playboy bachelor lifestyle. The situation with Marcus was made even more complicated because he was entwined in every aspect of Joey's life, even more so than me.

Marcus was a constant fixture in Joey's and my social life and in our relationship. He was sitting at the table or in a suite with us at almost every event we attended. I always felt uncomfortable around Marcus, but excluding him was not an option. Whenever we were at dinner with Marcus, I would order my signature drink, a vodka and cranberry martini, and he would say, "A perfect stuck-up drink for a stuck-up princess." Joey would make light of Marcus's comments, and didn't see anything wrong with them. I, on the other hand, was offended, but I didn't make a big deal out of it, because Joey would think I was overreacting. The truth was, I would have preferred to throw back a few shots of tequila whenever I was in the presence of Marcus just to stomach him, but that would not have been appropriate.

As I got to know Marcus better, it was clear that he did not share the same affection for Joey that Joey had for him. He was jealous of Joey, but whenever I tried to tell Joey about Marcus' true nature, he didn't believe me. The closer Joey and I became, the more Marcus seem to despise our relationship and me. His conversations with me were full of sarcasm; just like the nickname he called me frequently, "Stuck-up Princess." While being condescending to me in one breath, Marcus flirted with me constantly in the other. He often made snide comments about Joey behind his back, indicating that he was weak or a punk for being so kind and generous to people. Engaging in a subtle war of words was the type of interaction that occurred between Marcus and me whenever we were in the same space together.

At times, it felt like Marcus was in direct competition with me for Joey's attention. He also expected Joey to behave like he was still single even though Joey and I were engaged. He barely acknowledged our engagement, let alone showed any respect for it. On occasions when Joey canceled plans with Marcus, either to hang out with him separately or to participate in one of their boys' night only events, Marcus would get angry with me. He generally found a way to convey it to me, but he did it mostly behind Joey's back.

Both Marcus and Joey were expert marksmen, having won trophies in shooting competitions. They both owned rare and expensive guns and usually walked around strapped, like most Georgians. One of their shared passions was going to the gun range early Saturday mornings during the off-season. Of course, that changed once I entered the picture. Joey and I had started spending all of our weekends together, even on those days when he had his sons, which disappointed Marcus. Joey would still invite Marcus to join us in whatever we were doing, but he would decline, and then we wouldn't hear from him for a few days, as if his feelings were hurt and he was sulking somewhere. I found Marcus' behavior childish, but I didn't dare say anything about it to Joey.

Marcus and Joey had established a tradition of taking an annual hunting trip with some other male friends for the past few years. However, when it came time to confirm the logistics for the trip, Joey pulled out so we could spend more time together. When Joey told Marcus that he wasn't going, Marcus flipped out.

"Look at you, acting like a bitch for her already. Are you going to let Astrid run your life? This is how it starts. First, she tells you to cancel your trip with your boys, and then she starts telling you when you can and can't hang out. Man, you know how we do on this trip; we hunt, and then we party hard. I have some bad hoes coming up this time. It's a brand new crop, and they're fine as hell."

"Man, things are different for me now. I love Astrid. You know we're engaged, and when we get married, I intend to honor my vows and commitment to her. That means no other women, period."

"Well, you're not married now. Just stay engaged a few years, and we can still have our fun."

"Marcus, you don't get it? I love her; I don't need extra curriculum pussy anymore."

"What about Pilar?"

"She's just a baby mama and nothing more. There's nothing going on with us."

"Well, you can keep telling Astrid that, but I know better."

"Look, I don't want that lifestyle anymore. You need to accept that."

"Man, that bitch got you snowed. You've lost your mind."

"First of all, you need to stop calling her a bitch. "Her name is Astrid. You need to use her name when you address her, got it?"

Marcus was shocked by Joey's defense of me. He had never seen Joey react that way over a woman. He realized that Joey was serious about me and that it wasn't going to be that easy for him to get rid of me.

"Yeah, man," Marcus replied. "You know I meant no disrespect."

"I love her," Joey continued. "She's just as important to me as my sons. You're going to have to accept her. She's going to be around for a while; I hope forever."

When I saw Marcus later that afternoon, he went ballistic. He accused me of being deceitful and manipulative, which was why Joey had stopped hanging out with him and their other friends. He even accused me of being with Joey because of his money and celebrity status.

"I'm going to expose you for the thirsty fake whore you are, and then Joey's going to dump your ass like he's done to the rest of them," Marcus warned. "You're not fooling me. Don't forget, I was here before you, and I will be here long after all the Astrids come and go in Joey's life."

That's when I realized that Marcus saw me as a serious threat to his relationship with Joey. Our marriage would have far more implications than merely changing his social life. I was a risk to both Marcus's emotional and financial ties to Joey. While Marcus's identity was woven into Joey's life, his livelihood was dependent on it. But Marcus had it all wrong. Joey was the one pushing for the marriage, not me. While I loved Joey, I was still deeply confused about the future of our relationship.

I hated Marcus, but he was right. He had a special bond with Joey, and he probably outranked me, so I would have to be careful how I managed the dynamics of our relationship. I knew Joey would never cut Marcus off completely, not even for me.

Whenever Joey and I had a problem in our relationship, Marcus was the first to tell him to dump me. On numerous occasions, Marcus intimated to me that Joey and Pilar were still fooling around, and that's why Joey didn't want me visiting him often in California. Although I wanted a reliable source to provide me with information about what was going on with Pilar and Joey, I couldn't trust anything Marcus told me, because I knew he didn't want Joey and me to be together. Marcus would stop at nothing to get me out of Joey's life, even if he hurt Joey in the process.

It was common knowledge around our inner circle that Marcus had a private homemade porn collection; primarily starring him and the women he dated. He boasted about the professional high tech equipment that he owned, which cost him thousands. Joey had even commented on the high quality of Marcus's DVDs, claiming they looked like professional movies. I asked Joey if he was in any of Marcus's movies or if he had ever made any.

"No and never," he replied. "As much as I love you, I wouldn't want to make a sex film with us out of fear that it might get stolen. I also don't want a man jacking off looking at my girl or watching me make love to you. What I do with my woman sexually is private. It's between me and her only."

Every woman in Atlanta knew that if she slept with Marcus, she would likely be filmed with or without her permission. Rumor had it that Marcus had been sued several times over his so-called movie collection, but he settled those cases out of court. Marcus was one of Atlanta's foremost bachelors and was also known for having B&H parties at his house—parties where the only women on the guest list were paid by the hour. It was at these parties where Marcus often showed his friends his private porn movies.

I knew that if I ever wanted to hurt Joey, Marcus would be the perfect person to help me. Even sadder was that he would be happy to do it, because he was indeed the true hater.

21

SEASON II OF THE GAME

By the end of my second football season with Joey, our relationship continued to be strained. I knew Joey was still fucking Pilar. Even a blind man could see something was going on with them. During my last visit to see Joey in California, I found some pornographic pictures of Pilar that were date-stamped a month prior to my arrival. Most of the pictures were of her bending over, showing her large, wide-open anus. I guess that's why Joey liked her so much; she had a big asshole.

When I showed Joey the pictures, he swore he didn't know anything about them. He said that Pilar must have left them there intentionally so I would find them.

"I'm tired of arguing with you about her," he said. "You know I don't want her. She just happens to be the mother of my child."

I wasn't stupid. I knew that those long visits to see Aaron were not simply father and son bonding time. If Joey and Pilar's relationship was strictly about co-parenting, why did

Joey go out of his way to keep Pilar and me separate, and why was there drama with her whenever I came to California? Not to mention all the pictures she posted of them on social media, pictures of them looking like one big happy family. Although I tried to ignore it, I often felt embarrassed and humiliated by it. Of course, I had to deal with Gigi's constant negative comments about the situation—which ended frequently with her asking me, "Do you really want to marry a man with another family right under your nose?" Usually, I just ignored her and would never respond to her questions. I knew that no answer would be plausible.

The final straw for me was when I learned on social media that Joey had bought Pilar a house in an exclusive gated community just outside of Atlanta. When I confronted him about it, he explained that it was part of their settlement and he wanted all of his children to live in close proximity to him. That's why he had asked her to move to Atlanta. Not only would it be more convenient for him, it would lessen the strain on our relationship, because he wouldn't have to travel to the West Coast to see Aaron. He said he was waiting for the right time to tell me, but it was leaked to the media before he had a chance. That was bullshit. We both knew it was Pilar who leaked the news about her new home.

"I'm going to share this with you," he said. "I don't really trust Pilar to raise my son alone. My lawyer said that since Aaron's a baby, it will be easier to seek joint custody if we live in the same state, so that's why I persuaded her to move to Georgia, and for no other reason."

He tried to reassure me that it would not affect our relationship but I didn't buy it. I was in love with him, and he knew it, and now he was setting up his playground for three: him, Pilar, and me.

The news about Joey buying Pillar a house left me feeling betrayed. I had given him everything, and just like that, he tossed my feelings aside. I had yielded to all of his demands, indulged in all of his sexual fetishes no matter how disgusting or perverted. I even allowed him to debase me with his constant obsession with my rectum. During the off-season, at least once a week, he liked to give me an enema and then engage in some sort of scatophilia act with me. Even when he saw my apprehension and tears streaming down my face, it did nothing to sway his appetite. As much as these acts sickened me, I did them anyway, because I loved him, and making him happy made me happy, or so I thought. Contrary to what Abby said, pleasuring Joey's sexual needs and fantasies did not give me the power I was seeking. It actually made me feel weaker. I knew Joey loved me, but I realized that his love for me was far less than my love for him. The hurt was even worse for me, because I never intended to fall in love with him. In the end, he was just like Philip. He could love me, abuse me, and betray me all in the same breath. But this time, I wasn't going away quietly. I would destroy him first. I wanted to see how much pain he could endure, since he disseminated it so easily.

Football season ended, and Joey was spending most of his time in Atlanta once again. By then, our relationship was on a downward slide. We were off-and-on and had hit an impasse due to the three-ring circus he had created with Pilar. I was ready to call it quits, but Joey wouldn't give up. He kept coming back for more punishment, and I kept giving it to him. We were in the throes of a vicious cycle of break-up and make-up, which was turning me into an angry bitch. I was growing tired of him and knew just how to get rid of him permanently. When I was finished with him, he wouldn't know what hit him, except that the pain would knock him off his feet. When he regained his balance, I would acknowledge my parting gift and say goodbye forever. We would finally be free to go our separate ways. Little did I know how these words would come back to haunt me.

I decided to put my plan in motion at an upcoming party hosted by one of Atlanta's movie moguls. Atlanta's A-list would be there, including Joey and Marcus. Since I had been staying at my condo, I told Joey that I would meet him at the party. I planned to wear something really sexy that I knew Joey would want to peel off me. Of course, it wouldn't be anything black, since most women wore black to this event. I decided to wear the sexy red dress Joey had bought me recently. I really liked it. Its form-fitted design was definitely a head turner, a perfect display of my physical assets.

I arrived strategically late so that I could walk around and be seen. I finally found Joey huddled with Marcus and his usual crowd. I walked over and kissed him.

"Hey, beautiful," he whispered. "I can't wait to taste you tonight."

I smiled and started to walk away, making sure that Marcus knew I saw him starring at my voluptuous breasts and cantaloupe ass.

After I found my way downstairs to the restrooms, I texted Marcus and said I needed to talk to him about something. Just like the dog he was, he replied to me that he was on his way.

"What's going on with Joey?" I asked as soon as he arrived.

He shrugged. "I'm not sure. You know, sometimes a man doesn't know what he has until he loses it. But me, I'm not like that; I would never let a prize like you get away."

"Cut the bullshit," I replied. "We both know you've wanted to fuck me since we first met."

He laughed and was about to say something, but I interrupted him. "How about I let you get lucky tonight?"

He looked shocked, but he replied without hesitation. "Hell yeah!"

"Why don't you leave now, and then I'll meet you at your house in an hour."

"Cool," he replied. "I'll make it a night you won't ever forget."

I smiled. "Likewise."

Marcus would indeed play a major role in my plan to hurt Joey. I would hook up with him and make sure everyone knew it, including Joey. I knew that if I ever slept with Marcus, he would tape it, and Joey would see it and finally get a taste of his own pain. Our relationship would be over and done for good. He would be free to play with Pilar, and I would be free to go back to the life I had before I met him.

I went upstairs and found Joey sitting at our table. I could tell he wasn't happy with me.

"I don't know what's wrong with you lately," he said, "but I'm not going to put up with this shit much longer."

That was all I needed to start an argument with him so I could leave for Marcus' house.

"We wouldn't be in this place if you had kept your word," I replied. "You promised me that Pilar and your bastard son wouldn't be in the picture. But every time I turn around, she's on Twitter, Facebook, or Instagram posting pictures of the baby and the happy family."

"Look, how many times do I have to tell you that I don't want her?" he asked. "I'm sorry I couldn't turn my back on my son. My dad was there for me, and I have to be there for my boys too. I thought you understood that."

"We both know that Pilar has another agenda," I replied. "That bitch wants to take my place; she wants to be your wife."

"Well, don't let her," Joey replied. "Stop acting like you don't care about us anymore. You won't even set a wedding date."

"You're telling me 'don't let her'? You shouldn't let her. You should be the one protecting our relationship from her, but you can't do that when you're still fucking her." I stood up. "I'm leaving. Now you can go home and play with Pilar. I give up. She can take my place, and now you can have ass and shit twenty-four seven just the way you like it."

I walked briskly out of the ballroom to where the valet parking was located. Joey came up while I was waiting for my car.

"Don't do this," he said. "Come home with me, and let's fix this."

I shook my head. "I need some time to think. We can't keep doing this."

"I miss you," he said. "I need you."

I scoffed. "You don't miss me. You only want me to come over tonight so you can fuck me in my ass."

"Baby, don't do this. We need to stop this now."

I didn't respond as I stood there waiting for my car. A few minutes later, the valet pulled up.

"Tip the man, and I'll call you in a few days," I said. Then I got in my car and drove away.

When I pulled up at Marcus's house, I called and asked him to let me park my car in his garage in case Joey stopped by.

"Smart move," he said. "We don't want to get killed for having a little fun together."

When I walked in, Marcus was wearing only a robe.

"Here you go; it's your favorite drink, vodka and cranberry martini, right?"

I smiled. "The perfect drink for a stuck-up princess."

He didn't respond. He looked away momentarily as if he was slightly embarrassed.

"See? I pay attention to you all the time. That's how I know what you like."

"Make me another," I said as I walked toward his bedroom.

I looked around the room for the cameras, but they were well hidden. I didn't care. I wanted him to tape us having sex so he could show it to Joey. I took off my dress and laid it on a chair. Wearing nothing but my nude colored body-shaper, I sat on his bed, took off my shoes, and finished my drink.

Marcus came in the room and sat down next to me as he handed me my second drink. As I sipped it, he started kissing me, and then he stood me up and began rubbing my butt and making these exaggerated groping motions. I'm sure it was all for the camera effects.

He stood up and took off his robe, and he was butt ass naked and hard as a rock. "Now, take off your teddy—unless you want me to do it for you. I can't wait to taste that sweet pussy Joey's always bragging about." For some reason, once he mentioned Joey's name, my entire mood changed. At that moment, I thought about how much I loved Joey.

"I can't do this. I'm sorry; I need to go."

As I walked toward the chair, Marcus grabbed my arm. "Where do you think you're going? You can't leave me like this."

Suddenly, a familiar wave of fear came over me. I felt short of breath, and then I started having flashbacks of Ricky throwing me on the bed when I was a little girl. I saw images of him smiling and saying, "I told you I'd be back to finish what I started." I swung my arms, trying to pull away from Marcus, but I kept seeing Ricky's face instead.

"Please, let me go," I cried.

"Listen, you stuck-up bitch. You came here to get fucked, and you're going to leave here fucked. I'm going to give you the kind of fucking that your stuck-up ass deserves."

He pushed me down on the bed and climbed on top of me.

"So you're going to rape me?" I asked. "You're going to actually videotape yourself raping me? That should be a slam-dunk case. I think it carries a minimum of twenty-five years in Georgia."

I must have struck a nerve, because he stopped and pointed at the door. "Get the fuck out of here, and don't come back."

My heart was racing a thousand miles an hour. I was scared. I grabbed my dress, shoes, and purse and then ran to the garage and climbed into my car. Marcus opened the garage door as I was leaving.

"Bitch! You ain't shit! You're just like the rest of them."

I was glad to get out of there. I got out of my car at the end of Marcus' long, winding driveway, put on my dress, and then drove home. Once I got to my condo, I took a shower and then climbed into bed and cried in confusion, eventually falling asleep.

The next morning, I noticed that Joey had called and texted several times. I listened to him say repeatedly how much he loved me and to please call him. Finally, I called him back. He said he had stopped by my condo after I left the party, but the doorman said he hadn't seen me. He asked me where I went. I told him I had stopped by Zoe's house and had too much to drink so I spent the night at her house.

"I've been thinking about what you said about Pilar, and you're right," he said. "I'm the one who should be protecting our relationship from her. She's around us because of me, not you. I know how to fix this, but I can only do it if you're up to it. My attorney said I have a good case for joint custody. Thanks to Pilar's social media activity, we have ample proof that I am active in Aaron's life. So her efforts to humiliate you have only served to strengthen my case. A shared custody arrangement is the only way for us to have some control over the situation. She won't be able to use Aaron to run interference in our lives. Besides, she knows that joint custody is a prelude to full custody. Without my child support, she'll have to go back to waitressing, since her acting career hasn't taken off, and I know she doesn't want that. I know this isn't what you signed up for, but it's the only way for us to deal with Pilar. Don't worry, I'll hire a live-in nanny, but it will definitely change our lives. We could potentially become full-time parents.

"Please think about it," he continued. "I don't want to put any more on you than you can handle. I know how you love your freedom. I love you, and I want to spend the rest of my life with you. I'll do whatever it takes to make you happy. I'm sorry I come with this type of baggage, but I can make it up to you in other ways. Besides, you know that if I didn't already have these boys, you would have to give me children. You know I make big babies, and we both know you don't want anything large coming out down there."

That broke the ice. We both laughed.

"Fuck the big wedding," he said. "Let's go to Vegas next week and get married. I'm ready for us to quit playing these games and move on with our lives. I miss you, and I need you. Can't you see that?"

"You're right," I agreed. "It's time to stop playing games and get on with our lives. I love you, and I can't see my life without you in it. Besides, it's better for us to work on our problems together than apart. I'm down with whatever we need to do to keep us together."

"That's my girl," he said. "Now, baby, go run your errands and then bring your butt home to me for good when you finish. I mean it. I don't want you going back to your condo anymore. It's time for you to lease it or sell it. I want your driver's license to have my last name and address on it."

"Okay," I said. "Let's do it; we can elope. Fly to Vegas next week and get married. I love you."

After the call, I felt light and happy and excited about Joey again. For the first time since we started dating, I felt that I was finally ready to truly open my heart to him, to take a second chance on love. I was ready to risk it all for Joey. I would trust him implicitly. I would close all those doors I had opened to hurt Joey, starting with Marcus.

I sent Marcus a text: "I'm sorry for misleading you. It will never happen again. Please keep last night between us. I hope we can go back to just being friends."

He never responded.

I got dressed and met Zoe at the spa where we had our monthly girls spa day, which consisted of a deep tissue massage, a mani-pedi, a haircut, wash and style, wax and facial treatments, along with a few glasses of champagne. When we finished about five hours later, I noticed that Joey had called me several times and that he had also texted me

"911" a few times. I called him back immediately. He sounded shaken and upset.

"Where are you?" he asked. When I told him, he told me to stay there and he would come to me. "I need to talk to you right now."

The tone in Joey's voice had me worried. I had never heard him sound so upset. Whatever he needed to tell me was serious. I figured it had something to do with my son, Gigi, or some other close family member. Whatever it was, he wanted to tell me in person so that he could comfort me when he broke the news. He was kind and loving that way.

As Zoe and I left the spa, I told her about Joey's call. She said she hoped everything was okay and to call her later if I needed anything. Then she walked to her car, which was in the opposite direction of where I parked.

As I approached my car, Joey pulled in the parking lot and then slammed on his brakes. I heard the squeal of his brakes and smelled the burning rubber from his tires. He got out of the car and rushed towards me. As he got closer, I saw tears in his eyes.

"How could you do that to me?" he asked. Then he pulled out his gun and pointed it at me. I heard a loud blast, and just like that, it was over.

22

THE AFTERMATH

I woke up six weeks later in the hospital with Zoe and Val standing over me.

"Do you recognize me?" Zoe asked.

I nodded.

"Can you speak?"

"Yes, why wouldn't I be able to?"

I didn't know why I was in the hospital, and had no memory of the events that precipitated me being there.

"Where's Joey?"

She ignored my question.

"Gigi, your sisters, and Junior were all here when you were first hospitalized. Gigi had to go back to Detroit to take care of some things, but she's coming back," Val said. "Everyone took turns staying here so that at least one family member would be with you when you awoke." She kissed me on my forehead. "Girl, the whole world's been praying for you. You've been in a coma the last six weeks. I knew you would wake up. I felt in my heart that you weren't going to leave us right now."

"Where's Joey?" I asked again.

Val didn't know how to answer. Then Zoe stepped in. "Honey, there's no easy way to say this, but Joey's gone. He's dead."

An indescribable pain came over me, and then a river of tears came rushing down my face along with shivers and screams.

"No, it can't be true!"

I was so upset that my doctor sedated me. He was concerned about how the stress of Joey's death might affect my recovery.

Over the next few days, still heavily sedated, I was in a foggy conscious state, but I couldn't move or speak. All I could do was cry. Val and Zoe took turns giving me water and cleaning the dried tears from my face.

When I finally woke up again, Zoe was sitting on my bed holding my hands.

"Tell me what happened," I said.

"Are you sure you're ready?" she asked. "It's not a pretty story. I'm still in shock over everything that happened."

"Please, tell me everything. I need to know why I lost my Joey."

As Zoe told me the story of the events that led to that horrific day, I closed my eyes so that I could picture how everything unfolded. This is what she said.

The day Zoe and I had our spa day, Marcus had one of his tailgate cookouts prior to watching an NBA playoff game. Joey and I usually went to Marcus' cookouts, but I assumed this time we would skip it, because we were trying to mend our relationship. Unbeknownst to me, Marcus had called Joey earlier that morning to confirm we were attending, which was really a ploy to show Joey the sex tape and expose me as being THOT or something less in Joey's eyes, causing him to break up with me for good. Joey told him that we would not be able to make it, but he would stop by later for a few hours, because he had a special makeup date planned for me later that night.

Joey and Marcus continued their phone conversation in their usual bromance way. As Joey often did, he shared intimate details of our relationship, our problems and our happier times with Marcus. "Man, we're about to do this," Joey said, "make it official. I'm taking her to Vegas next week to get married. We can have a big wedding later. I need to put my last name on her now. She's not a THOT or one of those weave-wearing wanna-be model chicks. She's got her shit together. She's beautiful, intelligent and educated. She's got her own money—not like mine, of course, but she's doing okay."

"Dude," Marcus replied, "you can have any woman on this planet. I wouldn't marry anybody yet. Make them hoes wait. You don't have to be in a rush. She'll wait just like the rest of them with her snobby ass. She's okay, but how do you know something better isn't out there for you? Then you're going to end up like the rest of them, cheating on her and then giving up half your shit when she wants a divorce. But worse of all, she's almost ten years older than you. You're supposed to want young pussy, not old pussy. And in ten years, if you make it that long, you're going to be stuck with old ass pussy. Man, you're crazy, there's no way in the hell I would marry her stuck-up ass if I were you."

"Dude, hold up. You need chill out on the hate," Joey replied. "When you find a good woman, you'll know it, just like I know Astrid is the one for me. She doesn't care about this NFL shit. She just wants a good man. She's got my back twenty-four seven, and I got hers. If you learn how to treat women, maybe one day you'll find your own Astrid."

Marcus shook his head in disbelief. He couldn't understand why Joey felt that way about me. "I think you're moving too fast with her. I don't trust her. She's not the person you think she is. Just wait and see."

"Man, you're going to have to get some acceptance about Astrid and me," Joey said. "That's my girl. I love her, and we're getting married next week. I want you to be my best man, but I'll understand if you don't want to do it."

"It's all good," Marcus replied. "I'll be there. If you love her that much, then I'll welcome her into the family with open arms. Man, you know I got your back always. But make sure you get an ironclad pre-nup before you marry her, just in case."

They both laughed.

"We can talk more about Vegas and your impending nuptials when you get here," Marcus added.

By the time Joey arrived at Marcus' house, the other guests and couples were already there. The men were in the recreation room playing pool, watching the pre-game show, drinking beer, talking, and laughing the way they usually did at his gatherings. Then Marcus, true to form, mentioned the latest conquest that he taped. He told the guys that this tape was his best production to date.

"It's so good I could probably sell it for millions."

He went on to describe how he had sucked and fucked his co-star in every orifice on her body and how she sucked his dick so long that it was chafed. He said that he would definitely consider "wifing" her if she wasn't already engaged to someone else. He teased them about whether or not he would play the tape for them.

"I'd better not show it," he said, "because some of you might recognize her, and that's not cool." He laughed. "There are some freaks you need to keep private. This movie is fucking great. It's special. My dick gets hard just thinking about it. Hell, it might be Oscar-worthy because of my freaky co-star. She walks around like she got a stick up her ass, you know, like a stuck-up, snobby princess, because she's educated and shit. She's got most people fooled, but I know the truth about her. She's nothing more than a groupie whore like the rest of them."

By then, Joey had become increasingly curious about the sex tape, because he recalled several occasions on which Marcus referred to me as a stuck-up, snobby princess. Joey insisted that Marcus show them the tape, but Marcus kept taunting him.

"Man, you don't want to see it. I'll show you in private some time."

Joey became angry and raised his voice. "Man, stop talking shit. I want to see you fucking your stuck-up, snobby princess now."

The room became quiet, and everyone gathered in the billiard room. They could see this was turning into a showdown between Marcus and Joey. Marcus realized what he had set in motion and that he was heading down a path of no return. His ruse with this sex tape could cost him his friendship with Joey forever, which he didn't want to happen. Marcus attempted to reverse his antics, trying to laugh it off.

"Dude, I'm just playing around. There's no tape."

But Joey didn't buy it. He knew where Marcus kept his private homemade porn collection and that he labeled and organized them by dates. So he went to Marcus's study and looked through the most recent DVDs. Then he found the one dated from the day before, entitled, "The Stuck-up Princess."

Joey put the DVD in the player, and sure enough, it was Marcus and me, but he had edited the tape. It started off with me in Marcus's bedroom, sitting on his bed, sipping a drink, and wearing only my nude body-shaper with Marcus standing in front of me, wearing nothing but his bare ass. Then the tape showed Marcus pause and dim the lights further. This is the part where Marcus had spliced the tape he made of us, inserting part of another sex tape he made with another woman. The tape showed the woman performing fellatio on him while he stood in front of her and then showed them lying in the sixty-nine position, and other images of her performing fellatio on him, like it was her last supper. It ended with Marcus penetrating the woman from behind, with rough exaggerated thrusts. The quality of the edits was seamless and deliberate, such that it did not show a close-up of the woman's body or her face. Without any prior knowledge, it was obvious that the woman in the tape was the same woman from the beginning to the end. I was clearly the co-star in that movie. As everyone stood around quietly watching the tape, shaking their heads in horror and shock, no one said a word, not even to question the authenticity of the tape or to raise suspicion that it might have been edited from its original format. As Joey watched the movie, he just stood there stone-faced.

Then, without saying a word, Joey started to beat Marcus savagely, hitting him so hard that he fell to the floor. He continued to stomp Marcus until he was barely conscious and unable to move. But Joey didn't stop there. He picked up a pool cue and hit Marcus repeatedly across his head until the cue broke, spattering Marcus' blood all over the walls. The guys finally wrestled Joey away from Marcus. Joey got up and ran to his car. That's when he began texting and calling me. When I didn't respond, he drove to my condo and waited for me to return. A few hours passed, and he continued to patiently wait for me to get back to him. When I finally called him, that's when he came to the spa and shot me in the head before turning the gun on himself. Joey died at the scene, and Marcus died a week later from head trauma due to the severe beating he received.

Dr. Bolton, my neurologist, said that I was very lucky. The bullet only grazed the left side of my head. However, what was even more perplexing was the unknown cause of my comatose state. I did not have the type of head trauma or the usual complications that caused a person to go into a coma. The police said Joey probably did not want to kill me, because everyone knew he was an expert marksman, and he definitely knew where the kill zone was. He most likely grazed me with the bullet intentionally. Even in his deepest despair and anger, he loved me so much that he would rather die than kill me. I was responsible for the death of two people and for almost losing my life. How was I going to live with that, with all of the lives I had destroyed? Where would I go from there?

I stayed in the hospital another two weeks. Each day I cried and lay in bed except when the nurses made me get up and walk around. I wanted to be left alone in complete darkness. I wanted to close my eyes and never wake up. Occasionally, I would roll over and see images of both Philip and Ricky pacing in my room as if they were waiting for me to wake up. Each one saying, "Now I have you all to myself—come with me." But I had no strength to fight or scream. I didn't care anymore; they could do with me as they wished.

During that time, I was also vilified in the press as a Svengali, a cougar, and every negative name that described an older woman who dated younger men. The press made me sound as if I was a desperate, old, waitress who had a love triangle with two younger men, creating jealousy between them that ultimately led to their deaths. The press even alluded to the fact that I squandered Joey's money, convincing him to purchase vehicles, a condo, and vacation properties for me. Not once did they mention that I was a senior partner at one of the most prestigious law firms in this country. Never mind that my net worth was in the millions, and when did the age of forty become the new age of the senior citizen? Joey was a beloved NFL football player and considered a golden boy. Unlike a lot of professional athletes of his time, he had a spotless image and reputation. His star shone bright with the public, especially with children. I was the one responsible for putting out that sparkling light; it was as if I had actually killed Joey myself. As hard as the media was on me, it paled in comparison to how I felt about myself. They could never punish me harder than I could.

On the last day of my hospital stay, Dr. Bolton stopped by my room to say goodbye. He had a very pleasant bedside manner and was very kind to me. He could tell that while my head injury was recovering, my emotional state was still fragile. He gave me the business card for a psychotherapist.

"She's a colleague and a good friend," he said. "She's discrete and will honor your privacy. She will even come to your house if you can't go to her office." He leaned in close. "Listen, I'm not saying you're mentally disturbed, but you've had a very traumatic experience, physically and emotionally, and you need to heal your whole body in order to live a healthy life. I can take care of your physiological recovery, but you need someone more specialized to deal with your emotional recovery. Just give her a call and see what she has to say. It won't hurt anything. Goodbye. Stop by and say hello sometime."

As he was leaving my room, he paused at the door. "Oh, before I leave, do you do remember me? We met at a party once. It's been a while, almost two years ago. I gave you my business card. But anyway, that's neither here nor there. You know where to find me now."

While I was momentarily curious about what he said, that thought quickly faded in the sea of other things that were consuming my mind. I could not recall ever meeting him before my hospital stay, and I did not care to ponder it.

Later that morning, Zoe picked me up from the hospital and took me home. She arranged for us to use the delivery entrance to avoid the press, which was camped in the front of my condo. When I entered my condo, I noticed that Zoe had opened all the window shades and put fresh flowers in vases throughout the place. She had packed up all of Joey's things, including our photos, and placed them in a box in one of the spare bedrooms. She had planned to spend the night with me, but I insisted that she leave. She made me promise her that I wouldn't do anything to hurt myself and that I would call her if I needed her. After she left I closed all the shades and took all the flowers out of my bedroom and bathroom and climbed into bed, where I stayed the next few days.

After sleeping for what felt like a week straight, I finally decided to take a badly needed shower and get dressed, since Zoe was picking up Gigi from the airport that afternoon. Gigi was coming back to stay with me for a few weeks to help me get back on my feet. Truth was, I didn't want her to come down, but it wasn't like she had asked for an invitation. I didn't want to get back on my feet, I didn't want to think or do anything except sleep until it was time for me to die.

When Zoe and Gigi arrived, they came in with several grocery bags.

"You know we had to stop at the grocery store, because I knew you didn't have any real food here," Gigi said. "Last time I was here, you didn't have anything but butter and expired egg whites in that big fancy talking refrigerator of yours."

As I put the groceries away, Gigi went through the house and opened every window shade and a few windows throughout the condo.

"If you're not going outside, at least let some of the outside air in here," she said. "You got all this sunshine down here. You need to enjoy it."

Zoe made us mimosas, and then we sat in the great room catching up on the gossip that didn't pertain to me.

A few hours later, Zoe left, and I decided to go lie down and take a nap. That proved difficult, because Gigi kept disrupting me. Even though I had a weekly maid service, Gigi insisted on cleaning. She had a way of making herself feel at home anywhere. She had done the same thing when she visited me with Joey in California.

Later that evening, Gigi made me homemade soup and biscuits.

"Are you feeling okay?" she asked as she set the food tray on the bedside table.

"Yes," I replied.

"Then why are you lying around in bed so much?"

I didn't respond.

"Lying around isn't going to cure a broken heart or bring Joey back. God let you live for a reason. You can't stay in this room the rest of your life. You're going to have to rejoin the living. Get a good night's sleep," she said as she closed my door.

The next morning, I awoke to the smell of coffee and bacon frying. Gigi came into my room.

"Get up, 'cause we have a lot to do today."

I grabbed my robe and slippers and went into the kitchen and sat at the counter.

"I want to go to the grocery store, and then I want you to take me to the farmers' market," Gigi said.

"I can't leave the house right now with all the press hounding me," I replied.

"You can't hide in here forever. You have to get on with your life."

I started crying and ran into my bedroom and climbed into bed.

A few minutes later, Gigi came in with a warm towel and wiped the tears from my face. Then she climbed in bed with me and held me.

"You go ahead and cry as much as you need to today, but you had better dry it up by tomorrow. You have got to move on with your life."

"How can I move on when I'm responsible for the death of two people?" I asked. "I destroyed the love of my life. I'm a terrible person. Because of me, his kids will have to grow up without a father. You don't know all the terrible things I've done."

"Listen, I'm in my seventies, and I am no saint," Gigi said. "I've made mistakes. I've been hurt by people, and I've hurt people, too. My mother raised me in a whorehouse, and one of the patrons forced himself on me and made me pregnant with Di. After I was spoiled, I didn't think anyone would ever love me. I didn't think I deserved to be loved, so I became reckless. I used to party when I was young. I believe you all call it 'swinging' now. I've also done some things that only God and I know about, and I'm going to keep it that way. Nobody's perfect, but we're supposed to try to do better when we know better, but sometimes it's still difficult then."

I tried to explain how I played games with Joey, because I wanted to hurt him to get back at him for hurting me, but it backfired. I hurt him so deep that he snapped, and I lost him forever. Instead of me giving him a parting gift, he left me with one. By the time I realized how much I loved him and that he truly loved me, it was too late. How could I live with that?

"Babygirl, you hurt him because you were hurt. You were hurt long before you met Joey. I know that when you were a little girl, Ricky hurt you, just like some man hurt Di when she was a girl. But by the time I realized what happened to you, it was too late. The damage had been done, and you had moved on, just like Di did. I'm sorry I didn't protect you. Let me help you now. I don't want to fail you the way I failed your mother. If I had saved you from Ricky, then perhaps Philip might not have lured you into his web of misery for all those years. I knew Philip was abusive to you throughout your marriage, and so did the rest of the family. While you hid your physical scars, you couldn't hide the psychological scars. They were as noticeable as neon signs. But I wouldn't let anyone intervene, because you were so obsessed with trying to conceal the abuse. I realize now that I made a mistake by not getting involved."

I didn't respond. I sat there in shock as I realized that, all along, my family knew that Philip was abusing me. I wondered what other secrets they knew.

"Living with that kind of hurt can damage you and cause you to act out in ways that you're not even unaware of," Gigi continued. "You're no different than anyone else. Trust me, if you live long enough, people will hurt you, and you'll hurt people, too, whether deliberately or not. I can't erase the past, but let me help you get through this crisis and help you get rid of those shackles of destruction that Ricky and Philip have attached to you. I know you're dealing with the loss of Joey, but while you're trying to put Joey's death behind you, you have to put those other two tragedies behind you as well. Otherwise, this cycle will only repeat itself. There are doctors out there who can help you with this emotional turmoil in your life. You can always get counseling from the church if you don't want to see a doctor. I want you to take care of all this stuff now so you can live a normal, happy life. It's not too late. You're still young and beautiful. You have plenty of time to find love again."

Just when I thought I had escaped it, Gigi went on to give me her religious lecture. "Life is complicated. You know what they say, hurt people, hurt other people. That's just the way of the world. You're going to have to pray and ask God to forgive you, and then you need to forgive yourself. Don't forget, you're not in control of anything; God is. You don't know why things really unfolded the way they did. Things are not always as they appear. You don't know what burdens Joey was carrying. You don't know why God called Joey home so early, but I'm sure it wasn't to take him away from you. You need to trust God and have faith that he's handling everything. I know this is hard for you, but you'll get through it. God doesn't bring a crisis to you unless he's going to bring you through it."

While Gigi's words were heartfelt, they did nothing to soothe my pain. After Gigi left my room, I continued to cry throughout the night until I fell asleep.

The next morning, Gigi came into my room fully dressed. "Get up; I'm ready to go the store. Fix yourself up so that you look pretty. Put on one of those designer outfits you wear when you're going to one of those fancy ladies luncheons."

I tried to get out of bed, but I couldn't, so I just lay there. A few minutes later, Gigi came back and spoke to me in French using a very angry tone. The only words I could make out were, "obtenez votre cul maintenant," which meant, "Get your ass up now!"

I finally dragged myself out of bed and into the shower. I threw on a jogging suit, but Gigi took one look at me and shook her head.

"There's no way you're leaving the condo in those clothes."

After trying on a few different outfits, we finally agreed upon a navy blue khaki dress. Of course, I completed the outfit with my pewter color Chanel clutch and matching sandals. I pulled my hair back in a ponytail, put on a little soft makeup and a pair of sunglasses, and then we jumped in the white Aston Martin Joey had bought me, and off we went.

As Gigi and I attempted to run our errands, as expected, the press followed us everywhere. Against my wishes, we stopped at my favorite restaurant for lunch. I could tell people were staring and whispering about me, but surprisingly, a few older ladies came by our table and said things, like, "God bless you, my church was praying for you." Those kind words from strangers meant a lot to me. Although I wasn't looking for it, I needed the validation that the whole world didn't hate me. I still mattered to some people even though Joey was gone. We finished our lunch and then headed back home.

"I hope you can see that the entire world doesn't hate you," Gigi said as I drove. "Some people have sense. But sometimes it's easier to misplace blame than to accept the truth about people. You don't know what was really going on with Joey and his friend Marcus. It's not natural for two men to be that close."

"Please, Gigi, don't go there," I said. "I know what you're implying, and it's not true."

"I'm just saying their friendship could have exploded the way it did with or without you in the picture. Anyway, I don't want to keep talking about the past. It's just going to keep you in a sad, unhealthy place. We need to get you back on your feet so we can focus on your future."

"Yes, I guess you're right," I replied.

At some point, I needed to start thinking about my future, whatever that entailed. But first, I needed to learn how to get through the day before I could make plans for tomorrow, let alone my future.

"Oh, I forgot to tell you that that Pastor Jay is stopping by later," Gigi said.

"For what?"

"Nothing in particular; he just wants to talk to you."

"Why?"

"Look, don't be difficult. Just take a moment to talk to him; he might be able to help you."

"Help me with what?"

"Your grief. I don't know; just talk to him, please. Okay?"

I didn't want to upset Gigi any further, so I agreed reluctantly to talk to him.

Pastor Jay came over at about six that evening. After a few minutes of idle chitchat with Gigi and me, Gigi excused herself and left us alone sitting in my kitchen.

Pastor Jay went straight to the point. "I know you're still grieving about Joey, but how do you feel about his death and the role you think you played in it?"

I was shocked, because with the exception of me, no one really knew what happened, unless you believed one of the many rumors that were circulating.

"I feel guilty, like I pulled the trigger on the gun that killed Joey myself," I responded.

"Well, you didn't, and you can't blame yourself for a decision that he ultimately made. You know most people who commit suicide experience suffering for a significant period of time long before they actually attempt to hurt themselves. The underlying cause of a person's suicide is usually something much deeper than what appears on the surface. I don't want to spend time speculating or trying to understand why Joey did what he did. It's unfortunate, but we will never know the truth behind his decision. I would like to try to help you get beyond your grief and suffering though. Your mother is very worried about you. I think I can help you. A good place for us to start is with a few scriptures on forgiveness. That will help you deal with the guilt you're feeling."

I was thoroughly confused. How was forgiving anyone going to change anything or make my life better? I agreed to read the scriptures, but I knew they would not alleviate my pain. Nothing would. I was only meeting with Pastor Jay to placate Gigi, so I pretended go along and adhere to his suggestions. Little did I know this wouldn't be my last visit from Pastor Jay.

23

REDEMPTION

I had been out of the hospital for almost a month, but despite Gigi's efforts, I couldn't seem to shake off my depression. I still cried endlessly and wanted to crawl into bed and sleep until whenever. I missed Joey, and the pain and sorrow of losing him was debilitating. It felt like I had a knot in my stomach that churned and twisted all day. My pain became my constant companion, reminding me that it would always be with me, never subsiding. Part of me welcomed my new companion so that I wouldn't forget Joey. It also reminded me that I needed to punish myself for the game I played; the one that had resulted in the death of two people. During those times, Abby's words echoed in my ear, "Men can be very fragile. The same power and passion that makes them love you can also make them hurt you." I did not heed her words back then. I never thought they would apply to my life, but I had learned the hard way. My relationship with Joey was a fiery triangle. We had all the ingredients to ignite at any time, but I didn't know it. Our passion and love was full of all the heat and oxygen we needed, but it also had that third lethal component from outside agitators like Marcus and Pilar, making it combustible and creating the ramifications of where I stood, heartbroken and guilt-ridden.

On some days, the grief was so unbearable that it choked my semi-lifeless body, leaving me questioning whether or not I wanted to keep breathing. But Gigi always sensed when I was in this aphotic place and was right there to throw me a rescue line, pulling me back from the cliff's edge. Sometimes, she held me like an infant, squeezing me tight as if she was breathing life back into me, resuscitating my lifeless spirit, reminding me that the darkness I was in would subside one day and that I still had much to do in my life. I needed to keep fighting and hold on to fulfill my life's destiny. "Babygirl," she would whisper in my ear, "you got to hold on and fight back. You can't go out like this." Unfortunately, we would repeat this episode a few times without warning.

At times when Gigi was nagging me or if someone stopped by for a visit, I mustered up enough energy to pretend I was doing fine. If nothing else, I had become quite skilled at putting on a facade when necessary. While I could fool most people, I could never fool Gigi. She could always sense when something was wrong with me; she could read me like a newspaper. But this time was different. She knew that whatever was wrong with me was beyond her capacity to help.

Late one evening, Gigi and I were drinking herbal tea. I was lying on the sofa staring into space while she sat on the chair working on a crossword puzzle.

"Babygirl, I have something very important to talk to you about," she said, looking up from her puzzle. "I know you don't believe in psychotherapy, but I think you need to reconsider it. Everyone needs help sometimes, especially for ailments beyond our normal sphere. It's not a sign of weakness. If anything, it's a sign of courage and intelligence to get healthy using every resource available. I'm afraid that if you don't get professional help, you might not ever fully recover. You're going to be carrying around guilt and those two demon seeds with you the rest of your life. I know you're still tormented by memories of Ricky and Philip, and that's why you're still having those nightmares. I've had to come in your room several times during the middle of the night to wake you. You cry, yell, and swing your arms as if you're trying to fight off someone. Once you're awake, you seem to have no memory of the nightmare. Sometimes, I've heard you call their names. I can't help you with this."

I didn't say a word. I was shocked. This was the first time Gigi had mentioned my nightmares. "I guess you're right, I do need help."

It was hard to admit that I couldn't handle everything in my life and my efforts to do so had resulted in calamity. I always believed that only weak-minded or psychotic people needed professional counseling, and I certainly did not fall into either of those categories. But Gigi was right. I needed help to recover from all the baggage I was carrying. I was especially fearful of how Joey's death might exacerbate my anxiety attacks, so I swallowed my pride and started seeing the therapist that my neurologist had recommended.

Her name was Dr. Bina. She was very personable and not clinical in her approach, which made it easy for me to open up and talk to her. She also made it convenient for us to have our sessions by coming to my house once a week. For the first time in my life, I was revealing my purest emotional nakedness to someone. I had never done that before, not even for myself.

One of the things that Dr. Bina helped me to understand was how issues from my early childhood created a daisy chain effect on my entire life. My problems started once I learned that Di gave me to Gigi to raise, supposedly because she was not prepared for motherhood. Her complete absence from my life left a hole in my spirit, an emptiness that contributed to my fragile self-esteem. No matter how Gigi tried to polish and refine Di's story, it didn't lessen the pain of knowing I had been abandoned. I still felt worthless and inadequate, even though Gigi provided me with a loving surrogate family. Once I knew Di was my mother, I had a longing to know her, but Gigi refused to let me open that door. She would not allow me or anyone else to talk about her. But that did not dampen my thirst to know her—my mother, the person who created and birthed me. I was always curious about why she didn't fight harder to try to raise me and why she surrendered so easily back to the streets. While I was in graduate school, I tried to locate her, but it seemed as if she had fallen off the planet a few years after I was born. However, I did learn that she was incarcerated during the first seven months of her pregnancy, and that's how she was able to stop her drug use, otherwise she might have kept prostituting herself or either aborted or miscarried me.

My father's absence didn't seem to bother me as much, especially given that he could have been any of a hundred tricks. While growing up with a father would have allowed me to see the virtues of a man, my issue was much deeper. I needed something even more basic and intrinsic, a man who played the role of my protector. Although Gigi inundated us on a daily basis with the attributes of Big John, he had no effect on my life. He was merely a photograph, since he died before I was born. Further, since Gigi rarely dated or remarried, there were no other males around who could serve as a father figure in my life.

Although Gigi was able to protect us inside our home from would-be molesters, she failed to prepare us for the predators that lurked outside the home. The only warning she ever gave us was about forbidden and inappropriate touches from a boy or a man. She had no clue about the savvy seduction and manipulation of the pedophile, and that's how Ricky got to me. He presented many faces to me, as a friend, a big brother, a father figure, and, most importantly, a protector. He devastated me further by making me believe that, at eight years old, I was complicit in my own molestation, as if I wanted him to assault me. For a long time, I felt I could not reach out for help, because I had engaged in an intimate relationship with him willingly. Now that Ricky had violated his role as a protector, I had no one left to protect me. Now I needed protection from him. The incident left me carrying shame and fear on my shoulders, which deteriorated my self-esteem and robbed me of my innocence and my childhood. Even worse, it left me susceptible to more abuse in my adult life.

The same characteristics that lured me to Ricky drew me to Philip as well. Philip's nurturing qualities and constant concern for my safety were what attracted me to him. There again, I was drawn to the perception of a protector. However, once Philip revealed his true face, I felt overpowered by him and succumbed to his abuse. He created a fear in me such that I was afraid to leave him or challenge him. Just as there was no one to protect me from Ricky, there was no one to protect me from Philip.

In the end, Philip was just like Ricky, starting off as my friend and protector and then ultimately becoming my abuser. Both of them taught me a costly lesson that a man could care for me in one breath and destroy me in another. Because of my experience with those two individuals, I recognized that I had to start protecting myself. It was during this epiphany that I became confused about the role that power and sex played in relationships, which led to my defensive, offensive, and equally destructive behavior.

By the time I met Joey, I was damaged goods. We were doomed from the start, because unbeknownst to me, my PTSD was in full effect. From the moment he said hello, I had already made up my mind that our relationship would be short-lived and that it would end with him as the victim of a broken heart. But Joey caught me off guard with his love, kindness, and sweet serenity. While his sexual proclivities blurred the sex and power lines, I knew that deep inside, the love he had for me was real. I felt it in every fiber of my being. But my sickness would not let me see the purity of his love, so I played a treacherous game with him. By the time I realized his love was genuine and interminable, it was too late. Regardless of my efforts to thwart the wrong I set in motion, my actions resulted in the loss of two lives and altered the trajectory of so many others. There were no power and sex lines, unbalanced or even, in my relationship with Joey. I just didn't know it at the time. He loved as hard as he could without limits, and I should have done the same.

Against Dr. Bina's wishes, I stopped our therapy sessions after only three months. She was concerned that I had not completely resolved the issues surrounding my anxiety attacks. When she told me that I probably needed at least two years of therapy, and possibly psychotropic drugs, I decided it was time for me to find a new therapist. I thought two years of therapy was too much for any sane person. That length of time was needed for crazy people, not me. So what if I had a few hiccups in my life? That didn't make me crazy. It just made me another sad statistic on the victim list. I was temporarily depressed, but I wasn't crazy. There's a big difference between those two states of mind. Besides, any therapeutic treatment that required any mind-altering drugs stronger than my weed was unacceptable to me. That's where I drew the line. I would do some research on other therapeutic options and resume this therapy stuff later. I was done seeing shrinks for the moment.

Nonetheless, my time with Dr. Bina was well-spent. She helped me in many ways to understand and resolve many problematic areas of my life, even those areas that were foreign to me, such as being married to a closet homosexual and not noticing how profound the effect was on me. She also helped me to confront issues in my past that were keeping me from having a healthy relationship with a man. I was able to acknowledge my emotional voids and wounds, thereby allowing me to end my cycle of "hurt people hurt people." I was like so many people today, walking around clueless and asymptomatic of their mental health ailments. I was sick, but I didn't know it. I was a ticking time bomb. There's no telling how much destruction I could have caused in the midst of dispensing my wrath of pain and deception.

In parallel with Dr. Bina, I continued to see Pastor Jay as well. Later, I learned that without my knowledge, Gigi had arranged for Pastor Jay to aid in my recovery. He said that Gigi called repeatedly and wrote letters pleading for his help while I was hospitalized. When the doctors told Gigi there was no medical explanation as to why I was in a coma, that's when she became frightened. She thought that the traumatic events of my life had finally collided, sending me into some kind of self-induced coma, as if I wanted to retreat from life. She was worried that I might suffer a psychotic breakdown, or even worse, need long-term care in a psychiatric facility. Gigi had become quite religious in her later years and developed a strong belief in spiritual healing. She felt I was in desperate need of it, which is why she sought help from Pastor Jay.

Among my many discussions with Pastor Jay, I struggled constantly with the virtues of forgiveness. He explained that forgiveness was more than merely flipping a switch and saying the words. It required an absolute, time-bound follow-through commitment. It took me a few sessions before I grasped his definition of forgiveness, but I got it eventually. I also realized how crucial it was to have forgiveness in my life's toolbox. Without it, I could find myself standing in emotional quicksand, unable to move forward with my life. Over time, Pastor Jay convinced me that I needed to forgive a lot of people in my life, primarily Gigi, Di, Ricky, and Philip for their role in hurting me. I also needed to forgive myself for my wrongful deeds. I promised to do just that.

While Dr. Bina had given me the psychological treatment I needed, Pastor Jay provided me with spiritual healing. Their combined efforts helped to rebuild my strength, laying the foundation to the path forward in my life. I was a long way from feeling perfect, but I was in a much better place. I still cried each morning when I awoke and each night before I went to sleep, tortured by thoughts of Joey and my role in his death. But with each passing day, the pain lessened, and my memories shifted toward the love and happiness that we shared while the other painful memories became more distant, far off in a hazy fog.

I would always have regrets and guilt about Joey and even Marcus, but I would not let that define my future. My life would be filled with joy and pain, success and failure, lies and deceptions, and hurts and mistakes, but also redemption based on living and breathing on life's terms. I would step out in faith and try to be the best person I could be. That's all that I or anyone else could do.

Now that I was feeling better, I was ready to put the pieces of my life together, hour by hour, day by day. Thanks to Burke's public relations firm, the attention from the press had dissipated, and we had successfully countered most of the negative publicity I had received. My image and integrity was being restored gradually, which was paramount in my profession. I was inching forward, checking off all the items on my list that were necessary for a complete revival of my life.

I was feeling content and looking forward to going back to work. That sense of dread that had been my bedside companion for so long had finally disappeared. I was settling back into my old routine of starting my day with a cup of coffee while I scanned the Wall Street Journal. I even started going to the fitness center in my building a few mornings each week. However, my feelings shifted quickly to apprehension when I received the mystery package.

I had just returned from the gym when the bellman called and said that a courier service had a package for me and that I was the only person who could sign for it. I was startled, wondering who was sending me a certified package.

I rushed down to the lobby with my identification and signed for it. As I walked back to my condo looking at the package, I felt extremely nervous. I knew the contents had to be very important. As a lawyer, I used legal courier services often, and I understood the circumstances that necessitated using them, which was usually not good news for the recipient.

I was anxious to open the package, so I went straight into the kitchen, where Gigi was sitting. When I opened the box, it contained a yellow legal-sized envelope from Burke. That was a bit surprising, because Burke or someone from his office usually notified me in advance when they were sending documents to me. What puzzled me even more was when I noticed how secure the envelope was taped. It was sealed with the type of clear tape used for packing and shipping boxes and then wrapped again with red confidential tape.

"What's that?" Gigi asked. "It looks mighty important to be wrapped up like that. Did you check to make sure it doesn't contain anthrax or a bomb? You know there are some crazy folks out there."

"Relax, Gigi, it's not a bomb or anything deadly," I said.

Despite my words, Gigi continued to stare at the envelope. She could be very nosey at times.

I grabbed a pair of scissors and took the package into my bedroom and closed the door. After opening the envelope, I saw a smaller, white letter-sized envelope inside marked "Read First" and a couple of other smaller yellow envelopes. The letter read, "Here's a little gift on behalf of the Atlanta PD. It's always good in my profession to have friends at the police department. Not to mention, you've got quite an impressive network of friends and associates, too. By the way, your friend Zoe is something else; she risked a lot to help you. You're lucky to have a friend like her.

"You will find the contents of the yellow envelopes most important. I think these are all the originals and copies, so you don't have to worry about these getting into the wrong hands. I'm sending them to you, as I thought you would appreciate the opportunity to destroy them yourself. I'll be in touch soon. Take care."

My eyes shifted to the small yellow envelopes. I opened the first envelope. Inside were six DVDs entitled, "The Stuck-up Princess," and then there was a tiny cassette tape from the video recorder and a flash drive. Wow, I thought, Marcus was really planning to make copies to sell or give to whomever for some devious purpose. I wondered briefly, despite his hatred for me, how he could hurt Joey that way, especially since he claimed to care about him. But then I remembered, Marcus loved Marcus first and foremost. He was just like Philip when it came to dispensing his wrath. He could see only his target and the pain he would inflict on it. He didn't care about the collateral damage even if it ricocheted onto him, because he was a true hater.

As I sat on my bed, I realized Burke had really saved my ass. That's why he charged such exorbitant fees for his services. But I could see now that he was worth every penny. Not only did he clean up the mess, he thoroughly sanitized it to make sure there were no loose ends and nothing came back to bite his clients later.

With everything I was going through, I had forgotten about the sex tape that Marcus made with him and me. Now that I was thinking about it, it was strange that with all the press that covered the incident between Joey and me, there was no mention of the sex tape. I assumed one of Joey's "real friends" must have destroyed it in order not to scandalize the situation even further. I never gave a second thought about the possibility of being blackmailed or that the tape could have been leaked to the media to embarrass me further and malign my character. This tape could have ruined my career indefinitely. Having a positive image and integrity were essential in my profession. I would starve without it.

I stared at the DVDs for a few minutes, wondering whether or not I should watch them. My initial thought was that I shouldn't, and that watching it would dignify it somehow. But my curiosity got the best of me.

I put one of the DVDs in my Blu-Ray player and pushed play. The movie began just like a real movie with intro credits and background music. Joey was right; Marcus was a professional when it came to making his home movies. As the film progressed, it was just as I had imagined it, sexually XXX with flawless editing. Seeing the DVD made me feel angry, especially because it was a lie, albeit very convincing.

No wonder Joey flipped out when he saw it. I could imagine the hurt and betrayal he felt at that moment when he thought he was seeing Marcus and me having sex; two people he trusted and loved. I started crying as I thought about my Joey. Then I thought about Marcus. He was a selfish, uncaring asshole, and he got exactly what he deserved.

After a few minutes, I calmed down, and something in my spirit wouldn't let me stay angry or hate Marcus. I realized that despite his ugliness, he didn't deserve to die the way he did. Just like me, he tried to hurt someone he loved, and it got out of control. He was probably hurt too, carrying baggage like me that caused him to act out as he did. But now we would never know the reasons for his actions. All we knew was that Marcus had made his last sex tape, and it cost him his life.

It was time to destroy the DVDs. I took a hammer and crushed them into tiny pieces. Even though I broke my garbage disposal trying to mulch the broken DVD pieces, it was worth it for my piece of mind. I also pulled the tape out of the mini cassette and cut it up into small pieces and flushed it down the toilet. The remnants of the sex tape were gone. Now, I could move on and not worry about the sex tape resurfacing and wreaking further havoc on my life.

The following day I received an unexpected visitor. I had made Gigi promise me to not let anyone visit me until I was feeling better, especially my siblings and Junior. While my family and friends respected my requests, Junior obviously felt different. But I didn't mind. When the doorman said he was downstairs, I felt happy immediately. Of course, he and Gigi were in cahoots together with his surprise visit. I think Gigi was happier than I was to see Junior. She was used to having lots of company in Detroit, which was a far cry from how we were living in Atlanta.

Around nightfall, Junior and I went down to the terrace to catch a breeze and look at the skyline.

"Mom, I'm sorry about what happened to Joey. I really liked him. He was a cool guy. How are you really doing? Gigi says you seem to be doing much better."

"Yes, I am doing better. I still have bad days occasionally, but they say that's a normal part of grieving. How have you been?"

"I'm good. I've been worried about you, dealing with your injury and all that stuff the media has been saying about you. I know it's not true."

I didn't respond. A few minutes later, he pulled out two white envelopes.

"Here. I think you might want these. I found them sitting on the table when you passed out."

They were the missing letters that I had written a few years earlier when I was going through my divorce that were addressed to both him and Deana. I was shocked. He was the last person I thought would have taken the letters.

"Once I read the letter addressed to me, I knew you were in deep despair. I didn't know what to do. Since you and Dad were really going at it back then, I didn't want him to find the letters and use them against you, so I took them. I know you were just blowing off steam. I didn't believe you would really hurt Dad anyway. Mom, I hope you never become so sad that you want to hurt yourself again. I don't want to lose my mom again."

At first, I didn't say a word as tears streamed down my face. I reached over and hugged him. "I'm okay; you don't have to worry about losing me. I plan to be around until I'm a hundred years old."

As I continued hugging Junior, Philip appeared standing in the background with a smirk on his face, reminding me that he would always be in my life. I closed my eyes, trying not to freak out in front of Junior. Then the voice in my head said, "There's only one way to get rid of him, and you need to take care of Ricky while you're at it. That's the only way you'll ever be free from them."

When I opened my eyes, Philip was gone.

Junior and I went back to my condo and went to bed. That night, I found it difficult to sleep. For some reason, the little voice in my head would not shut up. It kept saying that I had to get rid of Philip and Ricky. I tried to ignore it, but it wouldn't stop talking. I finally took two Ambien and fell asleep.

When I awoke late the next morning, Junior was already gone. I forgot that he had an early flight back to DC.

24

THE KOKURAN

Gigi and I had settled into a routine of ending our day by sipping herbal tea and talking about her garden and its exotic flowers. One particular night, she talked about her orchids and their alluring beauty.

"You know, orchids have always been my favorite flower since I was a child, and that's why my garden is full of them today. The orchid is like us. If you look at it closely, it looks just like a woman's vagina. The anatomy of its beauty is analogous to us. It has lips and a clitoris, too."

I laughed and shook my head, because Gigi always had sex on the brain, even in her seventies.

"You know, you're like one of the orchids in the Liparis Nervosa species, the Kokuran."

I didn't respond, but she could tell by my facial expression that I was puzzled by her remark. She went on to explain the meaning and significance of the Kokuran. It literally means "black orchid" in Japanese. There are all kinds of legends and myths about the black orchid. Some people associate the black orchid with evil and death because of its color. For many people though, it symbolizes many positive things such as fertility, ecstasy, mysterious beauty, power, authority, and submission.

"We don't have to talk about fertility and ecstasy because you got my blood running through your veins, so I already know you're a firecracker in bed," Gigi said. "The one thing I know for sure is that I gave all of my girls a hot, juicy coochie, and Lord knows it's a blessing and a curse." She smiled. "Mine is still hot today. That's why I had to buy one of those things. I only use it every now and then."

"Quit it, Gigi, you're too old to be talking like that," I said, laughing.

"When you're my age, you're still going to have those feelings; just wait and see."

We both laughed, and then she became serious again. "Look at you; you're like the Kokuran. You're a mysterious, beautiful woman who commands authority and great power. Your looks alone are mysterious. No one can tell your true ethnicity simply by looking at you. If I had not been in the delivery room when you were born, I would not think you belonged to us. You have those blue eyes, blond hair and other European features. It's a shame that Di didn't have a clue about your real father.

"Your intelligence and distinctive beauty give you 'pretty privileges'. In this country, doors open wider for attractive people, providing greater access to opportunities and a foundation to develop or inherit various types of power. I know it sounds ugly, but it's the truth. Your appearance throws people off. They don't know how to identify with you. This gives you an upper hand when dealing with them. You can take the lead and be preemptive with any task at hand.

You also have the advantage of being able to choose whichever world you want to play in. You can check one or multiple ethnic boxes based on your ancestry, whether it's your European, Native American, African, or Creole roots. But you've always been smart when it came to matters like this. That's how you were able to obtain scholarships to afford that fancy education so that you could become successful like you are today.

"I thought Di was high on drugs when she named you Astrid, but she wasn't high at all. Your name means beautiful goddess, divine strength, and godly strength. People with your name are great leaders who obtain power and wealth. That's you; that's who you are. I believe it was Di's maternal instincts that gave her insight as to the person you would become—beautiful, intelligent, strong, and bold. Your accomplishments are a testament to those attributes.

"You have a quiet strength that's unpretentious but razor-sharp and as strong as tungsten steel. You are a true survivor. You never let your hardships stop you from pursuing your goals or your dreams. As a little girl, you were victimized, but you didn't crumble. You stayed the course and found a legitimate way out of the Gardens, getting a scholarship to Brookhaven and then to all those Ivy League colleges. You were only eighteen, still a baby yourself, when you married Philip and had a child and still somehow managed to complete your college education. Even though Philip, with all of his ugliness and unnatural ways, tried to break your spirit, you held your family together and remained a good mother to your son, sacrificing beyond the limits of any normal person. Through all that adversity, you went on to achieve great success and professional accolades. It was your strength that allowed you to confront and overcome the impediments in your life, and it is that same strength that will carry you forward.

"You're a natural leader, brilliant and accomplished, as if you came from a lineage of those kinds of people. No one can tell that you grew up in the Gardens. You have excelled at everything in spite of your circumstances. Although you were shy while attending Brookhaven, your classmates recognized there was something special about you, nominating you for several key positions, captain or leader of this organization, club, team, and so forth, and the same thing carried over into your college years and adult social life. People respect and trust you. That's why they follow your lead and submit to your authority. Why do you think you were the youngest person among the highest ranked executives in your company? It's not just because you're smart. You have that X factor that makes you different and gives you an edge over other people. Just as the Kokuran stands apart from other orchid species, so do you. You are so much more than you know. Girl! You need to recognize your own greatness."

Gigi was always full of words of wisdom, but I didn't know if her affirmations of me were biased because of her motherly love. While I wanted to believe I had all those wonderful traits, they were not readily discernable to me. Like anyone, when faced with an obstacle or in the midst of a crisis, I did whatever was necessary to overcome it. This is when we draw on those resources in our life's toolbox that enable us to fight or flee.

We all have skills and attributes that we acquire along the way or receive in utero that lie dormant until triggered into action. It's the latter that makes us unique and is a determining factor in how far we travel through life. The key is whether or not someone is smart enough to use his or her passive attributes when they are released.

In my case, I never hesitated. I always trusted and believed that I could overcome anything and had the fortitude to use whatever resources were at my disposal. I was born with a characteristic of being instinctively resourceful. Yes, I was gifted at birth with those unique traits, which gave me the strength I needed to navigate my passage through the stormy seas and rough terrain of life, but I am no different than anyone else. We all are blessed with unique survival traits. Some of us just get lost along the way, taking the left road instead of the right road, which can manifest into undesirable consequences. I would continue to stay the course, using all the resources at my disposal and keeping faith that I would always prevail over the obstacles in my life.

While I was finally comfortable knowing the depth of my power and the strength of my character, I was still uncertain about the correlation between sex and power in intimate relationships. This lingering uncertainty had nothing to do with my sexuality or self-esteem, because both were now intact. I had matured and evolved sexually, released my inhibitions, and allowed myself the freedom to conquer all my sexual fears and curiosities. However, I still struggled with the dichotomy between sex and power. I knew there had to be a perfect scenario that provided a delicate balance between them, but I couldn't see it. I needed to get an understanding so that I could stop playing games to avoid getting hurt in relationships. I recognized that my obsession and beliefs about the linkages between sex and power were grossly distorted. The major source of my confusion stemmed from traumatic events in my life with a common theme, having to do with a man who was an important figure to me. These experiences left me feeling weak and powerless, like a victim. Naturally, I concluded that there were two roles in a relationship—the victor and victim. To stop being victimized, I felt I had to dominate and hold the power in the relationship. I had to flip the script and use my sexuality to derive my power. I believed this wholeheartedly. After all, it had already been confirmed through my life experiences.

It started with my conception, which resulted from a simple business transaction—an act of prostitution. These circumstances left me without my biological parents and a sense of abandonment. While adopted and loved by my maternal grandmother, I still yearned for the real or imaginary love of my biological parents. But that would never be, as my parents were merely the reproductive vessels that created me. Of course, if the story is true that a man, Di's boyfriend, tricked her into using heroin just to gain power over her for his financial gain by becoming her pimp, then Di's boyfriend used sex and drugs to exert power over her in their relationship, thus making her the victim. There again is the linkage between sex and power.

The molestation I experienced from Ricky was my introduction to the triangular effect of sex, manipulation and power. Ricky sensed my hunger for a father-like figure, and he used it to prey on me. Ricky used emotions to lure me into his web of deception, which gave him power to assault me, thus making me a victim. To make matters worse, Ricky planted a fear in me, creating a belief that all males wanted sex and would take it if necessary. This fear robbed me from experiencing normal pubescent interaction with males and stunted my development into a woman. There again was the linkage between sex and power.

The icing on the cake, the crème de la crème, was none other than Philip, my prince charming and beloved husband. He was supposed to be the one who made life wonderful for me, erasing the pain and misery of Ricky and the hurt from Di's absence from my life, but he didn't. He waged the ultimate war on my spirit. I loved and trusted him and gave myself freely to him. I was open to any and everything he wanted. But instead of cherishing me, he tried to break me for the purpose of masking what he could not accept about himself—his homosexuality. My youth and inexperience was perfect in his quest to hide his flaws and imperfections. Due to my naiveté, I never saw it coming. I was the perfect victim. He caught me while I was young, dumb, and still chewing bubble gum. Philip was the most evil and methodical of them all. He derived his power over me by seizing my soul, dangling my child over a cliff, and leveraging a mother's love for her child. Through sex, we created a child together, which became his ultimate weapon to exert control over me. There again the linkage between sex and power.

Through those experiences, I learned that there was always a power play in relationships and there was never a healthy balance. The person with the upper hand was usually the victor while the other person was merely a victim. Therefore, since sex was always used in these entanglements, I would have to leverage that which gave me my sexual power, that thing his testosterone craved, that thing he could only get from her—the jewel of her soul that protected her pearl. Hence, I could be successful in my endeavor because I held the true source of this power. But it wasn't quite that simple, there was more to be revealed. While the prowess of a woman's sexual anatomy gave her power, it was in a different context from my initial thinking. I thought I needed to have sexual power in order to have control in the relationship. I went as far as to think I could use this power to manipulate and abuse a man if I so desired. I'm not sure how I postulated that idea, perhaps it was part of my sickness.

To the contrary, I learned through my relationship with Joey that I could have a normal, healthy relationship with a man without feeling like I needed to conquer him sexually in order to feel empowered and balanced. Sustainable power is freely given, not taken, and that's the only way you can have it in a healthy relationship. I finally understood that I could submit to a man without sacrificing formidable boundaries to please him and still have the connection I desired. Sex had nothing to do with my power or my feelings of being powerless in intimate relationships. A woman's real power is derived from within, not from threats, dependencies, or leverage over others. It is truly a sublime supernatural characteristic. We all have it, but many of us don't recognize it or know how to use it. So, in the end, I realized that there could be a healthy imperfect balance between sex and power in an intimate relationship. But it had to be based on the terms and limits set by each couple within the context of their relationship as long as each person's inputs were given freely.

By then, I was on the upside of my recovery. My mind, body, and soul felt whole again. For the first time in a very long time, I felt safe and normal. I didn't feel worried, scared or nervous about anything, nor did I have anything to prove, not even to myself. I was finally ready to re-join the living, as Gigi would say. After being off work for almost six months, I finally made arrangements to return. I would have gone back sooner, but my firm kept trying to force me to accept a promotion to an undesirable location. However, thanks to

Burke and his team, my firm quashed all conversations about me relocating to another office. In fact, they rolled out a red carpet for my return. I don't know what Burke did or how he did it, but I was glad it worked out in my favor.

That Monday morning, my first day back, I felt anxious, like a small child going to school for the first time. I must have changed clothes at least five times before I settled on the right outfit, because one thing was certain, all eyes would be on me. But then as I sat in the chair putting on my Louboutin pumps, I paused and realized stares and glares were nothing new for me. It had been that way since I was a child growing up in the Gardens. I had no reason to be nervous; this was just another day for me. After digesting that moment of clarity, I was pretty much dressed and ready to go, but I needed to give myself one more look over. I went back into my bathroom where I had a full-length mirror to check my attire. I smiled and then stepped back and thought to myself, I liked what I saw. I still had my swag. Maybe one day I would muster up enough courage to stop by the hospital to see Doc again. And then that little voice inside my head said, "But this time we're going to take care of Philip and Ricky for good. Don't worry, I'm not going away, we will revisit this matter later." I simply ignored the voice, knowing it would subside eventually like my other ailments.

As I applied a few minor touch-ups to my makeup, I stopped dead in my tracks and stared at the mirror. I saw the real me for the first time in a long time. I saw the woman I was before I met Philip, the woman who had survived a childhood rape, the woman who had pulled herself out of poverty, the woman who had survived an abusive marriage, the woman who had beaten cancer, and now a woman who had known the loss of a great love. I was a strong woman.

More importantly, I was a strong person and a true survivor. At that moment, I felt that I had the courage to confront life in all its glory. Whatever it was, I could play the cards dealt to me, I would know when to hold and when to fold. After all, I was a living proof that someone could survive catastrophic events and still flourish beautifully, like the orchids bloom and propagate in their natural and foreign environments.

All along, my exterior was a reflection of my interior being. They were, in essence, one and the same. Just as my name Astrid implied, I was divine and full of strength. I had spent the past few years blazing a horrific trail full of cataclysm and casualties in my quest to regain my power without realizing I had never lost it. I had power all the time. Gigi was right. I was like the Kokuran—a rare, beautiful, distinctive flower with an esoteric symbology that was mysterious, beautiful, strong, and powerful.

I am the Kokuran, and the Kokuran is me.

THE END

JORDIN MACK - AUTHOR BIO

Jordin Mack was born and raised in Detroit where she attended college and earned a master's degree in Business along with a lifetime degree in Hard Knocks from the streets. It is this duality that provides her unique urban style and perspective in her literary expression. In parallel with her corporate vocation, she continued to pursue her passion for writing, which finally culminated in her debut novel, The Kokuran.

31885252R00242

Made in the USA
Middletown, DE
15 May 2016